Book Four ...nnai Mage
By J.L. Mullins

Copyright © 2023 by J.L. Mullins

All rights reserved.

No part of this publication may be reproduced, distributed, or transmitted in any form or by any means, including photocopying, recording, or other electronic or mechanical methods, without the prior written permission of the author, except as permitted by U.S. copyright law.

The story, all names, characters, and incidents portrayed in this production are fictitious. No identification with actual persons (living or deceased), places, buildings, and products is intended or should be inferred.

# Contents

Chapter: 1 – That Seems Bad
Chapter: 2 – Practice
Chapter: 3 – Potent Creature
Chapter: 4 – The Dark, Cold Forest
Chapter: 5 – Nightshift
Chapter: 6 – Leshkin
Chapter: 7 – One Way to Protect the Caravan
Chapter: 8 – Outside the Defenses
Chapter: 9 – On Overwatch
Chapter: 10 – Welcome to Makinaven
Chapter: 11 – Less Than Ideal
Chapter: 12 – Needed Support
Chapter: 13 – Higher in Makinaven
Chapter: 14 – Espresso?
Chapter: 15 – Into the Constructionist Guild
Chapter: 16 – Jevin
Chapter: 17 – Venturing Food
Chapter: 18 – Crocheting
Chapter: 19 – As Expected
Chapter: 20 – Shift
Chapter: 21 – A Lot of New Things to Test Out
Chapter: 22 – That Seems Wise
Chapter: 23 – Kit Was Full
Chapter: 24 – Reactions
Chapter: 25 – Happy to Assist
Chapter: 26 – A Mild Combat Application
Chapter: 27 – Murder Dell
Chapter: 28 – Choose Wisdom
Chapter: 29 – Together
Chapter: 30 – Great…
Chapter: 31 – What Is Happening to You?
Chapter: 32 – Foundational Understandings
Author's Note

# Chapter: 1
# That Seems Bad

The second day of the venture to Makinaven was much like the first, excepting crystal entities and arcanes and Archons dropping through.

The guardsmen drove off more than a dozen arcanous creatures, varying from the quite common thunder bulls to a few massive reptiles. One of those seemed to have been stalking one of the thunder bull families and took exception to the guards having driven them off.

Rane took care of a half-dozen more minor threats to their progress.

Tala never left the wagon top.

Instead of begrudging her restriction—after all, she could see that Mistress Odera was correct in every instance—Tala kept a ready watch on their surroundings, usually being among the first to notice any potential threat. All the while, she continued her study of Holly's texts. She wanted her knowledge surrounding her inscriptions to be as deep and thorough as possible.

They made camp late that afternoon, just more than two hundred yards from the close edge of the reaching canopy, far overhead. The hard part of the journey would start the next day, it seemed.

The forest was an interesting presence beside the camp; the trees, starting at almost a hard line, were taller than anything she had ever seen, short of a mountain. Their branches spread out wide, interlacing with those around them. Their shape seemed much more like maple trees than pine.

Even the somewhat shorter specimens, at the near edge, were tall enough that Tala thought they might be able to strike the wagons, should they fall their way.

*Let's hope that doesn't happen...* She could probably catch such with a Restrain, but she'd never attempted to affect something that large before, and Restrain was a more complex working than Crush.

*Yeah, I could Crush a tree no problem, but that wouldn't help us if it were falling our way.* She put it out of her mind, though, as it was quite unlikely in any event.

Rane and Tala sparred before dinner, to the great enjoyment of the passengers and off-duty guardsmen. Their display caused more to brave the cold for longer periods, many opting to eat their dinner while continuing to watch.

Eventually, however, night had truly fallen, and Tala had eaten a quadruple portion of dinner. *Pasties never get old.*

Tala was given the first part of the night-watch as Mage Protector, and Rane and Mistress Odera bid her goodnight. Mistress Odera gave her several bits of advice and requested that she be roused if anything of note seemed to be happening.

Tala agreed with a smile.

That first part of the night passed with similar non-issue. Terry slew a night puma, a great cat that used shadow magic to stalk its prey.

He detected it, somehow, and slew it outside of the area between the wagons, near the edge of where she could see in the poor light.

He also ate it before Tala could notify the guards to log the encounter. When she checked with those on duty with her, none had seen the beast to corroborate the kill. *Ah, well. At least he got a meal out of it.*

She still found it marginally intimidating when Terry swallowed things much larger than his standard form. The night puma had been more than eight feet in length, nose to rump, and Tala would have guessed it weighed more than she did, even accounting for her gravity enhancement.

Still, it was handled. *No issue at all.*

She hesitated at that. *Is there no issue, because nothing has happened, or do I think there's been no issue, because the arcane returned, and removed memory of such?*

She shivered at the thought, causing Terry to shift on her shoulder, though he didn't open his eyes.

*Well, I suppose if it had returned, it would have manipulated me, causing me to not even consider its interference.* Great, so she only had to worry about the arcane's involvement when she didn't consider that it could have been involved.

She felt her left eye twitching. "Tala… you are making yourself crazy. You cannot possibly allow that to be how you think of this…"

She shook her head. *All I can do is keep on, and resist anything that I can.*

It was small comfort, but it did seem to help.

When Rane took over the watch around midnight, Tala gratefully slipped into sleep atop her reinforced cot, happy to end an unremarkable day and happy that it had been just that.

\* \* \*

The next morning, after her daily routine, a sparring session with Rane, and breakfast, Tala noticed Mistress Odera walking her way.

"Mistress?"

"Good morning, Mistress Tala. Walk with me, will you?"

"Sure."

Tala fell into step beside the much older woman, moving toward the forest. "What do you know of this forest?"

She thought back to the information she'd read up on in preparation for this trip. *Summarize, she doesn't need a recitation of all of that.* "It's full of magic, though not specifically in the air. The trees have more power than those in other low-magic regions, and there are more arcanous creatures than on the open plains. I haven't looked closely at the trees' power-flow, though." Her magesight had noted it at a great distance, and she hadn't focused on it since.

"Go on."

"It'll be colder? Not much direct sunlight reaches the ground. There aren't established roads through the trees, obviously, so the travel time is much less certain."

"All true."

"Almost no undergrowth? The trees deeper in grow massive and block even more of the sun, leaving the forest floor mostly bare of vegetation." She looked up at the trees which literally scraped the sky, uplifting branches creating trailing crevices in the lowest clouds as they moved past.

Mistress Odera nodded. "So, you know the basics."

"They are as big as I was warned." Tala grunted. "Even yesterday, I thought I was just mis-seeing, somehow."

"They truly are spectacular. The Mezzannis used to make their homes in these trees."

"Mezzannis?"

"An arcane species. Never enslaved humanity, per se. They were one of the few to completely collapse when we gained our freedom."

Tala frowned. "That's terrible. We wiped out an entire race which wasn't doing us any harm?"

Mistress Odera quirked a small smile. "They didn't enslave us, Mistress, because you don't put your beef cows to work in the fields."

Tala hesitated, narrowing her eyes at the older woman. "Wait…"

"The Mezzannis subsisted on ambient magic and human flesh."

Tala shuddered. "I feel like you purposely led me astray, there."

"Of course I did. I was curious how you would react to the elimination of a supposedly peaceful people." She nodded, her smile growing. "I am glad of your response."

"So… All gone?"

"Gone? No, but the decrease in magic, both natural, ages ago, and then that induced by our cities, caused the majority to wither away into lesser versions of themselves, all those that didn't die outright."

"So… most are not dead?"

"Some melded with the great trees, losing most of their sentience, and all of their sapience, in order to live on. It is because of them that these giants can move on occasion, though rarely while observed. That is one added difficulty in traversing this part of the human wilds."

"…the trees move. Like an ending-tree? They'll try to hit us? Or, do you mean…?"

Mistress Odera gave a small smile. "The trees can migrate. They move through the ground without truly disturbing it, and often reposition to hamper travel through the region using either trunk or roots as barriers. Though, they aren't clever or inter-connected enough to

# Millennial Mage, 4 - Bound

block the route entirely. When humans aren't around, those that can move tend to drift away from each other, making it less obstructive over time."

*And now the references to varying routes and lengths of travel make a lot more sense.* She hesitated. *Wait...* "You said that *some* of them melded with the trees, but not all?"

"No, not even most. Most that still remain are no longer conscious beings. They are arcanous humanoids. We call them Leshkin."

*Leshkin? This is their original home? I knew that some were found here, but this is where they come from?* She found herself giving an involuntary shiver. The Leshkin waged a mindless war on humanity every millennium or so. *Now that I think about it, wasn't the last one almost that long ago?* She thought through her memories of the various informational texts she tried to devour in the last week, adding them to stories from her youth. *Maybe a hundred or a hundred and fifty years out if the pattern holds.* "That isn't great, is it."

Mistress Odera shook her head. "Pernicious creatures. From what we've learned, each has a heart of sorts, hidden well beyond human reach: a seed from which they will re-grow if killed. As such, they lack even animalistic instincts for survival. Any that catch wind of us will attack and will continue to do so until they are obliterated. They will not retreat and cannot be driven off."

The two women stopped walking, a bit past halfway between the wagons and the forest edge.

"Their hatred of humanity is deeper than even the arcanous animals' aggressive instincts." Mistress Odera's eyes flicked to Terry. "Your companion will have some trouble with them, as their form is nothing more than animated, magically altered vegetation. You will have trouble because that plant matter has a caustic sap flowing through it, under high pressure."

Tala had read of that. "Wouldn't that be an issue for anyone?"

"Of course, but most people are used to being wary, of being in danger. You are accustomed to being invulnerable."

Tala found herself nodding. "Noted. Acid will definitely stress my inscriptions more than a sharp cut or blunt hit, but I should be able to endure, so long as I'm not submerged, or the like."

Mistress Odera gave her a long-suffering look. "Funny you mention submersion."

Tala did not like the woman's tone. "Oh?"

"There are, on occasion, pit-traps filled with their sap, usually in hollows. A misstep will break through the thin layer of turf and drop the unlucky into wells of acid."

"That's just lovely."

"Quite."

Tala sighed. "I have been thinking about releasing my increased weight. It's very useful in some few circumstances, but not many. In all others, it's actually pretty irritating to deal with. Do you think that wise?"

Mistress Odera hesitated. "Possibly. There are creatures that will snatch a person up, and carry them up nearby trees, and they are more numerous than the pit-traps. Your weight would be an advantage against such foes."

"Certs, right?" Human-like in form, but much bigger and with much shorter legs, proportionally. As a result, they were just taller than humans, on average, and they could easily run on all fours, while remaining mostly upright. Their heads were more like elk or rams, with horns or antlers, depending on the subspecies. Their feet were as dexterous as their hands, and they moved through trees more easily than a horse ran across open plains. Tala glanced up at the canopy before them. *Yeah… that could be… bad.*

"That's correct. They can survive a fall from the canopy and are known for attempting to drop directly onto wagons, or oxen."

"Great, so keep my eyes above us, too." *As expected, I suppose…*

"The guards are very good at watching for branches moving irregularly, but if you can, keep your magesight perceptive in that direction. Yours is always active, correct?"

"It is."

"Good. That should help, as well."

Tala nodded. As she thought about their talks, a question came to mind. "So… Leshkin are about human in size. What should I watch for, specifically? Are there any common signs of their presence or approach?" She'd studied many creatures from this region, but she knew that her knowledge wasn't complete.

"Lesser Leshkin are closer to child-sized. Though, if two combine, they will match a grown man in height and bulk. As to your question, they move about in human form most of the time. Otherwise, watch for fast-growing plants, filled with unusual power."

"Hold on a moment, combine?"

"Oh, yes. Two of the lessers can meld into a warrior. Those even use wooden approximations of human weaponry, blessedly mundane, but made of some wood that leaves them more effective than any human metal."

Tala nodded. *Ingrit's list had Leshkin weaponry as one of the most lucrative harvests on this route.* Tala had read about the warriors, but she'd missed the part where they were just combined lesser Leshkin. *Too much variation and nuance to fully read up on in advance…* "Can two warriors join? Wait." She shook her head. *If the pattern holds...* "That's a Leshkin knight, right?"

"Correct. They have something akin to plate armor, but again from mundane, if sturdy, wood. Some knights will have magically enhanced weaponry or armor."

"And two knights…" Tala thought back. "A juggernaut?"

"Precisely. Twice the height of a man, everything they use is strongly magically empowered. If we attract that much attention, we are in a *lot* of trouble."

*Two to a warrior, two of those to a knight, and two of those to a juggernaut.* "That's just eight. Eight are so much trouble?"

"Only if they have time and forethought to join. It isn't instantaneous and the process seems to require connection to a great tree for magical energy. It usually only happens if there isn't an easy chance for them to attack, so they take time to prepare before joining the battle."

*Okay. So that's why the information I found discussed how to counter groups of the lessers. Groups won't be combined as much as possible.*

"The lessers are *much* faster, so they usually try to soften up a target first, or act as distractions, when units fight together."

*Historical enemy of mankind, indeed.* "So… why do we have cities in here?"

Mistress Odera snorted, humorlessly. "Because the cycle of cities through this region is all that beats them back, even if just briefly. The centuries, between when the last forest city fades and we establish the next, see the Leshkin swarming deeply into the plains. They are more an annoyance than anything, but they make every route, every city, less safe."

*And the last forest city will wane in a little over a century and a half...* That lined up with her understanding of historical conflicts with the Leshkin. "Alright. So, what else will we be facing in there?"

They spent a few more minutes discussing what to expect.

Belatedly, as they were finishing up, Tala asked, "Shouldn't Rane have been here for this?"

"We already talked. He fills a much more standard role as a protector and has read up on the proper actions and strategies for someone like him on this route. You are a bit out of the ordinary."

She grunted. "I suppose I can see that."

Mistress Odera met her eyes with a searching look. "So, I noticed that you didn't do any practice with your new gravity manipulation yesterday."

"I thought it better to focus on the caravan and improving the efficiency of the inscriptions I already have active."

Mistress Odera gave her a long look, then shook her head. "Oh, child. You really are trying, aren't you."

Tala frowned in irritation. "What's that supposed to mean?"

Mistress Odera waved her off. "Unimportant, now. I want you to begin practicing as soon as we get underway. Keep your eyes out, but work on using that inscription. Until you have it under control, you are working with an incomplete powerset, right?"

"True enough."

"I'm heading back to take up my post on the cargo wagon. Why don't you take a more detailed look at the trees with your magesight, then join me?" After a moment's pause, she added, "Don't get closer. Don't start an engagement with anything, if you see it."

Tala nodded. "As you say, Mistress."

Mistress Odera moved back toward the caravan, and Tala, for her part, turned to regard the giant trees before her. She focused, allowing her magesight to really dig into what she saw.

Her eyes immediately widened in shock.

Each tree seemed to have sent its roots further down than she could easily discern, as well as so far out that she stood well inside the radius of their reach, even though the canopy ended another hundred yards in front of her.

That wasn't what had evoked the reaction, however.

*Power.* The forest was drawing in power from all around it, almost like a human city. Most of what she could see flowing into the forest came from *deep* in the ground. The trees, after using some of the power, seemed to release the rest from the tips of their branches to fill the air.

Even so, the magic didn't stay there long, and the results weren't even half as concentrated as the magic around Alefast. The power in the air seemed to be steadily flowing deeper into the forest. *Toward Makinaven.*

*How dense would the power be, if the city wasn't here to lessen it?* She shivered at the thought. *So, anything in there will be more power-dense than the arcanous beasts of the plain.* That was a lovely thought.

She briefly wondered why the Archons hadn't just burned the whole thing down, but as she considered, she doubted that the arcanes would allow such, and the action might even bring some of those uninterested in humanity down upon them. *We're in a strange stalemate. We have to defend ourselves, but we can't do anything that's too effective, or we could be starting an active war that we couldn't win.*

She grimaced. *The more I learn, the more I wish I'd been content with ignorance...* She snorted at that. She knew, very well, that even if she could go back, she wouldn't. *Blissful ignorance is a false paradise.*

# Millennial Mage, 4 - Bound

She sighed, moving to turn back toward the wagons when Terry perked up, his eyes locked on the trees.

Tala followed his gaze and saw what looked like a pile of flowers, slowly growing up from the forest floor, near one of the closest trunks.

Her magesight showed a complexity of power that she couldn't comprehend at this distance, and she *almost* moved to investigate. *Is that what Mistress Odera meant?*

Thankfully, her better reason prevailed, and she stayed put. *It's not because Mistress Odera told me to stay back. I'm choosing the wiser path on my own.*

Once the flowers had reached a height roughly equal to Tala's chest, they condensed, forming the shape of a small person, eyes of vacant darkness regarding her from its place, near one of the closest trees. Though Tala's normal sight saw only unending night in those black holes, her magesight saw blazing beacons of power. *Is that what I looked like to others?*

The depictions she'd seen in informational tomes did not convey the *wrongness* of the creature. *I really can see detail at a crazy distance...* She'd not encountered many instances where she focused so closely on something so far, but that was hardly the most pressing thing at the moment.

The thing tilted its head to the side in clear confusion. *Don't anthropomorphize, Tala.*

The small form continued to look her direction for a long, silent minute. Finally, it slowly began walking forward. Its movements were fast but jerky. The result was faster than a quick walk but looked more akin to a puppet's movements than that of a man. *A puppet controlled by a drunken child...*

"Terry, go get Mistress Odera's attention." Tala began walking backwards, unwilling to put her back to the advancing creature.

Terry vanished. The flickers of dimensional power behind her indicated that he was doing as she'd asked. *At least, I hope so.*

She moved with careful but quick steps. *No reason to trip while escaping that horror…* As such, the flower-being was gaining on her, steadily, leaving dragging, irregular footprints in the snow. Even so, it didn't, yet, seem hostile. More than anything it seemed… curious?

*It can't see me properly. Do I look like one of its own…? Why doesn't it see the caravan?*

Tala was about fifty yards from the caravan when the Leshkin reached the edge of the overhanging canopy. When it did, it froze in place, head jerking back and forth, seemingly seeing the caravan for the first time.

It threw its mouth wide, thorn-like teeth growing larger, stretching toward the center of a wholly inhuman, circular maw. A screech, high and wild, issued from the churning depths. Blessedly, there were no answering cries from behind it, within the forest.

The flowers of its exterior shifted into a pattern reminiscent of scales, and much larger thorns sprouted from its fingertips and toes.

Without warning, it rocketed forward with a sudden burst of speed, leaving a trail of flower petals in its wake.

The being seemed to have forgotten Tala and was aiming to pass her by, seeking the caravan.

*Yeah, no.* Tala drew Flow, connecting void-channels to it as she pulled it free.

The weapon blossomed into a sword, and the Leshkin seemed to take notice but didn't alter its path.

It whipped past her in a rush, Tala striking out and cutting through it with seeming ease.

Behind her, the Leshkin sprayed a bubbling yellow fluid from the cut Tala had made in its side.

Some of that acid splattered Tala's back, immediately eating through her elk leathers, and began burning at her skin. *Why aren't the endingberries stopping it?* The part that missed her sizzled through the light layer of white snow.

Allowing a moment's distraction, she looked within. Tala saw that something about the creature's blood was pushing against her magical defense, moving the endingberry power back more effectively than that of her inscriptions.

Tala growled, spinning around to face the creature. She bent her will toward her endingberry reserves and forced that magic back into the areas still under assault by the acid.

The power began diminishing but not too quickly. That removed the strain on her inscriptions and most of the strangely burning itch. *Well, Xeel did imply that I'd have trouble with some of the forest creatures...* And hadn't Ingrit mentioned something along those lines, too? *She definitely mentioned the Leshkin, but I don't think she discussed their effect on endingberry power.* But endingberries had fallen out of favor during a Leshkin war. *I think I might be starting to understand why.*

Tala fully faced the Leshkin as it tumbled to a stop, immediately picking itself back up and facing her in turn. It hesitated, seeming to examine her before glancing over its shoulder, the head turning far more than a human neck could.

It shrieked again, spinning and launching itself toward the caravan.

Tala cursed. *That... that seems bad.*

The guards had seen the beast, now, and Mistress Odera was clearly looking their way from atop the cargo wagon.

A single quarrel *thwacked* into the creature's chest, and Tala saw the scripts on the shaft's length ignite, inverting the Leshkin's power for use against the beast.

The Leshkin lost all cohesion, the blooms exploding outward to be carried back into the forest by a wind that Tala couldn't feel or detect.

# Chapter: 2
# Practice

Tala sat on the wagon top as it trundled toward the trees. The caravan was underway, and Tala had a task before her.

Per Mistress Odera's instructions, she was preparing to activate her active gravity manipulation for the first time. *I really should have done this a week ago...* But there had just been too much else to do. *I still haven't even started experimenting with spell-forms in my lungs, either...* No. This took priority.

She placed her palms on her elbows, left arm going above right. She carefully positioned her fingers per Holly's instructions, getting into the very awkward and specific position required for the initial activation. *I know we didn't want this to activate on accident, but this is a bit ridiculous.*

Even so, she followed the instructions given, closed her eyes, and entered the required mental state.

*Control.*

Power whipped through her, filling the gold inscriptions in her left breast and radiating outward into the others linked to them. A few of the forms made subtle additions to her magesight as well, utilizing the base scripts to give her needed information.

The miniscule copper links placed to kick off this first activation burned away, leaving her with another active draw on her power.

# Millennial Mage, 4 - Bound

It was a massive drain.

Tala's eyes opened, widening in surprise as she felt her reserves begin to steadily, if slowly, empty. With quick, practiced technique, she forged one of her standard void-channels and connected it to her body and the inscriptions there.

The added flow was just enough to satisfy the much greater demand for power. *Great...* Any time she didn't have an active void-channel, she would be losing power. *I need to understand this spell-working better. That should increase the efficiency and reduce the draw.*

She thought she could hold the single void-channel for most of a day. Even so, it wasn't enough to refill what she'd lost. So she quickly forged a second void-channel and dispersed it a few seconds later when her reserves were refilled.

That done, she opened her eyes, and had to blink back tears.

The entire world seemed to have a uniform, additional color layered overtop both her normal vision and that of her magesight. *Not quite a color, more an added depth.*

She felt her mind hitch at the additional facet of information.

Thankfully, given that the new portion of her sight was directly linked to her magesight, it functioned the same. Now that she had taken in the gravity of everything around her, it faded from her sight. *Only differences will be highlighted.*

She glanced down at her hands and was greeted by such a difference. The 'light' of gravity was deeper, coming from her body, the effect seeming to highlight the *weight* of difference. Tala huffed a chuckle at that. *Well, that's exactly what it is, so that's probably why I perceive it that way.*

Once she'd acclimated to that, her extra perception with regard to her own body faded as well. *Only changes will manifest.*

She'd picked up a small stone for practice and set it near her feet during the initial activation. As such, she picked it up to hold, focusing on it to bring back the 'other light' that indicated gravity's effect.

She brought her left, middle finger down to press against her left thumb, her other fingers curling naturally into the position she'd had Holly lock the ability behind. *I can't make changes, unless I have this hand position, for now.* It seemed a wise precaution.

*Increase.* She applied her will and felt a marked uptick in the power drain. She immediately created another void-channel. The 'light' increased minutely, but the increase in weight was much, much too little for her hand to register. *All that, for this?*

She thought for a long moment. *What am I doing, exactly?*

She was dumping power into an effect, without considering how it would be accomplished. She remembered her inefficiency with charging the cargo-slots before she'd fully utilized a mental model. She recalled how horrible her skin's defenses were before she understood the bio-chemistry behind inter- and intra-cellular bonds.

*Yeah, that's what's happening here. I haven't bothered to really understand how this is doing what it's supposed to do.*

She thought for a moment.

*It's exactly like my crush.* As soon as the thought entered her mind, solidifying into a mental construct, the new, added drain on her power greatly diminished. The stone got noticeably heavier, if still just minutely.

## Millennial Mage, 4 - Bound

*That's right. Take that ten percent extra weight and crack!* She shook her head, a smile tugging at her lips. *Hey, it's a start.*

She bent her will toward increasing it, and over the next hour was able to raise the stone's weight by nearly fifty percent, then slowly return it to normal. It was a colossally glacial process, but Tala thought she could make it faster in time.

*Practice it is, then.*

\*   \*   \*

Tala watched the false twilight landscape around their small caravan.

It had taken her nearly two hours to fully adjust to the dappled green light. Even still, she kept thinking that she saw movement out of the corners of her vision, but it was just the obscuring leaves and branches, high above, swaying in a wind she couldn't see. *Or, moving on their own…*

Now that they were past the forest's edge, the massive trees were actually spaced fairly far apart, with few exceptions.

Those exceptions seemed to be growing *just* too close together to get a wagon through, thus diverting them from their intended course. Whenever they came to such blockages, at least one of the trees was invariably one of the migratory variety. Tala's magesight told her that the magics within were much more complex than the average specimen of tree. Even so, they lacked the level of complexity of an arcanous creature.

As things would have it, it was always easier to divert to the left, or east, around the barrier. When they tried to go right, or west, the terrain became more difficult, often with great tangles of roots slowing them down or just making the path impossible.

The tree trunks were colossal, as befitted their height. If Tala was estimating correctly, the larger trees, past the leading edge of the forest, were close to nine hundred feet tall, and approaching two hundred feet across. In general, the trees grew around that far apart, making it a very dense forest, relatively speaking, while still having a lot of clear ground for them to traverse.

Thus, any given diversion took them only around four hundred feet out of their way, but it was still quite inconvenient, as the arrangement of the trees made it difficult to tell where paths through were, until they drew close.

*The whole scale of this place twists the mind.* She assumed that the trees got as much of their needs from the magic, which they were drawing up from the earth, as from sunlight, and that made the closer crowding less of an issue.

The fact that any light reached them at all was a testament to the sparseness of the canopy. *Those limbs are huge, though!* It was mainly the leaves that were sparse, barely forming a single layer between them and the clouds, all told. She even caught some glimpses of those clouds, occasionally.

It was cold enough under the trees that the ground was frost covered, but it didn't seem like much snow got through to the forest floor, at least not here.

The guards had attached an interesting device to the front of the cargo wagon's shaft, between the two oxen. It extended out in front of the animals on a hinge. To Tala, it looked mostly like a weight, resting on a set of wheels that moved up and down to stay in heavy contact with the ground. It seemed incredibly complicated, since it could move and swivel, while not hindering the turns or movements of the oxen and wagon in the least.

*To prevent the oxen from falling into a pit-trap?*

That was probably a good idea. The oxen were pretty key to the whole venture.

*Huh… what would happen if the oxen were slain?* It was probably worth asking. If it were up to her, now that she thought about it, there would be scripts embedded in the wagon that could do the work of the oxen, in the case of an emergency, but they would also be too expensive for regular use.

That in mind, she took a moment away from her practice, and watching their surroundings, to examine the wagon more closely with her magesight.

There wasn't active magic to stand out to her, but she *thought* she detected the intrinsic power of metal embedded, swirling through various parts of the vehicle.

*I wonder who can activate it, and how?* She was probably better off not knowing.

*I can be trusted not to activate it.* Tala decided to redirect her mind to other topics. Sometimes she felt like she was herding a toddler, while trying to direct her own mind.

*Rude.* She would get over it.

She felt a tickling from the edges of her magesight and looked up.

Something was moving through the canopy nearly directly overhead. As she opened her mouth to call out a warning, one of the guards on the chuckwagon beat her to it.

"Above!" He directed their attention to the one that Tala had seen, though she noticed some of the other guards pointedly looking elsewhere. *To ensure it's not a distraction?*

The Cert clearly seemed to notice their attention, vaulting off the massive branch it had been charging across.

Tala immediately brought her middle finger back to her left thumb, focusing on the falling animal and dumping five void-channels' worth of power through her mental construct, through the spell-form, and toward increasing the beast's weight.

In the roughly six seconds before it impacted beside the cargo wagon, Tala was able to increase its weight by only about ten percent, if she was understanding the new aspect of her sight properly. That barely increased the speed of impact, only increasing the energy of such by a bit.

The beast stumbled in its landing. The oddity of gravity's effect changing seemed to have caught it by surprise.

Tala continued to bend her will toward increasing it, even as guards jammed lances into it with passing charges from horseback.

This Cert didn't have any elemental abilities that she could see, and all the power in it seemed focused on its normal functions. *A bit like me, I guess…*

As such, the lances were mainly mundane, and didn't have the huge impact that those using the creature's own power would have achieved.

Tala glanced to Mistress Odera, but the woman shook her head. "No. Master Rane has it handled."

As if on cue, Rane swept by at incredible speed. Force struck the beast's chest and blew through it, while the creature's increased weight helped with anchoring the thing to allow for a through-and-through, upward cut.

Blood fountained into the air, and a chorus of deep, guttural notes rained from the canopy, above.

Tala swept her gaze across their green ceiling, seeing hints of creatures looking out from behind the power-filled branches, where they were very difficult for her magesight to pick out. *How many are there?*

Mistress Odera's voice was clear as she spoke. "They are ambushers more than fighters. They know we've seen them. Expect them to retreat but be wary just in case."

The next minutes were incredibly stressful as the wagons slowly left the pack behind. The beasts, for their part, didn't seem to be following, at least not those that Tala was able to pick out. Those watched the wagons depart until tree trunks blocked direct line of sight.

Mistress Odera finally breathed out a sigh of relief and nodded. "Return to regular observance."

The guards responded to her command, seeming to relax.

*Back to practice, then.*

The rest of the day passed with little of note.

They were attacked quite a few more times, but it was always by singular creatures.

Some ten lesser Leshkin total, five more Certs, a white stag that emitted blinding pulses of light, three medium-sized reptiles that reminded Tala a bit of Terry, and two night pumas fell before Rane and the guardsmen.

Mistress Odera only had to shield them once, when a Cert dropped from directly overhead. The woman angled her defense, shaped as a flat plane, so that the beast rolled off to fall the rest of the way to the ground. There, it was quickly dispatched, just like the others.

All told, Tala was an ancillary resource who barely helped, though she did get a *lot* of practice with her gravity manipulation.

By the time they made camp that evening, Tala understood how it worked well enough to be able to alter gravitational effects by close to ten percent per second, with sufficient power devoted to the task. Thankfully, her increased understanding also meant that the void-channel to her body was no longer required while she wasn't actively making modifications to the gravity around her. *That's good, at least. I don't want to think what would happen if I ran out of power in the night...*

The rate of change that she'd reached was still nowhere near fast enough to replace her Crush, but it was nearly six times her earlier pace.

*Every step draws me closer to where I want to be.* She knew that her future progress would be slower, but it wouldn't stop any time soon.

Their camp that night was in a slightly larger-than-average gap between several trees. She'd asked Mistress Odera if there was any danger of being fully surrounded and blocked in during the night, and the woman had simply said that it rarely happened. *So, not never...*

Still the older woman didn't seem concerned, so Tala had returned to her practice.

As Tala walked across the wagon top, thinking about her progress gave her an idea, and she decided to reduce her weight by ten percent, just to see what it would be like. The magic affected her easily. As it originated within her, her iron salve didn't block it.

She tripped immediately... on the smooth wagon top. *Seriously?*

Her every movement felt *wrong*. Even so, she gritted her teeth and went through her exercises with the altered gravity, forcing herself to adjust. *Alright, then. I need to practice under as many different levels of gravity as possible.*

She didn't really know how, exactly, it would be useful, but she didn't like that she was so incompetent with such a minor variation.

# Millennial Mage, 4 - Bound

*But should I practice large variations first, or subtle ones?* She had no idea. *I should ask someone…*

It was too bad that everyone was busy with their evening duties. Rane walked in a wide circle around the wagons, checking for any hidden lairs or traps.

Mistress Odera and the guards seemed to be thoroughly checking the ground between and immediately around their campsite in much greater detail than Rane could hope to achieve with his wide sweep.

*I should go ask if I can help.* She sighed, dropping off the side of the wagon.

She slammed into the ground, fracturing the already frozen soil. She ground her teeth, feeling how much endingberry power had been required to absorb the blow. *Okay. I'm calling it. I can always put it back on, now that my active manipulation is up and running.*

As Terry appeared on her shoulder, Tala brought middle finger and thumb together, and she began dumping power into reducing gravity's effect on her. It took every void-channel she had and nearly a minute to reach a normal weight, or close enough to be irrelevant.

She was able to watch her hand and compare that to her sleeve as a way of matching the gravity 'light' from each, nearly perfectly.

*Yeah… I should have released that ages ago…* She hadn't really considered how easily she could place the effect back on, if she wanted. *I'm a bit foolish, sometimes…*

She approached Mistress Odera, a literal spring in her step. Thankfully, she got used to her lightness before stopping beside the other woman. "Is there anything I can do to assist?"

"I don't think at the moment, Mistress, but thank you for checking in." Mistress Odera glanced to Terry. "Now, you, good avian, would you be willing to do a sweep of the surroundings? You can move faster than all but a horseman and will draw less attention than one of the mounted guards."

Terry cocked his head, then glanced toward Tala.

Tala smiled at her friend. "If you want, might be nice to stretch your legs?" He'd been a bit lazier that day, not really leaving Tala's side very often.

He bobbed and vanished.

In less than an hour, the camp was as secure as they could easily make it, and dinner was being served.

Tala and Rane sparred once again, to the delight of the others in the caravan.

Tala was having a bit more trouble, today, given her normal weight.

She was a bit faster on sideways and upward movements than before, but she couldn't anchor against Rane's blows as easily, and the result was that she was flung about much more often.

It was a stark lesson in humility, and plainly showed just how complacent she'd already become in accepting certain hits. *I should probably practice with even less than normal gravity... but not today.* In truth, she should wait until she could match Rane before pushing further, but she doubted she would have the patience. *We'll see.*

After a particularly brutal bout, Tala was taking a break to drink deeply from her water incorporator when she felt something bump her shoulder.

Tala turned to see Terry, the size of a small horse, looking at her.

A silence had fallen over those watching. They seemed to be curious more than anything else, as they'd all seen the bird in his smaller form, and the guards knew he could get bigger. Many had even seen him at this size, over the last few days.

"What's up, Terry?"

The bird bobbed to her, then tapped Flow with his nose and flicked his head toward where she and Rane had been sparring.

"You want me to fight some more?"

He bobbed, then shuffled that way.

Her eyes widened. "You want me to spar with you?"

He bobbed again, seeming much more excited.

Tala swallowed, though her mouth had been empty. "Well, I suppose it could be good practice…" *What under the stars am I agreeing to?*

Terry did a happy little shuffle, then appeared in the cleared area, crouched and ready.

"Well, alright then. Let's see what we can do."

# Chapter: 3
# Potent Creature

Tala notified Mistress Odera, and the guards on duty, that she and Terry would be sparring so that they would not come to her aid. Then, she carefully stepped forward into the already well trampled area of forest floor.

Terry seemed to have grown bored while she took care of the particulars, and he'd curled up on the ground.

Tala took a moment to regard her avian friend. *He looks so comfortable there.*

Her focus expanded just slightly, and she saw him in the greater context. He was curled up alone, no others of his kind nearby. *I wonder how long he's been alone?*

She gave a sad smile. *And he chose to join with me.* She never wanted him to regret that.

"Are you ready, Terry?"

The bird opened one eye and let out a soft squawk of assent.

"Alright, then. Let's—" Tala's words were cut off as her mouth filled with detritus: broken sticks and half-rotten, icy leaves. There was a weight on her back, and her ears were filled with a triumphant cry of exaltation.

She heard those watching gasp in alarm; she even heard several weapons clear their scabbards before the weight vanished.

She pushed herself up, her eyes finding the bird, back where he had been. She glared, grimacing at the avian. "That wasn't much of a bout."

Terry's eye opened, again, and the look he gave her was one of smug superiority.

"No, I'm not conceding." She took Flow into her hand, keeping it in its sheath, and used void-channels to extend it. Taking up a high guard, she nodded. "Again."

Even as she spoke, she moved Flow through a defensive sweep close across her back. She felt the briefest fluctuation of power as Terry again appeared behind her, but he seemed to notice the sword and immediately flickered to her side, behind the sweeping blade.

His taloned foot again knocked her down, this time with a blow to her side, and his weight held her against the cold soil.

Now, however, she could see him; he met her gaze and let loose a happy chirp.

"Yeah, yeah." Thankfully, her enhanced strength made it easy for her to draw breath, even with most of Terry's weight on her, and that gave her an idea.

She muscled through Terry's resistance to roll onto her back, grabbing the bird's leg with her off-hand and thrusting Flow upward.

Terry flickered again, and his foot was now over her face. With no time for her to react, he slammed her head down, pushing it into the ground.

Tala's off-hand closed on now empty air.

She growled in irritation. Even so, she didn't let her irritation slow her, and she used her anchored head to leverage her body up, coiling around the massive avian limb.

He was gone.

She'd already been in motion, so her inertia carried her all the way over, causing her to fall back to her stomach.

He returned, now standing fully on her back.

Tala let out a muffled yell of frustration into the freezing cold muck beneath her and *pushed,* vaulting up despite the few hundred pounds atop her.

She swept out, putting less strength into the strike, so that she could immediately reverse it. Her attack and quick reversal caused Terry to have to blink away in rapid succession, spoiling his next attacks.

*Alright, then. Let's do this.*

Flow was now in constant motion as Tala warded away the arcanous beast with a chaotic, but flowing, defense.

Every time she was too slow or too predictable, Terry would knock her aside, capitalizing on the further disruption to pin her down.

It was an exercise in utter helplessness, and she started to breathe heavier, unable to get space to think, to plan, to feel in control.

*Why can't I defend myself, here?*

Tala began to feel tears building in her eyes as her desperation grew.

*I am utterly outclassed. Even with all my defenses, he now has my measure.* Her breathing continued to pick up, but not due to the exertion. *He's been watching us practice. He knows exactly what we are capable of, and he knows, now, how to counter it.*

She forged one more void-channel for her body and inscriptions, giving her a marginal boost to her strength and reaction rate. *I'm glad Holly didn't put any power limiters on my enhancements.* Even so, it wasn't enough.

She wrought a second void-channel. In the corner of her vision, she saw that a faint golden glow was now easily evident from her exposed skin and the inscriptions set within.

*Still not enough.*

## Millennial Mage, 4 - Bound

She made a third, and there was now a distinct glow, casting shadows on her clothing, and hair, but not yet strong enough to light up the ground around her.

She was sweating profusely, her hyperactive muscles generating incredible amounts of heat. They were working with more power, and under more strain, than they ever had before. *Still too slow. What is wrong with me?*

She threw together a fourth void-channel for her body and inscriptions, while maintaining those to Flow. She was at her limit, and the light from her inscriptions now highlighted a circle around her on the ground.

Steam was visibly rising from Tala's clothes, skin, and hair in the frigid evening air.

Every change in Flow's direction of movement produced a whip *crack* of sound, echoing and overlapping through the campsite. Flow never even brushed Terry.

The avian hadn't noticeably responded to her ever increasing pace. He flickered around her with an air of utter non-concern, exploiting any and all imperfections in her form or defensive patterns, and there were many.

Her increased capacities meant that those flaws were exposed for briefer periods, but they were also much more numerous.

She could do nothing against him. It felt like she was simply flailing uselessly at the air.

Tears had long since joined sweat, streaming down her face, and her nose was draining down over her lips and into her mouth.

She couldn't spare even an instant to wipe it away, though she did spit, when possible, to keep her airways clear.

*Why am I so weak?*

In an act of pure, thoughtless desperation, Tala tried to lock onto Terry for a *Crush*. He simply changed size briefly without slowing his probing assault, thus disrupting her connection before she could enact the attack spell. She didn't have the presence of mind or focus to make a more persistent lock.

Dread built atop the despair. *He could kill everyone here, and there is nothing we could do to stop him.* He wouldn't do that… right?

Her face was tingling, feeling almost as if it had fallen asleep as her entire body responded to her emotional state.

Her vision was blurry, though her eyes were useless in tracking Terry, regardless. A brief flicker of diverted attention showed that there were far fewer onlookers than there had been. The distraction also earned her another faceplant against the cold ground.

After another frantic exchange, in which she desperately fought back to her feet, there was finally a brief pause, barely a couple of breaths in length.

Tala locked eyes with Terry, and she saw, as if for the first time, the true depth of his age, experience, and power. *He is violence incarnate.*

She should have named him Violence. She shook herself. *That doesn't seem right. I shouldn't name him directly after something like that.*

She almost laughed, then, feeling a manic desperation. *I'm still frantically hoping he's not about to kill us all.*

Terry seemed to notice something in her gaze in that momentary eye contact, because he didn't resume his non-stop assault, instead cocking his head to one side and settling down.

Tala stood still, eyes locked on her tormenter, Flow held to one side, her entire body on fire, all but literally. Her concentration broke, and the void-channels crumbled.

Her body responded immediately, instantly feeling like every muscle seized up simultaneously.

## Millennial Mage, 4 - Bound

She couldn't even muster a cry of pain as she dropped to the ground, twitching.

Aside from portions of her musculature that simply clamped down, refusing to release, many other parts rippled in uncontrolled spasms, with a feeling like a thousand small, powerful feet kicking her over and over.

Her only comfort came in the form of a small, fluffy weight that appeared on her side, shifting ever so slightly to account for her sporadic movements.

What seemed like an eternity passed before Tala felt her arms forcibly extended above her head and held down. Additional hands met her palms, and power flowed into her.

"Her muscles were cooking themselves. They'd have already succeeded without the reinforcement." It was Mistress Odera's voice, and she sounded concerned. The older woman tsked. "For all I can tell, they might have been ruined and healed, but I think not. Her brain was sheltered from the heat, though."

"Can you do anything for her?" Rane's voice was clear.

"Yes and no." The older woman sighed. "I can't do anything more, magically; her body is already working at capacity even magically aided, but she should recover from this with a night's rest. Her own regeneration scripts are up to the task." She huffed a little laugh. "I could cut off her limbs and let them regrow. That would likely be faster, but more costly, and highly detrimental in the long run."

Rane huffed out an irritated breath. "Why didn't her defenses prevent this?"

"The damage came from the regular function of her body and scripts. There was nothing to defend against."

Rane grunted. "I'm glad we sent everyone back into the wagons near the beginning of the bout. I know I wouldn't have wanted an audience for this, if I were her."

Tala finally managed a groan.

"Hush, child. You'll sleep tonight and feel better in the morning."

A big hand, which she assumed was Rane's, patted her back. "That was quite the attempt, Mistress Tala. I don't think I could have matched that level of effort for as long as you did."

Her lips briefly stuck together before she croaked out a question, "How long?"

"Close to a quarter hour, if my reckoning is right."

*Fifteen minutes…*

Silence surrounded the campsite, and Tala allowed herself to glance at the few remaining, who had been watching. Every face had some form of shock or horror in place, though none seemed too fresh, and few were turned her way. *Just the on-duty guards.* That was a kindness.

Rane tentatively tried to lift her, grunting when he succeeded. "Your movements looked like gravity was normal on you, again. Glad I was right." He muttered to himself after that, much too quietly for him to have expected her to hear. "Still rusting heavy, though."

Mistress Odera went before them, clearing the guards from the common room as Rane carried her through.

Kit dropped her room-key to the floor, and Mistress Odera let Rane in to lay Tala on her bed. It now felt hard as a stone floor.

*Great… I'll be uncomfortable if I sleep at a normal weight.* Her body was starting to work through its issues, and she smiled weakly up at the two. "Thank you."

Rane smiled back, and Mistress Odera nodded. "Drink a lot of water, dear. We'll make sure you have a good amount of food available when you wake up."

## Millennial Mage, 4 - Bound

*Good.* She didn't have the presence of mind to verbalize her thanks any further.

The older woman produced a wet cloth from somewhere and quickly cleaned Tala's face of sweat, snot, tears, and grime. *That was kind of her.*

Tala was already fading, though.

Rane and Mistress Odera left without another word, leaving her with the key.

Terry, for his part, curled up beside her on the bed, giving no indication of concern or remorse, save to nuzzle close before they both fell into a dreamless sleep.

\* \* \*

Tala woke to the amazing smells of cooked and cooking meat wafting through the cracks around her door.

She was *sore,* but as she stood and stretched, her body quickly worked out that lingering pain. She moved through the stretching portion of her morning routine with practiced speed, taking time where it was needed without lingering unnecessarily.

Terry was curled up on her folded bedroll, which she'd previously set up for his use. His eyes were open, and he was regarding her with what she could only interpret as a look of expectancy.

Food was calling to her, but there was something she needed to do. "So… What was that?"

Terry stood and walked over to her.

She waited.

Then, in a display of teleportation power beyond anything she could have imagined, Terry began to flicker.

He moved back and forth between two positions, two sizes, acting out two parts in a silent display. The power rolling off of him was palpable, but still so much lower than she'd have expected. *He must have near perfect efficiency.*

That wasn't the point, though. She focused on the display.

The larger terror bird was knocking the smaller around, as the smaller desperately tried to fight back. It was fruitless, but neither stopped or gave up.

Over time, the smaller one slowly grew in size and competence, beginning to occasionally land blows on the larger specimen.

Through the course of the thirty second play, the two drew closer in ability until they were equals, testing and training each other, both improving greatly and advancing, together.

Terry stopped flickering and staggered slightly, clearly having used a *tremendous* amount of power for the short communication.

"You were training me, trying to lift me up?"

Terry flickered to her shoulder and head-bumped her cheek.

"It was…" She swallowed back her rising tears. "It was pretty humiliating."

Terry curled up, tucking his head down.

She nodded, feeling like she understood. "But that's how terror birds train each other: ruthless, without actually causing damage. No cushion, no coddling, just a continuous, overt display of skill."

Terry let out a happy, little chirp, and shimmied slightly.

Tala shook her head. "I'll… I'll try to learn from that, but I didn't have space to think."

He opened one eye to regard her from her shoulder.

"That was part of the point… wasn't it."

He closed the eye again, and she'd have sworn he was smiling, except he didn't have lips with which to make the expression.

"Well, I suppose we have to accept each other as we are, not as we wished we'd be." She patted Terry's head with her off-hand. "Let's get breakfast."

She left her room, locking it behind her, and headed outside.

They exited the cargo-slot through the propped open door to find that it was still a bit before dawn. There was a pleasant, cool crispness to the air, and a light dusting of snow helped highlight the terrain, even in the dim forest. There were some guards already eating, and Rane was atop the cargo wagon, clearly the Mage on watch.

Mistress Odera was awake as well, it seemed, and she smiled and waved to them as they walked over toward the chuckwagon.

"Good morning, Mistress Tala." After a moment's hesitation, her eyes flicked to Terry. "And to you, Master Terry."

Terry twitched but didn't otherwise react.

"Good morning, Mistress Odera."

Mistress Odera's skin was a bit too pale as the woman smiled at them. "Last night was… educational."

Tala grunted, noncommittally. "You said there would be food?"

Mistress Odera ignored the attempt at a topic change. "Are you alright, child?" Her voice was barely audible, even to Tala's ears.

Tala hesitated. *Am I?* She felt recovered, but that wasn't what the Mage had been asking about. "I… I haven't felt that helpless in a long time."

The older woman nodded. "I can understand that. He is a… potent creature."

Terry gave a happy chirp in return but didn't open his eyes.

With that topic broached and dealt with, if barely, Mistress Odera gestured back to the bustling chuckwagon. "They are ready for you."

Tala didn't delay in the slightest as she stepped up and received a truly monstrous portion of food. There were two bowls that each looked to be meant for either serving or mixing large quantities of food.

Amnin smiled but didn't try to engage Tala in conversation. Instead, she simply indicated that the smaller of the two bowls was for Terry.

The avian perked up at that and gave a happy, trilling flute of gratitude.

Each bowl was filled with fat, well fried sausages. Sliced bread, buttered and toasted, had been arranged around the edge of Tala's bowl. Terry's had a fence of bacon.

"Grab a seat. I'll bring you some water and your bacon, dear."

Tala smiled gratefully, moving over to the end of an unoccupied table. She set down the huge bowls and almost pulled out her reinforced chair, but then remembered that she didn't need it at the moment. *That's nice.*

She slid onto the bench, and fell to eating with abandon.

Terry ate more slowly, but he still finished everything in his bowl with almost horrifying speed.

Tala tried not to complain about the lack of coffee. Apparently, Mistress Odera had advised she avoid it this morning because of how much liquid she'd lost the night before. *Coffee won't dehydrate me…* She sighed. *At least I can get some later today.*

Amnin had promised to save her a jug, but she wouldn't get it until after they started out for the day.

*Sacrifices must be made, I suppose.*

Breakfast done, she moved through her morning routine. Because her weight was now variable, she held off on muscular exercise until everything else was complete.

Now that she could alter effective gravity at will, if slowly, she had a task to accomplish right before her physical training.

She concentrated, bringing her left middle finger to her thumb, and focusing on herself, acting within the protective shell of her iron-salve. Over the course of a minute and a half, she increased her weight as much as she felt she could stand. Tala had been careful, near the end, as she hadn't wanted to overshoot and kill herself.

She didn't have an exact number, but her feet were easily sinking into the frozen ground, despite the increase to her footing.

*Around six times?* It didn't matter that much. She could see the alteration with her new gravity sight, so she could track her progress in the future.

*Alright. Time for physical conditioning.*

# Chapter: 4
# The Dark, Cold Forest

Tala fell into a modified pattern over the next few days. Mistress Odera rarely let her engage the creatures that attacked them directly, but Tala used her gravity manipulation as often as possible to assist in the defense of the caravan.

She'd made great progress at first, but that had slowed to a crawl and was continuing to slow. The new manipulation ability was highly useful, and she had no complaint about that, but in a combat situation, especially against more than one opponent, it still seemed cumbersome to the point of worthlessness. This was magnified because distance greatly slowed the rate of change that she could impart, as well as increasing the amount of power required per second to enact the change.

*Yes, I've been working with it for two days, and I dub it worthless!*

She shook her head to herself. It had taken her weeks before she was able to use Crush at all, for the first time. She could dedicate a good bit of time to this, too. Worst case scenario, if she still didn't like these workings, she'd get something else in their place after the inscriptions ran out.

Her morning routine didn't change much, except for the increase to her effective gravity for physical conditioning and the reducing of such after. If there was time, she and Rane would engage in a few rounds of sparring. Since they were fighting with their weapons, she still only ever won through trickery. Unfortunately, no trick worked more than once.

She did improve though, and she was surprised to see Rane improving as well. Mostly, the latter amazed her, because she could tell he was getting better. *My perception is improving, at least in regards to combat.*

The days were filled with forest watching, physiology and anatomy review, gravity training, conversations with Mistress Odera, and periodic moments of high adrenaline, as magic-charged beasts threw themselves at the caravan.

The evenings were filled by her role as a Mage Protector, along with sparring against Rane and other basics such as eating.

After all the passengers and off-duty personnel had gone to bed, she sparred with Terry, and while she didn't feel like she was improving combat wise, at all, she never let herself fall into quite the same level of desperation as that first time.

Consequently, she felt like she was at least better able to perceive how badly she was losing. *Baby steps, Tala.*

With regard to the attacks, the first day had mostly been Certs, with the occasional Leshkin, puma, or species of deer. *Or had they been elk? They weren't moose...* It was hardly relevant. There had even been a couple of great reptiles, but those were incredibly easy for the guardsmen to drive away, so Tala only ever caught the barest of glimpses.

The guards had been *very* thorough in harvesting from any creature that left remains, which was all those they killed, except the lesser Leshkin. The wagons were slow enough through the forest that the off-duty guards were easily able to do the work in time. It helped that nothing was anywhere close to the size of a thunder bull. The forest had powerful creatures, but not many large ones.

The second day, they left the Certs mostly behind, and their encounters were, consequently, more weighted toward the other creatures.

The third day, lesser Leshkin became almost their sole attackers. On that day, Tala began to take note of something odd with the Leshkin. Every lesser Leshkin that died within her line of sight had its gaze fixed on her as it perished.

*That's not creepy or anything.*

Over these days, Tala watched the slow change in the direction of the currents of magic within the forest. Finally, on that third day, Tala's observations of the power flow told her they were even with Makinaven, at least in the north-south direction. The power in the air seemed to flow almost due west, now, and there was a *lot* more.

They'd been shunted in the direction of old Audel, one of the more recent ruins, and the magic density in that region was still quite high from the recent waning.

The forest continued to attempt to force them east or south. *Toward greater magic density.*

Also, on that third day, Mistress Odera began creating arching shields over the snarls of roots, which occasionally were the forest's obstacle.

*Easier than migrating so many trees to deflect us, I suppose.*

The oxen, as was their standard, didn't seem to care in the least, dragging the wagons over the magical bridges. The surface dimpled slightly with each of their steps, giving good traction. Mistress Odera had worked her magics with as gradual a slope as was reasonable, so the task wasn't too onerous.

The horses *hated* it.

## Millennial Mage, 4 - Bound

In the end, most of the horses had to have hoods pulled over their heads before being forcefully lead over the constructs.

That added distraction and difficulty, along with making it harder for them to maintain a good perimeter.

The head driver had several constructs that let him pinpoint their location, and he let the caravan know that they were still around three days from Makinaven.

*Rust, we went much further east than I'd thought.*

That night, as she and Terry were preparing for their sparring session, Tala's magesight alerted her to incoming threats.

A unit of four Leshkin warriors was upon them, breaking from beside one of the closer trees, coming from the east.

"*Leshkin!*" Tala's voice boomed out, the inscriptions on her lungs, throat, and vocal cords allowing her to get to a much greater volume without causing damage.

She dropped Flow's sheath into Kit as she assessed the incoming enemy.

Like all the Leshkin she'd seen before, these were made of seemingly random plant-matter. One was of mostly roots, two of bark, and the final of leaves.

They all seemed to be staring directly at her, an odd savagery on their inhuman expressions that was in stark contrast to the nearly blank expressions of the lesser Leshkin they'd been fighting.

Each warrior carried a weapon.

Root held a massive, two-handed club as it thundered silently forward. *How do such loping steps not shake the ground?*

Each Bark seemed to be wielding a long spear, leveled at her as they charged on quick, light footsteps.

Leaves? Leaves put an arrow into Tala's eye as her warning call was still echoing through their campsite.

The arrow exploded on impact, unable to penetrate her well-inscribed flesh. *Bless you, eye inscriptions.*

The endingberry power had, like previously, retreated before the attack. Leshkin arrows, as it turned out, were filled with the same caustic sap-blood as the Leshkin themselves.

Tala screamed in irritation and pain as the acid burned at her defenses. *How is it hurting when it isn't harmful to me?* Was it a secondary effect of pushing back the endingberry power? Was it lessening her defenses overall?

If she understood the quick glimpse she took with her internally directed magesight, her defensive scripts were almost entirely annulled, and so her eyes and skin were burning freely beneath the acid. The only reason she still had a face was that her regeneration scripts seemed utterly unaffected by the strange repulsion the Leshkin exuded, and were working perfectly, rebuilding the flesh even as it melted away.

*I am an Immaterial Guide! Rust me if I let some rusting plant dominate* my *power in* my *body!*

With a growl of irritation, she mentally seized her defensive powers and forced them into position, even as she swiped the sticky sludge from her eyes.

Those same eyes widened as she opened them only to see Root's club incoming, *fast.*

On instinct, Tala dropped backwards, taking the move from Rane's arsenal, even if her version wasn't magically-enacted.

Her magesight detected the blips of Terry's retreating power. Mistress Odera had warned him away from fighting these foes, and he seemed to be wise enough to have listened, at least in the heat of the moment. *Great.*

## Millennial Mage, 4 - Bound

Flow was already lashing out, and Tala took Root's closest leg off, just above the knee, before her back had even hit the ground.

As the man-sized Leshkin fell toward her, she swept her blade upward, bisecting her opponent groin to crown.

She threw herself to the side, pushing a bit awkwardly across the ground and barely avoiding the deluge of acid that rained onto the frozen soil where she'd just been lying. Thankfully, Flow seemed to have some blow-back on the horrid liquid, delaying its fall and even driving a lot of it up, first.

*One.* Or was that two, because two lessers had been needed to make this one warrior?

Now was hardly the time for such contemplations.

Leaves launched three more arrows toward her, but she was able to dodge two and strike one from the air. *Score one for improved reflexes and proper training.* The one arrow she shattered covered her hand and arm in burning acid, however, and her sleeve was much worse for wear.

She connected a void-channel to the elk leathers to keep them from burning through their reserves and losing their power.

She couldn't close on Leaves, especially with the two Barks almost upon her. Even so, she'd distracted the archer for long enough that two guards were able to strike it with specialized quarrels from their position atop the chuckwagon.

Bark and Bark were closing rapidly on her as she turned her attention from the now removed, long-ranged enemy. *How was their heavy hitter the fast one?*

Unfortunately, her time sparring against the Guardsmen had made at least one thing abundantly clear: spears, halberds, and other polearms were incredibly effective.

*I wonder if I'll be able to add a path for one of those to Flow in the future.*

It was an oddly disconnected thought as she backpedaled, using Flow to knock aside quick thrusts and probing jabs, leaving heat-darkened marks on their wooden weapons. *Don't let them flank you, Tala.*

She was hearing the steady rhythm of crossbow fire, but her two opponents seemed not to be the targets of any of the shots. *What are they shooting at?*

She rolled her head to one side, a spear tip going through the space her mouth had just occupied. *Rude.*

Exactly as Mistress Odera had implied, there was a reason the Leshkin were considered a bane to humanity's early attempts at civilization and magic: their natural aura seemed designed to suppress, or push back, endingberries' defensive power. *And I modeled my primary defensive scripts on that same mythos…*

The aura was a subtle thing. To reference Ingrit's analogy, it was like a light rain; the presence or absence of a fence was largely irrelevant.

Translation? Her iron salve didn't stop it. *Might be weakening the effect, though.* She wasn't dead, after all, despite taking an arrow to the eye. *I doubt my regeneration was fast enough to stop that in the way it was blocked. My defenses had to have done something.*

If she'd been told this enemy so directly countered a large part of her defenses, she'd have picked a different route. *If only some other Mage relied on this defense in modern times, so that the counter was more than myth and legend.*

She grunted. Bark thrust for her trailing leg as she continued moving backwards, very much on the defensive. Tala jerked the limb out of the way, mis-stepping, unbalancing, and taking a forceful thrust from other-Bark in her shoulder.

## Millennial Mage, 4 - Bound

Her scripts had a *lot* more staying power than the nebulous, free-floating endingberry defense, especially backed by her pre-prepared will, so the sharpened wood didn't breach her flesh, but at some basic level, Tala felt her inscriptions *bend* before the impact. Thankfully, they held.

Leshkin were *strong*.

The single, upward angled thrust lifted her free of the ground and caused her to whip in a full circle before she landed in a tumbling heap.

*Not good. Not good!*

The buzzing of bolts through the air announced two quarrels striking home, and one Bark immediately crumbled into a disjointed pile.

*They targeted the same one.* Was it bad luck, or did the warriors need two quarrels to go down? *Didn't the Leaves go down with just one?* In that crystalized moment, as the remaining Bark drove a spear toward her abdomen, her near perfect recall brought her the memory of two bolts striking the archer.

So, that had taken two as well. *Fascinating. Not currently relevant, but fascinating.*

A guard tackled her attacker seemingly out of nowhere. His short sword hacked and stabbed again and again as he took the beast to the ground.

The combination of stab wounds and the massive man's weight coming down on top of the Leshkin caused it to *pop*.

Caustic sap-blood splattered across the guardsman, and Tala thought she heard him gritting his teeth in obvious agony.

*Wow, how is he not screaming at that much pain?* She knew the barest fraction of what that felt like, and she'd screamed while gaining that knowledge.

"Mistress Odera! Healer!" Tala was able to get to her feet. At the same time, the guard stumbled upright, turning toward her before swaying. He slowly sunk back to his knees.

He was mostly silent because the lower half of his face and the front half of his neck were gone.

The nameless guard looked up at her with pleading in his eyes.

The moment stretched out as Tala looked back into the man's eyes.

She couldn't do anything for him. He was already dead; his body just hadn't caught up with that fact.

Finally, the guard collapsed, motionless on the forest floor.

Silence filled the clearing.

The attack was over, and reality truly hit home.

*He's… He's dead.*

\* \* \*

Tala stood, staring down at the unmoving guardsman for what felt like an eternity.

He looked perfectly healthy, now that his wounded front was pressed against the ground.

He could be sleeping.

*But he's not.*

Why had he done that?

*Why did he protect me?*

That was his job.

*It's not anymore.*

Tala felt a mirthless laugh bubble up from inside her.

He's dead, and he hadn't needed to die.

*He's dead, and it's because of me.*

This was far from the first person she'd seen dead or die. She'd seen Terry's slaughter of around a dozen men, but those men had been hostile toward her. This man—*I don't even know his name*—this man died because she had looked weak. He died because her death meant the end of the caravan. He died because she'd let the Leshkin get too close. He died because she'd let the Leshkin get the upper hand.

She felt a weight on her shoulder, and Tala realized that she was kneeling beside the body, silent tears running down her face.

"Mistress Tala, do you need healing?" Mistress Odera's voice was soft, gentle even, conveying the strength of her presence without imposing it upon Tala. It was her hand on Tala's shoulder.

Tala shook her head. She heard other footsteps around her and watched as a number of guards worked together to move the body, likely taking it to a cargo-slot to be brought home for burial. *To next of kin.*

Had he had a family? *What will happen to them, now?*

Tala stood, took out her copper incorporator and used a brief, moderate pulse of hot water to wash her face clean. The too hot water used a small bit her endingberry power but was otherwise a blessed relief. "What happened?"

Mistress Odera patted her shoulder once more, then stepped back. "Around ten lessers attacked the far side of the encampment, while these four struck over here. That is more advanced tactics than they usually use, but not alarmingly so. There were a few casualties, but he was the only death. The others were within my ability to fully heal."

Tala nodded. *What would have happened if the attack occurred during dinner?* "Something's changed. These are the first warriors we've encountered, and I find it hard to believe that there just happened to be four, together, along with a small contingent of lessers."

Mistress Odera grunted before replying. "We started making our way in a nearly straight line toward Makinaven, bypassing most of the things meant to divert us and slow us down. I didn't do so earlier because it is known to bring greater attention, but I deemed the risks acceptable."

"Do you still?"

The woman gave her an odd look. "Yes, of course. Today, we made more progress toward our goal than the two previous days combined. We need to reach the city, and I am unwilling to wander the forest for weeks to do it. That would only lead to more potential injury and death. This route usually claims at least a few of the guardsmen; it's why it is so well paid for them." She paused, seeming to see something in Tala, then. Her voice softened, ever so slightly. "The fact that our caravan is smaller, that you allowed that, has already kept us from receiving as many attacks as is standard. We should have suffered more casualties by now, if not more deaths. Your abilities have mitigated that."

Tala grunted. "I'll have to take your word on it."

"You can look up the statistics yourself, Mistress. What I say is true."

Tala just nodded. *I know you're not lying...* "Doesn't make it better."

Mistress Odera grunted. "You aren't wrong. I wish there were better ways. We've tried having only Mages as guards, but it takes so many that we end up drawing more enemies down upon us, and people still die. We've tried…" She shook her head. "We've settled on this because it's the best of our current options, not because it's good."

*Best of bad options, indeed.* Tala took a deep breath and gave Mistress Odera a sad smile. "Should we expect more attacks tonight?"

Mistress Odera sniffed. "Always expect attacks."

Terry flickered into being on Tala's shoulder, returning from whatever he'd been up to.

"But if you mean should we be extra diligent? I don't think that's required. Once things calm down, you should be able to treat this like any other evening."

Tala looked to where the guards were dragging off the vegetative remains of the Leshkin. They'd already taken the weapons for use until Makinaven, then for sale to improve the payout.

Her eyes flickered back to where the guard had died. *There's not even any blood.*

The acid hadn't opened any wounds, and the damage it had done had been fused closed as it happened. "I will try."

"See that you do. I'm glad that you are continuing your practice. It will improve the defensibility of the caravan and increase the survival rate of everyone here." Mistress Odera quirked a smile. "Even if just marginally. Such gains are slow; every day matters." She turned to go. "Good night, Mistress Tala."

"Good night, Mistress Odera."

The camp slowly settled back down into the sleepiness of night.

It was dark beneath the forest canopy, and Tala had never really considered how the guards on night watch were able to see well enough to be worthwhile. During dinner, and for a bit afterwards, magical lights lit the space around them, but those would soon be put away.

*Why don't guards have night-vision inscriptions?* The obvious answer was that such couldn't be turned off without a keystone, and during the day they would likely be more than a little inhibiting. *I'll have to actually look, after lights out tonight.*

Until then, she would follow Mistress Odera's advice. "Ready, Terry?"

He answered by flickering over to the space already cleared for sparring. He was smaller today, choosing to be closer to the size of a large dog, as opposed to that of a horse.

"Let's see how I can improve."

\* \* \*

An hour later, a guard called that the lights were being deactivated.

Tala was drenched with sweat, having pushed *hard*, even if not nearly as hard as she had during her first match with Terry. She weakly waved acknowledgement to the guardsman. "Thank you!"

She'd done markedly better tonight.

It wasn't that she'd managed to hit Terry, nor had she been much better at warding him away, but she had gotten to the point where she didn't feel escalating panic at her own mounting helplessness, and that emotional control helped her keep her mind centered and allowed her to analyze what was happening.

She didn't have a workable solution, not yet, but it was a monumental step forward.

*First rule: Don't panic.* She smeared some of her sweat across her face. *I need a towel…*

With a sigh, she pulled out her cold-water incorporator and blasted herself clean. The cold water was shocking and invigorating. *Night watch, here I come!*

The large constructs dimmed and went dark, one guard carrying each of the four items back to the cargo wagon for safe storage.

Now that she was looking for it, Tala noticed that each guard wore a close fitting, flesh-colored mask, minutely thin copper wire was woven throughout and fused periodically to form inscriptions for increased light collection. *Only active at need, when powered, able to be used by any.* That was an elegant solution.

As she thought about it, she couldn't decide if she'd get inscriptions were she a guard. Obviously, the ideal thing would be to become a Mage, but that wasn't possible for everyone, not by a long shot.

*The Guardsmen Guild probably doesn't pay for personal inscriptions, but they likely pay for inscribed items, like the night-watch masks. Anything I got would always be on, so maybe before a particularly long or dangerous route?* That made sense. She hadn't really looked closely at the guards, though her magesight had shown her that many had bits of magic circulating through them on occasion, likely the result of long hours of training.

*Well, time to take my post on top of the cargo wagon.* Normally, she read or practiced, but tonight? Tonight, despite Mistress Odera's assurances, Tala knew that she'd have her focus fully on the dark, cold forest around them.

## Chapter: 5
## Nightshift

Tala smiled as she sat atop the cargo wagon, the morning light highlighting the thin, green canopy above. *You know? Those are leaves, not needles, but they weren't shed for winter.* She didn't know if she'd ever seen an evergreen with leaves before. *Not that I make a study of trees.* Not that it really mattered, in the end.

The previous night had been uneventful, and her morning routine, camp breakdown, and departure had passed quickly. She was now enjoying the last of a large bowl of sausages, chasing them down with a healthy amount of coffee… Maybe an unhealthy amount… *I'm sure it's fine.*

The food had been given by Amnin just as they were departing. "You have to keep up your strength." The older woman had given her a wink. "Brand told me that your huge appetite has something to do with your magic. Don't want you running out. That would be bad for all of us."

Tala had been profusely grateful. Her enhanced stores were *almost* full, or that was the sense she got from her body and power, but she wanted to be topped off in case she needed the energy and materials. She had a sinking feeling and a suspicion that she would have need, soon.

She turned her thoughts from that unpleasantness. *I'm not letting that ruin my appetite.* That would be counterproductive.

## Millennial Mage, 4 - Bound

The guards had taken to cycling more often, in part to help counter the growing cold, and partly because the trip had already taken as long as the shortest estimate.

Long shifts made for more frequent mistakes and slower reactions. They had the ability for shorter rotations, especially with the 'extra' guards that had come for this route. So, they reorganized. If Tala had heard correctly, they had dozens of different schedules that the commanding officer could select from, depending on the particulars of the caravan's current situation.

*That's probably wise; don't force a stressed commander to come up with a new, hopefully-workable system in the field.*

Tala continued to play with her gravity manipulation, targeting things near and far to get herself used to as many aspects of the ability as possible. She was even able to do that practice while reading, so she was hitting several key points for her advancement at once.

*At some point, I'll have to start investigating the fusing of my body and soul...* But that seemed *much* too critical and delicate; she wanted to wait until she was safely within a city's defenses.

She also kept her eyes lifted just enough, while reading, that her magesight would quickly respond to things in front of the caravan.

*I can do everything!*

Well, except advance toward being Fused, and—

*I can do many things!*

They were an hour away from their morning campsite when the first group of the day attacked them, coming from behind.

Thankfully, Rane had been in the rear when they came into view, and he, along with a healthy number of bolts, dealt with the six warriors and five lesser Leshkin.

*I don't know what we would do if those bolts weren't reusable.* From the looks she'd gotten at the items, each bolt had at least a half-dozen activations, assuming it wasn't broken or rendered unusable in some other fashion.

The Leshkin weaponry was collected with the caravan proceeding without changing pace.

Less than an hour later, Mistress Odera again created a bridge over a dense snarl of roots. Once the cargo wagon and horses were over, and when the chuckwagon had just started traversing the magical construct, the second attack came, sweeping up from the south on their left-hand side.

That assault had only been composed of lesser Leshkin, Twenty lesser Leshkin, all told. A few had managed to put some gouges into the chuckwagon before the last one was dispatched.

Apparently, Mistress Odera was at her limit with the bridging shield, because she had to manipulate and maintain the properties to greater extremes for it to be able to function in that way.

That was the reason that she hadn't been able to shield the wagon while the bridge was active. The fact that the chuckwagon had been half on that bridge made dismissing the spell-working a *bad* idea, as the oxen would likely have broken their legs from the drop onto the roots.

Those attacks set the tenor for the day.

By the time they made camp for the night, all the guards, even those newly on rotation, were twitchy, and Tala had completely given up on reading, her gaze constantly moving across everything around them. She was still able to continue her gravity manipulation practice, though. *Small mercies.*

Tala had lost count of the number of Leshkin they'd slain. Blessedly, they'd not seen anything more powerful than a warrior, but they'd dealt with more than a hundred of those, as the weaponry they'd collected testified. Tala had even been sent to assist Rane in one particularly desperate defense.

Near midafternoon, another guard had been slain.

Tala hadn't even seen it happen, but when she heard the news, her mind filled with visions of a pitted, all-too-visible lower jaw; of a melted neck; of confused, pleading eyes, begging for her help.

Only her inscriptions had kept Tala from emptying her lunch across the wagon's roof.

*Another one dead.* Could she have saved him if she'd been allowed to engage the enemy, instead of waiting out the attacks from up here?

*My presence didn't help the other guard…*

Aside from the one death that day, three guards had received severe injuries that Mistress Odera couldn't fix, at least not well enough for them to return to duty. Many more had been injured and healed, ready to get back to work thanks to her.

*We need to get to Makinaven.*

When Tala had asked Tion, the head driver said they were likely less than three days from the city, assuming they continued using Mistress Odera's bridges, and there weren't too many tree trunks moving to increase the length of their route.

*One can hope.*

The mood around the camp was subdued.

The passengers, while not exposed to the horrors directly, were quite aware that the trip was taking longer than it could have. On this route, they knew what that meant. Part of the purchase of passage was understanding and agreeing to the risks.

True, that was a part of any caravan trip, but for some routes, like Bandfast to Alefast, it was usually just a formality. For this path? It was a stark reality.

Tala and Rane still sparred, but they put less energy into it, using the opportunity to perfect form rather than fighting at full speed and strength. Tala even began altering her gravity during the fight to try leaping around Rane.

It didn't work very well, and Rane almost universally swept her from the air. *Falling slower makes me easier to hit; who would have thought?*

To make it effective in actual combat, she would need to be able to become lighter for the initial jump, then heavier than normal to drop back to a defensible position more quickly. Or she would need to be strong enough to make the heavier effective gravity not lessen her ability to jump.

To make the first idea work, she'd need to be able to change her effective gravity much, much faster. *That will only come with practice.* As to the second, the stars knew she'd tried just being heavier for long enough. *I could have been practicing this variability that whole time…* There was no going back, now, and not every crazy idea she tried would turn out well.

Tala and Terry's bouts, after most people had turned in, were likewise less strenuous. Terry seemed a bit twitchy, too. If Tala had to guess, the avian didn't like how nonlethal he was against the Leshkin.

He'd helped out in a couple of tense situations throughout the day, and each time, he'd barely been able to act as a delaying force. Any attack that harmed the Leshkin would, as a result, cause him to be hit with acidic blood, even if only the part of him that made the strike. Neither Tala nor Terry wanted to risk that.

# Millennial Mage, 4 - Bound

Because of the danger, he'd limited himself to tripping and destabilizing those that he had engaged. It had been fairly effective, but as the terror bird was used to being a one creature killing machine, it was obvious how much it frustrated him.

It was an unideal situation all around.

"We'll take a different route next time. Eh, Terry?"

He let out a low thrum of agreement.

Before the nightshift truly began, Tala was able to grab a quick bath. *Stars be praised.*

As she scrubbed, she contemplated their situation, and her wonderful friend who'd signed her up for this particular route. She would have to ask Lyn why she'd thought this would be a good second trip.

*Maybe I annoyed her too much, and she's decided to get rid of me...* That was unlikely.

*She's in league with the Leshkin and is sending them tasty, tasty Tala meat.* Where had that even come from? *I doubt I'd be very tasty...* Terry had seemed to enjoy her finger. *Bleh! Moving on!*

The Leshkin weren't intelligent enough to be in league with anyone, so that was unlikely to be Lyn's motive.

As she finished her cleansing and was ready to get to her post for the nightshift, Tala felt a couple things click into place.

*This route is more dangerous, meaning a higher pay for Mage Protectors. Lyn knows I am in need of funds, and I should have a better survival rate than the average Mage.*

Endingberry use was anything but common, and Tala doubted that anyone else had inscriptions based on the myths surrounding that power. Therefore, Tala had no reason to believe that Lyn knew Tala's defenses would be at a disadvantage against the Leshkin.

*Xeel had known, or at least suspected, but he's ancient. I'm sure very little is new to him, these days.*

So Lyn had been trying to ensure that Tala had a profitable trip, while sending a Mage that, from her understanding, would have a better chance of success.

When looked at in that light, Lyn's choice of route had been exceptional. *I'm still going to give her a hard time about it, even so.*

Tala took up her post, scanning the forest around the dark camp. *Stars be praised that arcanous beasts are less active at night.*

\* \* \*

Near midnight, Rane relieved her of duty, and she was about to climb down when she had a realization. "Hey."

Rane turned back toward her, a questioning look on his face. "Yeah?"

"How are you holding up?"

Rane gave her a long look, then sighed. "It's a bit rough. The experience is really good for me, and my scripts move me out of the way of the acid, but it's… pretty gruesome. Mistress Odera can heal anything short of a missing limb… or death." Rane glanced away.

Tala settled down, sitting near the ladder. Terry opened an eye to glance at her, then flickered away. *I guess he's going to hunt or something.* She looked back to Rane. "Were you there when the guard died today?"

"Yeah."

Tala waited, feeling like pushing would be a mistake.

Rane kept his eyes moving, but he seemed more burdened than usual.

She continued to wait. *I can give him a bit if that's what's needed.*

## Millennial Mage, 4 - Bound

Finally, Rane glanced her way, then sighed. "It was pretty awful."

"Oh?"

"I haven't lost anyone since…" He gave a sad smile and gestured to the faded scars on his face.

*Since the family died in front of him.* "Are you… Okay?"

He snorted at that. "I have to be. If I get in my own head, more will die, and I can't allow that." He said that with some finality, seeming to think the topic was closed.

Tala nodded, almost moving to go. Then she hesitated again. After a long pause, Tala spoke. "Last night… that guard died because he thought I was in danger."

Rane looked back her way but didn't say anything.

She pulled up her knees, hugging them to her chest. "I was on the ground, a Leshkin warrior standing over me, about to stick a spear into my stomach." She shrugged. "I don't think it would have killed me." She shook her head. "No, I'm almost certain that it wouldn't have. He died for nothing, simply because I looked like I was in trouble." She closed her eyes, resting her chin on her knees.

"He was doing his job."

"And I wasn't doing mine."

He gave her a confused look.

"I am a Mage Protector. I shouldn't have been on my back, seemingly in need of a rescue. I fell, and a man died."

"Mistress Tala, I got the after-action summary. You went down because you took a spear strike. You didn't trip over your own feet or stumble when fleeing danger."

"There are after-action summaries?"

Rane gave her a puzzled look. "Of course. How else can you learn from what happened?"

Tala just gave him a look. "How do you get them?"

"I just ask. Either Mistress Odera or the head guard."

"…I'll ask about that, then…"

Rane laughed. "I imagine that Mistress Odera would have passed anything relevant along. She is… guiding you, after all."

"Getting the information directly, even if not directly applicable, would be nice." Though, now that she thought about it, many of the things Mistress Odera had conveyed in their discussions had the tenor of being pulled from or built off of such a report.

"Fair enough."

They fell back into silence.

After long minutes, in which Tala waited and Rane kept his eyes on the forest, he finally let out a long breath. "You're still here."

"You still seem like you need to talk."

"A guard died. I couldn't have stopped it, but I was there. Maybe…" He shook his head. "There is nothing I could have done differently." He barked a laugh at that. "Rust, that sounds arrogant. 'I acted perfectly. Nothing to change here!'" He shook his head, again.

"So… could you have acted differently?"

"Of course. If I had perfect foreknowledge, I probably could have kept everyone alive, but with what I knew at the time? I wouldn't change a thing."

"I'm glad you have that, at least."

"Oh? Would you have acted differently?"

"I could have begun retreating toward the wagons sooner, kept a better footing, or moved to better positioning."

"Did you act to the best of your ability, with the knowledge you had at the time?"

Tala grimaced. "I'm not asking you to make me feel better, Master Rane."

Rane hissed a short laugh. "Of course you aren't, but you still need it."

"And you don't?"

He shrugged. "I don't blame myself for his death, I just…" He glanced away. "I wish it hadn't happened. I wish that I was better, more powerful, so that his sacrifice hadn't been needed."

Tala grunted her agreement. "It makes you think."

"Oh?"

"Yeah. I mean, these caravans are dangerous, but they'd be less so with a higher-powered Archon along. What are they doing that is so much more important than this?"

Rane made a non-committal noise. "There are probably too many caravans for them to commit an Archon to each."

She gestured at the two of them. "They sent two, here."

He laughed at that. "You know what I meant. We hardly count. We're barely more than Mages, at least for now. Even so, I know that the Caravan Guild has quite a few Archons, just not enough for every trip on every route to always have one who would have magics of a type to be useful."

*That's a fair point.* "Still seems like this route should have one…"

"Between any two forest cities is supposedly just as hazardous." He frowned. "Though, the fact that we were shunted so far east likely made this more dangerous than average. I've also heard that the caravans that have to go south, between the forest cities, encounter much more powerful beasts as well, so I might be overestimating the uniqueness of the hostility we've encountered."

"Fair enough, I suppose."

They lapsed into a companionable silence, then. Eventually, Rane looked back to her, smiling. "You really should get some sleep."

"You're probably right." She pushed herself to her feet.

"Mistress Tala?"

"Hmm?"

"Thank you."

She smiled in return. "Good night, Master Rane."

"Good night."

# Chapter: 6
# Leshkin

Tala rocketed through the air, momentarily confused as to what had happened.

*I was practicing reducing my own effective gravity. I thought I saw something moving in my peripheral vision, then—*

In an instant of clarity, she remembered a heavily armored Leshkin lunging from a nearby trunk and striking her with incredible force.

She was in perfect health, despite her new ballistic trajectory. *Oh, that's where so much of my endingberry power went...*

She saw the two-wagon caravan in the distance as a wave of lesser Leshkin seemed to fall like rain toward it. *Oh... that's bad.*

She saw movement closer as she continued arching through the air. *Lower gravity really allows for greater distance in ballistic arcs.*

Two shapes, clearly armored, were sprinting at impossible speeds after her, across the frozen ground.

*I've got to land safely.* She twisted in the air, less than three seconds having passed since she'd been on the cargo wagon. She reoriented just in time to see a *massive* wooden hammer coming for her face. *I guess this one was planning on flanking me.*

She couldn't decide if she was lucky for having come face to face with the flanking opponent before she engaged the others, or unlucky for coming into their striking range so perfectly.

In either case, she threw her arms up to catch the blow just as it landed. Both her arms broke with sharp cracks. Her scripts didn't impart invincibility, just a much, much higher resistance than was average.

She had a tight control on her endingberry power, keeping it internal, in her core, and allowing her inscriptions to handle surface level and limb protection. That freed up her mind to focus outward. *And left my arms exposed...* Not that endingberry power would have resisted this creature's blow very effectively.

Her now limp hands were driven against her face, stifling her instinctual scream of pain.

The blow caused the top half of her body to reverse directions, flipping her in a crazy spiraling twist to land in a tangled heap on the ground.

*This is becoming a repeating theme for me...*

Tala's scream morphed into one of frustration. It had already been a *long* day.

The first, renewed attack had come an hour after morning travel began, and they'd been increasingly hard to deal with. This was the third attack in as many hours and the first from ambush.

Leshkin knights had proven to be a *lot* harder to fight, and now she was separated from the others, potentially facing three. *I've got to get back.*

Her arm bones clicked back into place, pulling back into proper alignment before the structure reknit, her regenerative scripts eating into her reserves to get her back in fighting shape. Vaulting to her feet, she pulled Flow to her hand, instantly pushing power through the weapon to change it into the form of a sword.

*I need to be at normal weight. I'm not practiced at fighting effectively while lighter.* Her left middle finger touched her thumb, and she focused on herself, ramping up the effect of gravity, aiming for a 'normal' effect as a result.

The war-hammer-wielding Leshkin knight was approaching with deliberate, careful strides, as if expecting some sort of trick. *Or waiting for the others to catch up.*

Terry appeared behind that armored giant as it was advancing on Tala.

*No, just regular sized…*

The armor just made them look much bigger.

*But it's a part of their body, so… they are bigger?*

Now was hardly the time to consider such things.

Terry struck the creature's back, center mass, knocking the attacking beast forward, causing it to stumble as Tala lashed out with Flow.

The knights were fast.

Its war-hammer came up, knocking Flow up so that her blade sheared off the top of its head and helmet, instead of separating it at the neck.

They'd learned the hard way that this wasn't a lethal strike for warriors or knights.

*Full head removal, bisection of the body horizontally or vertically, complete obliteration, or solid hits from specialized, guardsmen weaponry.* Those seemed to be the only guaranteed kills.

Strangely, a diagonally-bisecting cut left them with some ability to fight on. *We're probably missing something critical.*

Sadly, the Leshkin seemed to slowly change over time, so the knowledge from previous wars was never precisely accurate.

She whipped Flow around in a tight circle for another cut, but the knight lunged forward, punching out with its heavy weapon.

## Millennial Mage, 4 - Bound

The impact threw Tala back, across the open forest floor.

The endingberry power took a large tick downward as it protected her ribs and organs from being pulverized; the blow had been greater than an ox kick. *I need some space to drink more endingberry juice.*

Thankfully, she'd gotten her weight back to normal. Unfortunately, it didn't really matter. She slammed into one of the great trees, actually denting the massively magically enhanced material. *More endingberry power used.* Thankfully, she'd managed to keep her head tucked, and she'd taken the impact mostly with her spine.

She snorted at that. *Who'd have thought I'd be trying to take damage on my spine…*

She jerked herself out of the tree, calling Flow back to her hand. *Wait; when did I lose hold of my weapon?*

Remembering back, it had been at the moment that the massive hammer had hit her sternum. *Understandable. Have a nice day.*

Tala shook her head. Her thoughts were a bit scrambled. *What is going on?*

*Right! I'm fighting knights.* She refocused on the space before her.

Terry was a flickering blur, engaging the three knights, trying to give her time to recover.

She almost laughed. When she thought about it, this was probably how he'd been sparring with her. *He's operating under the limitation of 'contain, don't kill.'*

The acid was a serious risk for Terry, especially if it came from a wound he was actively creating.

*Focus, Tala!*

She locked on to one Leshkin, which had a war-pick, clearly the greatest danger given its deep penetrating potential. The creature's form seemed to be composed mostly of long, fruit-like plant matter of varying colors. Its armor was a gray, tight-grained wood.

Tala's left middle finger touched her thumb once again, and she began pouring power into increasing its effective gravity. In the time since she'd been forcefully ejected from the top of the cargo wagon, she'd been too focused on fixing her own effective gravity to target one of the knights. *Until now.*

While Tala was dumping power into the gravity increase, she also pulled out her flask, downing a large amount of endingberry juice. She strode forward, returning the flask to Kit, continuing to increase the knight's weight more and more.

The creature was tripping and stumbling all over the place, and every time Terry knocked it down, it struggled to get back up.

*Next.* She switched targets and began ramping up the effective weight of the sword-wielder. That Leshkin seemed to be composed all of fine roots, like the hair thin ones that she often saw around weeds when she'd helped cultivate her father's garden. *Get it together, Tala.*

She was almost to the skirmish, and Terry anticipated her arrival, appearing opposite her approach and screeching.

Hammer swung for the avian, and Terry simply flickered, allowing the weapon to harmlessly pass through the space he'd been in.

Tala took that hammer-knight-Leshkin from behind, quickly cutting it into quarters with a practiced pattern of two strikes. Flow pulled a little more strongly on her power as it overcame the natural resistance of the being, but it wasn't significant.

The extra pull of power would also have cauterized the flesh of any being made of mundane material. Unfortunately, the Leshkin weren't. Their vegetation-substance simply caught fire, and the acid-blood bubbled and whistled as the force of her blow caused it to spurt away from her, through where Terry had been.

Terry gave her a bit of an irritated glare, and she returned an apologetic glance. *Oops.*

He didn't let her error slow him, however, and he quickly engaged the now-stumbling sword-knight-Leshkin, and Tala took a moment to behead then bisect the downed and struggling pick-wielder, coating the ground in more corrosive gore.

As she stepped around the ick, she glanced at her left hand, and contemplated the gravity scripts that were responding to the gesture from that hand. *These are awesome! Exactly what I needed.*

The gravity manipulation wasn't a quickly lethal skill, not by a long shot, but it was an amazing support ability.

While intelligent creatures could likely compensate for a time, Leshkin seemed almost to function along preset lines of action, rarely having good responses for odd tactics when used against them.

The sword-Leshkin followed the other two knights in death shortly thereafter.

Tala stood panting, the heavy breathing more from adrenaline than true exertion.

In the moment of silence, she heard Leshkin screeches from a distance, along with cries of pain. *The caravan!*

She snatched up the Leshkin's weapons, dropping them into Kit, and only *slightly* regretted leaving the armor behind. *They need me.*

She began running, but Terry was immediately beside her. He let out an implicative squawk and hunkered a bit lower as they continued to run. "Right! Thanks, Terry."

She hopped sideways, her great strength allowing the running leap to give her quite a bit of air.

She landed on Terry, and the terror bird bent lower still, greatly increasing his speed.

Tala tucked down, gripping his collar to gain better purchase as they quickly caught up to the still moving wagons.

*Come on, come on, come on!*

Lesser Leshkin were *everywhere.*

There must have been a hundred. Thankfully, more than half were dead or dying, if the piles of out of place vegetation were any indication.

A quick assessment showed her a group of three guards who were hard pressed by a Leshkin warrior along with a pack of lessers. "There!" She pointed, and Terry veered to the side, taking them that way.

Tala leapt from her partner's back and swept Flow outward, cutting four Leshkin. The warrior was bisected at the waist, and three lessers were cleanly beheaded. She put enough force behind the strike to knock the bodies aside, which directed the spray away from her allies.

Terry body-checked another two off their footing, and the guards were able to use the slight reprieve to finish off the remainder that had been within reach.

"Next enemies! Let's move!"

\* \* \*

It was getting closer to evening, and the attacks just kept coming.

Twelve guards had been injured beyond Mistress Odera's ability to heal.

Two more had died.

Tala didn't have the mental space to process that, but she knew it would hit her hard later. One had died just before she'd reached him.

*If I'd been faster…*

But now was not the time.

There was an outer perimeter around the city of Makinaven, inside of which the inward pull of power was greatly increased. That draw-down of power was a strong deterrent to the majority of the most powerful arcanous beasts. Leshkin were among those that usually stayed out of that zone.

The head driver and Mistress Odera had just finished a quick consultation, before letting everyone know that the caravan was less than an hour from that line, if they could keep the current pace up.

The spaced out, unit-based assaults had been replaced by an almost constant, steady inflow of Leshkin.

As such, Terry had been placed on get-the-bolts-back duty. He couldn't flicker while holding a quarrel in his beak, but he could still move *fast* and then flicker straight to the next to be retrieved. Thankfully, something about the quarrels' method of execution caused a banishment of the acidic blood as well, thus better preserving the ammunition.

It was a good use of his skills, especially with his understandable reticence in subjecting himself to the Leshkin's acid blood.

*Yeah, definitely blood. These things move around; I don't care what they're made of to start with. It's blood.*

Between Terry's efforts and how on top of retrieval the roving defense was, they had only lost a couple of pieces of ammunition throughout the long slog of the day.

Near the beginning, they'd been able to strip the fallen warriors and knights, claiming all the armor and weapons to help increase the payout for the trip, but lately, they'd had to struggle just to claim the weapons.

Kit had quite a stock of Leshkin weaponry, now, but the pouch was far from full. *This will be a good haul... if we survive...*

They'd actually been getting into a good pattern and rotation, since the enemy had stopped arriving in units. The building exhaustion across all the defenders was the only true difficulty. Unfortunately, shortly after Mistress Odera's announcement, something changed.

Almost as soon as the defenders had been informed that they were closing in on relative safety, groups had rejoined the ever-present lesser Leshkin assault: warriors led by knights.

Worse still, it turned out that the warriors and knights weren't alone in their renewed assault.

Tala was fighting behind the caravan, acting as rearguard to give Rane a momentary breather.

As she struck down yet another warrior, taking an ineffective blow to her leg from the creature in order to land a killing strike, movement caught her attention at the edge of her vision.

She lifted her gaze to stare through the horrible light of the seemingly endless forest, and her eyes locked onto a fear made manifest.

The sound of booming footsteps, somehow striking at the pace of a charging bull, overrode the sounds of routine battle around her.

Even at the great distance between them, Tala could still see that the creature was three times her height, and vaguely in the shape of a man.

Its armor was reminiscent of some of the latest designs she'd seen for heavily armored guardsmen, though those were usually only used in the plains routes, where mounted guards could easily sweep away enemies on open ground. *The Leshkin really do evolve over time.*

A massive glaive was held before it. The wicked blade was leveled at her chest. Even at such a great distance, she had no doubt of its target.

It was at least six hundred yards away; only a fluke in trunk alignment allowed her to see it at all.

Even so, it was growing closer at an alarming rate. *It will be on us too soon.* She looked around at those fighting with her. Each was winning their engagement; the caravan was protected, but none of them were free to face this new threat.

*If any actually could.*

Her eyes returned to the new, fast approaching foe.

If she had any guess on its speed, it would be upon them in less than ten seconds. *How can anything move that fast?* That was at least double the speed of a galloping horse. *If not triple!*

It was an insane pace. A forest of destruction, condensed into the body of a giant. *If it gets here, we're dead.*

Her right hand came up on pure instinct. Her first two fingers extended upward, her ring finger and pinky tucked down, all four pressed together, palm pointed toward what was obviously a Leshkin juggernaut, her thumb tucked in tight. She channeled magic into the activation and focused.

*Crush.* One gold ring burned away from the back of her hand.

Immediately, the massive creature stumbled, and it fell into a tangle of limbs, plowing a deep furrow through the hard-packed, frozen soil. Somehow, it kept its great weapon whole and free of the tangle. *Good instincts.*

It didn't stay down.

With obvious effort, the beast forced itself back up and lunged back into motion, quickly building up speed once again.

A second ring burned away on the back of Tala's hand, and the Leshkin went down much harder than it had in the first fall. A screech that froze even the other Leshkin washed over the caravan. An ancient creature of ridiculous power was *livid.*

The juggernaut forced itself up once more, cocked back its arm and whipped it forward.

The third ring blazed to life on the back of Tala's hand, and the Leshkin juggernaut simply flattened. *Sixteen times effective gravity wasn't enough.* That was a horrifying amount of force to have been shrugged off. It had required three full activations. *Sixty-four times gravity.*

Tala's relieved mind barely caught the blur of motion, high up through the trees, her enhanced senses focusing in on the unusual movement.

A flicker of dappled, late-evening light across the dull wood was the only confirmation Tala saw.

It wasn't enough to save her from harm, even with her physical enhancements.

Her eyes widened, and she began twisting away from the incoming, thrown weapon.

The motion unquestionably saved her life. *Or at the very least saved a* lot *of regeneration.*

The razor-edged sword blade of the juggernaut's weapon hit her right shoulder, in the divot between her chest and shoulder, right at the joint. Her rotation had shifted the point of impact away from the hollow beneath her throat.

The sheer force of the blow overwhelmed her defensive inscriptions, draining all of her endingberry power.

A distinctly resonant *pop* reached her ears as her humerus separated from her scapula.

The feeling of a *deep* stretch in all the muscles of her shoulder was followed closely by a tearing sensation that felt like nothing so much as the ripping off of ten thousand scabs or having each hair on her head pulled out one at a time. Her flesh tore as the weapon continued, unrelenting.

Now coated by an aborted spurt of her life's blood, the glaive moved through her to kill a guard who had been fighting behind her.

His spear dropped to the ground, left behind as he'd been jerked away, his lifeless body now pinned to the back of the chuckwagon, twenty feet beyond her.

Tala watched in horror as her right arm fell free, somehow not thrown backwards.

Her arm was gone, and it had been replaced with agony; every nerve that was no longer connected to her seemed to be screaming in horror, all at once.

She staggered, suddenly off-balance and disoriented.

Her active spell-lines, those that had failed to save the arm to begin with, hung in mid-air, clearly in the shape of her now missing arm, connected to her bloody shoulder but utterly beyond her control.

The limb, no longer attached but still clothed in an elk leather sleeve, lightly bounced as it settled onto the detritus of the forest floor, twenty-seven golden rings shimmering obviously on the back of the hand that was no longer hers.

Power ripped through her and on instinct she directed every void-channel she could create into her regenerative scripts.

Blood flowed out, through the gold inscriptions that had, just moments ago, surrounded, reinforced, and enhanced her vascular system. As that was filled, bone blossomed outward, marrow forming from the fine network of vessels that connected to it.

The hard casing of compact bone came next, again following the scaffolding of inscriptions, blazing with power in the dim light.

Her soft and connective tissues came quickly after that, the whole process taking less than five seconds, and draining her magical reserves almost entirely.

Her physical reserves had taken an incredible hit as well.

*And I lost the reserves stored in my arm.*

From the jagged tear around her shoulder, her elk leathers regrew her right sleeve. It looked strangely similar to how her arm had returned; small tendrils first, which then expanded outward, weaving into the lattice of magical skin, now bent toward Tala's use. She instinctively directed a void-channel into the garment to keep it powered. Given all the stress the garment had been under throughout the day, she just barely caught it before the reserves fully emptied.

In a daze, she looked down at the limb, bleeding out on the ground before her.

*That's my arm…*

Her vision unfocused, and she stumbled again.

*Oh, rust. I just lost my arm.*

Her mind refused to listen as a small part of her tried to point out that it had already grown back.

*By all that shines,* I lost my arm*!*

# Chapter: 7
# One Way to Protect the Caravan

Tala looked around in a panic, her mind both refusing to accept the loss of her arm and refusing to accept that it was already back.

Her eyes swept across the combat going on around her. The temporary pause caused by the juggernaut's rage-filled cry hadn't lasted.

*My arm is gone...*

Tala's arm was fully regrown.

*I've... I've lost my arm.*

Her inscriptions had returned the limb completely back to full functionality.

She forced herself, mechanically, to run and check on the guard who had taken the remainder of the blow.

*The blow that took... my... arm...*

With her augmented strength, she easily pulled the massive glaive from his chest, allowing him to fall free of the wagon as she almost absentmindedly slid the weapon into Kit.

She checked his pulse unnecessarily. He had no heart left, a vertical slit punched cleanly through his sternum and spine.

She stared down, the visage of a cat's eye seeming to stare up from the wound.

*Would he have survived if I took the blow?*

He was dead; she should turn her focus elsewhere.

## Millennial Mage, 4 - Bound

*Could I have saved him, for the simple price of some inscriptions to heal myself?*

It was not the time for deep introspection. More guards might be dying around her.

Her head snapped up at that. *Protect now, think later.*

She quickly lunged between several different individual engagements, giving aid where it might not have been strictly necessary, but where it would free up a guard to go help others.

After a few such interventions, her eyes moved over to where the juggernaut had fallen, only about three hundred yards away, behind the retreating wagons.

Like light from heaven, a beam of sunlight came through the trees and canopy at her back, lancing out, highlighting the helmet among the fallen vegetative matter. An irregular circle of the forest floor, a splash zone, was still lightly sizzling from the gushing outpouring of the Leshkin's demise.

*I could combine that armor with my elk leathers.* That would be an *incredible* defensive resource.

She took a step toward her spoils.

A guard screamed in pain nearby. She needed to protect the caravan.

*But that would be so useful! Even if I can't meld its form and magics with my clothing, I could sell it for so much!*

Her eyes found the wounded guardswoman, and Tala moved that way, throwing Flow into her opponent's head before pulling it back to her hand. It wasn't a lethal blow to the Leshkin but the guardswoman used the momentary reprieve and distraction to finish off the beast herself.

*I need to get that armor.*

Tala turned, taking one step in that direction, still feeling disoriented.

Her arm was before her, laying on the ground. Somehow, her zig-zagging and overlapping path had brought her back to the limb.

Trying not to look at it, she picked it up and immediately stuck it into Kit. *I'll deal with that later. I need to get that armor.* Now.

She took another half-step, stumbling as she warred within herself.

What was she doing? The caravan needed her. Her post, her job, her obligations lay behind her.

*But that armor would be so useful!* She felt blood flickering around the edges of the thought. She shouldn't be short on blood; her inscriptions were designed to maintain optimum blood volume. *What's going on?*

She shook her head. She *wanted* the armor, but she *needed* to stay with the caravan.

Hesitantly, reluctantly, she turned her back on the wealth, neatly piled in the woods.

She had a job to do.

\*   \*   \*

The caravan made it to the draw-down line at around sunset, fighting mostly lesser Leshkin and warriors along the way. Though there had been occasional knights sprinkled through the other ranks.

Tala had been rotated back to the top of the cargo wagon, and she absently noted that Mistress Odera was watching her more closely than usual.

Tala still felt twinges from her right arm that she knew were purely mental. *My arm is in perfect health.*

The back of her hand felt naked, even after the reapplication of iron-salve. There was not even a single ring for her Crush and Restrain spell-workings to implement.

They reached the draw-down line that Mistress Odera had referenced, and Tala took in the world around her, looking more closely.

The power in the air picked up speed, moving much more quickly toward Makinaven, still out of sight through the trees ahead.

She felt her gaze move downward, even as the last of the attacking Leshkin were being finished off by the rear-guard.

In the ground, beneath their feet, was an absolutely impossible-to-differentiate tangle of roots. Yet, somehow, she could *feel* that throughout all the tendrils of these great trees, existed the influence of something greater.

*Is it a bigger tree nearby, or something else?* She couldn't tell, and if she were being honest, she found it hard to care.

*What am I going to do with my arm?* She could burn it, to retrieve the gold from the inscriptions that hadn't been active when the limb had been separated.

In her perfectly healed shoulder, there were an unhealthy number of spell-form bits, ending at a jagged line, showing her exactly where her arm had regrown from.

She'd examined those remnants and didn't *think* they were valid spell-forms, but she meticulously kept every hint of power away from them, nonetheless. Given that she didn't know what they would do, they *shouldn't* activate, but she wasn't going to risk losing her arm. *Not again.*

Turning around, she felt an odd sense of disconnect in the suddenly silent forest.

The guards rarely yelled while fighting, and the Leshkin's only sound was their horrifying screech, which they didn't seem to use very often. The result had been a day filled, mainly, with sounds of grunting and physical strain, coupled with noises usually associated with the wood-cutting trade.

And the sound of tearing flesh.

And if a guard was just unlucky enough, the screams resulting from sizzling, burning injuries.

Tala shook her head. *No, it's not time to consider that.*

Mistress Odera looked up at her, from her seat near the back of the wagon. "Mistress Tala?"

"Hmm?"

"You seem… lost. Come, sit with me."

Tala obeyed. *Why not?*

"I received the reports about your arm. I am glad to see it back in working order. Is everything alright?"

Tala looked down at her right arm, whole and hale. "It seems to be functioning just fine."

"And how are you?"

Her gaze returned to the older woman. "They seem able to bypass my defenses…"

Mistress Odera nodded. "Your inscriptions aren't designed toward invincibility, correct?"

"Well, no."

"That is why you also have the regeneration spell-forms?"

"That's right."

After a moment's consideration, Mistress Odera smiled softly. "You've never taken such an injury, have you?"

Tala shook her head.

"It can be disorienting." The older woman was nodding again. "And to have the limb restored, before you've had time to really process the loss? That must have made it much worse."

"Why? I've not lost anything, not really. Why do I feel that I have?"

"When I was very young, my eldest sister lost her husband. At that time and place, a woman of her station couldn't be unmarried for long without complications. So she immediately remarried, this time to her deceased husband's brother." Mistress Odera gave Tala a meaningful look. "His identical twin brother."

Tala frowned. "That would have been… confusing."

"Quite. Whenever she looked at her husband, she knew he was there, knew he was her husband, but she also saw the one she'd lost. They were identical in almost every way. She hadn't even been married to the first for very long, and it had been a union of convenience." Mistress Odera snorted a laugh. "She'd actually liked this second brother more, but he had been less favored by his own family at the time, so she'd been united with the other."

"Why are you telling me this?"

"She never let herself truly process the loss. It felt like a figment to her mind, and therefore, unworthy of consideration."

"Sounds unhealthy."

"Precisely."

Tala grunted out a breath. "What do you suggest?"

"Take time to consider the pain you experienced, and what it would have meant for you."

"What the first casualty on this route is going through right now."

"The young man who you saved by cutting off his arm?"

*Does she really see it that way?* It was true, Tala supposed. "That's the one."

"Yes, that might be wise. I don't want you wallowing in that place." Mistress Odera tsked. "That would be horrible in a different way, but you cannot become desensitized to such injuries. They cannot be meaningless, and your body knows this. That is likely a part of your current state."

Tala found herself nodding as she stood. "Thank you. I will do what I can." She glanced back the way they'd come. "But right now, I should focus. Why are the Leshkin attacks stopping?"

Mistress Odera looked up at her, seeming to consider. After a moment, the Mage shrugged, apparently accepting the change in topic. "I assume you don't mean 'what changed?'"

"Correct. I can see what changed, and I remember you stating that they would turn back at this line. But why? They attack deep into the plains often enough. The open plains have less magic than here."

"Then, that is an excellent question, to which I do not have an answer."

Tala huffed a laugh and smiled. "That's fair, I suppose. Do you know what causes the change?"

"Yes. Makinaven is built in the great tree of this region."

Tala was nodding. "Yeah, I read about that. I imagined that it just meant it was more like a massive treehouse, network of such structures, or some similar thing. Bridges going between various high up platforms among the trees. How does that answer the question?"

Mistress Odera gave her a long look. "Not 'trees,' Mistress Tala. 'Tree.'"

Tala hesitated. *What?* She thought over what she'd read and what Mistress Odera had just said. *Makinaven resides within the great tree of this region.* The city was in *a* tree, not trees. Her eyes widened. "Wait. There's a tree bigger than these?" She hesitated. "Well, of course one tree has to be the biggest, and the chances of it being one of these is basically zero. That's not what I meant. I mean there's one larger to the point of being considered the singular great tree?"

"For this region, yes. It is a beautiful thing, and we have built within it."

"How does that work with the different defensive rings?"

Mistress Odera smiled. "I think it would be easier for you to see it before a full explanation, but the simple answer is that some of the city's stages are not within the tree, and it is the only great tree within the city proper."

"Ahh, yeah, that would do it." Tala smiled, feeling her tension slowly ease. "Will we be making camp soon?"

"Soon, I think, yes."

Tala considered for a long moment. "Did your sister really marry twins, one after the other?"

"Does the truth of the story change its utility?"

Tala laughed. "No, I suppose not." She hesitated. "In case you didn't know, my two quickest offensive spells are no longer available to me."

Mistress Odera cocked an eyebrow at that. "I did not know, though I suppose I could have intuited." She cursed. "Well, we shouldn't face anything else that needs such a heavy hit on this last leg."

"We logged the juggernaut kill, right?"

Mistress Odera grinned widely. "Of course, my dear. You'll be paid for that."

"How much should I expect?"

Mistress Odera considered. "You'll be getting roughly twenty-five percent of the payout to the Mage Protectors, equivalent to me, with that one exception boosting your portion. Master Rane was much more active and used far more of his inscriptions on this route."

Tala almost protested, but as she thought about it, she realized that Mistress Odera was correct. "About how much do you think that payout will be?"

"Well, I don't know the conditional rates, currently. There will be slight penalties for the delays, and we will be paying out our portion of the death benefits for those that died in defense of the caravan and assisting with the costs to heal those who were beyond my skill, but all told, those shouldn't be overmuch. As to the reward: two hundred ounces gold? That's probably an over-estimate, though."

Tala's eyes widened in shock.

"Total, dear, not to you."

"Still, that means that my portion, as Mage Protector, will be around fifty gold ounces." *I got into the wrong game, being a Dimensional Mage.* Then she thought about how she could have been tucked in the wagon, safe, warm, and well fed while other people fought around her. She also considered her expenses as a Mage Protector.

She would need all of her rings replaced, along with the accompanying scripts, and that would be a minimum of five gold. *Probably a lot more…*

She suspected that Holly had been giving her a steep discount, in consideration for her financial state, and her ability to take Holly's… oddities.

*I'll need to get them redone in Makinaven…* She scrunched her face. "I'm going to need a really good inscriber."

Mistress Odera nodded. "You don't have a slate, so you probably don't know: Mistress Holly has a list of inscribers, one in each city that she…" Mistress Odera seemed to hesitate. After a brief pause, she shook her head and continued, "Inscribers that she said she would *allow* to do any needed touch-ups." She sighed. "There is a list of things that she will, and will not, allow each to work on."

Tala frowned. "Can she really do that?"

"Well, no, she can't stop you, nor any inscriber, from completing a legal transaction. Effectively, though? Absolutely."

## Millennial Mage, 4 - Bound

"I think I understand, but can you lay it out for me?"

Mistress Odera quirked an amused smile. "She is, first and foremost, a frontrunner in the field of inscriptions and inscribing. Her inventions and discoveries are used in every city, by nearly every inscriber, even if not on every Mage they inscribe. She can easily cut one of the inscribers off, and they will be reticent to anger her. She could also refuse to work on you, if you do find someone who can and will do the work. From what I can see, there is no other inscriber in Bandfast who could work with most of your schema, and I'd bet my last copper that there is much more that I can't see."

"Fair enough. Don't anger your inscriptionist. They have proven able to stab something ten thousand times with horrifying precision."

Mistress Odera gave her a long look. "You think in some very unusual ways."

"Ahh... Sure... So! Who can I go see in Makinaven?"

Mistress Odera pulled out a slate, her fingers flying over the surface. "It looks like... Master Hawthorne. Oh! I've worked with him. He's very professional, skilled, and reasonably priced." She was nodding. "I believe that he touched up my scripts last time I was through this area. He's a busy fellow, though."

"Good to know. Will you be going to him, this trip?"

She thought about it for a moment. "I think that would be a reasonable choice, yes. I could get back without issue, but it never hurts to be careful. I'll happily go with you."

*Well, that was transparent of me...* She decided to lean into it. "Thank you."

Tala was looking at Mistress Odera when she saw the older woman's eyes widen in shock, her hand coming up in slow motion.

That was Tala's only warning.

It wasn't enough.

\*      \*      \*

A pulse of power exploded from the base of Tala's skull, and she returned to consciousness, violently.
…Just in time to slam into one of the massive trees.

\*      \*      \*

A second pulse of magic exploded from the base of Tala's skull, and she returned to consciousness, hesitantly.
She was surrounded by broken, splintered greenwood.
Tala groaned, pushing herself toward her right, the direction that felt more clear of obstructions. Splinters longer than her arm scraped against her, fighting with the elk leathers. Blessedly, none had succeeded in piercing her body.
A shiver ran through her from head to toe, and a sense akin to her magesight picked up the signature of what had awoken her. It had been the silver inscription, set to watch for any loss of consciousness not due to falling asleep.
*Did it bring me back once already? I didn't know it could do so in quick succession…* It made sense, though.
-*DING*- The all too familiar sound, almost like a bell, hummed through her thoughts, and she found the note calming.
She felt herself relax, slightly. *I am protected.*
Then, her own voice came to her as if she were thinking, without being her own thoughts.
*-Consciousness lost for 0.01 seconds due to heavy impact and whiplash of dura-matter within the cranium. Unconsciousness was the mind's natural defense. Neurochemical cocktail utilized for near instantaneous resuscitation.-*

## Millennial Mage, 4 - Bound

*-DING-*
*-Error, secondary loss of consciousness mid-cycle.-*
*-Secondary unconsciousness caused by heavy impact with a hard, fibrous material. Consciousness lost as a result of simultaneous activation of all head defenses, washing the brain in energy. Defenses have now returned to a normal level, allowing standard mental operations.-*
*-Critical note: Sequential losses of consciousness are ill-advised.-*
*-System recommendation: Consider the acquisition of an empowered helmet.-*
*-No lasting effects detected, despite predictive models.-*
*-Log complete.-*

Tala groaned, trying to ignore her inscription's sass. *I really need to talk with Holly about that…*

She pushed her head free of the tree, in which she'd been embedded, and her ears were assaulted by the rhythmic cadence of crossbow fire.

The day had been such that they'd increased the number of guards on duty in that role. They were firing as quickly as they could, but it didn't seem to have much effect.

Tala was high above the ground, nearly halfway up the trunk of a tree some three or four hundred yards from the caravan. The forest was mostly clear between her and the slow-moving wagons, and as such, she had a perfect view of what was happening.

A juggernaut stood beside and just in front of the cargo wagon, seemingly having stepped from behind a tree as they passed.

*It must have hit me with something like an uppercut to send me up here.*

It held a massive tower shield, easily fifteen feet in height and brimming with reinforcing power. The shield was between it and the bowmen.

The cargo wagon was surrounded by Mistress Odera's signature defensive shield, and the Leshkin juggernaut was slamming its empty fist into the protective barrier, sending rippling waves crashing across the surface.

Rane was standing beside the wagon, trapped within the protection, unable to get out.

The guards who were outside seemed reasonably hesitant about engaging the giant.

Tala, still a bit frazzled, brought up her right hand, first two fingers extended upward, her ring finger and pinky tucked down, all four pressed together, palm pointed toward the Leshkin juggernaut and her thumb tucked in tight. She channeled magic into the activation and—

The magic sparked within her shoulder, hitting the end of the broken inscription lines and searing through her.

She clamped her mouth down against a scream, even as she stopped the flow of power and her regenerative inscriptions dealt with the damage.

*Stupid! I can't use Crush.*

She had to do it the slow way. Her left middle finger touched her thumb, and she locked onto the Leshkin.

Before she even began to increase its effective gravity, the head whipped toward her, seemingly bottomless eye sockets locking onto her. The shriek that issued forth caused the caravan oxen to stumble and sent even Rane to his knees clutching at his ears.

The beast vaulted over the still-protected cargo wagon, obviously intent upon Tala.

*Well. That's one way to protect the caravan.*

# Chapter: 8
# Outside the Defenses

As Tala hung out of the depression in the big tree, her peripheral vision caught signs of movement around her, but her eyes were still fixed on the juggernaut moving her way.

*Every little bit will help.* Tala started dumping power into increasing its effective gravity.

However, even with such an obvious threat approaching, she couldn't ignore movement nearby, so she turned to look back at the tree she was in the side of.

She was hanging out of a relatively shallow, shattered hole, nearly four hundred feet up the trunk of a massive tree. *Relatively shallow.* She almost laughed. *It's practically six feet deep.*

As her gaze swept what amounted to a wooden wall that she was stuck in the side of, she saw Leshkin, so many Leshkin.

*Oh… Oh wow.*

There were at least a hundred lesser Leshkin in easy sight, hanging on the bark of the tree, like bees clinging to their hive, and each and every one seemed to be looking her way. The closest was only a few feet from her.

In fact, the splatter pattern of still-burning acid on the tree's bark implied that she might have gone *through* one or more, in order to impact as she had.

*Mistress Odera said they'd stop at the draw-down line…* Either the Mage had been mistaken, or there was something else influencing the Leshkin's actions. *Just great…*

The shield around the lead wagon dropped, and Mistress Odera's voice snapped out. "Get back to the wagons!"

The command hadn't just been directed at her, if it had been aimed at her at all. *Did she even see where I went?*

There were guardsmen ranging around the caravan, ostensibly to prevent things exactly like this, but now was hardly the time to throw stones. *Unless it was a really big one… Maybe I should get something like that for Kit? So I can drop the stone on enemies, if I'm up high?*

*Focus, Tala.* Her head was still ringing a bit. *I should talk to Holly about that… My head really should be better protected… Focus!*

*Okay. Get to the wagon. Mistress Odera can raise a shield around everyone, and we can proceed entirely inside it.* It wouldn't work if a snarl of roots blocked their way, but such shouldn't exist in this zone.

*Neither should the Leshkin…* It would also be a tremendous strain on Mistress Odera's power and inscriptions.

*Worth it if it keeps us alive.*

So, Tala had a choice.

On one hand, she could fight in the relative safety of her little indent, until the juggernaut arrived. She could use that time to increase the giant's effective gravity to the point that it would die, if she was lucky.

Her other option was to make a break for the caravan and safety.

*If I don't go now, Mistress Odera might not be able to keep the shield down for me, and I'd be stuck outside until we reach true safety…*

Put that way, there really wasn't much of a choice. *Break for the caravan.*

But she needed to do it intelligently.

Tala ducked back into her impact crater; it was almost as deep as she was tall. All her contemplations had taken less than a couple of seconds. *Bless my mental enhancements.*

Drawing Flow, she thrust the weapon into the shattered side of her resting place within the tree, angling outward so that Flow's tip would exit the tree, away from the opening. Tala moved the sword a full circle around the gap, attempting to cut out a conical chunk, as large as Flow's length would allow.

She still had a lock on the juggernaut, and with her left middle finger pressed to her thumb, she was increasing its gravity steadily. That wasn't her priority right now, though.

*I can't waste this time.* Reluctantly, she switched her lock to herself, left middle finger still firmly pressed against her thumb. *Decrease.*

The wood before her groaned as the large section of the tree began to slide free. It wasn't as large as she would have liked, but she would work with what she had.

The entrance would now be clear, and there was a good distraction for the Leshkin attention, at least momentarily.

She dove out after the falling bit of tree.

Humorously, several Leshkin looked up at her through the hole in that chunk, which had been the entrance to her divot. They would be crushed by the fall and the heavy chunk of wood momentarily.

With a tremendous sideways leap, Tala cleared the tree and looked back.

Waves of Leshkin were leaping off the main trunk after her, their own jumps far less impressive than hers, given her strength and ever-reducing effective gravity.

# Millennial Mage, 4 - Bound

There were also quite a few more than she'd been able to see before her leap.

*Why are they so fixated on me? Is that why they're here when they shouldn't be? Is something about me drawing them or angering them?*

She glanced down and saw the juggernaut, its gaze also fixed on her. Her gravity sight told her that it was now subject to nearly thrice normal gravity. *It took between sixteen- and sixty-four-times gravity to kill the last one.* Her meager increase would barely inconvenience the beast.

Her own gravity was now low enough that she was arching down *much* further out than she should have been able to. Unfortunately, she hadn't decreased it enough before her jump, so she would still fall short of the caravan, if not nearly as much as she would have with a normal fall.

*I'll have to have a good proportion of gravity once I land, so that I will be able to run the last bit.* But when should she re-increase? *In either case, I'm light enough, now.*

She switched the lock back to the juggernaut and continued to increase its weight.

Tala was still accelerating downward, but not nearly as fast as normal. It took her more than ten seconds to reach the ground, and the last half of her fall was punctuated by the rotten-log sound of the lesser Leshkin splattering themselves on the ground around the base of the tree.

As each lesser Leshkin struck the ground, among the roots, it was turned into a pile of mulch by the impact, the acidic blood fountaining in all directions.

Tala's drifting fall had managed to get her more than a hundred yards from the base… and almost on top of the juggernaut.

As the last couple seconds of the fall came and went, Tala switched back to herself and moved her weight back toward normal.

The impact was… more than she'd expected. Her increased weight, due to her large physical stores, factored in. In addition, she was imbalanced as her right arm was significantly lighter than her left. That didn't even factor in that the forest floor was far from perfectly flat.

All that came together for an awkward landing, and her leg broke on impact.

She went down, hard, but before she could scream in pain, her scripts had realigned and healed the damage. Her eyes had involuntarily squeezed shut against the momentary agony, and when they shot open once more, the juggernaut was bringing its shield down at her head.

*Not good!* This was becoming a pattern for her.

She jerked to the side as the massive wooden monument drove deeply into the frozen soil. *How much strength and weight are behind that?* Her gravity sight told her that she'd gotten the Leshkin up to almost four times effective gravity. *Right. That would make downward blows stronger… and I'm shorter… Great.*

She might not have thought through all the implications thoroughly enough.

Now was hardly the time, though. *Come on, head, get back in the fight!*

Tala moved her lock to the big creature once again and took off from the ground, hitting a full sprint almost instantly.

Behind her, gravity's influence continued to increase on the Leshkin juggernaut. *In for a copper—*

That Leshkin shrieked, and it was answered by another, equal in power.

*No… Oh, rust no.*

## Millennial Mage, 4 - Bound

She glanced over her shoulder and saw portions of the mulch and acid pile pulling together against the great tree. The form of a giant began to be visible among the remains of what had once been more than two hundred lesser Leshkin. *Another!? That isn't fair. They shouldn't be able to merge after falling to their destruction.* She cursed her luck.

In all likelihood, eight had survived the impact and had taken advantage of their incoherent state and the proximity of the tree to combine as much as possible.

Tala cursed again and threw her focus forward once more.

She promptly tripped, falling into a tangle of limbs. *Eyes on the prize, Tala. Focus forward!*

"*Get to the wagons!*" Mistress Odera's voice was being amplified, somehow.

The ground shook while Tala tried to get her hands under her to push back to her feet.

Just as she lifted up, the closest juggernaut's foot lanced out, connecting with her torso and sending her flying over the caravan to land in a tumbling heap on the other side.

She coughed, spitting blood onto the ground before sucking in a gasping breath. Her ribs realigned, and her punctured lungs reinflated. *This pain is wildly distracting.*

Oh, and her endingberry power was gone. *When did that happen?*

She thought back in a panicked haze and realized that it had been when she impacted the tree. *Oh… that would have been good to rectify.*

Even after the blunt force damage was healed, her body still seemed to be screaming at her about her injuries. Though the cries reached her more as distant echoes than as someone yelling into her ear.

She came to her feet, sweeping Flow in a circle to clear the area, as she'd practiced countless times against the guardsmen back in Bandfast. Bless the stars that she did.

A small swarm of lessers had been almost upon her, and Flow neatly decapitated many… drenching Tala in a flood of acidic blood.

She screamed. First at the pain, then again as some of the acid got into her mouth.

She spat furiously and stumbled in the direction of the caravan. She fumbled toward Kit and felt her hot water incorporator fall into her hand.

As she continued to move, she blasted herself. First her face, then as much of the rest of her as she could do quickly, to clear away the caustic substance. She even moved the void-channels away from Flow, allowing it to return to the form of a knife, so that she could use more water, more quickly.

With eyes once again able to properly see, she looked toward her destination. If her perception was right, the last of the guards were now clustered close between the still-moving wagons. Most had crossbows, and they were firing in all directions as quickly as they could rearm the weapons, their companions feeding them ammunition just as quickly.

Mistress Odera was looking back and forth between Tala and the other side of the wagon train. If Tala had to bet, she would have said that Mistress Odera was trying to decide if Tala or the two juggernauts on the far side would reach the caravan first.

The Mage couldn't change the size of her barriers, once created, and the larger they were, the harder they would be to maintain.

*She can't include me, here. It would ruin everyone's chances.* Tala stumbled into a run, getting her feet under her and pouring on the steam.

*Come on, come on.* Run, Tala. Run*!*

Her vision tunneled, her entire focus on the wagons before her.

Despite her own urgings, she pulled up short just as a massive blade came down, breaking the ground and embedding deep within. An instant later, the ground shook, the new juggernaut having leapt over the wagon-train to get to Tala.

Mistress Odera's shield snapped into place; the Mage was unable to wait any longer. *She waited longer than she probably should have, if the juggernaut was close enough to jump over.*

The juggernaut had reached her, and she was trapped outside the defenses. *Well… rust me.*

Tala turned to take her first good look at the incredibly heavily armored giant. Made almost entirely of vines, this one held a greatsword.

*Yeah… nothing else will fit that moniker ever again…*

The massive wooden blade was nearly fifteen feet long, two feet wide, and embedded nearly halfway into the ground, between Tala and the magical shield that protected the retreating caravan.

The Leshkin was staring at her with a look of unrestrained fury and… sadness?

*Betrayal? That doesn't make…* Her eyes widened. *Without my aura control, I would look like they do, at least to magesight. Can they see through that control, somehow?*

That didn't make sense. Why would they think she was one of them? *Do I have a better explanation?*

She didn't. Maybe they were seeing what seemed to be endingberry power, but if she was being honest, it really didn't matter.

The greatsword wielder stepped forward and punched down into her head and left shoulder, while its off-hand remained on the sword's handle.

Tala was thrown to the ground, something that Rane had made her incredibly familiar with. Her bones popped back into shape, and Tala found herself unable to care about the pain.

*Focus, Tala. You're alone, again. On your own, again.*

The strange squeal of frozen earth, forced to move, accompanied the greatsword's extraction. A whistling filled the air, as the massive blade moved in a deadly arc.

*Fight!*

She vaulted to her feet, moving Flow into a guarding position, even as she reconnected the void-channels, returning Flow to the form of a sword.

Her movements were just in time, and Flow perfectly intercepted the falling strike, edge-to-edge.

To her joy, Flow sheared straight through the oncoming weapon, clearly more magically powerful and able to overcome whatever magics or material properties reinforced the blade.

To her consternation, that resulted in the attack continuing. The now-severed end of the sword struck her at nearly full speed, though without the follow-through of a properly delivered attack.

She was thrown backwards, to the side, and to the ground.

*Rust you!* She stood and threw Flow at the giant's head, maintaining the void-channel connection to the weapon.

It sunk into the beast's eye.

*Nice shot!*

It did nothing.

*Right… I have to behead it…*

# Millennial Mage, 4 - Bound

She called Flow back. As the weapon flew toward her, Tala was struck by the now much shorter greatsword. The flat of the blade threw her sideways, into the caravan's shield.

She stopped instantly, robbed of all kinetic energy.

Her bones realigned, again, and she groaned, feeling *famished.*

*I need to get away. I can't fight this thing.*

The ground shook as the tower-shield juggernaut vaulted over the caravan and landed twenty feet from Tala to the west, closer to the front of the defensive field.

Tala whimpered in frustrated anger.

*No. This is like fighting Terry. Don't let your emotions rule you!*

Tala briefly bemoaned the loss of her repeating hammer. She could have thrown that and obliterated one of these creatures with relative ease.

She would give her left arm to have it back.

That struck a chord in her mind, and she twitched. *Well, no. I wouldn't give my arm...* She shivered. She did *not* want to repeat that experience.

Her gaze flicked back and forth between the two juggernauts that she could see. *Is there a third, or is this all the rusting bad luck I've earned?*

She didn't know but she decided to assume the worst. For some reason, the sword wielder was waiting for the shield bearer to flank her fully. *Precious seconds.*

A voice, incredibly muffled, came to her from behind the shield.

"Mistress Tala! To the back of the caravan!"

Tala turned and saw Rane waving at her frantically, but with huge and exaggerated motions. She looked toward the back and saw an incredibly small opening left in the magical shield. If she belly-crawled, she might be able to squeeze through. *Mistress Odera left me a way in!*

She smiled widely, hope filling her.

Rane's eyes widened in horror, and Tala felt something impact her back.

*I stayed in one place for too long.* The world went white for a brief instant as even her enhanced nervous system couldn't handle the sheer quantity of pain signals.

She somehow maintained consciousness. *No more sass, today!*

Tala was thrown forward, slamming against the shield once more, feeling what seemed like all her bones and connective tissue simultaneously pull back together. *How hard was I hit?*

Near half of her power reserves were gone, and she didn't have time to analyze the state of her physical stores.

Purely on instinct, Tala dropped to the ground just in time for the shortened-greatsword to bisect where she'd been standing. *Yeah… that would have been bad. It nearly killed me with a blunt hit. Given the caravan's shield as a cutting board, that sword would have been…* She turned away from the images that her mind began to conjure.

Tala rolled from her position on the ground, and as soon as her feet were under her, she sprinted toward the back of the caravan, to the hole in the defenses. As she did so, her hip popped back into place. *Why didn't that realign before?*

Some lesser Leshkin seemed to have noticed the weakness in their enemies' defenses and were attempting to crawl inside.

Rane had already run ahead of her, and he thrust Force out, through the opening, throwing the invaders back to clear her a path.

Tala dropped into a slide, coming to a stop just close enough to stick her hand through the opening.

Rane had flattened himself to the ground, and he thrust his hand out, snatching her outstretched fingers.

Once he had a firm grip, he *pulled.*

Tala shot through the opening, tucking her shoulders in close and pointing her feet to be as streamlined as possible.

The world shook as she slammed into Rane, falling in a tangled heap with him, inside Mistress Odera's shield.

Tala looked back through the opening and saw the sword blade embedded in the ground just outside the shield.

"Well… That was close." She barely managed a whisper as she clung to Rane, breathing heavily.

"Rust me. Yeah, it was."

A few of the guards swarmed over them, checking them for injuries and helping them stand.

Five stayed at the small opening to defend the vulnerability, each armed with a crossbow. The remaining led Tala and Rane back to the front wagon where Mistress Odera was visibly straining.

As soon as they were up on the roof with her, Rane spoke, "What can we do, Mistress?"

"Don't distract me. Keep the wagons moving, and keep them from breaching the opening I had to leave."

Rane nodded, beginning to climb back down.

Tala stayed, regarding the woman for a long moment.

"What is it? I'm a bit busy."

Tala didn't know how to say what she was thinking, so she decided to just go for it. "Thank you."

Mistress Odera opened her eyes to give Tala a look. "Now is hardly the time."

"Even so, thank you. You could have left me out there, and no one would have blamed you."

The older Mage grunted. "You are my responsibility. I don't care if anyone else would have blamed me. I would have blamed myself." She grimaced, closing her eyes once more. "Now go. We can't afford distractions."

Tala silently nodded acknowledgement and followed after Rane.

*We can survive this. I know we can.*

\* \* \*

Somehow defying the two Leshkin juggernauts' efforts, Mistress Odera's defensive shield held, and the oxen continued their unchanging pace. Blessedly, there had only been two of the giants.

The lesser Leshkin spent their lives trying to crawl through the small opening, and they died one by one.

The light had long since faded from the sky, and the caravan was only lit by their massive, empowered lights, the illumination barely piercing the shield to show their pursuers.

After hours of failing to claim their prize, and long after the last lesser had died, the Leshkin juggernauts ceased their useless assault and slowed, allowing the caravan to pull slightly ahead.

"Did we do it? Did we win?" one of the guards asked in a quiet, strained voice.

*They never retreat.* Tala frowned. She was walking backwards near the opening. She was there to support the guards and Rane, if the need arose.

As they watched, the juggernauts broke apart, falling into eight lessers each. Somehow, the juggernauts' equipment dissolved as well, the energy and material of the tools going toward recorporating the weaker Leshkin. Those lessers screeched their rage and charged the opening.

At that point, the defense of that vulnerability was well practiced, and the sixteen lesser Leshkin died quickly.

As the final died, the shield that had been protecting them for so long seemed to waver. Then, it vanished.

Mistress Odera's voice floated back to them. "We aren't stopping tonight. We need to get to Makinaven as soon as possible." There was a hesitation to the magically enhanced voice. "And I need to rest."

Several guards had rushed up to the top of the cargo wagon, following some instruction that Tala hadn't heard. They carefully helped Mistress Odera down, and into the cargo-slot that she would sleep in.

"Well, Master Rane, it seems like we're on overwatch for the night."

Rane nodded. "You take the wagon top, and I'll do sweeps of the surroundings. Terry, you able to circle counter to me?"

The avian flickered to stand beside Tala, once again roughly the size of a horse. He let out an affirmative whistling squawk.

"Thank you."

The two of them turned outward in opposite directions and began their sweep. Tala, for her part, headed to the cargo wagon and climbed up.

As she sat down and thought over the insane afternoon, she had a realization. Tala slapped her own forehead. "I could have increased the juggernauts' effective gravity, after I was within the shield."

She groaned. That likely would have shortened the whole encounter greatly. *Well, I'll do better next time.*

She began sweeping their surroundings with her magesight and enhanced vision; it was going to be a long night.

# Chapter: 9
## On Overwatch

The cooks worked through the night, getting energizing meals for the Mages and guards, along with keeping them supplied with coffee.

Tala got a bit more than the average of both food and coffee, but she still felt hungry down to her bones. *Which broke so many, many times…*

It did seem like they were mainly out of danger, as no further attacks came before the light of dawn broke across the canopy overhead.

Tala recharged the cargo-slots as her last act before stumbling into her room and crashing into deep sleep.

It felt like as soon as her head hit the much-too-firm pillow, a loud knock sounded against her door.

Tala rolled over and sat up with a groan. She was *sore.* The bed was designed for someone four times her weight, and so it resisted her downward pressure with ease. *I should have increased my weight before sleeping…* Maybe next time.

Her eyes flicked around the small space. The walls were simple in construction, made of interlocking panels that could be taken apart and removed from the expanded space with ease. Even so, there weren't cracks to affect privacy or the darkness desired for easy sleep, and they seemed to have been constructed with sound isolation in mind as well.

# Millennial Mage, 4 - Bound

Her eyes landed on Terry, sleeping in his corner space. *When did he get back?*

The knock came again.

"What." She didn't make it a question. *Don't encourage them.*

"Mistress Tala?"

*What kind of idiotic question is that? Who else would be in here?* "Yes."

"Lunch has been prepared for you; can I give it to you, now?"

*Lunch?* Well, that meant that it was later than she'd thought it was. "Yes. One moment." She stood and walked to the door, unlocking it and pulling it open.

One of the guardsmen stood outside the door, bearing a large tray that was laden with an absolute feast.

Tala grinned, taking the tray. "Thank you!"

He gave a half-bow. "Of course." Without another word, he closed the door for her, leaving her to her meal.

Tala came back to sit on her bed, placing the food on her lap. Her stomach growled at the slight delay. *I was not going to start gorging while standing.*

There was a large bowl of fresh berries, a platter of raw veggies, a whole loaf of heavy bread with copious amounts of butter, and meat enough to feed a small army. *Well, not quite.*

There was bacon and sausage, then pulled pork and ground beef, and finally what seemed to be garlic-flavored chicken.

Tala devoured the meal with abandon.

She drank deeply from her cool water incorporator. *You know, I bet I could brew tea with the hot water one...* If she knew how, she could probably make coffee as well. *Might be better to not learn that secret...*

She had a thought, then. *What would happen when the water discorporates? Would it just leave behind a powder?* She blinked a few times. *If I were to make a solution with a large portion of incorporated water, the saturation and potency would rise to an absurd degree, after the water discorporated.*

It wouldn't be useful in every situation, and might actually ruin quite a few concoctions, but it could be worth investigating. *If nothing else, cleaning iron-dust would become almost trivial… if I did that anymore.*

She smiled. It was worth experimenting with at some point. *I'll have time, eventually.*

The meal complete and her dishes scraped clean with remnants of the bread, Tala dipped the dishes into Kit for a final cleaning. *That is really, really handy. I do need to figure out what happens to all the gunk that Kit cleans off at some point.*

But that could wait for another day. She absentmindedly topped Kit off with power.

Tala felt refreshed but still ravenous. *More food!*

She and Terry left her room, the bird only coming awake enough to flicker to her shoulder as she departed before snuggling down to continue his rest.

Tala was almost blinded when she pulled open the outer door, looking out on the sunlit, forest landscape, slowly moving by. The white of frost and snow patches increased the harshness of the view.

After her eyes adjusted, she swung out, grabbing the ladder up to the cargo wagon's roof and pulling herself up.

Rane stood on the top, on overwatch for the two-wagon caravan.

Tala sat on the edge of the roof, beside the ladder. "Any excitement this morning, Master Rane?"

Rane smiled her way. "Mistress Tala, good afternoon. Nothing of consequence. A pack of upright reptiles made a play for the oxen, but they were driven off before we could get a good enough look to judge their species."

Tala grunted at that. It was a frustration for such creatures: Human eyes, even enhanced, weren't good at picking out the subtle differences between the large reptile species.

Sure, overarching groups were obvious; walking on four legs versus two was quite distinctive, and those with a long neck or massive, backward sweeping neck-plate were also easy to differentiate. Unfortunately, most of the obviously varied ones either weren't present in the forest or didn't seem as inclined to attack.

*All carnivorous lizard-things look really similar….*

Rane rolled his eyes. "I can guess what you're thinking."

"Oh?"

"All a bunch of featherless chickens?" He quirked a smile.

She paused for a moment. *What?*

Clearly, by the twinkle in his eyes, he thought he'd said something immensely clever.

*Come on, Tala. What does he— Right…* "Very funny, Master Rane."

He cracked a full grin. "All in all, Mistress Odera was correct. This portion of the forest is positively tame."

Tala smiled in return. "Ahh, yes. I'd like a home…" She looked around. "On top of that hill." She pointed to a nearby rise. Sun streamed down on it, showing that it lay beneath a break in the canopy.

Rane shook his head. "That would be horribly indefensible. All that light coming down would make the surrounding woods look almost black for much of the day."

"I thought you said these parts were tame?" She put on a mock air of confusion.

He laughed. "Not city-safe, Mistress."

"Fine." She took a deep breath, ready to continue the banter, when her stomach let out a gurgling roar. She felt herself blushing. "I… should probably get some more food."

Rane nodded. "Yeah, it looked like you did a *lot* of healing yesterday." His eyes flicked to her right arm. "Are you… Okay?"

Tala glanced down at the arm in question. "I…" She took a breath and let it out slowly. "I think so. The loss barely registered before it came back. I think I'm more irritated at the loss in reserves and inscriptions than the limb." *Is that true?*

He had an incredibly serious look on his face. "Severe injuries, even if they're healed, can be rough to weather. Take some time when we get to Makinaven to recenter yourself." He gave a half-smile. "We missed our earliest departure date for the return trip, so we'll be there for a bit more than a week."

Talal nodded. That sounded wise. "Thank you, Master Rane."

He waved her off. "Go, eat."

She nodded, swinging back onto the ladder and climbing down. Terry kept his eyes lightly closed, but his feet gripped her shoulder quite firmly, implying that he was awake.

Amnin greeted her warmly when Tala knocked on the chuckwagon's rear door, another massive tray of food already ready and waiting for Tala to devour. This one also had a large jug of coffee along with it.

"Bless you, mistress of these kitchens."

Amnin just laughed and waved her off. "Eat, please. Send word if you need more."

## Millennial Mage, 4 - Bound

Tala took the tray back to her room in the cargo-slot after briefly checking in with Rane. He told her to eat, then return so he could go sleep for a bit.

Mistress Odera had yet to come out, though her servant had gotten her a few meals, reporting that the Mage was resting after the massive expenditure.

*Makes sense. Even with her ridiculous efficiency, it must have been taxing to the extreme to maintain against the assault for so long.*

Tala sat down and dug into the smorgasbord. The variety in this meal conveyed the idea that the cooks were clearing out their leftovers before arriving at the city that evening, rather than making new dishes.

That was fine with her. The variability helped alleviate the oddity of just how much she was consuming.

In truth, she'd retreated to her room, mainly because she'd felt some embarrassment at the spread and hadn't wanted anyone to watch.

Terry dutifully kept his eyes closed. His only sign of wakefulness was an occasionally open mouth, which Tala placed food within. He ate happily, leaving her to her private gorging.

*This is taking a lot of the fun out of eating...* Too much of a good thing and all that. *Fine. I'll try not to lose any more limbs...*

She still had to decide what to do with the arm.

She did not consider the options while eating. She needed the calories and couldn't risk being put off by the grisly thoughts.

That said, once she'd basically licked the dishes clean, she did allow her thoughts to move to the limb.

*I could let Terry eat it.* He'd probably love that. Given how packed it was with calories and energy, it might feed him as well as many big-game beasts.

She wouldn't have to think about it again, that way...

*But what about the gold?* It was something to consider. There were at least five ounces of gold within the limb, probably closer to ten. She didn't often consider the scripts that had stretched through the arm in order to link those in her hand to those in her right breast. *And I'm going to have to get those replaced...*

Mistress Odera had a 'Holly-approved' inscriptionist to take Tala to, so that would take care of finding someone who could correct her lack of quick, offensive spell-forms. The cost would be cut in half now that Tala was officially a Mage Protector. *But if I were an inscriptionist, that would cause me to charge more.*

Tala wouldn't count on too much of a discount from her earlier inscriptions.

In fact, as she thought about it, she was pretty sure that Holly had already been undercharging her, given the other woman's desire to experiment with Tala's inscriptions and capabilities. Tala hadn't really let herself consider it fully before, because she hated being beholden to anyone. Still, she hadn't really had any other options. *So, don't think about it.*

She let out a tired sigh. *So, expect more expensive inscriptions...*

Thinking of inscriptions, she swept her magesight through her body, checking the integrity of the active scripts that she still had. They were *much* more worn than she would have liked.

*Six months? Rust you, Holly. These won't last six weeks.* To be fair, she had been stressing them quite thoroughly.

She shuddered, remembering the juggernauts knocking her around like a child's ball.

*Yeah, I prefer worn inscriptions to death.*

Still, this meant that she'd have to visit Holly as soon as she was back in Bandfast, just to be safe.

## Millennial Mage, 4 - Bound

*I'll need her to look at this, too.* She brushed her hand across the base of her neck, thinking of Xeel and the supposed encounter with an Arcane. *I hope she can get something from it.*

So, back to her arm.

*I should get the gold out.* Maybe the inscriptionist would have an idea as to how.

A thought occurred to her, then.

*Wait... the elk leather.* She opened Kit and reached in, seeking to get just the sleeve instead of the arm that was within.

She felt the supple leather in her hand and pulled it out.

It was that and only that; wonderfully high-quality, dyed, and treated leather. No magic remained.

*I wonder if I could cut my outfit in half and get two outfits out of it?*

What would the purpose be? She didn't need two of them, and they wouldn't be able to be sold; they were bound to her, after all.

*Maybe as a back-up? In case something manages to completely obliterate the one I'm wearing, and I survive?*

There was some merit to that, but she didn't want to experiment on her own. It wasn't worth losing the garments, especially when she'd be near a branch of the Constructionists soon enough.

She sighed, putting the leather back in her pouch.

"Thank you, Kit."

The pouch did not respond.

She'd finished her meal and was just delaying at this point. "I need to go relieve Master Rane." She glanced to Terry. "Want to stay in here or come with me?"

He cracked an eye then closed it without moving.

"Fair enough." She smiled to herself as she left her room, locking it behind herself.

She gave all her dishes over to the chuckwagon workers, along with her profuse gratitude, before she climbed back up onto the cargo wagon's top.

"Ready to take overwatch?"

She nodded. "Go, eat, sleep. I'll be fine for this last stretch."

"Thank you."

"Rest well, Master Rane."

He gave her a parting, tired smile before disappearing over the edge of the wagon, leaving Tala basically alone with her thoughts.

The afternoon passed uneventfully as they continued to draw closer to Makinaven.

The guards drove off a few lesser arcanous beasts, but nothing of note; no true attacks and nothing close enough for her to even see what it had been, through the low-light and trunks.

Terry came out of the cargo-slot and vanished for a couple of hours in the middle, likely off to hunt or for a final run before they were to be within a city for more than a week's time.

*Good thought, my friend. Burn off some energy.* She'd initially felt some irritation toward Terry. After all, he hadn't helped her when she was reduced to a training pell for the Leshkin juggernauts, but a little time and a little thought had shown her the folly of those feelings.

*He couldn't have done anything except get hurt. I survived. If I'd been seriously hurt, or truly trapped, he likely would have come to help me.*

She didn't actually know that, but she hoped that it was true. After all, he'd come to her aid in the past. *Never against creatures that could seriously harm him, though...* Well, he had helped her face Leshkin knights. *I might be over thinking things.*

To be fair, she'd never put herself on the line for him, had she? *Maybe with Xeel. I think that man would have killed Terry if I hadn't vouched for him, or if I had hedged too much.*

Her partnership with Terry was still incredibly new, and though she was coming to understand the value of sparring with the avian, it was quite intimidating, traveling with a creature that had so thoroughly demonstrated his martial superiority.

*Well, he can't outright kill me.* She snorted a chuckle. *That just means that I'll still be breathing as he kills everyone around us. Then, I'll have plenty of time to rue my choices as he bleeds my defenses dry.* But he wasn't hostile to her, so that wasn't a concern.

Nope, she wasn't worried in the slightest.

*Nothing to fear but a slow death, surrounded by carnage, at the hands of someone I trusted.*

Friends were great. Tala should find more.

Finally, they came out from around one of the large trees, and she was able to look down, across a cleared space before them, upon Makinaven.

Nothing that she had read or heard, prepared her for the sight.

A truly gargantuan tree stood in the center of the wide clearing, and nothing about that description accurately conveyed the scale.

The tree was a titan compared to the children they'd been traveling among, and no other great tree stood in the area before them, the space involved being close to four times the area of a normal, new built city.

It wasn't that much taller, at most double the smaller trees in the forest at around one and a half thousand feet in height. The trunk, however, looked to be a thousand feet in diameter at least, and the amount of magic flowing through the entirety was colossal.

Now that she was closer to the source, she could see that the draw-down line they crossed the previous day was likely the very edges of this great tree's roots. The Builders had obviously added to and augmented the power-drawing nature of the tree, using that natural framework to exceed the draw of most cities.

The tree, itself, then functioned as the others in the forest did, raining the power down from its spreading canopy. And oh, how the canopy spread.

*What sort of magics are in the wood to allow that?* No amount of mundane material could allow such cantilevered limbs, and certainly not of that size.

There was no city below or around the tree at first glance, and Tala was already seeing lights sparkling in the trunk in the early evening dimness. As she focused more fully, she saw buildings on the lower branches, melded with the bark.

*The streets must run down the middle of the branches with buildings on either side.* Makinaven *should* be firmly in the bureaucratic phase, preparing for its waning and abandonment, but if anything, it looked livelier than Bandfast, a city less than half its age.

"Beautiful, isn't it?"

Tala shifted her gaze to see Mistress Odera climbing the rest of the way onto the roof.

"Makinaven, Retindel, Truhold, Namfast, and Manaven." Mistress Odera took a deep breath and let out a deeply contented sigh. "Those are our remaining forest cities, this cycle. They are truly something special."

"Makinaven doesn't look like a city in the bureaucratic stage."

Mistress Odera nodded knowingly. "That is because the forest cities are able to maintain nearly every stage for their full life-cycle. Only the mining operations fade at the usual time. The great tree that each is built within makes the foundational inscriptions more efficient, long-lasting, and powerful. The result is more danger around the cities but a longer lifespan for most of the cities' functions."

Tala was awed, and true to Mistress Odera's words, Tala could see orchards and farmland tucked around the base of the tree, spreading outward to cover almost the entirety of the space beneath the reaching canopy.

"The entirety of the city is within the tree, only the food production and now closed down mining operations are located outside."

The wagons did not slow their pace as they headed down a slight incline, down into the valley in which the great tree flourished.

# Chapter: 10
# Welcome to Makinaven

Tala and Terry watched as Mistress Odera sat facing them, allowing them to take in the city while she only watched them.

"So, have you had a chance to think on your encounter with the juggernauts?"

Tala snorted, a rueful smile coming across her face. "Absolutely."

"And?"

She took another moment to put her words in order. "I'm too durable."

Mistress Odera cocked an eyebrow but didn't comment.

"I don't mean in absolute terms, more relatively speaking."

"Go on."

"My spars with Terry showed a part of it, but the juggernauts really brought it into focus. My offensive power is atrocious, especially in comparison to my durability."

Mistress Odera shrugged. "Yes and no. You took a juggernaut down with your ranged attack the other day."

"And the loss of a limb took that ability from me."

The older Mage shook her head. "Do you know how many Mages could continue after losing an arm?"

"Most?"

Mistress Odera rolled her eyes. "Very few. Few combat-oriented Archons, even."

"That can't be right."

"Mistress Tala, most combat-oriented Mages wouldn't have been in a position to lose the arm to begin with."

*Oh… Yeah, that makes sense.*

"The fact that you are still an asset to the caravan after receiving such a blow is a testament to the wisdom of allowing you to take up the dual role."

Tala gave a small smile. "Thank you. That's kind."

Mistress Odera waved that off. "The truth is true, Mistress. My point is this: You are not too well-defended, nor are you offensively ineffective. You have limited use at range, for now, but you also have tools that you haven't fully explored. You're judging half your deck against half that of others. That is foolish."

*There she is.* "So then, what is your assessment?"

"You need something to affix you in place, at need. You could also use something to take damage on your behalf, rather than simply hoping for the best and healing after."

"Yeah, I have been violently removed from this wagon top a few too many times…" *What could I use? Straps? They wouldn't hold up to the things that have knocked me free.* "Is there any form of magic to lock me in place?"

Mistress Odera gave her an odd look. "You're the Dimensional Mage; you tell me."

Tala's eyes widened. *I didn't think of it in that way. If I approach it from a dimensional standpoint, teleportation could be the field to start with.* Teleportation receiving scripts had what amounted to dimensional anchors, fixing them in place, relative to Zeme, so that incoming travelers wouldn't be reconstructed across a wide area. *Would that work?*

It wasn't perfect, as teleportation anchors were a combination of functions, including a beacon to aid in targeting specific destinations, and she did *not* want to be a beacon if she could help it. *Worth talking to the Constructionist Guild about, though.* There had to be something there…

Even if that worked, the result might be her taking more damage from any given attack. So, it would solve one of the two issues raised by Mistress Odera, while making the second one worse.

"It seems like that might have triggered something. I'll leave you to your thoughts." The older woman lifted her feet and spun around before resettling to gaze at the city before them.

*Let's assume I get the dimensional anchor all worked out, what would the consequences be?*

She would have to take the full force behind any blow, rather than allowing a large portion to be translated into kinetic energy and thus motion.

*So, I'll get hit harder, but wouldn't move.*

Depending on how it worked, could she hit harder as well, or would her entire body be locked in place?

*I'll have to investigate the different options. I'm sure there will be cost differences as well…*

Also, if it were to be truly useful, it would have to have a variable lock, letting her lock herself in place in relationship to the cargo wagon. Otherwise, she'd only be able to use it while at a dead stop.

*So many possibilities, and possible restrictions. An inertial lock?*

She looked up as they came under the farthest-reaching limbs of Makinaven's tree. Tala immediately felt a suffusion of power moving through her from above, into the ground below.

Rather than being a waterskin of power that she could draw and drink from, it felt more like a heavy mist, something that changed the environment without giving her anything to use, directly.

*Not that I can use ambient magic, normally.* But something about the feeling made her think that arcanous creatures wouldn't be able to draw on it either, unlike normal ambient power.

Tala found herself breathing more deeply, drinking in the sensation, if not the power.

*I've been in a desert and come to an oasis.* Those never-experienced geographic features seemed to accurately convey how she felt. *Bless books and the provision of a wider view of the world.*

The guards visibly relaxed as well, reminding Tala of her homecoming to Bandfast.

*Wait…* She looked around. *There aren't any defensive towers surrounding the farmland.* How was it defended?

She looked up, noticing that she hadn't heard the repulsion of any arcanous birds, either. "Where are all the defenses?"

Mistress Odera looked back, a smile on her face. "Most are passive; the claiming of all power in the near-region starves out and drives away beasts before they can attack."

That made some sense, but there would always be beasts that were outliers. *They can't be defenseless.*

"Look up. Tell me what you see."

Tala did so, and focused, trying to see through the haze of power in the air. After a long minute, she shook her head. "I can't see through the power in the air. It's too mobile, varied, and aspected. My magesight won't dismiss it, so I can't see through it."

"And what does your normal vision see?"

Tala blinked. *I'm not used to dismissing my magesight.* With a thought, she suppressed the added layer of information. Immediately, she was able to see what looked like long, steel gray fruit hanging around the outer reaches of the branches. "Those don't look natural."

"And they aren't. They are solid tungsten, an incredibly weighty metal. They have inscriptions to allow for faster acceleration, once released, as well as guiding spell-workings."

Tala's eyes widened. "How big are they?" They were visible from her position, even though the tips of the branches from which they hung were well over a thousand feet up.

"I don't know the exact specifications, but my understanding is that, near the waning, a single one can obliterate a half-dozen juggernauts, if properly aimed."

She found herself nodding. "The striking power is…" She shook her head, then. "That would be incredibly lethal, if they didn't see it coming."

"Did you not hear me say it has spell-forms for speed and guidance? The time between detachment and impact is only a second or two, and the projectile can track a target over a half-mile range."

*Ah, yeah. No dodging that.* She couldn't think of anything that could easily move nearly two thousand miles per hour. It would take almost that much speed to escape. *And that's assuming the defenses can't compensate, if something comes in moving that fast… somehow.*

Mistress Odera lifted her face toward the sky, closing her eyes and smiling in the cool breeze.

"So, well defended." Tala nodded to herself. "What about things that come from above?"

"There are inscribed defenses in the upper branches that dissuade or ultimately destroy any flying threat."

Tala found herself nodding again, this time feeling a bit of awe. Before her was a city that was able to stay at nearly full size for most of its lifecycle. It was truly impressive. "Why haven't we planted such trees for every city?"

Mistress Odera's smile widened. "Some of the Builders want just that. However, the trees we use for our forest cities are not replicable."

"The Mezzannis?"

"Precisely. Humanity can plant the seeds, and even nurture them to what would normally be an incredible size, some four or five hundred feet, but they don't grow bigger than that, and their canopy spread is miniscule by comparison."

Tala frowned.

"And while they still draw in power for redistribution, their roots don't go as deep, nor is the influx nearly as strong."

"So, those arcanes had some lost way of enhancing the trees."

"So it seems."

They lapsed back into silence as they moved onto well-worn roads. *Wait… are these paved?*

As she looked closer, Tala saw that the roads through the farmland and orchards were, indeed, paved. Smooth stone had been formed into a textured, even surface to easily support regular traffic. *I suppose if they will be used for most of the life of the city, it makes more sense to invest the time and resources.*

The smell of citrus came from the trees on their right, and Tala frowned in confusion. "How…?" She stopped herself, taking a moment to really *feel* her surroundings.

It was significantly warmer at ground level under the Makinaven tree than it had been even half a mile back, in the forest.

*A micro-climate?* The differences seemed more extreme than that. It was practically a late spring day, by the feel. *We left winter behind.*

No wonder Makinaven and the other forest cities were popular. *More dangerous to get to, but such amazing opportunities for long-lasting gains.* Well, this city would enter its waning in just over twenty years, so that way of thinking was less true than it would have been in years past.

*I wonder what the waning will do, here?* The level of magic around the city was hard to determine, hard to compare to the cities she'd been in before, because it was just so different.

The last leg of their journey was peaceful and relaxing. A good portion of that was a moderately steep slope up, toward the base of the tree. When they were nearly to the trunk, Tala noticed one particular farm, and began forming a plan in her mind. *I want to do something nice for Terry.*

Massive roots were on either side of them as the caravan moved up the rise, and they drew together until they met at the trunk on either side of a gateway that was worthy of the city beyond.

The entrance was easily wide enough for three or four wagons to pass through, side by side, depending on the margin the drivers needed to feel comfortable. It was about half as tall as it was wide, making an almost perfectly half-circular opening.

The city guards talked with Tion, briefly, before waving the whole group forward. Several of the caravan guards also talked with the men and women at the gate as they passed.

A warm light filtered down from magically empowered fixtures embedded into the ceiling. They weren't too bright to look at, yet still illuminated the tunnel as well as a noon-day sun.

Now that they were inside the tunnel, Tala could see that the wood, which made up the structure, had been polished to a near-mirror finish, allowing the tight grain of the material to be on full display, showing amazingly intricate swirls and striations.

*Trees don't grow like this; how is the grain so convoluted?* Her focus triggered her magesight to tick back on, and she realized that she'd been keeping it suppressed until that point.

She felt like she'd been smacked in the face with information, and shook her head, eyes closed tightly to allow her mind to recover.

After a short moment, Tala reopened her eyes and found the sight more bearable.

The answer as to the origin of the odd grain patterns became immediately clear, and she huffed a laugh at her own folly. *Of course.*

The grain of the wood was the spell-lines.

While Tala's inscriptions were mostly gold in living, human flesh, these were living wood, within living wood. This was beyond even an artifact.

Artifact style items had spell-forms wrought of magic, itself, affixed or anchored to physical materials.

This tree, by its very nature, *was* the spell-form. It didn't matter if it ran out of power. As soon as power returned, the magic would come back to life without issue.

*And because it's living wood, any materials that would be used up are likely regrown in short order, if not effectively immediately.*

It was a stunning display of magic, so far beyond what humanity was capable of reproducing.

*We are primitives, excited by our log fire, while our betters just shake their heads and return to the forge.*

With those last thoughts echoing in her mind, Tala and the wagon she was atop exited the tunnel, coming into the open, central space, inside of the tree.

The ceiling was easily a hundred feet overhead, the far wall at least seven hundred feet away.

The central open space was dotted with towering buildings, several reaching all the way to the ceiling above, seeming almost like pillars in the vast space.

Directly opposite the entrance that Tala and her caravan had used, as well as to the left and right, were other exit tunnels, meaning that each cardinal direction had a main gate into and out of the city. *Probably for easier access to the fertile land outside.*

The perimeter of the large space had layers of activity. There were twelve roads spiraling in the same direction, upward from the city floor, starting at various points around the outside of this open space. Each had uncounted tunnels, periodically running radially outward, acting as streets through the myriad levels of this section of the city.

From what Tala could see with her enhanced vision, buildings had been carved into the wood throughout the tree. *How strong is this wood, to still be able to support the tree with so much material removed?*

She shuddered. If it were up to her, she would *not* trust the tree to remain standing. *Still, the Builders have used this tree on at least a couple of occasions, for hundreds of years. It must be sound enough…* She didn't like it, but she wasn't about to go wait outside until her caravan departed again.

Everything was carved out of the wood of the tree, though it did look like stone and other materials had been added in various places as ornamentation, to break up the monotony.

The wood itself was nearly universally polished to an almost ridiculous degree. In places, it was stained or painted to add color or hue for decoration, but in all cases, near-high-gloss was maintained. That reflectivity helped bounce light around the massive interior, giving the entire enclosed vastness lighting similar to a glen in some quiet forest. Though, the murmur of thousands of people, living their lives, put the 'quiet' part to lie.

As she set aside her trepidation concerning the city's structural integrity, she found herself utterly captivated by the beauty of it all. *This is so much better than the cities of stone.*

There was a lightness, a warmth to the space that spoke of life, growth, and power.

As might be expected, the smell reminded Tala of the best scents within a carpentry workshop mixed with culinary hints and undertones of smoke.

*Fire in here must be pretty highly regulated… right?* That gave her something new to be concerned about. Though, it only took a moment's thought to realize that if the city didn't have a good way of regulating and controlling fire within it, there was little chance that it would still be standing.

The normal sounds of a city were present. Though, again, the wooden walls added a unique character to the mutters, babbles, and other noises that Tala expected.

People moved around freely, going about their day, many more going back and forth through the gates than Tala was used to, if she were being honest. That made sense, though, given the somewhat unique layout of the city. *If cities can be in different layouts, what else is possible?*

It was a somewhat childlike thought. If she'd considered it, she would have obviously known that cities could have any number of layouts. Bandfast and Alefast had simply been in similar environments, so the Builders had built them off the same template. Marliweather was another of that type, but she'd spent years at the academy, which was almost entirely different, structurally, and easily as large as a later stage city.

As she considered the implications, she remembered a cold mountain, late in the night and a woman simply calling herself 'Mistress.' *She spoke of villages. I never looked into that.*

Mistress Odera moved, catching Tala's attention and interrupting her thoughts. The older woman smiled toward her. "Welcome to Makinaven, Mistress Tala."

Tala smiled in return. "It is good to finally be here."

Mistress Odera let out a mirthless snort and nodded. "Travel around the forest cities is always a bit brutal. It's why most people who can teleport in or out do so, rather than taking a caravan." A frown settled into place across her features. "Something did seem off about this trip, though. I imagine that a high-level Archon or three will be sent to sweep the Leshkin lands to the east and see if something is stirring them up."

The caravan turned right as they cleared the gates fully, heading north toward the closest work yard. "Has this happened before?"

"Exactly? No. But similar, yes. If I recall correctly, the last time there was an expanding magical anomaly that was making a section of the southeastern forest impassible and increasingly dangerous, thus driving the Leshkin our direction more than was standard."

"What happened, then?" Tala knew this was hardly the time for a long-winded story, but that was fine. She was mainly interested in the short version.

Mistress Odera gave her a small smile. "We corrected the anomaly."

"So, we removed something that threatened them."

"That is one way to view it."

"But not how you view it?"

"No. We removed something that indirectly threatened us."

*Quite the human-centric view, but it makes sense.* Tala almost laughed at her own thoughts. *Of course, we're focused on how things affect us.* "Were you there?"

"No. That was before my time."

Tala shrugged. *Worth asking.*

The wagons moved in a small circle to position themselves near a group of warehouses before pulling to a stop. "Shall we go make our reports?"

Tala lifted her eyes from the wagon top, where her gaze had fallen as she'd considered.

Laborers and administrators were moving their way to begin the processes intrinsic in the end of every caravan journey.

"Let's."

# Chapter: 11
# Less Than Ideal

Tala found herself to be in a bad mood.

With around sixteen guards in need of additional healing and the death benefits for five further guards, the Mage Protector payments had been less than she'd hoped.

*Not that I begrudge the guards their healing, or the families the money for the death of their loved ones...* She definitely wished that neither category had anyone in it, though. *That's a good, not-too-selfish thought.* She gave herself a mental pat on the back.

In the end, she'd received twelve gold as the caravan's Dimensional Mage; the increase to that figure was due to her verified status as an Archon. For her work as a Mage Protector, she'd received a token to use with any inscriber, so that they could charge half the inscription cost to the guild, and thirty-six ounces gold.

She now had more money than she'd ever had before, but it still felt like a ridiculously paltry amount.

Thankfully, she'd also gotten permission to stay in her room within the cargo-slot until the caravan left the city once more.

*At least that takes care of housing.*

Rane, Mistress Odera, and Tala all moved through the busy, but not crowded, ground-floor streets. They were heading for the spiral road on which worked the inscriptionist whom Holly had designated as 'competent enough to work on a portion of Tala's spell-forms.'

## Millennial Mage, 4 - Bound

Rane needed some touch-ups, and Mistress Odera had already affirmed that she could use the same.

The man had his workshop on the two o'clock road, which began quite close to the work yard that their caravan had stopped in.

The twelve spiraling roads were each named for the position on the clock at which they started, given the roughly circular interior of the tree. They had come in from the east, so that gate was at the three o'clock position, and the three o'clock spiral began at the gate tunnel. The two o'clock road touched the bottom floor to the north of the eastern gate.

Each road did a full circuit before the next major floor, the next tier, was reached. There, more than a hundred feet above them, another large open space held more buildings, parks, or common spaces, depending on the tier. This basic structure repeated for each level as the city went up.

Thus, each road intersected the floor of every tier at the road's clock position, holding true to its name.

Now, this could cause all sorts of frustration to the uninformed. If a pedestrian wished to get to a place that they could see, but which was above them on another spiral, they couldn't just walk straight toward it. To facilitate transition between the spiral streets, which were stacked one atop another and perfectly pitched for even spacing, there were inset ladder tubes every so often.

Anyone moving large vehicles around was not given such a convenient way to change between the spirals.

That said, as Tala inspected the city more closely, she noticed that each spiral had a color combination theme to it, which made it much easier to determine which o'clock spiral would be needed to get to any given location, assuming she could see her desired destination. The two o'clock street, on which they needed to walk, had red and white banding on the outside railing as well as most of the buildings.

When they reached the entrance to the spiraling road, they turned to the right, walking beside the buildings to leave the inner portion of the road, that which was closest to the railings, open for vehicle or animal traffic. There were some horses and a few oxen, but those were really the only beasts that Tala saw. *There are probably all sorts, but they just aren't as common.*

Terry eyed each passing creature with interest but settled back down on Tala's shoulder after they passed without doing more.

The walkway they used on the building side of the road, designated by more white and red stripes on the roadway, was wide enough for five or six people to pass with ease.

Tala glanced down the side passages as they moved past. Some were gated and clearly marked as private sections of the city. Some of those seemed to be entirely owned by a single family with unifying styles behind heraldically emblazoned gates. Others seemed to belong to trading groups, or one of the Guilds. *Probably mostly farming or crafting related.* It had seemed like most of the buildings on the first-tier main floor were oriented toward crafting or production of some kind.

Other roads were simply that: roads through a short side district, leading toward the outside of the great tree without penetrating to the open air.

There were residential streets, along with shops either of mixed types or of a unified kind.

"Food!" Tala turned down a side street, and Rane shook his head, smiling.

This particular side-street had alternating red and yellow magical lights down the length, and every shop they could see seemed to be oriented toward food of one kind or other. They were a mix of restaurants and supply stores, if Tala was seeing correctly. *I could get ingredients here and cook for myself, or just buy bulk food more cheaply.* It was a good thought. Her consumptive needs did not lend themselves to a reasonable budget.

Aside from the lighting, the obvious features of the street were a series of tables, trees, and low shrubs artfully spaced throughout the area, giving plenty of places for people to enjoy their food, as well as some privacy and nature. *The plants were selected to be the most pleasing in the oddly colored lighting, too.*

Mistress Odera gave the other two long looks. "We should get to the inscriptionist."

Tala stopped, turning around to face the older woman. "Of course we should, but I need some food." Tala hesitated. "I should have gotten the Caravan Guild to pay for half my food, too…"

Mistress Odera huffed a laugh. "You could probably make a case for it, given your need to eat so much because of your inscriptions, and for your inscriptions to use."

"Can you authorize that?"

"As a blanket allowance? No, definitely not, but I can speak to it once we're back in Bandfast." She got a thoughtful look on her face but didn't say more.

"But I need food *now*." Tala stopped, realizing just how whiny that had sounded. "Sorry about that. I meant, my reserves are *incredibly* depleted."

Mistress Odera opened her mouth to say something but stopped as Rane walked back up to them. *When did he leave?*

He held out something to Tala. "Eat. We can get you more after our inscriptions are refreshed."

Tala took it without thinking. It was a thick flatbread that had been slit open and stuffed full of meat and vegetables, and then drenched in sauce. The bread was such that nothing leaked out. The thing was *heavy*. "Thank you!" She smiled to Rane. "What do I owe you?"

He waved her off. "I think you helped more than the pay distribution represented. It wasn't worth fighting about, but I can correct the slight imbalance with a couple of meals."

Tala opened her mouth to object, then considered his words. *Yeah, it probably wouldn't be worth contesting the division of things for less than a gold, and there is no way this cost that much.* "Very well, then. Thank you, Master Rane."

Mistress Odera sighed, likely in part because she'd been a guiding hand behind the distribution of their pay as Mage Protectors. Even so, she didn't interject with regard to the food or pay. "Can we go, then?"

"I'm good for now, yes."

They went back out to the main road, and Tala took a huge bite of the meal-in-a-package. *There really are a lot of variations on this concept. It's like a pasty, or a little caravan, or a pot-pie, or so many other things I've come across, while being just a little different.*

It was… mildly disappointing. It was good, especially because she was hungry, but something about the way the bread had been made gave it an odd, fibrous texture and almost no flavor. *Meh, they can't all be winners, I suppose.*

As they spiraled upward, Tala devoured the less than ideal concoction.

*Wait a minute… do the defenses work the same within the city?* The errant thought almost caused her to pause, but she decided to keep walking as she contemplated, glancing at Terry.

"Mistress Odera?"

"Yes?"

"Would Terry be safe in here without the collar?"

Terry perked up at the question, looking intently at the older Mage.

"Yes, but no." Mistress Odera smiled. "He wouldn't be struck down instantly, as he might be in some other cities, but his presence would trigger all sorts of alarms. The defenses would shift, and he would quickly be subdued or killed. In the worst case, an Archon defender would be summoned to deal with him, and the fine that would be leveled for such a thing is *expensive*." She gave Tala a meaningful look.

Tala nodded. "Fair enough."

Terry flickered a bit away and his collar began glowing yellow, just like it would have if they were in Bandfast. He returned without further testing.

Mistress Odera nodded. "He would also be very ill-advised to leave the inside of the tree without an active collar, as any space outside would be subject to… less gentle repercussions, as we discussed."

Terry let out a small squawk of acknowledgement but didn't open his eyes again.

Rane cleared his throat, without slowing his pace. "Are you sure you want to stay in the cargo-slot while we're in Makinaven?"

Tala shrugged. "I have to come to the work yard every morning anyway, so there isn't much benefit in staying anywhere else. It would just add to my daily travel time."

Rane thought for a moment, then nodded. "I can't argue with your logic. Still, Master Grediv recommended that I get a room in the Soaring Heights Inn. It's in one of the highest branches, reaching well above the canopy and giving commanding views of the surroundings from every room."

"That sounds amazing! I'll have to at least drop by for the view."

Mistress Odera clucked her tongue. "There are quite a few observation areas that allow anyone who wishes to see views just as good, if not better."

Rane crinkled his nose, then sighed. "Even so, I think that's where I'll be staying." He glanced to Tala once more. "There are some sparring areas available there, as well."

"I'll take a look, sure. Not sure when, though. I still need to sell off some of the harvests I managed to grab after I drop by the Constructionist Guild."

Mistress Odera stopped walking, pointing to a door just to their left. "After inscriptions."

Tala looked up to the sign hanging over the door, an inscription needle imposed across a circular spell-form. It was a keystone, if her interpretation was correct. "Ah, we're here."

The storefront wasn't large, but through the glass in the door, they could see that the business inside seemed to extend quite a way back into the tree.

The three Mages entered, and a chipper attendant stood from behind a small counter. "Welcome, Master, Mistresses. How can the Hawthorne Inscribers serve you this day?"

Mistress Odera took over communication, quickly explaining that they were Mage Protectors, newly arrived and in need of reinscription.

The young woman's eyes seemed to glitter the more she heard. It made her look younger than she had before.

*Or revealed her true age? I bet she's related to the inscriber, somehow. I know the look of avarice.*

Tala remembered that feeling when a particularly wealthy and needy patron had come to her family's shop.

## Millennial Mage, 4 - Bound

The attendant pulled a cord, causing a bell to ring somewhere in the back. "We are fairly booked with appointments for the next week, but Master Hawthorne has some time right now, and we can make time tomorrow and then two days after. Who would like to go first?"

Both Rane and Mistress Odera turned to look at Tala. Tala gave a self-conscious smile. "I guess that's me. I probably have the most foundational work needed. They both just need some reinforcement of existing lines." She glanced to the others. "Right?"

They just nodded.

A middle-aged man came from the back, a slate in hand. "Welcome! Who am I helping?"

Tala raised her hand. "I suppose I'm first."

The man extended the slate to her. "I'm Master Hawthorne."

Tala ignored the available sharp protrusion, intended for use in drawing blood, and simply placed her thumb on the flat stone, allowing her power to brush the device.

Hawthorne took the slate back. "Archon Tala. Welcome. Let's see what we…" All expression left his face. "You're one of Mistress Holly's?" He looked up at her, seeming to take in her appearance for the first time. "Where are your inscriptions? I don't…" His eyes narrowed, then widened. "Impossible! How did she make them so minute?"

Without seeming to move, he was suddenly standing directly in front of Tala, his nose almost brushing her cheek. Tala was too startled to move.

"I can't see the details even from here!"

Terry hissed, causing Hawthorne to step back.

"Ahh, right… My apologies. I was…" He cleared his throat. "That was unprofessional of me. Yes. Let's see what we can do. Hmmm?"

Tala glanced at Mistress Odera and Rane, who both smiled. Finally, Tala shrugged. "Alright then…"

Hawthorne looked to the other two Mages. "I won't be able to work on either of you at this time, unfortunately. Has Lana scheduled your appointments yet?"

The assistant, presumably Lana, smiled and motioned for the two to come to the counter as Tala followed Hawthorne into the back.

The inscriber, for his part, was looking over the slate in his hands, muttering to himself in incomprehensible fragments.

Based on her glances into side rooms as they passed, Tala would guess that this space expanded to the sides as it went further back. Most of the workrooms were empty, though there were a few closed doors that Tala thought she heard people beyond.

After the hall took a few turns, they came out into a courtyard with a large tree growing in the center. *A tree, growing in a tree?* She'd seen them before, most notably in the food-oriented side street, but it was especially odd in what was basically a building. *A tree in a building, within a city in a tree.*

Magical lights seemed to mimic the natural light outside, at the moment doing a good job of making the space feel like it was open to a sunset sky.

"Are you really that busy? It seems like most of this place is empty."

"Hmmm? Oh, well, this is after business hours for most of my workers. They're eating dinner with their families and will be back in the morning."

"Oh… Did we interrupt your meal?"

"Oh no, not at all. There's always too much to do, so I live here, sleep when I can." He smiled her direction. "I find it hard to turn away any in need of inscriptions. It just feels like I'm robbing them of a tool. Does that make sense?"

Tala found herself frowning. "Well… I understand seeing inscriptions as tools, but aren't there other inscribers?"

"Yes and no. Yes, of course there are others, but they are just as busy as I am." He shook his head.

"Didn't you turn away Master Rane and Mistress Odera this evening?"

"No, not at all. I can't simply drop everything for every person who walks through the door, but I can make time for everyone who needs it." He smiled. "Ah, here we are."

They had crossed the courtyard, skirting the spreading tree-within-a-tree, and come to a large archway, leading into what was clearly an inscriptionist's sanctum.

One wall was covered with racks of inscribing needles of Holly's design.

*Right, of course he wouldn't have an auto-inscriber.* She thought for a moment. *That might just revolutionize his scheduling.* Tala considered telling him about it for a moment, then dismissed the idea. *I'm sure Holly will make it known when it's ready.*

Tala almost stumbled slightly as her mind connected that thought to her own experiences with the device and hitched. *She used an unproven method on me.* That wasn't news, precisely, but Tala had assumed that the auto-inscriber was relatively new, not utterly new. *No, Tala, she even said that she tested it out by printing the books.*

Tala grimaced. *Well, that's a bit terrifying. I guess I didn't really think through what she'd said, and what it meant.* Tala promised herself that she'd listen more closely to the madwoman and consider what she actually meant by what she said.

Hawthorne sat on a wooden stool, still looking at the slate. "I must say, I don't think I can help you with most of these."

Tala brought her attention back to the present and frowned. "What do you mean?"

"Well, these are too delicate for me to work on." He huffed a laugh. "I'd say they are too delicate for *anyone* to do, but I see them in place within your flesh already." He shook his head. "What has Mistress Holly come up with, this time?"

The question wasn't directed at Tala, so she didn't reply.

"So, how about you tell me what you were hoping to have done, and I'll see what I can do."

Tala glanced at her right arm, trying to decide how to explain. "Well, I need a refresher on my activation rings, for my offensive casts."

Hawthorne moved a few things around on the slate, then nodded. "Oh, I see, yes. I can do that." He grabbed a sheet of what appeared to be inscribed glass and brought it to a chair in the center of the room. "Come on, sit here."

He pointed to the chair, beside him, and Tala sank into it.

"Let me take a look at what we're working with." He sent power into the glass and held it near her right arm. "Wait… Oh, my apologies, can you please lower your magical defenses? They are blocking my scan."

Tala hesitated. *Oh… my iron-salve.* "I apologize, do you have a private room? My magical defense is physical, and I neglected to remove it."

He arched an eyebrow at that but didn't comment. He showed her to a back room, and once the door was closed, she dropped into Kit, stripped out of her top, and scrubbed her right arm clean with near-boiling water, soap, and a scrub brush she'd bought ages ago.

Less than five minutes later, she was dressed and back in the inscriber's chair.

Hawthorne looked like he wanted to ask but restrained himself. Instead, he held up the inscribed item and looked through it once again. What he saw seemed to drive thoughts of her unorthodox defenses from his mind. "Remarkable. Truly remarkable."

Tala glanced over and through the glass. The organic material of her arm was invisible, only the metal of the inscriptions could be seen. She shuddered and looked away. It looked *much* too similar to how the inscriptions had looked after her arm had fallen away.

Hawthorne frowned. "Wait, I don't see the connecting scripts." He consulted his slate, then looked back through the glass. "Did you burn through all the secondary inscriptions for those castings?" He seemed to be talking to himself as he moved the glass up her arm. "You did, they are utterly spent—" He stopped, the glass allowing him to look at her shoulder. "Mistress Tala." His voice was flat, utterly bereft of inflection.

"Yes, Master Hawthorne?"

"Tell me what happened. Your secondary inscription channels are gone past a jagged point in your shoulder."

"Well, you see… I lost my arm."

"You lost your arm."

"That's right."

"And it grew back."

"So it would seem."

"Maintaining all the other inscriptions." He cocked his head to the side. "Well, of course it would, if they were active, and these are active." He frowned, then shook his head and sighed. "Alright then. Let's get to work. It's going to be a long night."

# Chapter: 12
# Needed Support

Tala sat in the inscribing chair for what felt like hours, Terry asleep in her lap. Thankfully, with Holly's needles, and the pane of inscribed glass to allow Hawthorne to see where he was working in detail, she didn't need to even roll up her sleeve.

"The fact that most of your inscriptions are intact makes this so much easier." Hawthorne leaned back, stretching his back.

"What do you mean?"

"Well, with all the inscriptions already there, my scripts here," he tapped the piece of clear material, "have something to lock onto easily, without having to worry about the exact positioning of your arm. It aligns the scripts that are present, then tells me where the missing ones should go. I'm basically just tracing." He looked at the inscribed needle in his hand. "Tracing with really expensive colored pencils."

Tala snorted a laugh. "Glad it's that easy."

"Easier, I would say. It's hard coloring within the lines."

Tala gave him a side-eyed look. "You don't inspire confidence."

"Good luck going anywhere else to get this fixed." He gave her a mischievous smile. "We're just lucky this was a part of what Holly dubbed me capable of working on."

Tala shook her head. "Isn't that a bit insulting?"

He shrugged. Before responding, he reinserted the needle, injecting another fleck of metal into the proper place.

She grimaced at the additional swelling pressure.

"I think it is more an acknowledgement of my skills by a master than anything else."

Tala looked him over again, seeing a new side of the man. He wasn't an Archon, at least not that she could tell. He was a Material Guide, and he used his magic almost entirely to improve his ability with inscriptions. Even as she watched, a flicker of power went through a spell-form in his hand, and she felt the newly added gold shift by less than the width of a hair. *No, he didn't move it, he rotated it, reoriented it for better conduction of power.*

She'd never considered the orientation of the metal as important, but he manipulated almost every injection he made.

*Is it like a magnet?* She could just ask. "Why do you reorient the metal?"

"Hmm? Oh, the metal in the injection medium isn't perfectly uniform, despite what we'd prefer. So, by orienting and concentrating the precious metal on the long axis, along the channels we want the power to flow down, we improve efficiency and reduce the total number of injections required. It isn't a lot, but over the course of a spell-form or an entire set of inscriptions?" He smiled. "It's better."

"But you used your own power, your own inscriptions, to enact the change."

"That's right."

"So… doesn't that take more power and metal than the efficiency gives?"

He chuckled at that. "Yes and no. In the beginning, it definitely did, but my efficiency has increased to the point that it's a net gain. Even before that, though, it was worth it."

"Why?"

He gave her a long look before shaking his head, smiling, and turning back to his work. He continued to inject and reorient as necessary. "You fight for civilization. A drop in your power, in your efficiency, in your effectiveness, could mean the death of others, the failure of a caravan. That means needed supplies don't make it to their destination. Letters are lost between loved ones, and so much more. I can't allow that." He shook his head again. "Not if I can help it."

Tala just nodded.

After a moment, he cracked a smile. "Also, in your case, there is a danger of interference or cross contamination with your surrounding inscriptions. Any misplaced metal could be disastrous."

They fell into silence, then. With nothing to distract her, Tala gritted her teeth against the unpleasant sensations, and kept her regenerative scripts from activating. She needed to wait until he was finished.

It took hours more, and Tala gained a renewed appreciation for Holly's strange device. *I hope it spreads soon. I can't imagine how much it will help humanity.* What if they'd had one in the caravan? Could Tala have gotten her inscriptions refreshed as soon as they were lost?

*Those two juggernauts would have been squished for sure.* She frowned at the thought. *Why were they after me so intently?* She didn't have any doubts, now. They had been after her.

The juggernaut had left the caravan behind to pursue her, even if just briefly.

At the time, the chuckwagon had been all but undefended, but the Leshkin had chosen to pursue her.

## Millennial Mage, 4 - Bound

She allowed her mind to think through the various possibilities as the night wore on.

Terry continued to sleep in her lap.

"There we go." Hawthorne set aside another spent needle. "That's the last of it." He swept his viewing item across her arm, and up to her shoulder, once more. "I just need to correct the connection here. When you lost your arm, the blow seems to have moved some of the dormant gold out of position." He placed his hand on her shoulder, and a series of spell-forms lit up across that arm.

The sensation was akin to a mass of worms wriggling in her palm, but *inside* her shoulder. Tala winced and felt like vomiting at the *wrongness* of the feeling but held herself still. *I'm not meant to have something wriggling around inside my muscles…*

"Are you alright? That can be disconcerting to some."

"It wasn't great… How does it look?"

"We're done. Your inscriptions are refreshed."

Tala relaxed, allowing her regenerative scripts to fully activate. Her flesh tightened around the new metal, seamlessly integrating it into her spell-forms. She let out a relieved breath. "There."

"I won't ask you about your other work. It's… It's detailed beyond anything I've ever seen before. I'll bet Holly's close to an announcement." He didn't ask, though it was clear he wanted to.

Tala gave an awkward smile. "Something like that."

"There's a schema in here for connecting your other hand to the same spell-workings. There's even space to add another set of rings on your other hand. We could schedule another appointment to do that?"

Tala almost said yes immediately, but then she hesitated. *I am trying to remove my dependance on those. I need to be practicing, using, and digging deeper into my*

*active manipulation, not leaning on a well-loved crutch.*
"Thank you, but I think I'll hold off."

"As you wish. We should settle up now, then."

"Oh! Wait, one more thing." Tala reached into Kit and pulled out her naked arm. "As a Material Manipulator, could you get the gold out of this?" It didn't seem to have begun decaying, yet, but it was still… icky to hold.

Hawthorne gave her a longsuffering look. "Is that your arm?"

She rotated it, so that he could see the gold rings on the back of the hand. "It is."

He stood, seeming to take a deep breath to calm himself. After a moment, he went a grabbed some gloves and came back, taking the arm from her. "It is deeply disturbing that you kept this, Mistress Tala."

"Should I have left it for the beasts to eat?"

"Well, probably not…" He sighed, holding up his left hand. To her magesight, a series of inscriptions lit up with power across that arm and onto his chest. With a squelching sound, gold pulled itself out of the dead limb, exiting away from Hawthorne, before floating over to an empty dish on a side table.

Without a word, he went over and rinsed the gold, before drying it on a cloth and dumping it into a small pouch. He returned and held out the pouch. "Here. Mage gold is often prized by the Constructionist Guild, and while not difficult to get, few like providing it."

"Thank you. What do I owe you for helping retrieve it?"

He waved his hand. "It took little effort or power. We can call it an addition on the other services." He glanced to her arm, which sat on the side table. "I'm going to have that burned."

Tala decided it wasn't worth arguing, especially since she really didn't have a better idea. She nodded, taking a breath and bracing herself. "How much for the inscribing work?"

Hawthorne quirked a smile. "Ten ounces. I wish I could offer it for cheaper, but the needles are *expensive,* and I had to use quite a bit of power manipulating the gold to be in the right position, given your inscription complexity."

*Ten ounces gold... that means that this will get him twenty, total, and he's acting like it's as low as he can go. How much, exactly, was Holly undercharging me?* "I can do that. Thank you for fitting me in immediately."

He waved that off. "I couldn't let you be hampered." He pulled out a slate, did a few things on its surface, and then handed it to her. "Put your token, there, and confirm the transaction, if you would."

Tala looked closely, verifying all was right. She then placed the token she'd received as a Mage Protector on the slate and confirmed the exchange. "There we go. Thank you."

He waved her off. "I did the work; you paid; no thanks needed." He yawned. "I do need to get some rest, though. Lana!" He called out the last.

The attendant from before came a few moments later. "Yeah, Dad?" She hesitated. "Oh! My apologies, Mistress Tala, I didn't realize that you were still here."

Tala gave a seated half-bow. "More than fine. I was apparently difficult to work on."

"Oh?"

"Master Hawthorne can tell you, if and when he deems appropriate." She smiled.

Hawthorne shook his head to clear the sleep. "Lana, could you escort Mistress Tala out? There isn't anyone else, right?"

"No, the apprentices are all finished. I'll lock up, after."

"Thank you."

"Um... is that an arm?"

Tala and Hawthorne looked to where Lana was pointing. "Yes, dear. I'll be dealing with that before I sleep."

"But—"

He shook his head. "No buts. We can talk tomorrow." He smiled toward Tala. "Good night."

Tala stood. "Thank you, again."

He shrugged and waved, using rote movements to clean up his space before he dealt with the limb and slept.

Tala followed Lana out and bid the girl 'Goodnight.'

"Remember us when you need a refresh."

"I will."

Tala turned away from the now-locked front door and looked out at the nightscape of Makinaven's first tier.

The interior light had been dimmed, but it was still bright enough to see clearly. Traffic had slowed, but it was far from nonexistent.

Tala began to walk back down, toward the work yard and her accommodations for the night. The cooks had given them all food as they'd approached the city, but even with that, and Rane's offering, Tala felt *famished*.

She came to the food-oriented side street once again and stepped back into it. The restaurants all seemed to be closed, and only one of the general stores looked to be open for business.

Tala knocked as she pushed the door open. "Hello?"

"Hello!"

Tala looked at the young man who sat behind the counter. "Are you open?"

He gestured. "Seems so."

Tala gave him a flat look, then shook her head. *Kids shouldn't be sassy with adults...* She walked in and looked through the wares. She quickly picked out some fruit, jerky, and what seemed to be small bag of day-old pastries.

"One silver, please."

It was an exorbitant sum for what she was getting, but she wasn't in a position to be too picky. *I really, really need to replenish my food stores.* She hesitated for a moment. *Could I use my incorporator to make soup, with dried ingredients?* That would be amazing. *I'll look into it.*

She paid and left.

While she ate her newly acquired food, she got out some of the arcanous jerky for Terry.

She took the time to stretch her legs and just let herself walk. *Tomorrow, I'm going to walk through the city... but not without good food.*

Tala could probably find open vendors in the upper reaches of the city, even at this time of night, but she wasn't willing to do a long hike in the hope of such bounty. *Tomorrow.*

They got to the work yard all too soon, and she found her cargo-slots set off to one side, standing free of any wagon.

*Oh...* Tala stood for a moment, staring at the fourteen identical, empowered constructions.

*Which one?*

With a sigh, she went down the line, glancing inside each, until she found the one that she wanted. "There you are."

She hesitated in the eerily silent work yard, looking into the equally silent, dark interior of the cargo-slot. She didn't really want to go inside. At least not yet.

*I don't know how much I'll sleep in. I should charge them now.* With a sigh, but not of relief, she let the door swing closed and walked over to a nearby warehouse.

There, she grabbed a short stepladder that she'd seen leaning against the side. Little ladder in tow, she went down the line, recharging each cargo-slot.

*There. Now, time to sleep.* She returned the stepladder to where she'd found it, then walked to the correct cargo-slot.

*No hesitation, that will just make it worse.* She strode inside, allowing the door to close behind her.

The space was… a bit creepy, in all honesty. She was used to it being quiet—it was well built and designed for such—but she wasn't used to the utter silence that now surrounded her.

With hurried, quiet steps, she moved through the dark interior to her door.

She unlocked her room, jumped inside, slammed the door, and relocked it behind her.

*That's right, Tala. The darkness almost got you.*

She shook her head but didn't let herself laugh.

*Make no noise…*

She was *tired*, despite having slept past lunch the day before. *I can't sleep that late, today.* Only a short sleep, then. Just like six hours.

She flopped down on her too hard mattress and touched middle finger to thumb, increasing her effective gravity until the bed was comfortable. That sorted, she closed her eyes to sleep.

\*   \*   \*

A soft knock on her door jerked Tala out of a heavy sleep, filled with nightmares.

She sat bolt upright, her heart pounding. *No one else is supposed to be here. Who's knocking?*

# Millennial Mage, 4 - Bound

She gasped in a breath, her mind telling her that her ribcage was shattered, lungs ruined. *No. That was a dream… Or two days ago…* She grimaced.

She stood slowly, eyes locked on the doorway. Terry lay motionless in the corner.

*Doesn't he sense the danger?* She had a horrifying thought, then. *Is he dead?*

She stared at him, her gaze unmoving despite her half-awake mind screaming at her to watch the door. Finally, she saw his chest move with an inhaled breath. *Good, not dead.*

Her eyes returned to the door as she drew Flow, leaving it in the form of a knife. *A knife is a better weapon for close quarters than a sword.*

The knock came again, a little louder this time, booming in the otherwise silent cargo-slot.

Tala grabbed the doorhandle to fling it open. Instead of throwing the door wide, her quick pull jerked her forward, slamming her face and chest against the locked door. Flow stabbed easily into the wall, where it stuck.

"Ow…"

"Mistress Tala?"

She recognized that voice. "Mistress Odera?"

"Yes, dear. Are you alright?"

Tala shook her head, pulling the key from Kit, unlocking the stubborn door and pulling it open.

"I brought you breakfast and thought that we could take a bit to talk."

Tala looked to the woman's hands but saw nothing. "Do you have a storage item?"

"Well, yes, but the food isn't in there. Come on."

Tala rubbed her eyes and glanced toward Terry.

"We aren't going far. He'll be fine." Mistress Odera smiled. "I'm not even sure the city defenses would register his presence regardless, while he's in here."

Tala nodded and followed Mistress Odera out to the common area of the cargo-slot's interior. On one of the tables, a massive spread of food was laid out, along with what appeared to be several earthen carafes of some kind. *Coffee?*

She almost sat in the closest chair before remembering her increased weight. *It's nice that it hasn't been causing me issues in moving. I'm getting more used to variable gravity.*

She brought her left middle finger to her thumb and focused on herself, returning her effective gravity to standard.

It didn't take too long, but it was long enough for Mistress Odera to move around and take the chair opposite.

The older woman began building herself a breakfast sandwich, pulling from the various platters of food with the implements she'd already set out.

"This is a feast, Mistress Odera."

"For most people, yes, it would be. For you? In your state? It's needed support for proper functioning as a Mage Protector." Her eyes were twinkling.

Tala grinned back at her. "I like the sound of that."

Mistress Odera nodded. "I believe I saw that you've recharged the cargo-slots already?"

"That is correct."

"Good, then we can eat now." She smiled. "I can't authorize this for every meal, but it seems reasonable to me to fund some calories after particularly demanding ventures."

Tala lowered herself into the seat, her effective gravity back to normal, some of her joy leaving. "It was… a bit demanding." The faces of the guards who had died flashed through her mind. Sometimes her near perfect memory was a curse.

She hadn't known them. She hadn't learned their names, and she couldn't convince herself that she cared about them as individuals.

In truth, she didn't. That said, they had died fighting alongside her, in spirit even if not physically, and that did matter. *Maybe I can care about their character, their actions?*

"What's wrong?"

"Hmm?"

"You aren't eating. What's wrong?"

Tala sat up a bit straighter and began taking food for herself. "I… I don't feel anything for the guards that died." She frowned, and Mistress Odera cocked an eyebrow. "No… No, that's not right. I am grateful for their sacrifice. I hate that they died, and I think well of them for their actions in defense of the caravan, but I can't bring myself to care about them as individuals."

Mistress Odera gave a slow nod. "You're dissociating from their deaths. You don't want to view them as husbands, wives, fathers, mothers, sons, or daughters. Yet you still see their sacrifice for what it is."

Tala shrugged, eating without really focusing on what she was consuming.

"It is so easy to hear, 'Thirty people died in this accident or attack.' It sounds tragic, and you wish it hadn't happened, but rarely do we consider the ripples such deaths will cause. It's uncomfortable to consider, and hard to deal with emotionally."

Tala nodded, continuing to eat mechanically.

Mistress Odera gave a sad smile. "You don't want to have to sit with the fact that Sergeant Fawn had a two-year-old daughter, who he will never hold again."

Tala set her food aside, looking down at her hands.

"We don't like considering that guardswoman Hida was newly married, and she'd decided that this would be her last round trip before settling down to have a family."

Tala's vision began to swim with unshed tears.

"Those are just two of the fallen. Each death is a tragedy of unmitigated horror for those who cared for and loved them. To us? It's unfortunate, but doesn't occupy more than a cursory place in our minds. It can't."

Tala lifted her head with a frown. "What does that mean?"

"Mistress Tala, across humanity, between five hundred and a thousand die each day. Now, a bit more than that number are born as well, their lives laid out before them. Do you know how many of those deaths are due to old age or similar causes?"

"I imagine very few."

"You'd be right." Mistress Odera had a sad smile. "We live in a violent world, Mistress Tala. Death is all around us, constantly. Yes, every death is a tragedy, but it can't be our tragedy. That sounds heartless, because it is. Death should never cease to affect us, but it should also never break us."

Tala huffed a derisive laugh, wiping her face. "You make it sound so easy."

Mistress Odera shrugged. "It isn't. We have a lot to talk about, and this is just the beginning. It is alright to not be Okay." She smiled. "You need to process through the losses. The loss of the guards under our protection, the loss of your arm, these are not small things." After a moment, she poured a mug of coffee, then handed it to Tala. "Here. Drink, eat, let's talk."

The next couple of hours passed slowly. Mistress Odera often seemed to be contradicting herself as she drew Tala through her emotions and thoughts on how the trip had gone and the results thereof.

## Millennial Mage, 4 - Bound

In the end, Tala decided that Mistress Odera was perfectly willing to spout utter nonsense, if it allowed Tala to properly think through a given issue.

*I'm glad she brought food… This is exhausting.*

The morning passed, and they made some progress, but as with most things, it was but a small step forward.

*One step at a time.*

# Chapter: 13
# Higher in Makinaven

Tala licked her fingers clean of the last of the massive spread of food that Mistress Odera had brought for her.

Even so, Tala really hadn't registered what any of it was. *She could have brought me food that was little better than scraps, and I probably wouldn't have noticed.*

No, that wasn't fair. In her memory, the food had been good, but Tala hadn't taken the time to savor it as she ate.

Tala's stomach gurgled. "Seriously?" She looked down at her own abdomen.

Mistress Odera smiled. "We should go get some lunch." She'd stopped eating hours earlier. "I also believe that I've kept you from your normal morning routine?"

Tala waved her off. "You've helped me talk through a lot of different things." A smile pulled up at the corner of her mouth. "And you brought food."

Mistress Odera nodded. "I'm glad it's been of use." After a moment's pause, she continued. "Please don't see this conversation as a solution or a fix."

Tala nodded in turn. "So you've said. Talking through how I'm feeling and how I perceive things is just a start."

"Good. Shall we?"

"One moment." She took a breath and directed a shout over her shoulder. "Terry!"

Terry flickered into being on her shoulder before regarding the empty plates on the table between the two women. He let out a disgruntled squawk and eyed Tala.

She laughed and tossed a much bigger than standard hunk of jerky. "We're going to get lunch. Shall we get you something, there, too?"

Terry was already happily enjoying his jerky. He bobbed a nod, then settled down into his customary resting place on her shoulder.

"I'm ready."

They stood and Mistress Odera swept the table clear of dishes, putting everything into a slim pack that almost hid against her back when worn.

Tala hadn't seen it before today. *But I suppose I've only seen her at a restaurant in her home city and on the road, when she had a room for her use.*

It was a storage item in the artifact style. If what Tala interpreted was correct, the space contained was easily four or five times what Kit had, within. *That's a valuable item.*

The three came out of the cargo-slot into the bustling work yard. The workers gave them passing glances, but they were, for the most part, ignored.

"Do you know anywhere good to eat? I wasn't impressed with the food from that little side street…"

Mistress Odera nodded. "That was closer to a quick stop-through for local workers than a place to get good food." She thought for a moment, then shrugged. "That said, such places are often some of the best food you can find. But that isn't what you asked. I know of a couple of excellent places in the upper tiers. Shall we?"

Tala nodded, and they strode off, turning to the south of the eastern gate this time. Mistress Odera said that the establishment they were going to was just off of the four o'clock spiral.

They talked about small things as they moved up the new path. This road had a green and yellow theme, designating it for easy identification from the main floor below.

The buildings were much the same as those they'd seen on the two o'clock spiral, and as such, nothing really caught Tala's attention. Even the green and yellow inner railing faded from notice after a short climb.

After a time, having made almost a full circuit of the city, they approached the top of this first tier and continued into that ceiling. The road remained largely unchanged, save the inner railing being replaced by a wall.

The lighting was still good, and there were still storefronts and side streets branching off, toward the outside of the tree.

*I wonder if this is more, or less, valuable space? There's nothing to distract potential customers from the shops here, but they aren't really visible from anywhere else.*

After less than a hundred yards, the top of the road began to open once more, letting in more light from the second tier. Shortly after, they came up, level to that tier's floor, and Tala stopped, eyes wide.

The center of the tree, here, seemed to have been turned into a vast parkland. The ceiling was, again, close to one hundred feet up. Though, magical lights and effects made it difficult to notice that it wasn't open, cloudless sky.

Gently rolling, well cared for turf filled much of the space. Small, white flowers sprinkled the ground near and far. *Is this all covered with clover?* She didn't know enough to decide if that was good or not.

Several stands of trees were artfully scattered around the space, along with several delineated spaces of flatter ground, further divided by lines or a change in makeup. *Sports areas?*

## Millennial Mage, 4 - Bound

Growing up in Marliweather, she'd seen a few of those, but they weren't *that* common. *A benefit of a more static population, I suppose?* The population in Marliweather, and most cities, was steadily declining, overall, while Makinaven's would be rather static for the majority of its existence.

There was a scattering of food vendors at a few points throughout the massive park, and they seemed to be doing a brisk business with those who were enjoying the space.

Mistress Odera had paused beside Tala, and she spoke up while the younger woman continued to examine the communal space. "We can get food here, if you desire."

"Maybe another day. I'd like to try wherever you're taking us."

"As you say." They began walking again.

"Do you know the usage rules of the park?"

"They are free for public use."

"Do you think they'd mind if I used one of the sand courts for sparring?" *I hate sand… It's coarse, and rough, and irritating. And it gets everywhere.* She'd prefer the green-covered areas, but she didn't want to ruin the vegetation.

"That should be allowed." Something about Mistress Odera's tone implied hesitation, however.

"What are you thinking?"

"I'd be concerned specifically about you sparring with Terry in such a public space. In the worst case, it could cause a panic if people thought he was a wild creature who had somehow penetrated the defenses."

"Yeah… that probably wouldn't be good." Tala frowned. "Any ideas on how to mitigate that?"

"Well, you could have Rane or a few city guards observe. Then, if anyone saw you, they'd see the armed men and women around you, casually watching. It wouldn't be a perfect solution, but it could work."

"I'll bet the Guards Guild has training spaces anyway. I'll just drop through there and ask."

"That could work, too."

They fell into silence as they walked the perimeter of the second tier, slowly climbing upwards. Both women had their attention focused inward, toward the park and the tamed nature it represented. *I wonder what the world would be like if all nature were so tamed.*

The buildings set into the outside of the road in this second tier seemed to be a bit bigger, but not by too much. There were also many, many more that looked like residences or complexes of such.

*How far are we walking?* She thought about it for a moment. *The interior is roughly seven hundred feet across, and we're circumnavigating it. Adding some variability because it isn't a perfect circle, and we are climbing rather than walking a flat perimeter, each loop is just about a half-mile.* Huh, that was somehow much shorter than she'd expected. It also meant that with the interior of each tier being about a hundred feet high, and with close to twenty feet between tiers, the slope was about four and a half percent. *Not bad, Tala.*

Sadly, that didn't actually answer her question.

"Mistress Odera?"

"Hmm?"

"What tier are we going to?" They were just about halfway through the tunnel from the top of the second to the base of the third tier.

"Oh, the restaurant I was thinking of is on a limb that we can reach from the base of the fifth tier."

*Okay, so just about five hundred feet up, and two miles of walking.* "Oh, Okay." *Just over a mile left.*

"Is something the matter?"

Tala glanced toward her bare feet. *The ground, here, is surprisingly comfortable to walk on.* "Well, I was curious how far we were going to be walking."

"It's just about three quarters of an hour from here. Do you need us to grab something on the way? I assumed that a little walk wouldn't be too much." She gave Tala an inquiring look.

"No, I'll be fine. I just wanted to know what to expect."

"Fair enough." Mistress Odera gave Tala a mischievous smile. "You know; we could run." She then glanced to Terry. "Or Master Terry could consent to carry us…?"

Terry opened his eyes and looked to Mistress Odera. He then glanced to Tala.

"Do you want to? We could get to food faster."

Terry huffed, rolling his eyes, but before Tala could comment further, he appeared between them, bumping them both away with his increased dimensionality.

As he settled down on the ground to allow them to mount up, Tala took in his size. *More massive than a horse, to better carry us both?*

"I think I should be in front; your arms are longer than mine."

Tala took a moment to look at Mistress Odera. *Huh, she is shorter than me. I never really noticed that… somehow.* "Sure."

Mistress Odera looked almost regal as she settled down right behind Terry's neck.

Several other pedestrians gave them odd looks or muttered under their breath about people with mounts in the walking lane.

Tala quickly settled right behind Mistress Odera, and Terry stood up. Tala just managed to grab onto the enlarged collar before he moved, her arms on either side of the older woman.

"Alright. Let's go—"

Terry crouched low and *shot* up the ramp. Each stride took him tens of feet as he bounded higher in Makinaven, along the road. He wove around the slower moving vehicle and mount traffic, blessedly not scaring any of the other animals beyond their handlers' abilities to rein in.

The third tier came into view, showing Tala a widespread market with interspersed greenery and soft lighting. The buildings inset beside them were huge blocks of interlinked guild headquarters. If Tala had to guess, most of each spiral path for this tier was taken up by one or two guilds, or guild affiliated residences, workshops, or peripheral spaces.

The fourth tier was another park, surrounded by residences.

Strangely, these didn't appear bigger than those Tala had seen on the second tier, though they did seem to be more intricately detailed.

When they reached the fifth floor, Mistress Odera pointed to an opening toward the outside of the tree, and Terry darted down it, causing a pedestrian to shout and shake his fist at them.

Light poured in through the opening ahead of them, and Terry pulled to a stop just as they exited the great tree of Makinaven.

With a flicker, Terry was on Tala's shoulder, even as she dropped the short distance to the ground.

Mistress Odera landed lightly, falling into a halfcrouch before straightening and giving Terry a critical look. "Thank you for the ride, Master Terry. In the future, I would appreciate some warning before the dismount."

Tala had stumbled sideways in catching herself, but she straightened without embarrassing herself too much.

As she stood upright, her gaze swept outward, and her jaw dropped open.

Like all the trees of this forest, the canopy was sparse and only really one layer, the leaves mainly sprouting from the tips of the branches rather than along their full length. The three of them were far below that layer.

The road continued outward and upward, along the flattened top of the branch, and structures were to either side.

The entrances of the buildings were almost universally set downward, reached by a short set of stairs or other such paths. If they were multi-floored, it seemed that those floors went downward. Some likely even went under the road.

The result was very little obstruction to the view, and what a view it was.

When arriving the night before, Tala hadn't noticed just how much the land had risen back up to the base of the tree, but it must have, because they were above most of the surrounding trees. *Or the tiers were taller than I thought, or… Too many options, really. It's probably a combination of things.*

A strong breeze blew through the massive branches, but it wasn't overbearing. Even if it had been, Tala would have had no concern of falling; there was a low wall bordering the road, anywhere the top of a building wasn't offering protection from a fall.

The cool, early-winter air held a pleasant chill after the comfortable warmth within Makinaven. *So, the warmth we felt among the farms at ground level doesn't extend this far up? Interesting.* It still felt warmer than back in the forest, below.

If Tala focused on it, she could feel a *slight* movement of the branch beneath her, likely due to the wind, but it was miniscule. *I'm so glad I don't get motion sick, or this would be awful.*

Under the midday sun, the forest looked like a sparsely snow-covered, hilly plain, spreading out all around them, with mountains in the distance to the north. Tala could just see those around the trunk of the tree in that direction. There were mountains further away to the southwest, and far to the east and south, but they were barely more than a hazy outline, even to her enhanced vision.

"It is an incredibly clear day."

Mistress Odera smiled and nodded. "Indeed, it is. Now, let's get some food."

Tala nodded and smiled in turn.

The nature of the tree meant that this tier of branches likely had the best views, at least until those at the very top. Those in the middle layers would be more obscured by leaves and other branches. *I'll have to go see what it looks like from up there. That might be a good place to meditate and contemplate Fusing.* She nodded to herself. *I'll do that today.*

Mistress Odera led them down the branch way for close to a quarter hour, traversing a bit less than half the branch's length and steadily sloping upward. There was still quite a bit of foot-traffic around them, as well as a few vehicles.

They likely could have continued on Terry, but Tala found herself thoroughly enjoying the walk in the open air.

When they reached their destination, Mistress Odera moved down a set of stairs to their left. She opened the door into the restaurant without hesitation, and Tala followed her through.

A graying man bowed to them as they entered. "Welcome to our humble establishment, Mistresses. Do you have a table preference?"

Mistress Odera spoke with him quietly for a moment, and he brightened. *Is there a hint of magic around them? Is that why I can't hear?*

Mistress Odera's workings were *incredibly* subtle, and Tala was still struggling to perceive them with any consistency.

*Unless they are overtly obvious, like a defensive shield.*

The hints of power in the air vanished before Tala was sure they had actually been there.

"Oh, certainly, Mistress! Right this way."

Tala frowned but followed Mistress Odera and the older gentleman. They went down a couple of floors then outward toward the north side of the branch.

They were seated at a booth hard up against the outside of the limb. A large section of the wall beside them had been replaced with glass or something like it. That, coupled with the distance they'd traveled down the branch, ensured that they could easily see the mountains in the distance.

It was breathtaking.

Their server came a few minutes later, bringing water without ice for both of them, along with the start of their meal.

Empty plates were set in front of each of them and dishes laden with food were set on the table between them. Rice was in abundance, both plain and fried, and most of the main dishes consisted of variously glazed and seasoned meats and veggies, intended to be eaten overtop of, and with, the rice.

Terry sampled a bit of everything before curling up beside the window to sleep.

After the server had dropped off the sixth and final serving bowl, Tala leaned forward. "Mistress Odera, how much is this going to cost?"

The older Mage shrugged. "It's their lunch special." A grin split her face. "For a family of six. They charge two silver and fifty copper. It's a real deal, if you ask me."

Tala looked at the food, realizing that she'd already eaten more than Mistress Odera was likely to, all told. "So… how much will I owe?"

"A silver is reasonable to my mind."

Tala cocked an eyebrow.

"I invited you. If you ate a normal amount, I'd happily treat you, but my budget won't handle your intake requirements."

"We can't charge it as a necessary expense?" Tala asked hopefully.

Mistress Odera grinned. "After thinking it through, I believe I can justify a meal each day but not more."

"Fair enough." After a moment, Tala smiled again. "Thank you."

"Enjoy. We won't be in this city for too long, and I haven't found food in this style in Bandfast." After a brief hesitation, she added, "Well, at least not this good."

"It is that."

So, without further comment, the two settled in to eat. Mistress Odera ate a careful amount, enjoying every bite but not overindulging by any metric. At the same time, Tala devoured her second feast of the day.

\*     \*     \*

After Tala had polished off the last of the food, the three of them paid and departed. The elderly gentleman wished them a good day and a speedy return.

Instead of heading back into the main tree of Makinaven, Mistress Odera led them further down the branch, nearly as far as they'd previously come from the main trunk, to where the road ended in a wide, flat circle.

## Millennial Mage, 4 - Bound

The branch continued on for quite a ways, but it thinned, becoming too slender to be a safe foundation for the street to continue upon.

The wide, flat circle was presumably for vehicles to turn around on, but it was currently vacant, and the variation in the branch left it largely hidden from the rest of the length.

True, the windows on the other branches, and those on this side of the tree within the trunk above, looked down on the space, but those were quite far away.

"This is the closest location I knew of, where you could do your regular exercises and stretching in relative privacy."

Tala smiled to the older woman. "Thank you, Mistress Odera. This was incredibly kind of you."

"Oh, I'm happy to assist. Now, I have much that I need to get to. I assume you can find your own way back?"

"Absolutely."

"Then, I bid you a good day, Mistress Tala. Do try not to fall off." There was the glint of humor in her eyes.

"Take care, Mistress Odera. I will do my best not to."

The other Mage departed, and Tala began her training.

There, high in the great tree of Makinaven, caressed by a pleasantly chill, winter breeze, hidden from most eyes save the most discerning, Tala strove to improve.

# Chapter: 14
# Espresso?

Tala thoroughly enjoyed her morning exercise, nestled in one of the lower branches of Makinaven's great tree, even if it was after noon.

*Mistress Odera really picked a great spot.*

Tala was even able to find a nice level nook, off to one side, where she could open Kit in a secure manner and quickly cleanse herself of the sweat she'd built up.

Terry perched beside Kit protectively while she was inside.

*You know, if I'm ever falling, could I just climb into Kit and wait until we land?* At some point, she would have to trust someone enough to have them close her inside so that she could see if she could get out.

That wasn't a terrifying thought.

Not at all.

*Necessary evils to get greater utility out of my items.* Kit was great, but Tala wanted as much utility from the pouch as she could get. *And if that works, I'll have to see if I can close myself in…*

But that was down the road a bit. Other things were jostling around in her head, demanding her attention.

*I wonder how much one of those tungsten rods costs.* Another thing to ask the Constructionists about. She'd probably never need it, but she was finding herself airborne far too often to not consider it.

As she climbed back out into a cool breeze, Tala took a moment to close her eyes and just enjoy the feel of the gentle currents. Her elk leathers shifted to allow the wind through to her skin.

The sensation was amazing. *So much better than the frigidness of the forest in winter.* Even if the difference was not as extreme this high up. *I wonder if it's cooler in summer too.*

She glanced at Terry as she clipped Kit back to her belt. "Willing to give me a ride?"

Terry grew to a comfortable size and crouched down.

"Thank you." As she climbed up, she tossed him some jerky.

He snapped out, catching it with his beak before it went out of range.

*Right, he doesn't want to teleport while I'm on his back.* "Sorry about that." She tossed another much closer, and he snapped it up much more easily.

He set off at a leisurely pace, just faster than she could comfortably jog.

Tala had a thought and glanced behind them.

Terry's talons were digging into the tree for better grip, speed, and balance, just as he would the ground, below. *Oh… That's—*

Even as she was considering the cost that she'd incur from all the damage already done, her magesight showed her that the wood was pulling back together, reforming and returning to its base state.

*Oh, that's wonderful.* She let out a relieved breath and turned to face forward once again. *Where to first?*

There was no contest, she needed to go see the Constructionists.

"Let's go back to the third tier. We can ask for directions to the Constructionist Guild from there."

Terry bobbed his head in acknowledgement then bent lower, increasing his speed.

*Might as well practice.* She locked onto herself, bringing her middle finger to her thumb. *Reduce.*

Terry began to speed up more, seeming to relax a bit as her effective gravity decreased.

*This is wonderful!* She laughed joyfully.

There was an ox cart in the road in front of them, making its slow way toward the tree. When he was almost upon it, Terry pushed off to move around the obstruction, but things didn't go as expected.

Something about moving from the straight run to a sideways diversion tripped up the avian, and he began to tumble. Terry immediately flickered away, appearing in a crouch on the short wall to one side of the road. He was now the size of a cat and wore a look of profound irritation clearly on his avian face.

Tala, with her effective gravity reduced, but her momentum maintained, tumbled through the air, straight into the back of the cart, hitting with a solid *thwack!*

She groaned, sliding to the ground in a comically slow fashion.

It seemed that the cart had been made very well; she hadn't damaged it in the least.

The driver must have turned around to look, but obviously didn't see her. Tala heard him flick his reins, and the cart pulled away, now moving a bit faster than before.

Tala lay there in the road for a long moment, glaring at Terry.

He preened while glaring back.

"I was just lighter, Terry. I still had the same inertia." She was actively returning her weight to normal.

Terry squawked and shimmied, still giving her an irritated look.

"Fine. I'm back to normal weight. Let's try again?"

He didn't move.

"I won't change my gravity while riding, not without talking to you first. Alright?"

After a moment, he bobbed and reappeared beside her, sized for easy riding.

"Thank you. I apologize for throwing you off."

He shook, settling her in place, and let out a satisfied thrum. It was almost a purr but with more music to it.

"Yes, you are a wonderful runner. As I said, I apologize."

He bobbed, and started out again, this time going a little slower as if a bit unsure of his footing. That quickly passed, however, as he took a few zigs and zags to get a renewed feel for it. By the time they'd passed the still plodding cart and ox, he was up to speed once more.

A few minutes later, they reached the trunk and passed through the entry tunnel. At the end of that tunnel, Terry took a hard right, down the four o'clock spiral. His claws dug deep to facilitate the change in direction, but he pivoted perfectly, barely losing any speed.

Terry let out a quiet trumpet of triumph as he continued. If anything, he increased his speed as they moved down the sloping road.

Behind them, the wooden road fixed itself, sending out minute eddies of power which quickly calmed, leaving no trace that the damage had ever been there.

They practically whipped down the tiers, Terry skillfully weaving around and through the traffic.

As they went, Tala occasionally thought she saw flickers of light from across the open space of the tiers that they were passing. It seemed to originate from larger tube-like vertical shafts. *I'll investigate that later, I suppose.*

It didn't seem dangerous, but something about it tickled at her mind. *Later, I said.*

When they reached the base of the third tier a few minutes later, Tala directed Terry out onto the main floor.

Giving a subtle whistle as a warning to Tala, Terry flickered to her shoulder, allowing her to drop and land on her own two feet.

"Thank you, Terry. That was kind of you."

He simply hunkered down a bit before opening his mouth.

Tala grinned and gave him some jerky.

She wandered the vast, open market of this tier, taking in the sights and sounds of bartering and merchants calling out to potential customers about their wares.

As she walked through a section that was oriented toward food, an odd-seeming stall caught her attention. It was manned by two older men and a boy: likely a father, son, and grandfather if their looks were any indication. The stall was smaller than those around it but was doing a brisk business.

They seemed to be selling dark-colored bars of some kind.

*Is that some type of dessert?* It almost looked like low-quality chocolate, but there seemed to be a teapot in front of each section, steaming away on magical heaters. *That's not cheap to maintain.*

The father smiled her way. "Welcome, Mistress. What can we interest you in today?"

"Pardon my ignorance, but what are you selling?"

The oldest of the three stepped forward and bowed. "No pardon necessary, Mistress. These are tea bricks, for the most part. I assume you have not come across these before?"

"I have not."

## Millennial Mage, 4 - Bound

He moved to one side, drawing her with him by the movement, so that they would not be blocking the front of the stall. "Well, once you have a brick of the tea of your choice, you cut off a small portion and toast it, usually over a flame, but hot air or a magical heater can work as well. This brings out the depth of flavor. Once that is done, you grind up the tea and place it into your mug or teapot, pour in hot water, and allow it to steep as appropriate for the given tea. It is a compact, efficient way of carrying a large quantity of tea."

Tala leaned forward, inhaling steam coming from the various pots. "These smell amazing." She felt herself relaxing as she took in the myriad herbal scents. She knew very well what it reminded her of, but she refused to acknowledge that since it would ruin her enjoyment.

"Thank you, Mistress."

"How many cups of tea can a brick make?"

"That depends on the strength of tea you desire, as well as on the type of tea. But in general, you can get ten cups per ounce of the stronger teas. For the herbal teas, you need closer to half or three-quarters of an ounce to achieve a robust flavor."

"And the bars are how heavy?"

"The smallest we sell are single-pot nuggets, and the largest, single bricks are a pound."

"And the cost?"

"It varies, Mistress." He smiled apologetically.

Tala shrugged. "I suppose that makes sense." She considered. "Am I right in assuming that you have some of each already brewed in these pots?" She gestured to the steaming kettles.

"You are."

Tala nodded. "Then, if you are willing, and they are available, could I sample your mint blend, a chamomile, and…" She hesitated, her nose catching a whiff of something. She frowned in concentration. "Do I smell coffee?"

"Ahh! Yes, we have a limited selection of espresso bricks."

"Espresso?" She tried the unfamiliar word.

"Coffee that has been processed to be stronger. Usually consumed in very small quantities."

She could tell that he had greatly simplified that explanation, but she didn't really mind. "I'd like to sample that as well." *My own supply of coffee?* It might work, at least until she got her coffee incorporator.

*I know they exist.*

The man bowed low as the other two moved, getting three small cups for her to sample.

They set them on a small, cleared space to one side, and Tala moved over to pick up the first.

She closed her eyes, inhaling deeply. *Mint.* It was a crisp scent. *At least pepper and spear… is that rosehip and lemongrass?* She hadn't actually delved back into alchemy or herbalism since Holly had given her the enhanced senses. *This is incredible!* She took another deep breath, then sipped slowly. *Hibiscus, too?* It was a masterfully put together blend. "Splendid. How much for the larger bricks of this?"

"As an herbal tea, the larger bricks we sell this in are just under a pound with indentations for easy preparation of twenty-four pots. The cost for each such brick is twelve copper."

Tala blinked at him. "Twelve copper."

"Yes, Mistress."

*How is it that cheap?* Ingredients were much cheaper than prepared products, and even prepared tea was cheap enough to be simply given to guests at many restaurants… "That seems very reasonable." *They must grow it nearby.*

## Millennial Mage, 4 - Bound

"It is actually the least expensive of our teas, and one of our most popular, Mistress. My brother's son has cultivated an expansive amount of mint to the south, along with most of the other ingredients we use." He smiled proudly. "Mint, we have in abundance; that grows quite prolifically."

"I think ten bricks of this." She took another slow sip of the tea, draining the small cup.

She passed back the teacup and reached for the next one they'd prepared.

"Ahh, one moment." He produced a cup of clear, cool water from behind the stand. "To cleanse the palate."

Tala smiled and drank the water gratefully before handing the cup back and picking up the second flavor on offer.

Other customers had entered, and the father had greeted them and was seeing to their needs. Tala paid them no mind.

By the smell, this second drink was the chamomile blend. *Chamomile, obviously. Hibiscus again. Spearmint?* She supposed if they had a ready supply, it made sense that they would integrate it wherever possible. *Rose petals this time, and blackberry leaves?* She continued to analyze the aroma, internally going through the ingredients that she could pick out. Finally, she took a sip, marveling at the flavor.

She wanted to wax poetic on the wonderfully subtle, balanced tastes, but the tea also made her want to curl up in a comfortable chair and watch the world go by. She settled for a contented sigh and a softly uttered, "Oh, this is fantastic."

"That blend is a bit more efficient in quantity to desired flavor by design, though it is still an herbal tea. The one-pound brick is segmented for thirty-six pots. The price for that is twenty-three copper."

"Yes, ten pounds of that, too, please." It had been much, *much* too long since she'd taken the time to enjoy good tea. At first, at the academy, it had been too much of a reminder of all-too-fresh wounds. And by the time that those aches had faded somewhat, she had been well out of the habit. *No more.*

Tala noticed that most of the customers that came up seemed to be regulars, not needing to sample before they bought a large amount of this or that tea. A few bought a selection but not many.

She took a final drink of the chamomile tea, finishing off the little cup. She couldn't help herself; she smiled and spoke her praise once again. "Wonderful."

"Would you like these bricks open or wrapped for longer, more secure storage?"

"Cost of wrapping?"

"Three copper per brick."

"Done."

The young boy began wrapping her selections individually in waxed paper. His expertly dexterous fingers tucked the paper back in on itself, sealing the tea away from the elements without need for string or other, additional fastener.

She handed back the empty chamomile cup, and took another proffered cup of water. That drunk, she picked up the last sample.

It was indisputably coffee by the smell. *No. It's espresso.*

"Now, this is brewed strong. Many will add it to water or milk, and most like it with a bit of sugar or honey. Would you like either for your sample?"

Tala breathed in deeply through her nose, reveling in the potent fragrance. "No, thank you. I'd rather taste it as it is, not masked by something else. It smells divine."

The older man gave a half bow. "Mistress is too kind."

## Millennial Mage, 4 - Bound

She took a sip, and her eyes widened. "There isn't any bitterness at all."

"Of course not, Mistress." He straightened himself, clearly proud of his offered goods. "We only buy from the finest roasters. We do recommend that you use water *just* shy of boiling, so that you don't burn the grounds as you brew it."

"And it's much stronger than I was expecting, even with your warning." Tala found herself staring down at the black liquid. There was no other way to put it; it was *strong*. If the coffee she usually drank was a bucking donkey, this was a well-trained team of oxen. *Smooth, powerful, amazing.* "How much?"

"This is usually brewed in smaller quantities. What you are sampling, here, was ground as finely as possible, and the espresso stays in, just as with the teas you tried. If you prepare it that way, you need one ounce for every pot. But if you intend to strain out the espresso, you won't want it as finely broken up, and you will need close to four times the amount."

Tala gave a slow smile. *So, it's expensive.* "How much?"

"Sixty copper per one pound brick." He said it with an easy, unapologetic smile.

*That's nearly three times as much as the more expensive tea.* "I'll take ten of those, as well, wrapped."

The man smiled. "Wonderful! That will be ten silver and forty copper. Can I assist you with anything else?"

Tala nodded. "I could use a mortar and pestle along with a teapot and cup."

He laughed. "Of course!"

They talked about the various kinds he had available. They were of high quality but limited in selection. He apologized for that lack. He worked with other merchants to have a few in stock for the occasional customer in need, but they were not among his primary wares.

In the end, she selected a lovely, black-granite mortar and pestle and a stunningly enameled, cast-iron teapot and matching cup.

The teapot and cup set got a raised eyebrow from the man, but he didn't comment. *The look is likely because I chose iron over one of the clay or wooden versions. He must know something of Mages, I suppose.* She'd been tempted by the others, but the one she'd ended up picking had just been too beautiful to pass by.

The one that she'd chosen was a squat thing, a bit wider than it was tall. The main color was a glossy black with the outlines of interconnected, dark-red hexagons overlaying the surface. The effect looked like ruby veins peeking through an onyx shell.

In total, the peripheral items cost her another three silver. Or it would have, if she hadn't negotiated. In the end, she got the lot for eleven silver. *Still a lot more than I probably should have spent…*

Even so, she was happy with her purchases. "Thank you, sir."

"Thank you, Mistress."

"Oh! Before I go, could you point me to the Constructionists' Guild?"

"Certainly. You can find the nearest public location that I know of at the north six o'clock of this tier."

*North? Six o'clock would be south.* She frowned.

"Oh, my apologies. That is on the six o'clock spiral, half-way to the next tier."

"Ah! So, to the north."

"Just so."

"And do you know where the Culinary Guild can be found?"

He gave her another odd look, then shrugged. "The closest public location can be found at south twelve o'clock of this tier." His eyes twinkled a bit.

"I think I've got it. Thank you!"

She tucked her purchases into Kit, waved goodbye, and departed.

Terry flickered back onto her shoulder shortly after, and she realized that he'd departed just before she approached the stall. "Where were you off to?"

He simply hunkered down in seeming sleep.

"Well, I don't hear any screaming, so it's probably fine." She shrugged and started toward the south to get onto the six o'clock spiral. After a moment, though, she hesitated. *I could just climb up one of the pedestrian tubes. It would be about a fifty-foot climb.* That would be faster than going all the way south, then circumnavigating the tier.

She spun on her heel, feeling a bit of a fool, and headed back north.

She waved to the tea merchants as she passed and walked quickly toward her destination.

Tala and Terry passed through the market, and Tala did her best to not be distracted by the wide selection of items up on offer. Blessedly, she succeeded. *I already spent too much time. I need to get to the Constructionists.*

When she reached the twelve o'clock road, she looked around until she saw a tube-like space, inset in the wall, which had a ladder housed within.

The one she found first was marked as 'down' so she continued to look around, until she found the one labeled 'up.' She grabbed on and climbed quickly, Terry gripping her shoulder tightly.

At each level, there were large, stylized numbers beside the exit. It was a bit of an odd thing as the numbers were counting down while she climbed up.

When she reached the large 'six,' she stepped out onto the six o'clock spiral. Just to her left, up the slope, she saw the sign for the Constructionists' Guild.

"Finally. Let's see if we can't get some of our questions answered." Tala found herself grinning.

# Chapter: 15
# Into the Constructionist Guild

Tala stepped into the Constructionist Guild.

It was still odd to her, being inside spaces so vastly composed of wood. It changed the feel of a place, the way sound moved through it, how it was lit. *I'll get used to it just in time to leave...*

Her magesight picked up the now-familiar scan from the guild's doorway, and a harsh, blaring noise sounded from deep within the building.

*What the rust?*

The world seemed to stutter, and there were suddenly three people standing around her, forming an equilateral triangle with her in the dead center. Magic flowed between them in an overlapping, interweaving three-dimensional standing-spell-form.

Tala could see the spell-lines as pure magic power, suspended in the air around her.

Instantly, all light from the room vanished save the Mages' aura and the spell-form.

Tala felt the magic within her body hitch, even as her iron-salve heated. Her power was *mighty* and with the screen of iron, the magic was able to keep flowing, if just barely.

Each of the three was indisputably an Archon, each just past true yellow to Tala's magesight. *Three Refined?*

Their auras lay heavily on the room, clearly the medium for the spell-form enacted around her. Strangely, it seemed that the three auras were each a unique medium, as the sense of the spell-form altered slightly as it transitioned from one to another.

The Archon standing directly in front of Tala was a young-middle-aged male. Even under his cloak, it was obvious that he was heavily built. Something about his build and the richness of the garment caused him to look a bit like a pretentious workman, a carpenter or stone carver wearing his finest to pass for a member of the upper class. His face was just barely visible to her enhanced senses within the cowl, and it was locked in a grimace of concentration.

Tala perceived all of this in less than a heartbeat, as her iron-salve moved from unpleasantly warm to scalding. In a pulse of light and heat, the iron dust within the salve flashed off.

The world's most incongruous *ding* sounded from the back room, and the lights came back on.

With the renewed light, Tala saw that Terry had flickered to one of the corners. He opened one eye briefly before closing it again, seeming unconcerned. *When did he move?*

Every flicker of power within Tala's body was now held in suspension, unable to move, unable to act. Her senses dulled, her body felt weak beyond imagining, and her thoughts began to slow.

A voice from the back yelled out, accompanied by quick footsteps. "What, by the rusted pile of slag you have for brains, are you doing?"

The man who strode out of a doorway to Tala's right was shorter than average, but that was far from the most apparent thing about him. His aura was unfurled and a deep blue-green. *Paragon, moving toward Reforged?*

No, his aura wasn't unfurled, that wasn't quite right. It was moving as tightly controlled tendrils. Then, her magesight winked out, the last vestiges of power stilling within those spell-forms as well.

The three Refined either hadn't heard the Paragon or had ignored him, their focus seemingly locked on Tala.

With quick motions, the Paragon's aura swept through the standing spell, disrupting and shattering it, utterly. It was so strongly manifest as to even be visible to Tala's mundane sight.

Tala could suddenly think clearly again. *Is that how I used to be? That was awful.*

From what her returned magesight picked up, the broken spell-form had blossomed outward with enough power to level half a city. Seemingly unconcerned, the Paragon's aura had simply absorbed it, draining magic from the air faster than Tala could blink.

Tala gasped in a breath, staggering. The return of her senses' enhancements hit like a physical blow. Her heart beat, the sensation painful. She hadn't had even a moment to realize that her biological functions had been arrested, too.

*Much longer, and I'd be dead. How long can you survive without a heartbeat?* She knew, somewhere in the back of her mind, but she shied away from the information.

It wasn't long.

The most recent arrival was an Immaterial Guide, and all of his inscriptions were… *What?* She couldn't understand them at all, and that was actually a bit terrifying.

Many of those that were visible were lit, clearly active and not perfectly efficient, but she couldn't see them with her magesight. *He's allowing his aura out and hiding the power from his inscription activation?* That was the inverse of what she'd seen on skilled Archons before. *How? Why?*

He was handsome in a simple sort of way. Dark black hair and a slender build were what stood out most prominently from his physical appearance.

Her enhanced vision saw a grain pattern in his skin. *Wood?*

No, he wasn't made of wood, but his physical form was clearly influenced by it. *He's some variation of a wood Archon, then?*

As she processed further, in the split second before events continued, she felt like the wood-like aspect of his appearance seemed in process of being… overwritten? It wasn't actively occurring, but she could somehow tell that this man was working to remove it.

*He is reforging himself, and what I'm observing is one point of evidence of that.* It might even be what was driving him to do the reforging. *Grediv did imply that it was a difficult, unpleasant process.*

The three Refined swelled with power, turning on the intruder.

Then, they stopped, all power leaving their building spell-forms and inscriptions. Tala saw the bigger man, who was still directly in front of her, blanch as he saw the much smaller Archon approaching.

"I'll ask once more. What. Are. You. Doing?"

"The alarm triggered. And—" The man in front of Tala responded.

"And you panicked!"

"We reacted to the alarm."

"And you assaulted the Blood Archon."

"The what?" That came from Tala's left. She glanced that way and saw a woman frowning at her.

Another voice answered, from Tala's right, and Tala looked at the new speaker. The man there sounded a bit mortified. "Oh… Rust… She was raised just over two weeks ago. Her title made information on her raising a bit 'unfriendly' for dissemination to the Mages, but her picture was in all the Archon lounges for days."

"Oh… I don't really… go into those…" The woman sounded a bit… contrite?

Tala was *not* liking being surrounded by people who she didn't know and who clearly outclassed her, at least as a group. That in mind, she stepped backwards to beside the door, out of the triangle, and watched as the woman turned to glare at the second male Refined. "You didn't recognize her, either! This isn't on me."

The bigger man sighed. "Mistress Yenna, Master Grent, bicker later." He bowed toward Tala. "Blood Archon. I apologize for our mistake."

Yenna muttered under her breath. "You don't even know her name. You don't follow new Archons, either."

Tala quirked an awkward smile. "While I won't say it was nothing, I will not take it as a hostile assault. I am unharmed…" Her eyes flicked to the Paragon, even as she let her magesight sweep through herself, searching for issues. "Right?"

The Paragon bowed in turn. "There should be no lasting damage. Mistress Tala, I sincerely apologize. I am Jevin." He then motioned to the bulky Refined. "That is Master Bob."

"Master… Bob?"

Yenna grinned. "Yeah, he hates it."

Bob grimaced. "Must we do this, Mistress Yenna?"

"You could change your name."

"It's. My. Name."

Tala felt like she'd stepped into an ancient couple's house and brought up some taboo subject. "Well… Nice to meet you Master Bob, Master Jevin, Master Grent, Mistress Yenna."

They gave half-bows to Tala, and when they straightened, Grent spoke. "You should join us for afternoon tea. It's about that time, and it's the least we can do."

Tala was going to object, but then she realized that she had a *lot* of business to do with this Guild, and it wouldn't hurt to accept some hospitality. "That sounds wonderful, thank you."

They led her out of the mostly austere front entry room. As they left, Terry flickered back onto Tala's shoulder, seemingly satisfied that any danger had passed.

Tala leaned her head a bit his way and whispered. "Traitor. You totally could have helped there."

He looked straight into her eye and somehow conveyed a depth of… parental fatigue?

*I'm reading too much into his looks.* "I know I was fine, but it would have been nice…" She trailed off, looking at those walking close by. Yenna was giving her an odd look, and the others seemed to be casting sideways glances at Terry, himself. "We'll talk about this later." Tala whispered the last even quieter, in a rush of words.

As they moved down a series of side hallways, Yenna cleared her throat. "He's not your familiar; is he?"

Jevin sighed. "Mistress Yenna, you know very well that that is an incredibly personal question."

"And I make a study of familiars. This is my area of expertise, Master Jevin."

"She doesn't know that."

"She does now." Yenna turned back to Tala, a smile on her face. "So?"

Tala cleared her throat, watching the woman out of her peripheral vision. "He is not. I was advised to not consider such a bond until at least Refined."

"Fascinating. I can see why that would have been said."

"Do you not agree?"

"Hmm? Oh, of course. If you are doing a traditional soul-bond, you need to be more powerful than the familiar, in raw strength."

"Is there another option?"

Bob groaned. "Not now, Mistress Yenna, please? We already basically assaulted the woman; let's not bore her with your theories."

"I am actually interested."

Yenna brightened, and Bob sighed, falling a little bit back. "Well, we're almost there, so I'll be brief. Traditionally, a familiar bond is when an arcanous creature chooses to swallow a willingly offered Archon Star."

"Yeah, that's my understanding." Terry had perked up and was looking intently at Yenna.

"Well, there's not really any reason you couldn't do a spirit binding instead."

Tala blinked. *Like my elk leathers? When I bound the two pieces together?* "How would that even work?"

Grent spoke before Yenna could. "It wouldn't. She's been trying for… a long time. Never been able to get the bond to grab hold. There has to already be a sense of commonality to fuse two things with that spell-form."

"But look at him! The power within that bird is vastly more than any other test subject. The commonality factor is only important for power requirements."

Tala didn't really like the sound of that. *But that's the second time I've gotten reference to the spell-form and fusing.* Well, in truth Grediv had been incredibly circumspect, but still. She should probably find out what happened to Yenna's earlier volunteers. "What's happened in the past?"

"Well…" Yenna glanced away. "The arcanous beast's power was quickly consumed to maintain the link, and they died, powerless and in pain…"

## Millennial Mage, 4 - Bound

Terry let out an unamused trill and lowered his head back into seeming sleep.

"But I've only been able to test it with the traditional familiars, young and weak, those who would be easily dominated by their Mage. You, you are clearly ancient and powerful." She addressed the last to Terry.

Terry lifted his head, looking at the Archon.

Grent leaned back from his lead position. "She's flattering you. My magesight is better than hers, and all I can tell is that you are *very* power-dense. Anything more is just a guess, meant to make you like her more."

Yenna glared at him.

"And we're here!"

Tala walked into a large sitting room with the others. The first thing to grab Tala's attention about the room was that one wall was almost entirely transparent, though her enhanced eyesight told her there were hints of wood-grain in the clear section of wall.

Through the wooden window, Tala looked north. She couldn't see the mountains, this room was below the distant treeline, but there was a commanding view of the farmland and orchards on this side of the city. *Beautiful.*

As the others moved around in the room, Tala pulled her gaze from the scenery. Off to one side, a tea service was already laden with several different pots of steaming tea, along with a dozen varieties of finger food.

"How… how is this already here?" Tala didn't try to hide her confusion.

Bob sighed. "Master Grent is *quite* fond of afternoon tea, and he funds this spread, daily. The assistants make it happen, and your timing is good." He looked her way apologetically. "Well, at least in some regards. I do apologize, once again."

Tala smiled and nodded his way. "Apology accepted."

Each of them got some tea and a little plate of food before taking a seat in one of the comfortable chairs, artfully arranged in a loose circle around a low table. Tala had considered loading down her plate, or stuffing some extras into Kit, but decided that that would be in poor taste.

"If you don't mind my asking, why no coffee?"

Grent shifted forward in his seat. "Well, I see coffee as more of a morning beverage. I'd love to do coffee in the mornings, and tea in the afternoon." He looked sadly toward the tea service. "But I don't have quite *that* much free capital."

Yenna leaned closer to Tala and spoke in a conspiratorial whisper. "Master Grent provides afternoon tea to every Constructionist Guild facility in the city, and tea, even good black tea, is *much* more affordable than coffee."

Grent moved back, nodding. "Don't get me wrong, tea is wonderful. But I do wish we could do morning coffee, too. I feel like I was close… Maybe I should try again? This time…" He seemed to become lost in his own musings.

Yenna took a sip and looked Tala up and down. "Now that we're a bit more comfortable, what was that, anyway? Why did the alarm go off? Why did you register as a cloaked threat?"

Tala cleared her throat. *She's a bit… odd.* "My magical defense is passive. I imagine that…" She trailed off. "Hang on. I have my aura restrained. Most Archons do. How did it detect anything? Why did it expect to be able to?"

Bob grinned. "You *are* new."

"That's been established." The more relaxed setting of afternoon tea was allowing the last of the tension from their unfortunate encounter to bleed away. *Probably partly why they do it. It helps form bonds and smooth ruffles.*

Jevin sighed. "I will gladly answer your questions. But first, I feel like we've rather stepped in it. How can we make amends?"

Yenna opened her mouth to pursue her inquiry, but silenced herself, so as not to override Jevin.

Tala oriented on him in an instant, and her look was apparently so forceful that the smaller man leaned back involuntarily. "Coffee. Incorporator."

He blinked back at her. "What?"

"I want a coffee incorporator."

Jevin hesitated. After a moment, he glanced at the other three, then sighed. "You're never going to be a Constructionist, are you?"

"Probably not. How is that relevant?"

"A coffee incorporator. It's not possible."

The three Refined looked at him with confusion; Grent was full on frowning. "Wait a minute, now. You told me to see what I could do when I asked about them. I was even considering giving it another attempt."

Jevin cracked a grin. "And that kept you out of my hair for a decade. Were she a Constructionist acolyte, I'd have told her the same."

Bob and Yenna suppressed laughs, and Tala heard them each say something about having given up after a year or two.

Tala ignored them. "Why? Why is it impossible?"

"Why? Dear girl, do you know what an incorporator does?"

"It turns power into a material."

Jevin just stared at her for a long moment, he then rubbed the bridge of his nose, closing his eyes. "It pains me to say that that is… accurate. I suppose it's the best I can hope for, from a non-Constructionist Immaterial."

"Coffee is a material."

"No, Mistress Tala. Coffee, like virtually any other consumable, is a *lot* of different materials in a precisely ratioed solution. Coffee has more than one thousand different chemical compounds within it, together making it what we know and love."

*Oh…* "Wait, then why hasn't anyone just told me that!"

Jevin pointed to Grent. "Because the quest for a coffee incorporator is usually a final step before an incorporation journeyman is acknowledged as a master. We use it to analyze a Mage's ways of thinking, how they function with an impossible task, what avenues they try. Will they ask for help? Will they consult others? What do they do when it seems like they've been sent on a fool's errand?"

Suddenly, all the odd looks she had gotten when she'd asked after the coffee incorporator made so much more sense. "Well… that's disappointing."

"That is usually the result, yes. We can incorporate many very complex molecules, so long as the resulting solution is pure. A true master can design an incorporator capable of non-pure results, but the best I've heard of have only managed three distinct compounds generated at once, in unequal quantities. Few have been useful enough to come into ready production, but they have been made." He cracked a smile. "That said, there was a master before my time who spent a century on the coffee problem. In the end, he actually succeeded, after a fashion."

Tala perked up. "Oh?" *What's the catch?*

"He created a device that contained more than a thousand individual incorporators, each producing one part of the coffee whole. Feed in power, and it was properly parsed out to the incorporators in the right ratios to create the proper mixture."

"So…?"

"First, would you like to pay more than three hundred gold for the incorporators?"

"Well… no."

"Then there's the magical matrix that is required to run and operate it. That's more complex than most city defenses."

"Oh…"

"On top of that, it couldn't create less than a gallon at a time."

*Well, that's not a problem.*

"The compounds discorporate at varying rates."

*Oh, that'd be odd.*

"And it took, at a minimum, ten thousand mana in a single burst to function."

"That's… That's a lot."

"So. Any more questions on a coffee incorporator?"

"What was his second prototype like?"

Jevin blinked at her, and Grent laughed out loud. "I like her."

Jevin took a deep breath and let it out slowly. "I don't think he ever made a second version."

"Quitter," Tala muttered under her breath.

"What?"

"Nothing."

He gave her a searching look, then shook his head. "That aside, how can I assist you? I would normally leave you to my assistants, but I'm already displeased with how they… greeted you." They were all nearly finished with their tea and treats.

"I appreciate the personal service. I do have quite a few items to inquire about. I'm also looking to do an integration of magical weaponry with my soul-bound knife."

"We can get that sorted, then." He stood with a smile. "This way, please."

## Chapter: 16
## Jevin

Tala bade goodbye to the three Refined and followed Jevin down a short hallway to a large workshop, deeper in the tree. Terry remained on her shoulder, content to play at sleep. *Maybe he actually does sleep, some of the time.*

She couldn't begin to understand what half of the tools were in the space, and the partially completed projects might as well have been arcane spell-forms for all the sense they made to her eyes.

There were weapons and parts of weapons; mechanical constructs, partially or wholly inscribed; bottles filled with glowing liquids; jars with organic parts held in suspension; a single glass cylinder with something that looked, and moved, like ambulatory mud; and there were books and notes in piles and stacks throughout.

Jevin spoke, drawing Tala's attention back to him, "So, Mistress Tala, where would you like to begin?"

"What do your inscriptions do?"

He paused, frowning. "That is not what… Why are you curious about that?"

"Well, when you broke up their spell-form, it looked like you were somehow manipulating your aura, and your spell-forms were clearly activating, even if I couldn't see the magic in them, specifically."

Jevin looked at her a bit closer before nodding in understanding. "You have always active magesight. Clever, if you can take it." He smiled and gestured to two reading chairs beside a large bookcase, positioned for easy conversations. "To answer your question, my scripts almost entirely deal with perfecting my dexterity with and authority over my aura. So long as my inscriptions last, if I am conscious, I have unbreakable control within my aura's reach." The words were spoken with utmost humility as a simple fact.

They settled into the chairs as Tala thought about his words. "That's a bit terrifying."

"For humanity's enemies, it is." He smiled, then, and Tala saw a fierce glint in his eyes.

*Glad I'm human.* "Thank you for sharing that." She frowned. "Wait. Why would you need to increase your authority over your own aura?"

"Oh! That's simple, if less so to explain. You can control gravity, yes?"

"I can."

"So, you have authority over gravity?"

"I do."

"So, why not immediately crush all your enemies, regardless of where they are, with a thought?"

"Well, I can, if I can target them. I mean, I have to take it in measured steps, ramping up."

"Why are you limited to those you can easily target? Why must you be measured?"

"Well, to do otherwise would require too much power."

"Why?"

"Well… it's harder?"

"Exactly." He smiled.

Tala was frowning. They sat in silence for a long moment, before she started to nod. "So, you're saying that I don't have complete authority over gravity. My authority is resisted, or contested, so I am limited in what I can do, and it is difficult to achieve certain things."

"Well reasoned."

Her eyes widened at the implication. "So… you are like a god within your aura?"

He laughed at that. "No, no. I simply increase my authority. I do not remove all resistance or gain unassailable power. My control is such that none should be able to shake it, but it can still be opposed."

There was a lot there that Tala would need to unpack, but she thought she needed more time to consider, before pursuing it further.

"Now, what else is on your mind?"

Tala pulled Kit off of her belt and began taking Leshkin weapons out.

"Wait. Are those the weapons you want to combine with your soul-bond?"

"That's right, if they will improve it."

"One moment, then." He went to a nearby table and rummaged around before he returned with a round pad, connected to a metal rod by a finely woven, golden cable. "Please set your weapon on this circle." He placed the circle on the side table that was between the two chairs.

Tala pulled Flow from her belt.

"Oh, please remove the training scabbard. That is what the sheath is, correct?"

"It is." She complied, setting Flow down on the device, blade bared.

Jevin picked up the first Leshkin weapon, a sword, and touched the rod to it. The rod turned red. "This is incompatible with the current state of your weapon. We could force a union, but it would ultimately weaken it."

Tala nodded, and continued to pull out weapons, saving the best for last.

Sadly, every weapon registered as red.

Finally, when there was a sizable pile of Leshkin armaments beside them, Tala pulled out the juggernaut's glaive. It wasn't easy to withdraw, given its size, but she managed to do it without feeling too awkward.

A pressure fell over the room, much more palatable here in the magic-poor, city air than it had been in the forest. Jevin's aura expanded, surrounding the weapon and containing its power.

"That." He looked to her, then back to the massive glaive. "It's a juggernaut's weapon?"

"It is."

"That must be some story."

Tala indulged him, trying to make it interesting without over-embellishing. It only took a couple of minutes, and when she finished, he was nodding.

"We should discuss your spell-workings at some point. I imagine we could learn a bit from each other."

Tala frowned at that. *What could I possibly teach a Paragon?* Still, she wasn't going to say no. "Sure."

He took the weapon from her hands with a flex of aura and touched the rod to it. The metal turned a yellow-green. "This is compatible, but it won't improve the strength of your weapon very much." He frowned, looking at something in the magic surrounding Flow. "That is a form changing weapon?" He nodded to himself, not needed her to answer. "That makes sense. Melding these two will give you another available form, as well as a *slight* improvement to the weapon as a whole. Mainly, your weapon will have more mass, both magical and physical, at its disposal. Thus, it will be able to hit harder, should it not cut through what it strikes."

*Flow has yet to fail in a cut, but I suppose hitting harder when it eventually happens would be good. And I can turn it into a glaive?* That was a pure win.

*I'll have to learn how to fight with one.* She could do that.

"Let's do it!"

He smiled. "We can schedule a time. Tomorrow morning work for you?"

She frowned but nodded in resignation. "I suppose. I'd prefer to do it sooner."

"I do apologize. Mistress Yenna is just finishing up a refresh of the workspace that would best facilitate this merger. I don't wish to give you a shoddy result. She only came down to this tier for afternoon tea with her colleagues and me."

"I appreciate that. So, we'll go to another tier for the working?"

"Yes, the facility on the sixth tier is more capable of working with Archon-level materials."

Tala gave him a searching look. "So… why are you down here?"

He smiled at that. "Well, my current work is on items without any sort of bond intrinsic to their design. I have a theory that items not built to be bound end up being stronger than those designed with that goal in mind."

"Oh? Why?"

"Well, if a table has two legs, is it stable?"

"Well, no?" She thought for a moment. "Maybe?"

"What if I told you that each leg was actually designed to hold a table on its own. Now, do you think the theoretical two-leg table is stable, or not?"

"I see what you mean. Something that is useful, powerful, and stable on its own will make for a better result after the bonding."

"That's my theory."

Tala nodded. *That makes sense.* "But back on the topic of my weapon, what would the cost be? I am a Mage Protector for the Caravan Guild, if that factors in."

He grinned back at her. "I think, as a show of inter-guild solidarity, we can do it at cost, then. Four gold should cover it. It might flex up or down a bit, but we'll know before we enact it."

"Four? Last time I melded something with this weapon it cost half that."

"And the weapon seems to have become more powerful as a result. It is now more stable, with greater magical weight, and it will require more power and material to work a true melding. I won't leave you with a magical patch that will explosively break off in a decade or two."

*That's fair...* She placed the Leshkin glaive back into Kit.

"Now, what else can I do for you?"

"Do you have use for those?" She pointed to the weapons that they'd tested and found incompatible with Flow.

"We would." He thought for a moment. "They would probably be worth near six gold, all together. But that would take you finding buyers for each, and it wouldn't be quick." He smiled again. "Would you be willing to accept four as a show of inter-guild solidarity?" His eyes were twinkling.

Tala found herself chuckling. "So, a straight exchange, then?"

"That would work for us."

"Done."

Inscriptions activated, and Jevin's aura swept all the Leshkin weaponry into a workbench drawer, which was obviously too small to hold them.

*Constructionists. They must be able to make all the extra-dimensional storage they'd ever need.*

"Next?"

"Why did the scan expect to penetrate my aura, while not being able to break through my passive defense?"

"I assume that defense is gone, now? I can't see any evidence of it."

"It is." She felt a bit exposed, but she also knew that the iron salve wouldn't help her much against this man regardless, if he chose to harm her.

He was nodding. "I apologize for that, as well. I will try to think of a worthy repayment for our… brutish response."

"That's kind of you, but I still don't really know what happened."

"Humans, even humans controlling their aura, have a… magical sense to them. A signature, if you will. Your defense likely masked that or altered it somehow. The scan detected you without the signature, and sounded the alarm." He shrugged. "That's my best guess, anyway. Master Grent designed it, though. He's a good lad, but he sometimes gets a bit too enthusiastic about his projects." Jevin quirked a smile at the last.

*Lad? Jevin is talking about a Refined like he's a precocious teen…* "Ahh, Okay, then."

Tala thought for a quick moment, running through the list in her head. *What should I ask next?* She settled on an easy one.

"Would a self-repairing item, split in half, recreate two of itself?"

"In general, no. The repair magics would stay with one piece over the other, and only that one would rebuild."

*That explains why the severed sleeve didn't regrow any of the rest of the outfit, at all.*

"That makes a lot of sense, actually."

Jevin smiled. "The truth often does."

"Not always?"

He barked a laugh. "Oh, stars no. Sometimes the truth is so much stranger than the competing theories, and it is almost always more complicated than it seems."

## Millennial Mage, 4 - Bound

As Tala considered, she realized that she'd seen that a time or two. "True enough." *What next… Oh!* "I think I'm looking for a dimensional anchor of some kind."

"You think?"

She described her encounters with the Leshkins as well as the night wing ravens and a few other incidents that seemed applicable. To her mind, she could take damage but kept getting knocked free of where she needed to be.

She did not mention the likely arcane encounter. *I… I don't want to deal with the complication.*

The very idea started a headache building.

"That is an interesting problem. Let me think on it, and I'll give you my suggestions tomorrow."

"That works for me. Do you have any advice that you'd give to me, as an Immaterial Guide? Or as a new Archon?"

"As a new Archon? Begin working toward Fused as soon as you can. It can be a long road, but you only know once you've taken your first step. Also, once you start, we can discuss, if briefly, what being Refined will mean. As an Immaterial Guide? Focus on that which Materials cannot do, but you've already done that, to some extent." He frowned. "No, you actually seem to have been bridging the Immaterial and Material quite a bit, though your offensive work is decidedly Immaterial."

"All my work is Immaterial."

He waved that off. "In enactment, yes, but in principle? Your defenses could be done with either, relatively easily. You need to focus more on your specific scripts. Some of them seem… ill adjusted? Do you have spell-forms that are fairly new to you?"

"I have a variable gravity manipulation, which I haven't had for long."

"That is likely what I'm seeing. Get used to it. Explore the edges of its capabilities. If I may ask, what does it do?"

Tala shrugged. "I can alter the effective gravity of items around me, so long as I can perceive them well enough to target them."

"Targeted… gravity alteration? How novel. Why not area?" He leaned forward a bit, clearly quite interested.

Tala shrugged. "Gravity doesn't work over an area. An object either acts on itself, gravitationally, or two objects act on each other. Gravity doesn't exist in a vacuum." She hesitated. "Wait… that's not what I meant…"

Jevin grinned. "I think I understand you. That is an interesting way of conceiving of that fundamental force. It doesn't seem quite right to me." He let out a little laugh. "I can think of a few things that seem to contradict your thinking off the top of my head, but I won't try to disabuse you of your working mental framework. Rust me; I was never able to understand gravity well enough to get scripts related to it. I might be the one who's mistaken."

Tala just shrugged. "No one's broken me of my understanding, yet. After all, I can see it working every time I use my offensive spells."

He shrugged in return. "Regardless, I do have a few questions. Can you do groups of targets? Can you increase gravity on one item while decreasing it on another, simultaneously? Is the change linear or compounding? Can you target an area instead? Can you change the direction of the resulting acceleration? Can you affect gravity on part of a thing, while leaving the rest unaltered? What about an item that is held by a hostile magic user?" His eyes brightened. "Have you practiced opposed enactment?"

"For this script? I haven't tried the first two. The changes are compounding. And I haven't tried the last five, either." She felt a bit embarrassed, if she were being honest. This was *her* spell-form, and she hadn't yet plumbed its depths.

"Then, that's a good place to begin. Your inscriber should have given you notes on the inscriptions. Read up, test, explore the boundaries of what that spell-form can do. If you need practice under opposition, let me know, and I can schedule some time." He smiled, again. "And pursue Fusing."

"I'll consider that. Thank you." She frowned. "Wouldn't your helping me take from your other projects?"

"Not really. I can hold a mild magic-nullification effect over an item within my aura while I work, and you could try to affect it." He shrugged. "It would take very little of my attention."

"There is no way that I could hope to overcome your resistance, though."

"Of course not, but by the same token, I wouldn't place much effort behind it. I'd ensure it was within your reach. To stretch your abilities, as it were."

That was… tempting. "I'll consider that, too. Thank you for the offer."

"Of course." He didn't press further.

Tala moved to the next topic. "Mage gold. Do you have need of some?"

"Ahh, your arm, right?"

Tala nodded. She'd told him the story behind the juggernaut's glaive, after all.

"We can use it. Honestly, using it in the merging, tomorrow, would probably improve the process, at least marginally."

"Really? Why didn't you mention that before?"

"If I told you that I could, maybe, improve the melding fractionally, would you be willing to cut off your arm, and get it reinscribed once it grew back?"

Tala shuddered. "No…"

"That's why. No one likes making Mage gold." He shrugged. "It is also most effective when used in conjunction with the one who made it. Even then, it usually can only grant a one or two percent increase in efficiency for some things. We should try to use it tomorrow. How much do you have?"

Tala tossed him the pouch that Hawthorne had given her. *Do not remember how that used to be in your arm, Tala.* She didn't. She didn't give it a single thought.

He caught it with raised eyebrows. "Well. Let me check this." He went and weighed it, then ran several instruments around the pouch, sticking some in. "Yeah, we can definitely use this tomorrow. If there's any left, I'll buy it off you at twenty percent more than its weight?"

She had no idea if that was a good price or not, but it seemed reasonable enough. "Alright."

"Thank you. We'll sort that tomorrow."

"Sounds great. Now, tungsten rods." She smiled, aiming for innocence. *Not sure why, but might help? I am asking after city defense weapons…*

Jevin hesitated. "Like the city defenses?"

*Precisely!* Well, the flimsy veil of innocence was gone. "Yup."

"I could get you an uninscribed one for… two hundred and thirty-five gold?" After a moment he nodded. "Yeah. That should be about right."

Tala's eyes widened in shock. "What?"

"Those are each close to eighteen thousand pounds, Mistress Tala."

"Oh… I probably don't need something that heavy."

He grinned. "Probably not. You want something to drop on enemies, likely augmented by your gravity manipulation?"

"That's the idea."

"I'll see what I can come up with. Talk tomorrow?"

"Sure." After a moment, she nodded. "If I fell from a great height, within my dimensional storage, would I survive?"

Jevin glanced to her belt, the scripts around his eyes dancing to life with power and subtle light. *He's not hiding his power anymore?* "A static space. Axis and kinetic isolation." He was nodding. "Yes," he answered simply.

"Could I get out?"

"Have you never been in your storage?"

"Well, I have, but never with it closed."

"Ahh, so you're more asking what would happen if you were closed inside or if it landed upside down?"

"Landed upside down?"

He smiled at that. "If it were open, upside down, what would you see?"

"The ground?"

"And could you push off of it?"

"To move the bag? No." Her eyes widened. "Oh! Oh… yeah… that would be bad."

"You'd need to close the bag and reopen it to correct the orientation. Or, you might be able to work your fingers between the ground and the edge of the storage item, then apply force to flip the pouch over."

"Kit has dimensional… Wait. How did you read the scripts within the pouch?" She looked down, noticing for the first time that Kit's magic was easily visible. *Their spell stripped Kit of iron, too.* Tala shuddered. *What would have happened if Kit explosively, dimensionally realigned with the world around us?*

"So, you had the bag defended as well, then. Kit? You've named your storage?"

"Seemed reasonable. I have to think about Kit in some fashion, and Kit is shorter than dimensional storage, pouch, or any other moniker."

"Fair enough, I suppose." He nodded. "I imagine that you were going to reference… Kit's dimensional defenses, the ability to minutely affect the world around it."

"That's right."

"It would probably land as you desired, yes."

"Good to know." After a moment. "So, would I be able to get out?"

"I've no idea. Let's find out." He gestured to an open space on his floor.

"I don't…" Tala hesitated. *If he meant me harm, there is literally nothing I could do about it…* "Alright," she answered hesitantly.

She still wasn't a fan of the level of trust it required in a stranger, but that requirement only existed if she ignored her utter helplessness, even outside of Kit.

*Okay, Tala. Let's do this.*

She shifted her shoulder, jostling Terry a bit. "Hey, wait outside?"

Terry opened an eye and then flickered away.

Tala set Kit on the floor, pulling it wide enough for her to climb in. Before she could reconsider, she dropped through. Tala immediately focused upward, watching the opening.

Jevin grunted. "Fascinating. It seems very capable of avoiding interference by most people. I'm having trouble grabbing the pull cords."

Tala absently refilled Kit. *I'm already in here, might as well.*

## Millennial Mage, 4 - Bound

A moment more, and he let out a sound of success. "There we go. Closing! If you don't come out in a minute, I will open the storage. Agreed?"

"Agreed."

The opening shrunk, then vanished entirely.

Tala controlled her breathing. *It's alright, Tala. You chose this.* She looked at the top of the ladder, in the dim but sufficient lighting.

*Nothing. Smooth.*

She climbed up and placed her hand there. *Still nothing.*

Blessedly, the space hadn't altered any. It was as both Ingrit and Jevin had said.

Even so, Tala wanted out.

As soon as the desire crystalized in her mind, her hand moved upward, pushing through the previously solid ceiling. She stuck her other hand up and pulled them apart.

The opening reappeared and easily opened to full size. She climbed out, back into Jevin's workshop.

She looked around and found it dark. *What?*

Terry was curled up on a bench to one side, apparently sleeping. *Nothing new, there.*

"Mistress Tala?" The voice sounded… off.

"Master Jevin?" She looked toward where the voice had originated.

"It is you! Stars be praised." A hunched figure came into the workshop on shuffling steps. He looked *old*. A white beard covered his face, and wrinkles decorated his features.

"What's going on?"

Terry lifted his head, regarding them with a hard to discern expression.

"You didn't come out, and I couldn't get your device back open." He gave a sad smile. "It's been…" His eyes unfocused. "Eight hundred years?" He nodded slowly. "Yes, nearly that."

Tala's eyes widened, and she settled back on a nearby stool. "No."

"I'm afraid so."

Tala looked over to Terry. Terry, for his part, looked between the two of them, then stood slowly, shakily raising one taloned foot toward her.

Her eyes narrowed. "Wait a minute. Archons of your rank don't age. Terry, what are you doing? You're probably as immortal as an Archon. Why would you be shaky?" She looked around, the lights were dimmed, but there weren't any windows. The only reason it would be dim is if Jevin had lowered the lights.

Jevin hesitated, then straightened with a smile. "Fine." The beard and wrinkles vanished. "It was worth a shot."

Terry flickered to her shoulder and bumped her cheek. She glared at the bird, but his expression seemed to convey amused ambivalence. So, Tala turned her glare on Jevin. "What was that!? That was horrifying."

He shrugged. "Thought it would be funny." He gave a cough, scratching the side of his nose. "Didn't work out quite as I'd hoped."

"Yeah, it wasn't that funny."

He cleared his throat, seeming slightly awkward. "Anyway. It seems like you had no issue getting back out. I'd suspected that the item would respond to your desires and allow itself to be opened from the inside. In fact, I'd wager that if you hadn't been willing, I wouldn't have been able to close it." He hesitated. "Well, at least not without breaking it in some way."

Tala was still a bit thrown by the odd attempt at a joke but tried to move past it. "Well… Okay then." *This is why you shouldn't trust strangers, Tala.*

"Is there anything else?" He smiled sheepishly, clearly feeling a bit bad for his clumsy attempt at humor.

"No… I think that's it."

"Very well. Then, I will see you tomorrow morning for the melding of the weapons?"

"That sounds workable. Thank you."

# Chapter: 17
# Venturing Food

Tala left the Constructionist Guild feeling conflicted. Jevin had helped her, but he was… odd. *All the older Mages I've met are odd, though…*

She would be meeting up with him the following day to meld Flow with the glaive, but she wasn't sure that she wanted to see him after that. *Being able to train myself against a Paragon, though…* The level of control and resistance he could offer would be unlike most others she could work with.

An old proverb came to mind: '*When training the sword, find a master.*' Though, in truth, she'd heard 'the sword' replaced with all sorts of things. *More a format than a true saying, I suppose.*

Tala decided to walk down the spiral to let herself have some time to contemplate. *I can climb up a pedestrian tube when I'm to the south. I'll avoid the market that way, too.*

The trip down the six o'clock spiral was uneventful, and she found the 'up' pedestrian ladder without issue. A short climb brought her to twelve o'clock south and a Culinary Guild office.

She squared her shoulders, put a smile on her face, and strode in.

The brush of magic moved over her as she entered, and a chime sounded from within the space. If Tala had to put an emotion to the sound, it would be one of cautious alarm.

An attendant immediately bustled out from a side room to intercept her. "Mistress? Did a courier miss a delivery or payment?"

Tala frowned at the man. "No? I just had some questions for a guild official."

"Apologies, but Mages are not permitted within culinary facilities unless specifically invited or seeking restitution. If no delivery or payment has been missed I must, respectfully, ask you to leave. We will gladly accept any inquiry via courier."

Tala was almost stunned into inaction, but she had slightly expected something like this. Instead of responding, she pulled out her iron medallion. The coin bore the deeply inset relief of a scythe.

It had been given to her by Brand in order to identify her as 'in the know.' *And as an apology for attempting to stab me in the heart…*

"I would really like to speak to someone of authority."

The assistant hesitantly took the coin, examining it closely. "Where…?" He swallowed involuntarily, his voice barely above a whisper, "Where did you get this?"

"From the head chef on a caravan venture. It was voluntarily given and gratefully received."

He gave her a long look, then nodded. "I will… I will see if the branch head can see you."

Tala gave a partial bow in thanks, but he was already gone.

*Well, I'm in it now.*

There were several notable sounds from the back rooms, and Tala tried not to overhear. It wasn't hard, given the number of walls between her and the raised voices. She likely couldn't have heard details even if she'd tried.

A moment later, an older man strode out into the entry hall. He wore expensive clothes and clearly was a figure of importance here.

The assistant hung back, walking behind and to his boss's left.

Tala opened her mouth to greet the man, but he cut across her.

"I'm not sure what your game is here, Mistress." He flicked the medallion her way.

Tala caught it from the air, examining it for a moment to ensure it was the same one. *At least of the same kind.*

"The inter-guild accords are clear, and you haven't been invited."

"Then I am requesting an invitation."

"Request denied."

Tala gave the man a flat look. "May I at least have the name of my denier? I am called Tala."

He hesitated, then seemed to decide it wasn't worth refusing. "I am Wannor. I do not wish to be rude, Mistress, but you are treading near many violations. You must leave if requested to do so. We have."

"Then invite me to stay. The problem will be solved."

He glowered. "I will not."

Tala let out an irritated breath. "Don't you want to know why I'm here?"

"No."

*Are you rusting serious?* "Or where I got the medallion?"

"No."

*Fine then; let's poke the bear.* "Or how much arcanous meat I've eaten?"

Wannor hesitated. "Why would I want to know that?"

Tala held up the coin. "Because of this!"

"No… I'm genuinely curious. Why the rust would I care how much you eat?"

Tala opened her mouth, then paused. *Well… that probably doesn't really factor in… does it?* "Fine. That wasn't really the point."

Wannor's features scrunched in irritation. "I don't know what you know. I don't really want to. I have six caravans leaving in the next three days, and I need to finalize the manifests and…" He trailed off, shaking his head. "I'm not going to justify myself to you." He locked gazes with her. "Please, go… Whatever it is you're here for, do it somewhere else."

Tala opened her mouth to argue further, but finally just shook her head. "Fine."

Wannor smiled.

"I'll leave." She didn't turn. *Maybe I'm being a bit mean…*

His smile slipped just slightly, but he made a visible effort to maintain it.

"I'm departing." She hadn't moved. *Still, he's been very rude.*

He lost the struggle, and his expression became blank once more.

"I'll go… just as soon as I know where I should go *to*. Where can I talk with someone from this guild?"

Wannor's eye began to twitch.

Tala stood there, smiling.

He grimaced, then sighed. "Fine. Go to the guild reception on the fifth floor. They'll have more time for your foolishness." Without another word, or backward glance, he turned and strode from the room.

"Well, that's something I suppose." She shook her head. "Have a good day!"

She didn't listen too closely to his response, but if she interpreted the tone correctly, it was filled with imaginative curses.

She had just left the building, and started walking away and upward, when an imposing figure stepped out after her.

She glanced back, taking in the man's appearance. *He might be taller than Rane.*

He towered over her. His hair was a smooth black, and he had a beard that almost caused her jaw to drop. It went down nearly to the man's waist, and it was skillfully braided in complex patterns, taming the otherwise voluminous locks.

His clothes were simple, but clean, and he had an apron over one shoulder. "Mistress Tala, was it?"

"Yes?"

"I'm Sarenor, a cook with the Culinary Guild, and I'm heading up to the fifth tier. Would you like company for the trip?"

Tala gave him an odd look. "Why?"

He just grinned. "Oh, Wannor is a grumpy sort. I caught a glimpse of the medallion. Please, don't let him sour you on our guild. He's up to his armpits in paperwork. Still, his advice to go to the fifth tier is good. Shall we?" He motioned.

Tala began walking, and he fell into step beside her.

"So, what did you want from us, anyway?"

She shrugged. "I've had good relations with several of your head chefs, and I have some food needs, so I figured I'd go to the source."

"Food needs?"

She smiled a bit self-consciously. "I need to eat. A lot."

"Like, 'I'm one of the guys; see? I eat so much!' or is this more of a requirement for your magic?"

She chuckled. "Requirement is probably too strong of a word, but that is the more accurate of the two."

"Good to know. So?"

## Millennial Mage, 4 - Bound

*Well, I'd ask Brand if he were here, or Amnin if I knew where she was. There's nothing really secret about it.* She quickly outlined what she was hoping. She wanted a large amount of food that would keep well, and easily be made edible and palatable.

"Oh, yeah! We do that sort of thing all the time."

"You do?"

He gave her an odd look. "Of course. The city has scouting parties that keep tabs on the forest around Makinaven, and they need to eat. The higher-level Mages within the city often go on missions for weeks at a time without peripheral support." He was nodding. "Yeah, you just want solo-venturing food."

"That sounds exactly right."

He grinned. "Glad to help! Yeah, we can get you some. I assume you have a storage device?"

They chatted about what tools she had already that would allow her to prepare, carry, and maintain the food. He outlined some suggestions on equipment for her to acquire so that she could improve what she would be able to eat.

They then moved on to talking about the various options she could select from. As it turned out, Sarenor was one of those who prepared food for the caravans, and the secondary role for his team was to make up this solo-venturing food.

When she learned that, Tala was instantly suspicious, but that lessened as she learned more about the Culinary Guild in general.

Those who worked in the guild offices were either bureaucrats or members of teams like Sarenor's. The other members of the guild didn't have much occasion to come to the offices. Even those who worked the caravans only sent a representative with their reports, manifests, and other required pre- or post-trip paperwork.

*I suppose I never really considered how such guilds would work.*

They came to a comfortable pause in the conversation around the time they entered the fourth tier, still climbing.

Tala kept glancing toward the man, still feeling a bit odd about the whole thing. He wasn't breathing hard, as she expected for someone who lived here, often traversing the tiers.

Finally, she asked what had been bugging her. "Wouldn't your beard interfere with your cooking?"

Sarenor grinned back at her, stroking his beard proudly. "Oh, so you noticed this?"

Tala gave him a flat look, and he laughed.

"Fair enough. In truth, it would be quite the issue, if I didn't have a nephew in the Constructionist Guild." He hesitated. "Well, I suppose I'm his nephew?" He shook his head. "Maybe great-nephew. The lad barely looks thirty, and I'm pushing fifty. It's just less confusing to modify familiar terms, right?"

She shrugged.

"But you asked about the beard." Sarenor pulled out what looked like a cloth mask, but Tala's magesight told her it was so much more.

With a clearly carefully-practiced motion, the cook somehow scooped the entirety of his beard into the mask before fixing it in place. The cloth didn't bulge at all, but still seemed to rest naturally against his face as if he were clean shaven. Not a single stray hair showed as evidence of the glory beneath.

"A dimensional… mask?"

"Yup! Somehow it's designed to only allow hair into the expanded space. That actually makes it more efficient, or so he tells me." Sarenor shrugged. "I've been able to keep my beard, and he gets to test out new theories."

The mask came off, allowing an almost comical explosion of previously well-contained facial hair.

*That seems like such a contradiction, but it's the only description that makes sense…*

They chatted about small things, mainly the variations to regional dishes, along with how the caravan's cooks chose the dishes to be served.

It turned out that the cooks in the caravans had almost universal discretion in what they served. It was a prestigious position but also a dangerous one. Due to both of those factors, it was high paying as well.

"I prefer practicing my craft by day and returning home each night."

Tala just smiled. She knew that it would be polite to inquire about his family, including if there was one, but she couldn't bring herself to do so. Too many things were reminding her of family already.

*Oh, Tala. You really need to sort yourself out…* She'd been fine asking others about family. *Yeah, but I hadn't been working through so much death, then.*

She shook her head and turned the topic to various spices and herbs.

It turned out that many of the regional differences to various dishes were directly linked to the availability of core spices that were required to bring out different flavors. That made sense, and if Tala had any notion of relative spice prices, she could have easily realized that connection on her own, but she'd never done any sort of investigation.

*Maybe this is why Mistress Odera hasn't found a good version of our lunch food in Bandfast? The requisite spices to do the dishes justice aren't available for reasonable prices.*

Probably worth asking. In all likelihood, the Mage would already know, one way or another.

When they arrived at the fifth tier Culinary Guild office, Tala was again asked to leave by the assistant.

Sarenor rolled his eyes at the assistant, but simply bid Tala farewell and went into the back.

Tala presented her coin once more, and the assistant scurried off to get someone with more authority.

Ten minutes later, Tala was enjoying afternoon coffee with thrice-baked cake to dip into the beverage. *I could get used to all these in-between meals.*

The coffee was strong, almost as strong as the espresso she'd so recently purchased, but it was cut with cream and sugar. It was a wonderful counterpoint to the dipping-cake, which actually wasn't very sweet.

A woman strode in without introduction and sat across from Tala. She was immaculately dressed, though Tala's enhanced vision could pick up the pressure lines from a recently removed apron.

She seemed to be an austere woman, holding her features under careful control. Her hair was gray and held up in a tight bun. That lent greater weight to the grandmotherly air about her. "So, Mistress Tala. Tell me what the Culinary Guild can do for you?"

Tala set her thrice-baked cake on the small, provided plate, swallowing her latest bite. "Well, aside from some solo-venturing food, I actually wanted to ask you what I can do for the Culinary Guild."

The woman blinked at her, seeming stunned. She tilted her head to one side, considering. "I apologize, Mistress. I am Atrela. I am the currently elected Head of the Makinaven Culinary Guild. I preside over the branch heads of every branch office within this city."

"It is a pleasure to meet you, Head Atrela."

"Just Atrela will be fine, Mistress."

"Then, Tala, please."

"As you wish, Mistress Tala."

Tala felt her eye twitch but didn't press the issue. "So?"

"Honestly, I am unsure how to reply. To speak with you, directly, violates our guild charter, but since you bear a medallion, to turn you away would similarly breach procedure."

"I apologize for putting you in such a difficult position. Will there be repercussions?"

"Honestly? Probably not. But if someone decides to make a play at replacing me, they could try to get me removed. That was assured as soon as you showed up."

Tala frowned. "Wannor, down on the third tier, sent me up here. Would that factor in?"

Atrela sighed. "It just might. Thank you for that warning. You said he sent you? Did he meet with you personally to do so?"

"He did."

Atrela nodded thoughtfully but didn't comment.

"So… I am aware that the Order of the Harvest has a *very* poor history with Mages, and I assume that the Culinary Guild is the public face of that order?"

"Quite correct."

*Honest of her.* "If I may ask… why haven't you approached more Mages through the years? You are a powerful guild, after all."

Atrela's mouth quirked into a small smile. "We have, Mistress. Every ten to twenty years, we ask for an unaffiliated volunteer to present our ideas to the local Archon council, or the Constructionist Guild, or some individual Mage or Archon. The response is always the same: 'That is not for you to pursue. Drop it, immediately.'"

Tala frowned. *That didn't seem right…* "What if I were to take and present it?"

The woman leaned back, considering. After a long moment, she poured herself some coffee and took a careful sip. "That would certainly be different."

"I am unaffiliated. I'd meet that requirement."

Atrela let out a short, soft chuckle. "True enough. I cannot authorize this, however, not on my authority alone. I can propose it to the guild council. Would you be willing to keep the guild and the Order out of it?"

"Yes? I don't want to lie, but I can obfuscate."

"That is acceptable, so long as you are willing to refuse to answer about certain things."

"I'm open to that."

Atrela nodded. "That could work. We've never worked directly with a Mage before." She hesitated. "Well, not openly and not on this side of things."

Tala frowned. "I find that very unlikely."

"Oh?" The other woman seemed genuinely confused.

"Has no member of the Order ever had a child who grew up to become a Mage?"

"Of course we have. One of my sons, and three of my aunts are Mages."

"So?"

"We are barred from discussing it with them, or anyone who is not of the Order. We don't admit any minors to the Order, so none ever become Mages after admittance."

"That seems foolish."

Atrela gave Tala a pointed look. "If I told you that we were studying and enacting necromancy within this building, and you believed me, what would you do?"

"That's hardly—"

Atrela cut across Tala. "What would you do, Mistress?"

Tala paused to consider. Academy doctrine was to kill them all, then hunt down anyone they had ties to and kill them as well.

If she did that, she'd probably be rewarded. *No, a law-abiding Mage should report it to the local council and then return with reinforcements, so that no one could escape.* But that didn't answer the question. What would *she* do?

Tala frowned. Necromancy. The animating of dead flesh. That portion was a bit gross, but hardly *that* immoral. *Disrespectful, though.* Even so, it wasn't actually outlawed. Working with the souls of the dead, however, *that* was utterly forbidden. *Does that include founts?*

Tala hadn't actually considered that association. Could every arcanous beast be considered the product of necromancy?

That had disturbing implications.

She glanced to Terry, who was clearly listening with interest, despite his closed eyes.

*So, what would I do?* "I would clarify what type of necromancy you meant."

"Mistress Tala. You know what—"

Tala held up her hand. "I wasn't finished. I do see your point, Atrela. If it was the forbidden kind, if I even suspected the forbidden form, I would burn this place to the ground." She hesitated, looking around at the wood and considering the tree around them. "Well, not literally. That would probably end badly."

Atrela quirked a smile. "Precisely. Mages do not respond gently to those pursuing forbidden knowledge or practices."

*There's good reason… for most of it, anyway.* "And you feel that you've been told the consumption of harvests falls into that category."

"From the best of our understanding, it does."

*But it doesn't!* At least she didn't think it did. *Am I willing to risk thousands of people's lives on my assumption?* After thinking for a long moment, she realized that she wasn't. "Very well. I will bow to whatever the Culinary Guild decides. I don't like it, but I won't pull back the curtain from your Order without permission."

Atrela visibly relaxed. "Thank you, Mistress. I hope that we don't put you in any awkward positions because of this."

Tala shook her head. "I'm already seen as a bit of an oddball. I doubt I'll be pressed too closely about anything I ask or attempt."

Atrela gave her a skeptical look but didn't comment on that. "Very well. So, you mentioned venture supplies?"

"Yes. I would like food and equipment to carry in my dimensional storage, so that I can always have food ready at hand."

They briefly discussed Tala's available resources, and the conversation actually went quite quickly, given it was a mirror of the one she'd had with Sarenor on the walk up.

"I think I can put together some things for you. What is your budget?"

"It depends a bit on how much food you can get me, but a gold or two?"

"That is… considerable for such things."

"I eat a *lot* of food."

"So you've said." Atrela was smiling. "Very well. I will see it done. Would you be willing to return in three days to discuss your offer and pick up your food?"

"That sounds perfect. Thank you."

"No, Mistress Tala. Thank you. I cannot express the stress I feel in the presence of any Mage. Even your offer to *potentially* alleviate that is valuable beyond what I can express."

Tala gave a seated bow. "I am glad to be able to help."

# Chapter: 18
# Crocheting

Tala had gotten the ball rolling on her business with the Constructionist and Culinary Guilds. It was time to handle some long-term items; she needed to delve into Fusing.

She knew that task was before her, a hurdle that she needed to overcome, but she hadn't given it the attention it deserved.

Toward that end, she'd decided to climb to the top of Makinaven, in search of a quiet place to meditate and contemplate the potential paths before her.

She was well on her way when she was startled out of her musings.

Tala had decided to walk to give herself more time to contemplate, so Terry was currently asleep on her shoulder. At the moment, she was passing by a large, open shaft.

The shaft itself wasn't that odd. Tala had seen a few scattered around the circumference of the city, though she had yet to investigate their purpose.

No, what caught her eye was the man walking very close, past it. That, by itself, was dangerous enough, but the man seemed to have a penchant for dangerous things. He was missing a leg, and seemed to have a round, short, thick stick grafted into the stump. Magic suffused both the wood and his leg around the joining.

*What is that? I should just ask him.* "Ummm… hi." Tala suddenly felt really awkward. She had spoken before thinking through exactly what she wanted to say, or even what she wanted from the interaction. *That was foolish…*

The man gave her a quizzical look. "Mistress? What can I do for you?"

She cleared her throat, forcing an attempt at a friendly smile. "Can I ask you a bit of a personal question?"

He shrugged. "I suppose you can always ask."

"Are those inscriptions I see, linking you with the wood?"

A grin split his face, and he looked down, lifting his peg. "You could see those, eh? Even through the pants?"

"I can."

"Mages really are something special." He shook his head, his smile staying firmly in place. "Yeah." He patted the peg. "Wood from this very tree." He gestured around them. "The inscriptions bind it to me, allowing me a degree of control over some things here."

"What do you mean?"

"Well, I can focus the great tree's energies to build walls or weaken the links to allow for walls or other structures to be moved or removed."

Tala hadn't thought about that. The great tree repaired itself so quickly; how could they ever modify the interior? Now, she knew. "Fascinating. So, why…?" She felt awkward, again, allowing her question to trail off.

"Why replace a limb? The wood Mages say that it makes us more 'one' with the tree. Gives our instructions more weight. Authority?" He shrugged. "Seems to work well enough for me."

"Why a leg? If you don't mind my asking."

"I like having my hands." He spread his fingers wide and grinned. "Some replace a hand or arm. A few opt for just a finger as that much, at least, is required to do any sort of construction work. The more flesh replaced, the greater the connection and authority. It's not the only factor, but it is a big one." He tapped his peg on the ground. "This is the largest section that most are willing to part with, even if it is regrown in retirement. I'm a foreman because of this beauty." He smiled proudly.

"That truly is fascinating." Tala took another moment to study his leg. "I'm Tala, by the way. What's your name? I apologize for waylaying you." She gave a genuine smile.

"I'm Ciaran, Mistress Tala. It is a pleasure to meet another of our magic wielders. I only dabble, and I can only guess at what it takes to be a Mage."

Tala smiled. "That is kind of you. It sounds like you do much for this city."

"I do what I can." He glanced to Terry. "That's a beautiful bird. Have a name?"

Tala glanced at Terry to see the terror bird returning her look, self-satisfaction practically radiating from him. "This is Terry."

"Good to meet you, Terry."

Terry thrummed happily and curled back up.

"Now, I do apologize, Mistress, but I must be on my way. I've a project site to get to."

"Absolutely! Thank you, again, for letting me inquire."

"Any time." He bowed and continued down the spiral. His walk was surprisingly normal, the peg not seeming to interfere at all.

As she watched, Tala saw the roadway flexing slightly as Ciaran moved, facilitating the natural pattern of his stride. *Control within the tree, indeed.*

Tala shook her head, refocusing on the task at hand. *To the top.*

## Millennial Mage, 4 - Bound

She fell back into her contemplations, allowing the world to fade around her as she climbed higher and higher.

Finally, after she-knew-not how many tiers, the spiral shunted outward, leaving them to decide to either turn back or go outside, which was no choice at all. *Outside it is.*

The sky was partly cloudy, highlighted in the late afternoon light as Tala came out onto an upper branch. To her right, the spiral continued, now a wooden walkway affixed to the outside of a central limb.

Buildings hung from limbs near and far, almost like oversized birdhouses. They were linked to each other and the central thoroughfares by arching bridges.

Even so high up the great tree, with wind almost constantly swirling around them, the swaying was negligible.

She turned and continued higher.

Every so often, signs pointed to divergences from the main way. The signs contained short descriptions of what lay up this ladder or over that bridge.

Many indicated viewing platforms or public walking trails, cultivated for immersion in nature and the occasional breathtaking view.

Tala grinned. *This place gives being a forester a whole new meaning.*

Still, she didn't turn, simply continuing up. She wanted to see what was at the top.

The road slowly narrowed until it was just wide enough for two people to pass.

It finally ended, along with some of the other spirals, at a large platform. That platform was built around a single upraised branch.

At some distance, scattered throughout the top of the canopy, Tala saw a couple other, similar platforms, likely the terminal points of some of the other spirals.

One of those other platforms, the one most centrally located, had a single spiral continuing up another hundred feet. As she followed that path with her eyes, she saw that an embedded ladder went higher still to the highest platform that she could see.

Given that she could see the sky and all the up-reaching branches, Tala was fairly confident that it was, in fact, the highest.

*Do I go back down and try to find the right spiral?*

She shook her head. There was no telling how long that would take. If she knew the city better, she could probably have found her way over easily, but she didn't, and there wasn't anyone around to ask at the moment.

*I have magic. Let's solve this like a Mage.*

Grinning, Tala climbed over the railing, holding on with her right hand as she crouched, facing the desired main platform.

Her left middle finger came to her thumb, and she focused on herself. *Reduce.*

It took her about twenty-three seconds to reduce her effective gravity down to roughly ten percent.

*Wind shouldn't be too much of an issue, as I still have the same inertia, but I should still account for it.* The wind was currently blowing left to right, from her perspective.

*Aim to the left a bit.*

The distance was over a hundred yards.

*Aim high. Worst case, I increase my gravity and drop faster.*

She felt the muscles in her legs coiling, relaxing, and preparing to explosively contract. *Jump powerfully. Spare no strength.*

*And, if worse comes to worst, get in Kit.* She grinned at that. *Not a bad worst case.*

"Terry, can you wait for me on that platform?" He might throw her off. *Reduce variables.*

Terry looked around, saw what she was going to do, and flickered over to her destination. His collar began to glow a deep orange of warning. *Right… I need to get over there, soon.*

She refocused on the jump.

*Okay, aim high, jump hard, don't hesitate, and don't look down.*

Before she could talk herself out of it, she *leapt.*

The platform and branch behind her had enough mass to not buck away from her powerful push.

Now, even with her enhanced strength, she'd consider a running long-jump a long shot if she reached forty-eight feet.

Basically, under normal gravity, she wouldn't have made it even a sixth of the way there. *And I started from a stand-still.*

But her gravity wasn't normal. The downward pull of the ground below was reduced to just less than a tenth what any other creature could expect.

Tala soared.

She kept her arms tucked in tight and her legs fully extended behind her, willing more thrust from them, despite the fact that that was utterly impossible for her.

After a long moment of flight, she reached the apex of her arc and began to descend, still moving forward with great speed.

Her eyes flicked to her destination, then to look behind her.

*Oh… I undershot.* Even though she'd tried to aim high, this was not an action that she'd practiced, so she'd estimated incorrectly and made mistakes.

That wasn't the end of the world.

The near vertical branch around which the platform was built extended from below. The spirals were wrapped around it to provide transit up and down. *This is fine. I'll just land on one of those and climb up a bit.*

But she had aimed off to the left, to counter any wind… and the wind had temporarily died.

*Don't panic. You'll be fine. There's always…* If she went into Kit and fell, Terry would exit the allowed range for his training collar. He would be subject to the city defense.

*Oh… That's bad…*

Alright, then. Emergency contingencies were off the table. *Grab the support struts, the railing, anything.*

The platform passed close overhead, just out of reach, and Tala was approaching the structures beneath quickly. *Focus, Tala, focus!*

She tried to grab one of the struts, but her fingers barely slapped against it as she shot past. She did hit it well enough to start herself spinning.

*Worse!*

At the last instant, a massive gust swept over Makinaven, shoving her to the right. She slammed into the spiral ramp, the wood cracking beneath her.

Tala groaned.

The impact hadn't been hard enough to harm her, given her enhancements, but it had been far from a clean landing. Her head was still spinning as she lay there.

She felt the wood repair itself beneath her, and she was bodily lifted just a bit to allow for that reformation.

A moment later, Terry flickered into being, standing on her chest.

He did not look pleased.

"Yeah… I could have handled that better."

## Millennial Mage, 4 - Bound

The avian shook himself in irritation, then moved to her shoulder, latching on and settling down, despite the odd angle.

"Fair enough. Let's go see if it was worth it."

Five minutes later, Tala sat on the highest observation platform over the city of Makinaven.

There were no rails around the ten-foot diameter space. It seemed that few people ventured up this high, especially when there were easier to reach places with views that were nearly as good. That was fine with her; she wanted privacy.

The small, artificial platform was easily two thousand feet above the forest floor below, solidly affixed to a singular branch that grew almost straight up from the great tree.

There was an easy path up from the platform, which Tala had failed to jump directly to. After that easy spiral ended in a viewing deck, Tala had found the simple ladder leading the rest of the way. It was composed of wooden dowels affixed and integrated with the branch.

She had climbed it with ease, especially after returning her effective gravity to normal.

The view had been stunning in all directions, even below her. The canopy of Makinaven, below, hid any evidence of civilization, save the series of walkways and platforms she'd already seen.

Even so, Tala's mind wasn't on the view, nor on the city below her. After taking in her surroundings, she had focused within herself. Her eyes were now closed, and her magesight swept through her body head to toes, fingertips to heart, again and again.

The Archon Star, which bound her body and soul, was deeper than the magic of her inscriptions. As was her gate, for that matter.

It seemed like magic was a dimension like any other, and as far as she could tell, it was infinite.

*That doesn't mean I can affect that infinity.* It did mean, however, that she could bind herself more tightly, body and soul, without having to overwrite her inscriptions.

*I really don't understand this very well.*

Her inscriptions were a feature of her body, and her keystone surrounded her gate, her soul. *Well, that part of my soul, anyway.*

The other part of her soul seemed to already be firmly established within her body but didn't interact with her inscriptions.

It was like, from a magical perspective, she had an entire un-inscribed body, superimposed upon her physical self.

It wasn't a physical body, obviously, so even if she could figure out how, she couldn't add more regenerative scripts, or other enhancements to her natural functions.

*No… it's a spirit body.* That tickled something within her mind.

*Grediv said what I'd done to my items gave me a head start.* She looked down at her elk leathers. She'd bound them to one another, making them magically and spiritually one with a simple spell-form that vaguely resembled an Archon Star from casual inspection.

The details were different, but that wasn't currently important.

Tala returned her focus to her implanted Archon Star.

It was like the weight at the end of a pendulum, dangling outside of the net of her scripts, while being encapsulated and protected by them at the same time. It didn't make sense, but that was how it felt.

## Millennial Mage, 4 - Bound

The tether between her star and her gate, like between her star and her spiritual body, was a two-way thoroughfare of power.

*So… I've really just bound my divided soul together, with the Archon Star acting as an intermediary. My body is still only loosely attached to my spiritual self. A fusing would incorporate all three… Right?*

Tala thought about her grandmother for the first time in what felt like ages. The woman would crochet in every spare moment, making everything from sweaters to toys. She had passed before Tala's departure for the academy. *That was about the time that he started…*

She shook off the sad memory and sadder thoughts. Tala had no desire to think of *him*.

*No, I'm considering crocheting.* One particular birthday, her grandmother had made a net into which Tala had placed three kinds of stuffing, layering them carefully. That done, her grandmother had tightened the stitching, and finished out the pattern, enclosing all three into a unified pillow.

It had been the most comfortable pillow in the house. Tala had even taken it with her to the academy, where she'd used it every night until it fell apart. *After nearly a decade and a half of heavy use.* She hadn't thought about that pillow in at least a couple of years.

Again, though, that wasn't the point.

*I know I can knot power into spell-forms that affect the spirit. I should be able to chain them together, crocheting a magical pillow, filled with my physical body and the two halves of my soul.*

She reached inside and tried to create the spell-form within herself, beside the Archon Star and using its tether as the yarn.

Her power resisted her, but she fought on. After what had to have been at least an hour, she gave up, falling back onto her back, staring up at the darkening sky.

*That didn't work.* It was more than her failing. The magic had fought her, and she *felt* like something was wrong with her approach.

She sat up, pulling out her tools to prepare some tea. *I need to focus.* She chose the chamomile. With careful fingers, she broke off the amount she needed and placed it within the cast-iron teapot. With an application of power, she heated the pot with her hot air incorporator, toasting the dry tea within.

That completed, she added hot water from the requisite incorporator. Once it was done brewing, she poured herself a cup, and turned her mind back to the matter at hand.

*Okay. I'm not making a pillow.*

Still, the crocheting mental image appealed on some deep level. *Maybe I'm adding a second layer to another blanket?*

She finished the first cup of tea, poured a second, and focused inward again, renewed determination filling her.

She made some progress, this time. She was able to pull up portions of her spiritual self, and thread the Archon Star's anchoring tether together with it. She could even move on and work her way across her spirit, moving outward in a circle from where the Archon Star rested in her chest.

But near midnight, when she simply *had* to take a break, she released her grip on her power, and it began to unravel.

Tala panicked, trying to snatch the threads and keep her efforts from being undone, but to no avail.

In less than a minute, it was as if she'd never done anything.

Tala growled, causing Terry to lift his head from where he'd been sleeping near the edge of their current platform. Finding no threat, he went back to sleep.

In irritation, Tala refreshed the water in her teapot, the first batch having discorporated hours earlier.

A new cup in hand, she contemplated through her frustration.

*Well, that can't be right. If it had to be done in one go, there'd never be anyone between red and orange. The same would be true if it would be undone with a moment's inattention.*

She leaned back, bracing herself with one arm as she drank and glared up at the stars, overhead.

*I should get a blanket from Kit.* She didn't want to move. She felt utterly spent, and in her dejection, she didn't want to put forth the effort. *Anyway, it's too cold for just one blanket. The tea helps, but I'd need at least two.*

*Two.* Tala blinked up at the night sky.

*Two blankets. My body and my spiritual self, each identical in dimension, but not really connected.* Her eyes widened. "Two blankets! I need to crochet the two blankets together!" *Like a sandwich held together with some sticky filling.* That wasn't a great analogy, but she wasn't interested in making a better one.

Tala sat up straighter, her exhaustion forgotten, but no less present.

She fought through the tiredness, taking a deep drink of tea before tucking those items away and stuffing her mouth with jerky. *I need the energy.*

Reaching deep within, Tala was able to perceive the space between her physical and spiritual bodies, and when conceived of in the right way, she could perceive her Archon Star resting between them, beside her gate. The star was a bridge of power between the three other parts of her.

Slowly, carefully, Tala grabbed the threads of power and interlinked the three points of connection with another loop of power. Using the Archon Star as hook and needle in one, Tala wove the spirit binding spell-form, the same one she'd used on her elk leathers and cinched it tight.

A wash of golden power rippled through her, and the point of connection seemed to solidify, locking in place.

As Tala pulled back, her magesight told her that her aura had taken an all-but-imperceptible tick toward orange.

Her final glimpse within herself was altered by her new understanding and perspective.

Within her there were two blankets, each the size of a city. At the center lay an infinite ball of yarn and a tool for using the last to unify the first two.

Most important though, was the last feature; there, at the center of it all, a single stitch joined the two great expanses, fusing them at a single point.

*I have a long way to go.*

A joyful smile on her face, she opened her eyes into bright, new light, and the dawning of a new day.

## Chapter: 19
## As Expected

Tala found herself glorying in the new-dawning sun's light, a self-satisfied smile resting comfortably on her face.

*I did it. I took my first step toward Fused!* True, it was just the first step of a cross-continental trek, but it was something. *Jevin said he wanted to talk to me about the transition to Refined, after I began the road to Fused.* One more thing to remember to ask him about.

Tala didn't let that weigh her down, however. She was giddy with excitement, despite her soul-deep fatigue. It had taken a *lot* of mental effort to figure out how to accomplish this first step, and the enactment had been no less taxing. Add to that a missed dinner, already low reserves, and a missed night's sleep, and she was lucky to be conscious at all.

Something about mornings tickled the back of her mind, but she ignored it for the moment.

The air was chillier up here than she really realized, and as she began to shift, her body felt stiff and cold.

Groaning with the effort, she went through a stretching and strengthening set, limbering and warming up.

"Good morning, Terry!"

Terry cracked an eye open, let out a grumpy little trill, and opened his mouth.

Tala laughed and tossed a bit of jerky over the edge.

Terry huffed but flickered and caught the treat.

She gave one last twist back and forth, sending a radiating series of *cracks* up her spine. "So much better." She reached toward the sky. "*Good morning!*"

She laughed and spun in a circle.

"Oh… I'm a bit loopy." She snickered. "Cause I'm spinning in a loop." *Or is a loop vertical…? It probably doesn't matter.*

She shook her head. *I wonder why sleep deprivation seems to hit me so easily?*

It might be due to her enhancements. Her mind was more taxed than most. *Or it's the night spent doing intense mental and magical work.*

"I need to go get some sleep. To the cargo-slots we go, for sleep!" She paused; the tickle came back, fully manifesting this time. "Right! To charge the cargo-slots we go! Then, sleep."

Terry could probably carry her down in short order. *Or… I could jump?*

Tala looked over the edge of the platform. "You know, it didn't work so well the last time I tried… Maybe when less hangs in the balance?"

She nodded to herself. *Wise choice, Tala.*

*Why, thank you. I do try.*

She stood for a long moment, looking down at the canopy below. *What was I doing?*

After another pause, she jerked, coming back to the moment. "Right!"

She needed sleep, sleep after cargo charging.

"Terry?"

He looked her way.

"You willing to carry me down? I need to recharge the cargo-slots."

He gave her a deeply skeptical look, then somehow conveyed irritation. Hadn't she turned down a room in an inn, because she didn't want to traverse the height of Makinaven?

"Well, not every day, no." *Wait… I'm projecting. There is no way I interpreted that from him, from a look.*

Terry vanished.

Tala swept her gaze around, eventually following the lingering dimensional energy as she looked over the side and down to the platform below.

Terry was there and already rideable-sized.

"Fine, fine." She swung over the side, maneuvering to the ladder and climbing down. Thankfully, her dexterity didn't seem too hampered, and she was able to navigate the descent without major incident.

Terry trilled at her, crouching so that she could mount up.

"Thank you, Terry." She climbed up, hooking her hands into the collar and tucking her head down against his neck.

She was asleep before the avian began moving.

\* \* \*

Tala heard a trill somewhere in the back of her head but didn't waken until she slammed into the ground, face first.

Terry trilled again, a bit of irritation evident in the noise.

She groaned. "What?!" Her eyes opened slowly, and she found herself looking at the Constructionist Guild's door. "Terry… I needed to go to the work yard. Charging cargo-slots and sleep. Remember?"

Terry appeared in front of her, leaving barely two feet between their eyes as he locked gazes with her. He took in a quick breath then projected a basso tone into her face.

She jerked upright, looking around, suddenly fully awake, at least for the moment.

A few people were within sight, but they seemed to be studiously avoiding looking at the odd Mage and her small, oddly loud bird. *Did they see him when he was bigger?* There was really no way for her to know.

Terry bobbed, moving his head toward the door.

"Right… I do need to come here…" She sighed, standing.

She didn't remember opening the door, but she was in the entry hall, so she must have.

"Mistress Tala?" Jevin came from the back room. "You're a bit early, but…" He looked her over. "Well, congratulations on your first step toward Fused."

Tala tiredly lifted one fist in the air. "Hurrah." *Wait… I thought I was fully awake.* She was slipping back, fast.

He shook his head, but he was smiling. "If I may be so bold, you seem exhausted. Please go, get some sleep. I'll bump the merging until later. Come back this evening, or late afternoon, after you've had time to rest and get your head on straight. Soul-work is not the type of thing you want to do while tired."

Tala mustered a slow nod. "I suppose that makes sense. Thank you."

"Sleep, Mistress Tala."

She nodded again and was back outside, slumping on top of Terry.

Terry, for his part, grumbled in an amusingly musical fashion, shifting beneath her until she was properly situated.

She again tucked her hands through his collar and dozed.

\* \* \*

Consciousness barely returned enough for her to charge the cargo-slots.

Her mental image was *terribly* fuzzy, while still being accurate. Thankfully, that just made it take a bit longer.

An instant later, according to her perception, she was standing next to her locked door, in the dark.

She felt a presence.

There was *something* standing beside her, staring at her with wide, intense eyes.

Tala slowly looked to her right, down the unlit hallway. Only her enhanced eyes allowed her to pick out the predator, regarding her from the gloom, always watching, always hungry.

She jerked sideways at the sight, slamming into the still-locked door.

*Come on, Tala, it's just Terry.*

Terry tilted his head in concern from where he watched her. "Squawk?"

"No. You speak in descriptions, not quotes."

Terry gave her a deeply confused look in response, trilling questioningly.

"Better. Now, where's my key…?" It fell into her hand as she reached for it. "Thank you, Kit."

"Feed me."

Tala froze, staring down at her pouch.

"Feed me all night long."

She cleared her throat, blinking slowly. "Okay… I think I broke myself, somehow." *Still, it wouldn't hurt.* She shrugged and topped off Kit's reserves as she unlocked the door, letting herself and Terry inside.

After blearily locking the door behind her, she slammed into the too-hard bed, increased her own gravity, and was asleep before another thought or oddity could delay her rest.

# Millennial Mage, 4 - Bound

\* \* \*

Tala woke slowly from a dreamless sleep.

The room looked exactly like it had when she'd fallen asleep. *As expected.*

She sat up, looking down at Kit.

"So… did you actually speak, or was I already dreaming?"

Kit did not respond.

"Do you want me to feed you?"

The pouch did not respond.

"Okay… just sleep deprived, then." She looked to Terry. "Did you hear anything from Kit last night?"

Terry lifted his head, giving her a level look.

"Fine, this morning?"

He let out a satisfied chirp, then shook his head.

"Yeah, I didn't think so."

That oddity addressed, Tala stood, stretching and returning her effective gravity to normal. As she did so, she noticed that some of the stretches felt deeper and more effective under increased gravity. *Oh, that makes sense.*

That in mind, she decided to integrate variable gravity into her stretching. After all, she already did her body-weight exercises with massive increases. Those, however, couldn't easily be done in the small space.

Her stretching complete, she carefully unlocked the door, checking both ways in the hall before she came out, and moved into the common area.

It was simple enough to clear space for her workout.

Once she was finished with her start-of-day routine, she bathed within Kit, refilled all her bonded items, and set out from the cargo-slot.

Terry, of course, came with her. Like the day before, she was largely ignored as she crossed the work yard.

This day, however, one of the men ran up to her. "Mistress Tala?"

"Yes? That's me."

He gave a bow and handed her a folded note. "Master Rane asked us to watch for you."

"Thank you."

The man hesitated.

*Oh… It would probably be reasonable to pay him for the favor…* Tala pulled out a silver coin and flicked it to the man. "Thank you."

He caught the coin and bowed. "It was my pleasure, Mistress."

*Look at me, giving tips like they're nothing.* She stood a little straighter as she walked toward the two o'clock spiral. It would slow the paying of her debts, but in the grand scheme of things, it was *just* one silver.

The note was simply an invitation to come to a reserved training room on the second tier. *Northwest seven o'clock.* Tala hesitated. *So, the seven o'clock spiral, but at the eleven o'clock position?* She nodded, that sounded right. *Alright!*

Wait.

*What time is it?*

She looked around until she spotted a clock. *Early afternoon…*

Jevin had asked her to return after she rested and cleared her head a bit. *A little training could help clear out the remaining fuzziness of sleep. I'll just go to the Constructionists after.*

"Terry, are you willing to carry me up to the second tier? I'd prefer to go across the park than through the city, here."

He bobbed from his perch on her shoulder but then waited.

"Ahh, yes. We should go all the way there, shouldn't we." She smiled and told Terry where they were going.

Terry flickered to beside her, sized for her riding.

Tala tossed him a big chunk of jerky that he ate happily as she climbed up. "Ready."

Terry took off at a comfortable jog, which meant that he was moving faster than she could sprint.

She tucked her feet under his vestigial wings while her hands gripped his collar, and she kept her head low.

It took a laughably short time to get up to the second tier, and the park therein passed just as fast as they crossed to the seven o'clock spiral.

From there, it was a short trip up, just over a quarter-way around the tree from where the road had left the park level.

Terry trilled then flickered to her shoulder, allowing her to land on her own two feet before a plain-looking structure.

A sign out front simply declared it as a training complex.

She pushed open the door and walked tentatively inside.

"Good morning, Mistress. How can we assist?" A young girl sat behind the counter, likely in her early teens.

"I am here to meet a friend?"

"Oh! You must be Mistress Tala."

Tala felt her eye twitch. *What did Rane tell these people?* "Um… yeah."

"Right this way. Master Rane reserved our largest training arena for the next six days. There should always be someone manning the desk, here. If they ask, you can simply give your name, and they shouldn't bother you further. If you need anything, we will do what we can to provide."

Tala nodded along but didn't verbally respond.

The girl led her down a few twisting hallways to a large door, set in the hallway to the left.

If Tala had tracked the orientation correctly, this would be close to the center of this section of the tree's perimeter. *The center of the training complex, then?*

The doors opened to reveal a massive room, fifty feet across and half as tall.

There were some viewing rooms near the top of the space, looking down through clear sections of wall, though they were currently empty.

Rane was in the middle of the space, moving through a form with Force. By the sweat covering his bare skin and his well-fitted shorts, he'd been at it for a while.

Their entrance disrupted his concentration, and he spun toward them, Force rising into an inside, middle guard.

As soon as his eyes focused on them, however, he let the blade drop. "Mistress Tala! Welcome." He smiled. "I apologize for my current state, but I was unsure when you'd arrive, and I thought it best to use the time while I had it."

"No apologies needed, Master Rane."

The attendant colored, bowed, and said her goodbyes, closing the door behind her.

"So, what do you have in mind?"

Rane grinned. "Well, I have a few things that I'd love to discuss with you, but I want to spar first." He lightly bounced on the balls of his feet. "I'm a bit wound up and could use the expenditure."

Tala shrugged. "Sure. Give me a minute to get my head on right."

His smile turned sheepish. "I was actually wondering if I could try a match against Terry? Just one, then I'd love to spar with you, too."

Terry squawked questioningly.

Rane nodded to the avian. "Yes, really. I may not be as durable as Mistress Tala, but I am harder to hit."

Terry glanced to Tala, who shrugged. The terror bird flickered to a position flanking Rane, letting out a deeper squawk. He'd increased his size to be a bit bigger than that which he used when Tala rode him.

"I'm ready." Rane said this as he turned to face the bird, lifting Force into a hanging guard.

Terry immediately appeared behind the man, striking for his back.

Rane's inscriptions activated, sending him into a front-flip. Rane took advantage of the motion, tucking Force in close, tip toward his feet.

As soon as he was horizontal, continuing the flip, Rane drove Force toward Terry, using his immense physical strength along with the motion.

Terry, of course, flickered out of the way, appearing beside Rane to strike again.

Rane's defense activated as expected, altering his trajectory once again. The large man, quite accustomed to his own power, reacted instinctively, and Force lanced out toward Terry once again.

The following sequence was both beautiful and somehow comical.

Rane continued to spin and twist, as much like a child's top as an acrobat. He used each motion efficiently to bring his blade to bear, threatening Terry and forcing the terror bird to flicker away.

The Mage only occasionally contacted the ground, and he used feet and hands almost interchangeably to keep himself aloft and moving.

After nearly two minutes of back and forth, Terry flickered away, settling down to watch.

Rane came to a stop, landing perfectly in a crouch, Force held out to one side.

To Tala's enhanced vision, the conflict had looked like nothing so much as a choreographed display, which she'd expect to see in an expensive play.

She hesitated at that. *I haven't seen a play in… years.* The last had been before her father's descent into addiction. They'd had some money, then, and the older kids had been able to go see plays with their parents.

She felt a sadness at that but shook it off.

Rane was breathing heavily, his arms trembling, ever so slightly. "That was… fantastic." He stood slowly, sheathing Force.

Terry chirped.

Rane laughed. "If I hadn't already had Force out and ready, I'd have been hard pressed to pull it free. With it, though, I think we should call that a draw?"

Terry stood, tilting his head.

"Fine, fine. You could keep going, and I'm almost spent." He pulled a thick cloth from his dimensional storage, the cloth seeming to appear as it was drawn from the leather loop on Rane's belt.

*Like a street performer.* She hadn't seen one of those in years, either.

"Give me a minute to catch my breath and get some water." He swept sweat from his skin and dried his hair.

Tala took the moment to look around, examining the training space more closely.

Gloriously, the flooring wasn't sand. Instead, it seemed to be wood, but there was an unnatural springiness to it.

Rane saw her bouncing up and down slightly, and he laughed. "There's an underlying structure that allows the hard floor to have some give. It lets falls and takedowns hurt less."

Tala grinned back at him. "So long as it isn't sand."

He smiled. "I thought you'd feel that way. How about you go a round with Terry? Then you and I can get some practice in?"

Tala glanced at the clock, high up on one wall. *It's not that late. A couple rounds won't take too long.* "Sure."

Her face slammed into the floor, and she had a fleeting desire for the cushioning softness of sand.

"Come on, Terry! I wasn't ready."

He chittered at her happily.

"Fine… I know I should always be ready." She vaulted up, drawing Flow and taking it into a two-handed grip. As subtly as she could, she touched her left middle finger to her thumb around Flow's handle, focusing on Terry. The lock stuck.

She didn't let anything show on her face as she slowly increased his gravity.

He didn't seem to react, instead circling her.

It wasn't wariness that caused him to circle, nor was it to taunt her. No, he was probably just trying to get her used to not knowing when an attack would come.

After fifteen seconds, his effective gravity was closing in on four times normal. *He has to have noticed.*

Tala frowned.

Terry stopped, a glint of mischief suddenly obvious in his avian eyes.

Her own eyes widened. *Oh—*

Terry flickered into being, standing on her shoulders, still full sized.

Despite her prodigious strength, Tala couldn't remain upright beneath the weight. Terry was heavy to begin with, and she had quadrupled the effect that had on him and anything below him.

Thus, Terry crowed in triumph, his talons latched onto her arms, as he rode her down to the floor, pinning her beneath his massive weight.

"Rust you, Terry. That's not fair."

He trilled at her and squatted down, sitting on her upper back.

She managed to squeeze out, "Get off."

He trilled again.

*He wants his weight back to normal...* She growled, but despite her irritation, she reversed her enactment and lowered his effective gravity.

In just less than fourteen seconds, he was back to normal, and he vanished from her back, changing shape to break her lock and ensure he remained properly gravitized.

Tala pushed back to her feet, glaring. "You should not be able to turn my tools against me that easily."

Terry simply curled up in one of the corners to sleep.

Rane, wisely, kept a smile from his face. "So, ready?" His breathing had leveled out, and he lifted Force slightly in indication.

"Sure… I can't do any worse against you than I did against him."

He laughed then. "Just so."

Tala called Flow to her hand, made sure the training scabbard was still firmly locked in place, and took up a guarding stance. "Ready."

## Chapter: 20
## Shift

Tala and Rane were both drenched in sweat by the time they'd fought a few bouts.

The winner was never in question; Rane still greatly outclassed Tala in terms of both skill and experience, and her strength, speed, and enhanced perception just weren't enough to close that gap. *For now.*

When afternoon was nearing its end, Tala called a halt. "I need to drop through the Constructionist Guild for an item melding."

"Oh? Can I accompany you? I still do have some things I'd like to discuss now that we've sparred."

Tala thought about it for a moment, then shrugged. "Sure, I don't see why not. I just need to get cleaned up first." She pulled out Kit and opened it on the floor.

Rane nodded and stretched. "There's a shower available with the renting of this training arena. I'll take advantage of that and meet you back here in twenty minutes?"

"That sounds like a plan." After she climbed down into Kit, she hesitated before speaking to herself, "I've got to do this eventually."

Before she could talk herself out of it, she pulled the pouch closed, with herself inside.

"I don't want you running out of power while I'm in here." She immediately topped Kit off. Somehow, that made her feel a bit less nervous.

For some unknown reason, as Tala was finishing up her cleansing, Kit began using an odd amount of power. Thankfully, Tala noticed so it was trivial to keep the pouch topped off. *Maybe my being in here, while it's closed, takes more energy?*

Tala was quick to finish up her ablutions, but Rane was still waiting for her when she opened Kit and climbed back out.

"Were you waiting long?"

"No, just a couple of minutes." He looked a bit… guilty?

"What happened." Her inflection removed the question; she knew he'd done something.

Rane grinned self-consciously. "Well, I was curious if I could move your dimensional storage."

Tala narrowed her eyes. "What would you have done with it, if you could?"

"Nothing!" He held up his hands. "I just thought it would be good to see if it could be moved."

She drew her lips into a firm line. "Fine. So?"

"Well, it kept slipping from my grip. I couldn't get a hold on it. Even trying to scoop it up," he made a bowl with his two large hands, "I couldn't budge it by more than a couple of inches. It behaved like water." He shook his head. "No, I've scooped up water that was easier to contain. In magical terms, its dimensionality was utterly pliant toward the goal of staying where you set it."

Tala was nodding. "So that's why I kept having to add power to it."

"You were filling it, while inside it?"

"It was hungry." She shrugged.

"Master Grediv always…" He trailed off. "You know what, it doesn't matter. Your way works for you." He smiled. "So, shall we go?"

"Terry?"

The avian flickered to her shoulder.

She nodded and smiled. "Let's go." They'd walked a short way from the training facility when Tala turned to Rane and broke the companionable silence. "So?"

"So what?"

"What did you want to tell me?"

"Oh!" He grinned. "I maxed out my Archon Star and have begun Fusing." He positively beamed.

She smiled in return, genuinely happy for him. "Hey! That's great, Master Rane. I've begun Fusing as well."

Rane's expression hitched. "Oh… you did?" He recovered quickly. "I didn't think you were working toward that yet, but that's great!" Then a frown stole over his features. "Why didn't you tell me?"

She smiled and shrugged. "I hadn't really had a chance, as I figured it out last night." She couldn't keep the smile from her face. "I know how to move toward Fused, now. I just need to take the time to do it. It won't be fast, and I'll have to devote time to doing it right."

Rane frowned. "Figured it out? Done… right? All you do is dump power into the Archon Star, thickening and strengthening the bond. It was the first thing I tried, and it worked just fine. Once I filled out my Archon Star, I bumped over the hurdle, and now, I'm moving toward Fused with every moment, with every extra bit of power I can spare."

"Um… no? Archon Stars can only take so much power. I hit that ceiling before I used it to become Bound."

He nodded. "Of course. Before it is integrated into you, it can only be sustained with so much magic. But after? It can soak up an ocean of power."

Tala groaned, scratching furiously at her forehead. "Are you kidding me? I didn't even think to try that…"

Rane gave her a quizzical look. "What did you do?"

## Millennial Mage, 4 - Bound

"I'm stitching my physical and spiritual selves together, using the Archon Star as a tool and my gate's power as the thread."

He simply stared at her, blinking in confusion.

"Master Grediv said I'd already done something relating to fusing with my items." She gestured to her elk leathers. "I bound them together spiritually." She grimaced in frustration. "Then, some of the Constructionist Refined referenced the same spell-form in regard to *fusing* with a familiar."

"So, naturally, you thought you should do that."

"It was worth a try, and it worked!" She grunted in irritation. "I need to think… Let's just walk quietly for a bit."

"Sure."

\*    \*    \*

There were two pleasant dings from the back of the Constructionist Guild when Tala and Rane entered.

Jevin strode out. "Well, I'm glad you got some sleep." He glanced to Rane. "A new friend? I'm Jevin."

Rane was standing, mouth open. "Master… Jevin?"

Jevin smiled. "Yes. And you are…?"

Rane was coloring deeply, so Tala came to his rescue. "This is Master Rane."

"Master Rane?" Jevin frowned for a moment, then broke into a wide smile. "Oh! You're Master Grediv's boy, his apprentice. That's right! I saw the announcement of your elevation. Congratulations."

Rane swallowed. "Thank you. Thank you, sir."

Tala frowned at Rane. "What's wrong with you? You're acting strange."

Rane cleared his throat. "Master Jevin is one of the foremost Constructionists on…" He shook his head. "No, he's one of the foremost Constructionists, full stop."

Tala looked back and forth between the two men. "That's great! Now, Master Jevin, are you ready?"

Rane turned toward her, eyes wide. "He's the one assisting with the merging?"

"Yeah."

Jevin had a half-smile. "Master Rane, it seems that your friend does not impress easily."

"You tried to convince me that I was trapped for centuries." She gave Jevin a piercing half-glare.

He scratched the back of his head. "Well, I thought it would be funny…" He shook his head. "But that is beside the point. Shall we go?"

Rane just nodded mutely.

Tala rolled her eyes but didn't try to hide her smile.

The short trip up to the Constructionist facility on the sixth tier passed in near silence, though Jevin engaged some of those they passed in brief dialogues.

Soon enough, Jevin led them into a chamber, much like the one that Boma had used in assisting her merging of Flow with the midnight ravens' feathers and talons. The walls were covered in lacquered iron plates, and the door was similarly warded with iron to prevent magic from leaking out, or penetrating in.

Terry simply flickered to a corner and settled down.

Jevin sighed, sitting cross-legged on the floor. "Before we do the merging, we should briefly have that talk I mentioned, now that you took your first step toward Fused."

Rane smiled happily toward Tala, nodding again in congratulations, though he was still a bit hesitant, given her earlier unhappiness. "We actually had a question about that."

"Oh?"

Rane and Tala each briefly described how they were progressing toward Fused. In the end, Tala gestured to Jevin. "So? Who's right?"

Jevin shrugged. "You each are correct, for yourself."

Both Rane and Tala glared at the Paragon, speaking over each other.

"Master Jevin, that is entirely unhelpful."

"Rust you, that's useless."

They looked at each other and both huffed a laugh.

Master Jevin shook his head. "You two are a strange set, you know that?"

"What is that supposed to mean?"

"Just that I'd have not pegged you as friends. You are both too alike and too different." He shrugged.

"So, care to explain?" Tala cocked an eyebrow.

"About the two of you? That's not for me to address." By the twinkle in his eye, he knew what she'd meant.

"About fusing."

He shrugged. "It's simple. Everyone fuses differently. There are always commonalities, but it's based on perception. I cannot impose my perception of fusing onto you and trying could break your gate."

Tala growled. "Same excuse as always."

"If I lift up a thousand different items and let them fall, would you give me a different answer as to why each accelerates downward?"

"Well, no."

"Precisely. Each thing with the same answer simply expands the universality of that answer."

"So, why is my method of fusing so much more convoluted than his?" Tala was quite irritated. "And why did Master Grediv try to give me advice?"

Jevin sighed. "Master Grediv has good insights into people, and how they work. My guess?"

She nodded, sinking to sit on the floor as Jevin had.

"This is just a guess, mind you: He thought that if you believed the answer was near at hand, you would strive for it more diligently. Is the solution actually that close to what he implied?"

"Well… No?"

"There you have it."

She jerked her head toward Rane. "That still doesn't explain why I have to crochet, and he gets to just dump in power." Her eyes narrowed.

"To allay your fears, Master Rane will need to manipulate his ocean of power, to use his language, for the final step of fusing. It will be a colossal effort of will. Yours is more difficult at the start but will likely get easier as you move forward. Your magic is, as a rule, more delicate and precise than Master Rane's. His is not necessarily more powerful than yours, but it is more focused on power, just as yours isn't really more precise than his, but it is more focused on precision." Jevin shrugged. "But that's mainly a guess. It could also be the case that because you believe it should be hard, it is hard for you, and Master Rane believes it should be easy, so it is."

Tala sighed. "Fine…" She hesitated, then brought up something that had been bothering her. "After I started my Fusing process, I was… very mentally strained. It was like I hadn't slept in days, and I think I might have been seeing and hearing things that weren't real."

Rane gave her an odd look, but Jevin simply shrugged as he responded, "That can happen, especially if you were trying a bunch of different methods. Working with magic and your own soul is incredibly mentally exhausting. In addition, fusing opens your physical body, meaning your senses, more fully to the spiritual and the magical. Some Archons see deep truths; others have disturbing hallucinations; and most land somewhere between those extremes." He smiled, seeing her nodding in understanding. "But we are off in the weeds."

"She does that to people." Rane sat down, forming a triangle with the other two. "So, what were you going to talk about?"

Jevin smiled Rane's way but didn't address the fact that Rane had tacitly added himself to the lesson. "To become Refined, you must purify your body. This is *not* a personalized process." He looked them each in the eyes. "I want to emphasize this again. Do not go your own way. Do not try your own thing. When you are fully Fused, we will simply tell you how to take the next step." He took a deep breath. "Please, for the love of humanity, don't try to Refine yourself unguided. Too many Archons used to incinerate themselves with various heat or power sources."

"That seems… drastic. How many really did something like that?"

"One would be too many for something so foolish, but it was dozens in the early years and a few since."

*That's not too many.*

"It's completely avoidable. Please just let us help you with that step. Any Archon, Refined or above, will give you the information as soon as you are Fused."

They both nodded their agreement.

"Alright then. We have a merging to do."

Tala grinned as they all stood. She absently topped Kit off, just in case. It did accept some power, but not much. She then removed her belt and set it in the corner, taking Flow from its sheath and the massive glaive from Kit.

Jevin had already begun manipulating the scripts in the room, creating the merging spell-forms. He motioned for Tala to move into the center of the building spell-form, and she complied, sitting cross-legged once again, with the two weapons balanced across her lap.

Rane, for his part, stood near Terry, well out of the way.

"One last thing, before we begin."

Tala met the older Archon's eyes. "Yes?"

"You are adding in a weapon of the Leshkin. Any… choice that you are presented, which seems to come from a place other than the Leshkin, will be your weapon attempting to assert dominance over you. Some of this can be acceptable, if the gains are appealing, but it will change you, fundamentally."

Tala frowned. "How is that different?"

"We are breaking down the glaive and allocating where its power goes. Let me give two examples: If, say, you choose an option which allows you to harden your skin like bark, this will result in a portion of the glaive's power settling into your body, instead of all of it joining with your knife. This is not harmful, necessarily, but most recommend against it, as it is a bit sloppy." He smiled. "Though, you must decide if the results are worth it to you. Now if, instead, you choose an option that allows you to harden your skin like the metal of your knife, that is the result of the knife extending itself to bond with your body. That *is* bad, almost always. If you allow too much of that, you will become subservient to the impulses of your bound items. For a weapon, that usually means you will grow in bloodlust and violent tendencies."

Tala found herself nodding. "Understood. Don't let the knife change me, change the knife."

"Exactly."

She nodded. "Let's do this, then."

Jevin took out a small pouch that Tala recognized. *My Mage gold.* The Paragon seemed to have reformed the gold into near perfect spheres; their only defects being a single flat spot on one side of each. He placed down the small lumps with what seemed to be careful deliberation, though Tala couldn't tell why he chose to place each one where he did.

"There." He contemplated the whole. "In looking at this, now, I believe that all of the Mage gold will be used, but it won't make the process less costly, it will just catalyze the merging more efficiently, allowing for a better merging. The cost will still be four gold, for which you've already paid that Leshkin weaponry. Is that still acceptable?"

Tala hesitated for just an instant before nodding. "That is acceptable."

Jevin smiled, moving to sit in the small, connected circle prepared for him. With practiced motions, he reached out, placing his hands on perfectly sized imprints on the floor to either side of him. The threads of power seemed to collect, moving across his skin until they all seemed to originate from his hands, flowing into the stone. His gate opened wide; the power flowing outward became a flood, and Tala's magesight was instantly overwhelmed by a wave of utterly pure magic.

Her vision went white as a torrent of magic slammed into the knife and, through it, into her.

\*     \*     \*

She was outside herself, without form, looking into a white void.

It wasn't bright; it wasn't dim; it simply was, and it was white.

An instant, or perhaps a decade, passed without anything violating the purity of the void.

Then, before her bodyless gaze, a scene unfolded.

This was not like the previous two ventures into this void. Instead of simply seeing a version of herself, Tala was presented with a tableau.

A Mage streaked through the air on powerful, black wings, a long glaive held in both hands.

The weapon was near black, and blood flowed along its length.

The Mage pivoted with ease, diving back down upon a sea of enemies, reaping lives by the score.

*Don't let the knife change me.* More than that, though, Tala somehow knew that the wings would always be out, and she would never again be truly comfortable on the ground.

This Mage was *not* her.

The vision shifted.

Vines shot forth from the Archon as she strode through a pack of wolves.

Each beast was captured and pinned to the ground, then easily dispatched by a flick of her sword.

*That's more like it! If I can get restraining abilities from this merging, I can get rid of those scripts and—*

Her thoughts cut off as the Archon turned, giving Tala a look at the other woman's face.

Her eyes were empty, bottomless pits of hunger and hate. She was little more than a Leshkin.

*And… no.* Tala sighed. This Archon was not her, either.

The vision shifted.

Feathers, blood, and rage.

Shift.

Inhuman thirst for destruction, and the slow crush of powerful roots.

Shift.

Shift.

Shift.

## Millennial Mage, 4 - Bound

Tala could not have said how many versions she'd seen and discarded, but she was beginning to despair. Everything she was being shown was so inhuman as to be entirely unacceptable.

"I don't want to change *me*."

She'd spoken mainly from frustration, but the void shuddered.

Shift.

Tala fought through an ever-shifting army, Flow in her hand, its form altering smoothly between knife, sword, and glaive.

The knife and sword forms were almost exactly as she currently knew them. The only difference she could discern was from the hints she got of the handles. Those revealed that the hilts were wooden in texture, now, instead of seeming like stone.

The glaive was, as expected, entirely new.

The wide, sword-like blade was just as the blade of Flow's sword form if a bit shorter. A brilliant haze of heat filled the outline, just as it did for the sword form, and that cauterized the insides of her enemies with every strike.

The shaft of the large polearm was a dark wood with flecks of gold and spirals of wire embedded throughout.

The weapon flexed as she wanted, while holding strong at need.

Moreover, just as Jevin had suggested, there was a weight to all forms of the weapon. Those she struck were driven back. The pieces she severed were sent flying, and the occasional opponent that managed to block her was clearly shaken even by the intercepted blow.

She approached the last manifestation and indicated acceptance.

Power shattered through her and the knife; her very self felt as if it was being scraped raw.

\*　　\*　　\*

Her vision splintered back into normal sight, and she found herself sitting cross-legged on the smooth floor of the room, knife resting in her open palms.

All traces of the glaive and spell-forms were gone, and Jevin was standing over her. Terry and Rane were still waiting in their corner.

"Success?" Jevin was examining her with his magesight, and after a moment, he seemed satisfied.

"I think so. How long does that take, anyway? I've never asked."

"For us, there is a bright flash of light, then it is done. A couple of seconds later, you return to consciousness."

"That's all? It feels like a *lot* longer."

"That's all." He smiled, holding out his hand to help her up. "You are making your choice, and having it enacted upon you, at the speed of the soul."

Tala took his offered help, coming to her feet, Flow in hand. "Thank you."

"I am happy to have been able to help."

# Chapter: 21
# A Lot of New Things to Test Out

Tala stood before releasing Jevin's hand and stepping away to gain a bit of room. She then gave Jevin a half-bow in thanks for his help standing up.

Carefully, she took Flow into a proper grip and reached out to her soul-bound weapon with her will.

Exactly as she'd expected, there was now another path for power within the magical matrix of the item.

Tala forged a void-channel as large as she could manage and connected to the new path.

Flow shifted in her grip, consuming power like a desert drank in water. In less than ten seconds, she held a glaive, perfectly sized for herself.

Unfortunately, the weapon's shape was wavering, its magic was barely stable.

Tala connected another void-channel, then a third, before it stabilized. Each of these was near double those that she'd been in the habit of making. Thus, this form seemed to take nearly double the power to manifest and maintain as Flow's sword form.

*Never enough power.*

Tala spun the weapon experimentally.

She had little experience with such massive weapons, but her improved physicality and perception ensured that she wouldn't drop it, at least not in such an undistracted moment.

On a whim, she turned and hurled it toward the doors.

Tala had never thrown a spear, and it showed.

Flow struck the door cleanly, perfectly flat and parallel to the wall.

The hit created a long, straight dent in the metal, and Jevin gave her an incredulous look.

Tala flushed, allowing Flow to snap back into knife shape as she called it back.

Jevin suppressed a smile, but Rane was openly grinning.

Terry was asleep.

She sheathed the knife at her belt and scratched her left shoulder. "Well, that wasn't the most climactic end, but thank you."

Jevin gave a slight bow. "I am happy to have helped." He waved toward the door. "That'll be trivial to repair, but please don't make a habit of it."

Tala nodded sheepishly. "Yeah... I apologize for that."

Rane spoke up then, likely trying to help by changing the subject. "The new form will be quite useful, though you'll need time to learn how to use such a weapon properly."

Tala just nodded.

Jevin was pulling things seemingly out of nowhere, but Tala didn't focus on the items themselves.

"Okay. You're the second Archon I've seen doing something like that."

He stopped, glancing her way. "You'll have to be more specific."

"I don't see your storage device. You're just pulling things out of thin air."

"Ahh." He smiled at her. "Watch closely." He reached out, and *something* opened before his hand, he immediately withdrew a small sphere, the opening closing behind. "Did you see?"

"Some sort of storage space? What is it connected to?"

"To me. To my body and soul. Whenever I need it, it is there."

Realization struck. "Soul-bound."

"Precisely."

"So… does every storage allow that, when soul-bound?"

"Oh, absolutely not, but it isn't a hard thing to arrange, if you work at it beforehand."

Tala glanced down to her pouch. "So…?" She looked back up.

"Oh, yes. It will be very easy to get… Kit? Yes, that's what you called it. It will be quite easy to prepare Kit so that it has this functionality once you soul-bond it. It will actually be easier than usual."

"Then what are we waiting for! Let's do that; I have a star. Let's bind and make this happen."

Jevin blinked at her a few times. "Aside from the questionable wisdom of having a star premade and ready-to-hand, I must caution you in three regards."

Tala gave him an expectant look.

"First, once the final merging of materials and magic takes place, you must soul-bind the artifact immediately, or it will be lost, forever."

"Easy enough."

He gave her a flat look. "You are effectively creating a storage space, untethered from physical reality."

*Then how…? Flow. Flow comes to me at need. Why would a soul-bound storage be any different?* "I see."

"So, while easy, it is *expensive* to pin the construct down even for the short time required to soul-bond it."

"Why not untether it after…?" She trailed off. "Because there'd be just as much danger of me losing physical connection." She frowned. "I just wouldn't choose that option."

Jevin gave her a wry look. "It is reasonable to assume that would work, and maybe it could. But we have *never* had a recorded case of untethering a soul-bound item without the Archon vanishing as well, never to return."

Tala thought for a moment. "What could be offered that was so tempting that no one would refuse?"

"Maybe transport to another, better existence?" He shrugged. "I've no idea, as it isn't my area of study."

"Alright, so that's the first issue. I have to have a star ready and—"

He spoke over her, briefly. "A fully charged star. It cannot be anything less than at maximum power."

"As you say. What else?"

"Once this is done, the capacity of the storage can never be altered in any way, magically speaking. Meaning it can never be increased in size…" He hesitated. "Let me correct that. You cannot increase it artificially. It will grow as you do, regardless, but that growth is proportional to its starting size. Its growth will forever be anchored."

"That makes sense, I suppose."

"Additional to the linear growth of the capacity being locked, you will not be able to add any other features."

"Other features?"

"There are some who have added magically simulated day-night cycles or weather systems within dimensional storages of sufficient size. Some add both."

Rane was nodding as he joined the conversation. "One of my great…" He hesitated, seeming to think. "Great, great, great uncles has an orchard in his soul-bound storage." Rane grinned. "He always had fruit aplenty, ready to hand."

Tala's eyes widened at the possibilities. "So I can't untether, after soul-binding, and I can't increase Kit's magics after untethering. So, effectively, I can't alter Kit after the soul-bond."

"If you wish this functionality. You'll also have to learn to do more than just pull with your soul, but that becomes easier once you reach Fused, and easier still at Paragon. That, though, you don't have to wait on. Work on the capabilities of your soul and its bonds. That will help you across the board. It will help you get the greatest utility from the items bound to you."

Tala grimaced. *Time, eh? And likely money, but how much?* "How expensive will all this be?"

"Assuming you don't find the items or magics you need? Very. I wouldn't recommend binding with a dimensional storage smaller than a modest house, and that's the minimum."

"That seems like it would require a lot of gold…"

Rane laughed. "Oh, yes. There is no quick, cheap fix in this area."

Jevin shrugged and nodded. "Master Rane is correct. In general, combining any two dimensional-storage items is additive, not multiplicative. By the spell-forms I can see, Kit looks to have just around two-hundred-twenty cubic feet of space; is that correct?"

Tala considered for a moment. "That sounds right."

"Alright. A modest house for one person would hold around eight-thousand cubic feet. So… thirty-six?" He shrugged. "Close enough. Thirty-six times your current size."

She paled. *Kit is worth about thirty gold…* That meant that she'd need dimensional storage items with a total worth of more than a thousand ounces gold to merge into Kit. *That doesn't even cover merging costs, let alone the costs for any other features or whatever magics are needed to untether it.* "Do… Do I really need to make it that big?"

"Need? No, especially not right now, but it would be pretty foolish not to. You are building something to permanently integrate with your soul. Why would you want to skimp?"

"That's true." Tala sighed. So storage was going to continue to be a resource drain, and she wouldn't be able to soul-bind Kit anytime soon. *What about defense?* Tala frowned, a thought occurring to her. "Wait… could I commission a magically reinforced wall, with the ability to self-repair, then untether it, bind it, and summon it as a defense?"

Jevin gave her a funny look. "That's quite the change in subject and an oddly specific idea." He lifted a hand, and Tala saw dimensional energy swirl, a portal flashing through the space in front of the Paragon.

Once the energy had passed, a solid wall of indeterminant material stood beside them, radiating power.

Tala's mouth moved, but she couldn't find the words. It was exactly as she'd described, a heavily magically-reinforced defense that would repair itself over time, if given enough power.

"So… you have that already?"

Jevin stepped around the wall. "No, of course not. If it were untethered, it wouldn't have any physicality with which to be a defense. This is just a wall, albeit a magically reinforced and empowered wall. I have several hundred housed in my dimensional storage. I can bring them forth almost as quickly as what you describe, and, as I said, they actually work to protect me. Additionally, they don't require individual soul-bonds, nor threaten the integrity of my soul whenever they are damaged." He quirked a smile.

*Oh… yeah, that would be a downside that I hadn't considered.*

"Wait… hundreds?" Rane was walking around the wall. "With hundreds, you could build fortifications almost at will."

Jevin grinned. "Precisely. The Leshkin war of this cycle is approaching, and I often function as a mobile fortress during those decades." He frowned. "Centuries?" He shrugged. "Both are probably true. Obviously, I also help with other threats, but that is the largest scale enemy we've dealt with in quite some time."

Rane ran his hand down one side of the wall. "This is prepared to fuse with any additional walls that touch it. There are power sharing workings and…" He seemed a bit overwhelmed. "This is a ridiculous feat of magical engineering."

"Where do you think all our wealth and knowledge go, lad? We are millennia into a never-ending war. We do not steal from the average members of humanity, but we do all we can with a clean conscience to build up our power, utility, and survivability."

Tala touched the wall or tried to. Her hand was lightly repulsed. The harder she pushed, the more the wall deflected her. She thought that a quick, full-powered punch *might* let her brush the surface. She glanced to Rane, his hand easily touching the surface.

Power was swirling around the hand, his scripts clearly working to negate that portion of the wall's defense.

"Do I even want to know what one of these would cost?"

Jevin smiled. "Probably not, no."

Tala sighed. *So… money will continue to be an issue for centuries to come.* She shrugged. "Very well."

"Now," Jevin smiled, "I have a few answers for your other issues." He waved a hand and the portal for his dimensional storage whipped over the wall, leaving the space empty.

Tala perked up. "Oh?"

Jevin tossed the sphere that he'd most recently pulled from his dimensional storage.

Tala caught it, her eyebrows rising at the weight. It was nearly ten pounds, while being barely bigger than her closed fist. "This is weighty."

"Solid tungsten. That's about twelve silver worth."

It was a comfortable size in her hand; it wouldn't be hard to throw. "So, what would I use it for?"

"Well, since you can lower effective gravity for items, you can lower that to virtually nothing. Then when you throw it, you'll get a lot greater distance. You're strong, so it will hit like a charging bull. With practice, you could get up to a hundred miles per hour, if not faster." He shrugged. "I don't know, exactly, how much stronger you are than average. Of course, that is just one possible use. I'm sure you can come up with many, many more. After you suss those out, we might want to make you different shapes, but a sphere should have the greatest universal utility, at least for now."

That was an interesting idea. Not novel, but interesting. *I could also increase the effective gravity and drop it… That would do even more, but I'd have to be above my target.* She considered.

If she had a couple with their gravity ramped up until she could barely hold them, they'd be great at pinning people down too.

As if reading her mind, Jevin lifted a couple light gray metal arches. The internal dimensions were just over five inches wide and little more than two inches tall. As Tala looked closer, she could see that the inside curve was a flat band of metal, with a perpendicular fin fused down the center of the span, clearly meant to reinforce the structure from the back, making the cross-section a T.

"What is…" Tala began to nod. "Increase the effective gravity, and I can use that to pin a person or something else down." Her eyes widened. "I can tuck my feet under two of those."

Jevin laughed. "I suppose you could use them to help hold you in place, supposing the material you're standing on can take it. But I had thought their utility lay in other areas."

Now that she thought about it, she could wear sturdy, gravity-amplified shoes. *That wouldn't help with the inertia problem, though.* And no one liked heavy shoes… *I don't particularly like shoes of any kind.*

"So, I considered your question about the dimensional anchor, and I think that you'll have to decide what tradeoffs you want."

Tala refocused on Jevin. She dearly wanted to stop being snatched, hit, or punted off the wagon top. *It would be nice to not be sent flying by Rane's strikes, too.*

The three of them fell into a prolonged discussion of the various possibilities. As they talked, Jevin led them out of the merging room and into a comfortable lounge, off a side corridor.

Terry came along, perched on Tala's shoulder as usual.

An assistant got them afternoon tea. They were a bit late for it, but there were leftovers aplenty.

They discussed dozens, if not hundreds of ideas.

Finally, Rane started pacing. "Let's walk while we talk. I'm starting to feel like a prisoner in here."

As the words left the Bound's mouth, Jevin jerked. "That's it!"

Tala and Rane turned to fully face the man, and Tala prompted. "What did you think of?"

"Prison!"

Tala frowned, but Rane's face shifted to one of consideration.

"Can someone explain? Is there something about prisons I'm not aware of?"

"Powerful, dangerous, or magically potent prisoners are all handled in virtually the same way, and it might be just what you need."

"I assume you don't mean execution… right?"

Jevin laughed. "No, no. Not execution."

Tala leaned forward, paying close attention.

"Most could break through any confinement, given enough time. So, a dimensional prison is used."

"Explain."

"It's an item in two parts, usually linked to the city's power matrix. One part is on the prisoner, to identify the target. It's affixed in some manner to prevent its removal, but that's not relevant, now. The other part is the anchor. Effectively, the item creates a donut of space, ten feet in diameter, which contains the prisoner. It doesn't create any visual effect, but if the prisoner walks further than ten feet from the anchor, space is expanded. That way, no matter how they run, walk, or move, when they stop, they are still no further than ten feet from the anchor."

Tala leaned back. *That's a little terrifying, actually…* It sounded a lot like the cargo-slots' working, if more active and dynamic.

"Similarly, if they try to approach within arm's length of the anchor, or draw it to them, space is expanded to keep them out of reach."

"So, it's immovable by the one it affects."

"When built as a prison, yes. That also allows a jailer to pick up the anchor and move the prisoner without being in danger. Even so, we don't need to include that inner working. You could pick up the anchor and affix it to anything you want."

"Wait, couldn't Mage prisoners just use their magic on those around them? Or the anchor?"

"The key locks onto the target: body, soul, and magic." An apologetic look stole over his face. "It was actually originally adopted from necromantic traps."

Tala gave him a flat look. "So, I'd be trapping my own soul." She frowned. "What would that do to my soul-bound items?"

"Anything with a physical presence would be, likewise, contained. This is a benefit when used for imprisonment."

"Could we leave out the soul aspect?"

Jevin considered. "I believe so. Like removing the inner working, that should increase the efficiency. I'll look into it."

"Ideally, I wouldn't want my magic contained, either. It *shouldn't* be an issue, because I just need to be able to perceive that which I target, and so my magic doesn't cross the intervening space…" She hesitated. "Would it affect things that I throw?"

"Depends on the sensitivity, but I think I can build it so that it's restricted to your body, not things that you are touching or have touched recently."

Tala hesitated. "Wait… what about my defenses?"

"What about them?"

"If I am immune to magic—" She cut herself off. "No, it doesn't act on me, it expands the dimensionality around me. Otherwise, it would become a contest of wills with the prisoner and have uncertain results."

"Correct. So long as the key is outside your defense, it should work just fine."

"Yeah, that should work." Her eyes narrowed. "How much?"

Jevin considered. "As an inscribed item?" He nodded. "Yeah, I'd insist on that. We don't want to attempt making an artifact style item with an untested structure."

He scratched his chin. "I think I can develop and create a first version for ten gold."

Tala's eyes widened, about to protest, but she hesitated, giving herself a moment to think. *The cost is for him to develop a unique variation on my behalf and create it. Even so, what really matters is how long I can use it.* "How long would it last?"

"Depends on use. You should be able to charge it yourself, assuming you haven't just been pretending to understand me. I'd say two months of moderate use, including as a sparring aid to get used to it and improve its utility to you, or a couple of years of emergency only use."

Tala sighed. *So, I'll be lucky if it lasts a few weeks....* "What will it cost after that?"

"A few gold to reinscribe, assuming we don't want to make a new version."

"Alright… So, four gold for the merging, already settled." She patted Flow at her waist. "One gold, twenty silver for ten of the tungsten balls, and forty silver for ten sets of the metal arches, right?" She wanted to play around with the items, to see what she could do with them.

"That sounds right." Jevin pulled out a slate, building out an invoice. "So, that's a total of eleven gold, and sixty silver ounces owed."

"How soon can you complete the… I really don't want to call it a dimensional prison…"

Jevin laughed. "How about dimensional tether? I believe I can have a working version in a couple of days."

"That's feasible." When Jevin held out the slate to her, Tala confirmed the transaction. *My money is not going as far as I would like…* And there were so, so many expenses looming ahead of her. She sighed. "Thank you, Master Jevin."

Rane bowed toward both of them. "Thank you for allowing me to observe the merging and participate in the discussion."

They both smiled toward Rane, responding overtop of one another.

"Of course, Master Rane."

"I wasn't going to kick you out, was I?"

Tala and Rane bid farewell to Jevin and departed. As they began walking back down the spiral, Tala glanced toward Rane.

"So… I need to test some things, and I need to learn what I'm doing, then practice, with a glaive." Her eyes flicked to Terry before returning to Rane. "I'm not to the point with this guy," she tilted her head toward the bird, "where it matters what weapons I use. So, that's no help. Willing to work with me?"

Rane grinned in return. "Absolutely. The training complex has a deal with some local restaurants, so we can get food delivered."

"That sounds like a wonderful way to spend the evening."

Thus, they headed straight back to the training grounds; Tala had a *lot* of new things to test out.

# Chapter: 22
## That Seems Wise

Tala growled as she threw three tungsten balls, followed closely by Flow in the form of her glaive.

None struck its intended target, and the backstop she and Rane had set up was now slowly toppling away from her, despite the bracing they'd added.

*I did manage to stick the glaive in point first. That's not nothing.*

Of the six, evenly spaced targets, three had been struck, but not in the center and not the ones she'd been aiming for.

"Hey! That's much better."

Tala glared at Rane.

The man was moving through one of his forms but had enough attention to spare to mock her.

"That's not helpful."

"What? You hit three out of four."

"Not the ones I aimed for…"

He gave her a quizzical look. "How was I supposed to know that?"

"I… That's fair." She groaned. *Two days.* She'd been training for two days, and she didn't feel like her aim was improving at all. *That's not fair. I am getting a little better, and it has only been two days.*

In irritation, she called Flow back, maintaining its glaive shape with effort, and dropped into the beginning of a form that Rane had taught her. He'd claimed that the early forms for this weapon were little more than modified staff training techniques, but they helped her build confidence in her use of the weapon. *The advanced techniques should be pretty awesome, when I get there.*

She kept a grimace from distorting her features. *Doesn't help with my throws, though...* She calmed her mind, using the now well-practiced movements to clear her head.

*Ha, well-practiced...* She'd learned the sequence only yesterday morning, though she had moved through them a couple hundred times since then. *Maybe it is well-practiced at that.*

The series of movements ended with a downward sweep. She exhaled sharply and held the pose for a moment before spinning the weapon back up to rest on her shoulder.

She released her void-channels, and Flow returned to the shape of a knife even as she sheathed it at her belt.

By her reckoning, Jevin would have the dimensional tether for her by now, and the Culinary Guild should have her venturing food as well.

During the past two days, she'd taken time to meditate and work within herself, adding two more stitches toward Fusing. *Two of...* No, she'd determined to not consider the magnitude of the task before her. *One at a time.*

"I'm going to get cleaned up. I've a couple of errands to run."

"Want company?" After the briefest of pauses, he clarified, "For the errands."

She shrugged. "I think I'll be Okay." Then, thinking of the Culinary Guild, she hedged a bit further. "It would probably be nice to take the walk by myself. I won't be gone long."

"Suit yourself." He simply continued his workout.

Once Tala was cleaned up and back on the city spiral, she asked Terry to carry her.

He agreed without hesitation. So, she made good time, arriving at the Constructionist Guild office where Jevin worked in short order.

The magical scan and pleasant ding greeted her.

"In the back!" Jevin's voice carried in such a way that she didn't think he'd been shouting, but he still sounded quite far back in the complex.

Tala shook her head and walked down the halls, trying to find her way to his workshop.

The few times she went to make a wrong turn, unknowingly, Jevin called out to her again.

Finally, she arrived, Terry firmly asleep on her shoulder.

Jevin's workshop was much as she'd remembered it, if a bit more organized.

The oddly moving mud caught her eye again, and Tala walked over to the heavily empowered glass jar, ignoring Jevin, who was working in another part of the shop.

"Don't touch that."

Tala hesitated. She had, in fact, been about to touch the glass. "What is it?"

"That, my young Bound, is living iron." Jevin walked over to stand next to her, shaking his head. "It's always awkward to address 'Bound' by that title."

"Archon? Mage? Mistress Tala?"

"Too vague, some would be insulted, and too long." He had a slight smile, seeming to indicate another attempt at humor.

Tala huffed a laugh, but otherwise decided to ignore the effort. "So, living iron?"

"It's a not-quite-magical creature that we've run across a few times. More frequently recently."

The reddish-brown mud seemed to be trying to crawl up the side of the container, but it couldn't get purchase on the walls or push the lid free. Interestingly, it didn't seem to leave any residue; the glass stayed clean.

Even through the heavy magic on the container, Tala's magesight was able to get a look at the creature. It did, indeed, look like any other bit of iron. *Like how I look, with my iron-salve.*

"We've found individuals of several distinct metals, but they die quickly when exposed to what we would call breathable air."

"What do they do?"

"No idea. That's why I'm studying it." He hesitated. "Well, obviously we know some things." He handed her a sheet of paper. "These are the gaseous mediums they can exist in, along with liquid, and solid."

Tala looked over it in passing.

"Whatever their metal, they seek out and consume it, adding it to their shape."

"So… not-quite-magical. Do they have magic or not?"

"No? No more than any other creature. We've found some with bits of magic, but we've not seen signs of intelligence sufficient for complex mental constructs, and they've no will to speak of; spell-workings take hold with almost no resistance." After another pause, he smiled. "Well, they do on those not composed of iron."

"But they could go through a fount."

He gave her a searching look. "Yes. Though I doubt an iron could."

"Why study them?"

His look changed to one of genuine confusion. "Because they exist, and we don't understand them."

"Ahh." *Right, knowledge for knowledge's sake.*

"It is fascinating. When damaged, they move the metal into the wound first, almost as we would form a scab. The biological aspect then back-fills."

"Can magic flow through it?"

"You mean like an inscription? They seem to exhibit all the same properties as their metal, so yes, at least in theory. Even though we've determined a lack of sapience, I'm still hesitant to experiment on them too extensively."

"You just talked about damaging them."

"Of course. Can you not imagine a scenario when a Mage might need to do so?"

Tala frowned.

"Metals, Mistress."

Her eyes widened. "What happened?"

"One of the more extreme examples occurred when a Mage slept on the bare rock of a cave. Apparently, that was close enough contact to let the metal be sensed, and a living copper… ate the copper out of him."

"That's… horrifying."

"Just a bit, yeah. He survived, but it was an enlightening experience." He hesitated for a moment. "That actually provides an answer to your question. Though, I hadn't thought of it in that light."

"Oh?"

"The Mage's inscriptions functioned perfectly, until the creature left, taking the copper with it. So, yes, magic can flow through them identically to the raw metal."

*Interesting…* Tala regarded the container once again. "Is there a name that covers all of them? Regardless of metal?"

"Dasgannach."

"Colorful name."

"Not a metallic one?"

Tala gave him a flat look.

Jevin suppressed a smile and shook his head. "Fine. The name comes from arcane records. These creatures were known but not often seen. They were a curiosity more than anything."

"So, why is this dasgannach so dangerous? I've no iron in me."

Jevin cocked an eyebrow.

Tala glanced his way, then froze, realization blooming. "No."

"And she understands."

"A blood eater?" As Tala asked, Terry shifted on her shoulder but otherwise didn't react.

"We caught this one because several people in a single family that didn't have any pre-existing conditions of note died of what seemed to be extreme anemia. They also each apparently complained of odd, random itching, leading up to their deaths." He shook his head. "Honestly, anemia doesn't really cover it properly, even though it is, technically, correct."

"So, that was… inside them, consuming their iron until they died?"

"Hmm? No, no. They were perfectly healthy until the creature left. It stayed until all the iron was under its control, every drop of blood from the heart to the smallest capillary. Then, it took it all, when it passed to the new host." He paused. "The iron, I mean. Not the blood itself. Left their blood almost entirely white, and utterly useless for carrying oxygen within them. The victim left behind suffocated with full lungs and strong hearts. Interestingly, each subsequent host felt invigorated, leading up to their death, likely due to the higher iron content, or maybe some chemical cocktail to keep the host functioning at peak form until the dasgannach was finished." He shook his head. "One of the stranger things I've come across."

Tala swallowed involuntarily. "That's not how any of that should work."

"Hence not-quite-magical."

She grunted. "And now, I have new fuel for my nightmares. Thank you for that."

"Better to know than live in ignorance."

Tala took another step back. "Yeah… I'll leave that thing be."

"That seems wise."

"So… the tether?"

"Ah! Yes." He led her over to a side table and pointed to a set of bracers made of leather and plated with heavily inscribed wood. Beside them rested a wooden spring-clip with inscriptions so intricate that Tala had trouble discerning them, even after she picked it up.

"Lacquered?"

"Yes, to protect the metal, at least until you activate it. Please don't throw it into anything especially hard. You won't be able to disrupt the active scripts, but you could reduce their effective lifespan. It should be fine, clipped to your belt, Terry's collar, or part of a wagon."

Terry cracked an eye to regard the device, then settled back down.

Tala nodded, clipping it to her belt. "Did you get the functionality you wanted out of it?"

"I did." He handed her a small booklet. "Read that before you empower the device. You'll get better efficiency."

"Fair enough." She examined the bracers more closely. They were small, not sized as armor, and their straps were both intricate and sturdy. "Can these take a hit? I don't exactly stay out of direct damage."

"That's why there are two. So long as one is intact, the anchor will continue to function."

## Millennial Mage, 4 - Bound

She nodded. *Not ideal, but it will work for now.* She contemplated for a moment. *You know, after we have these perfected, I could meld the artifact form with my elk leathers. That should make them effectively invulnerable.*

Jevin grinned, unaware of her wandering thoughts. "And I anticipated the issue might extend beyond even that precaution." He pulled out another set of bracers. "Wearing any one of these will be sufficient, and their power and metal use should be vastly less than that of the anchor. If you wish, you could affix these to your lower legs, but I think that might be a bit excessive."

Tala felt a bit better with such back-ups. Though, part of her felt like she should be insulted. *Oh, yes. The brilliant Constructionist correctly covered for a weakness. How dare he?!* She shook her head at her own immature thoughts. "Thank you. What's the extra cost?"

He waved that away. "Most of the cost was in the development, and I promised you a device that would work for *you.* Having backups is required in your case."

She did glare, then. *Eh, baby steps. No one matures overnight.* "That's hurtfully accurate."

He gave her a quizzical look, before shaking his head and smiling. "I aim to fulfill my commissions, not keep you happy."

Tala sighed. "Fair…" She crinkled her nose, pushing her mild irritation aside. "Well, thank you." With clumsy motions, Tala strapped on one set of bracers. She moved her arms around and felt the bracers pulling and pinching. Her sleeves were caught, cinched down against her arms and the odd constriction around her forearms made opening and closing her hands feel… odd.

Jevin sighed. "Here, let me." He reached over, working the buckles and straps, and subtly shifting the bracers and her sleeves, until they were quite a bit tighter than she'd managed by herself. Even so, after his ministrations, they *felt* looser, while shifting less. "There."

Tala moved her arms, stretching this way and that. There was no pinching, pulling, or constriction. "Huh… I'll have to learn how to do that."

Jevin nodded. "Take them off, and I'll walk you through it."

Together, Tala and Jevin removed and replaced the bracers half-a-dozen times. Then Tala did it herself half-a-dozen more while Jevin watched and commented. The Paragon was giving off a paternal air that made her slightly uncomfortable. It wasn't that his actions or attitude were unwelcome, unhelpful, or inappropriate; it was more that, for that brief time, she felt like this virtual stranger was acting more like her father than her father had, at least near the end.

Ultimately, she was fairly confident that she could get the right placement and fit, even if it would take some finagling.

"Thank you." She put her parental issues aside and gave Jevin a genuine smile, tucking the extras into Kit.

"I am happy to help." He was nodding to himself. "Now, I dug those out for you." He waved in a gesture toward a nearby cloth sack.

Tala frowned, going over and opening the bag. Within were six well-maintained, but obviously old, iron spheres of various permeability. Each had an identical wooden ball inside. *Well, I assume the last one does, too.*

One extreme of the set was a sphere of interwoven wire, with holes *just* too small for the wooden ball to fall out through. When she looked closer, she saw that the wires were welded at the crossings, to prevent the holes from opening wider.

The other extreme was a nearly perfectly smooth iron ball with no perforations or holes, at all. The four other balls were an even progression between those, two, and all six were covered with minor dings, dents, and scratches.

"What are these for?"

"For you to practice. You didn't seem enthusiastic about letting me oppose your will, so these will work. I wish all Mages would train with something similar, and I insist all my apprentices do so, but most have a reasonable dislike of iron. I assume you wouldn't have that issue."

Tala grinned. "Not even a bit."

"Good. You aren't my apprentice, so I can't make you use those, but I do recommend it." He was moving back toward his earlier project. "If you change your mind, I'm happy to oppose your workings, but those should be a good starting point, regardless. Just return them when each becomes too easy for you. I'm rather attached to them." His smile was one of fond memories, tinged with the sadness of a parent whose children were out on their own.

Tala was regarding the last ball, trying to ignore the awkward emotions. "I can't do a working through solid iron."

"I'm not asking you to."

She frowned. After a long moment, she began to nod. "You want me to see if I can affect an object's gravity from the other side. See if my scripting will allow that."

"Do you think they could?" He gave her a half-interested look. *He's trying to not put pressure on me, but he does think this might be possible.*

"Maybe. Gravity, at its most basic, is an interaction between two points. I should be able to affect one through the other... possibly." She didn't know how, but it seems like it *should* be possible.

"Good. If you can work that out, very few defenses will work against you." His smile lessened for a moment as he amended. "Well, other than direct opposition of will. So, no passive defense should work against you." He grinned fully once again.

"Well, I'll definitely add this to my training."

Jevin opened his mouth to comment, but hesitated, tilting his head to one side. "I believe someone is here to see you."

Tala grimaced. *I told Rane I would be back.* Couldn't he let her run two errands on her own?

"An older Mage Protector…" His face shifted slightly toward sadness, but he didn't say why. "Shall we go greet her?"

*Oh, Mistress Odera.* It seemed odd to Tala that he would come, but she didn't object.

Together, they walked through the building until they reached the entry room where Mistress Odera waited.

Mistress Odera gave a deep bow toward Jevin, hands clasped. "Master Jevin. I did not know you would be in residence at this location. I am Mage Odera."

"Mistress Odera, be welcome." His voice was soft, but still carried through the room with ease. "You said you were here to speak with Mistress Tala?" He gestured to Tala as she stepped up beside him.

*She said? She must have spoken when she entered, and he obviously has some way of perceiving the entrance.*

"I am, indeed." Mistress Odera turned to regard the younger Mage. "Greetings, Mistress Tala. Master Rane informed me that I was likely to find you here. Our schedule has been altered. A critical shipment is anticipated, and ours is the only caravan already within the city that can carry the cargo in its entirety. There have been increasing delays on incoming caravans, and they don't want to risk the lack of a sufficient caravan." After a moment, she smiled kindly. "Thankfully, we haven't confirmed the permanent loss of any caravan, stars be praised."

Tala frowned as she bowed. "Greetings, Mistress. By altered, what do you mean?" *At least Rane didn't come himself.*

"We've been asked to delay our departure by almost a month."

Tala balked at that. "Why? And why tell me now?"

"I just learned an hour ago, or I would have told you at our last meal. As a concession for the inconvenience, we will each be paid a stipend of two gold per day for each day past our previously scheduled departure. That will be a total of fifty gold apiece."

Tala's eyes widened in shock.

"Indeed. It seems that this load of goods *must* be shipped together, and the client is willing to pay to ensure such."

Tala nodded, finding herself a bit speechless.

"We will need to power down the cargo-slots. So you will have to find another place to stay, but you also won't need to return to the work yard each morning."

Finally, Tala found her tongue once again. "Thank you for bringing me this news."

Mistress Odera gave a slight bow. "Of course. If you can, please get any items you need from the cargo-slot this evening, and the local Wainwrights will oversee the deactivating of the slots tomorrow. You were not requested for that, but you would likely be welcome to observe, if you so desired."

"I will gather a few things. Thank you. I don't believe I will observe."

There was a slight lull as they ran out of applicable topics.

Jevin cleared his throat, stepping into the silence. "Mistress Tala, I believe that we have concluded our business for the moment. Would you be willing to depart, so that Mistress Odera and I could have a word?"

Tala frowned, giving him what she thought was an inquisitive look, but he simply waited for her response. "Alright." She bowed to each of them in turn. "Master Jevin, Mistress Odera."

They bid her farewell in return.

As she left, her enhanced hearing picked up the beginning of their conversation.

"Mistress Odera, I know what is in your pocket. Would you like me to take it from you? That is not a cure, but it will be a delay."

Mistress Odera's voice came back, obviously filled with relief, an edge of pleading apparent as well. "If you command, Paragon, I will obey."

The door swung shut, locking Tala out of the remainder of the exchange, and she and Terry started upward, toward the Culinary Guild office on the fifth floor.

## Chapter: 23
## Kit Was Full

Tala and Terry made good time to the Culinary Guild. The assistant on duty was obviously a bit uncomfortable with Tala's arrival, but he'd apparently been advised to expect her.

Atrela came out to greet her in short order, leading Tala down a side hallway into a spacious pantry.

The four walls were covered, floor to ceiling, in shelving. A counter ran the circumference in front of the upper shelves, and above the lower. That counter was only broken by the single door in and out.

A large work-surface anchored the room from the center, with a six foot walkway all the way around.

The room was bigger than most home kitchens. *And this is just a side pantry.* She wasn't sure what she'd expected from the Culinary Guild. If she was being honest, she'd not given it much thought.

The shelves of this pantry were stocked full of bulk goods, well labeled and tightly sealed.

On the central counter, a treasure trove of non-perishable food was spread out, awaiting Tala's inspection.

"We try to keep proper nutrition in mind." Atrela had a self-contented smile. "I oversaw the selection myself, bending the choices toward those we'd give a combat response group."

When Tala gave her a quizzical look, Atrela continued.

"We tried to ensure that you have the right nutrients for proper healing and bodily function."

Terry was looking around with interest, but he didn't leave her shoulder.

Atrela walked Tala through each section of the staggering array of food. *I need to expand Kit's capacity…*

There were dried fruits and vegetables of all kinds, grains en masse, and canned meats in ridiculous abundance. Tala had seen canned food before, but her family had rarely used it. As she considered, she actually didn't know how it worked.

Atrela grinned widely when Tala asked. "We use the same methods the supply masters use for city emergency stores. A marginal dimensional expansion on the food, which fades once the can is sealed. That causes a strong vacuum that helps prevent any seepage or contamination of the contents. Then, we have a powerful sterilization inscription that we activate on all the goods. It kills anything that might otherwise ruin the stores. It is more effective than home preservation methods and allows for the long-term preservation of items that can't take heat-canning."

Tala nodded appreciatively, glad for the explanation, but not really interested in a deeper exploration. *The preservation process works, it won't fail, and I don't have to be concerned about the food going bad.*

Atrela handed her a simple notebook, smaller than Tala's palm. "This contains the list of items and recommended preparations and meal-plans. Feel free to add your comments and ratings, then when you re-order, we can shift what we provide to match your specifications."

"Couldn't I just tell you?"

She gave Tala a long look. "Mistress, this is five-hundred days' worth of meals for one person who is expecting heavy exertion, and it will effectively never spoil, assuming it isn't damaged or otherwise despoiled. I deeply hope that you don't remember your impressions of the early meals when you finally reorder."

Tala's eyes widened, doing quick math. *I gave her a budget of two gold.* "How can you provide meals for fourteen copper apiece?" She hesitated. *No, that's not actually that cheap, is it…?* She could almost get three of Gretel's meat pies for that price, and that would be a reasonable meal for most people. Food from a restaurant or food-cart was almost always more expensive than it would cost to make it herself.

"We make all of this in colossal quantities. We pulled your order from a batch we're putting together to ship to the City Builders' Guild at the current construction site."

*The new city.* "The Builders eat this regularly? Why wouldn't they just get it from the closest city?"

"It is meant to supplement and insure against the loss of supply caravans, so yes this does feed them, but not exclusively. As to why from us?" She shrugged. "While we are on the far side of human civilization, all cities pull their weight in the support of upcoming bastions of humanity. At the moment, we have an excess of foodstuffs, so that is what we're sending." Atrela smiled. "If cities between here and there have need of the food, instead, they'll trade it out for other things of use to the Builders."

Tala nodded, thinking through all the implications. Most of her thoughts centered around the food before her, rather that the intricacies of inter-city trade agreements. *That makes a lot of sense. If they are making vast quantities of this type of food, they're likely able to be much more efficient and thus get the price much lower than it could be under other circumstances.*

"We still do recommend that you get some form of cauldron or cooking pot. Trying to cook this up without such a tool will be difficult. Obviously, you can eat some without preparation, but most will need some cooking."

Tala shrugged. "Any recommendations on a supplier?"

Atrela grinned. "We can offer some options. The best would be cast-iron, both for longevity and utility, but I understand that Mages want as little to do with iron as possible. We have several other options that should serve well-enough."

Tala waved her off. "Cast-iron will be just fine."

That threw the woman off for a moment, but she recovered quickly. Atrela turned, squatting to reach behind where she'd been standing, into one of the lower shelves, muttering under her breath, clearly not intending Tala to hear, "Not the strangest thing about her, I suppose."

Tala didn't comment.

With a soft grunt of effort, Atrela pulled out a relatively large, cast-iron cauldron. "This can be set over a fire without need of a grill or suspension." The woman set the heavy cookpot on the central worksurface.

Tala glanced to the bottom and easily saw three legs sprouting from the pot-bellied base. Those would hold it a good six inches above a flat surface or be sunk into ground to give greater stability and less distance above the heat. The cauldron itself was just under a foot in each dimension at the largest, discounting the legs. The sidewalls and lid were all thick, which would lend them longevity if Tala cared for it properly.

Atrela spent a few minutes extolling the virtues of the cauldron, pulling out several implements for use alongside it and explaining how it should be cared for.

"Alright, I'll give it a try. How much?"

"Ten silver."

Tala sighed. She'd expected as much, if she was being honest. That was twenty-five days of meals, at the cost she was paying here. *Still, can't eat the meals if I can't prepare them.* "Can you throw it in, with such a large order?"

Atrela gave her a long look. "I think if you are still willing to discuss the… other item, then yes. We can sell the food and these implements for a total of two gold."

Tala nodded. *It's always worth asking.* "Thank you."

After they'd finalized the transaction, Tala took Kit off her belt in order to make the loading faster. She didn't worry about organization within Kit; the dimensional storage would arrange as appropriate. *Yeah, I definitely need to give Kit some good upgrades. They are well-earned and heartily deserved.*

She thought about it for a moment as she continued moving items into the pouch. *I have a bit more free funds than I was expecting. An upgrade to Kit's capacities is likely one of the better investments I can make, at the moment.* She would investigate it at least.

She hitched for a moment. *I forgot to ask about a clock of some kind.* She sighed. *I really do have too much going on…*

Once all the items were tucked away, she regarded Atrela once again. "So, did the Order make a decision?"

Atrela was looking through notes on her slate, and she glanced up. Noticing that Tala was done, Atrela tucked the slate away and nodded. "We have. If you allow us to add you as a member of the Order within the Archive, we will not oppose you taking the question to one you deem appropriate."

Tala thought about Ingrit's answers in the Bandfast Archon's library. *My being a member might allow me to unlock the records to a librarian, for investigation. Then, I can progress from there.* "I agree." She hesitated. "Wait… You have Order membership logged in the Archive?"

"Of course. We have to, so that we can properly restrict access to our research."

"But you're trying to hide from Mages… Aren't you being a bit trusting?"

Atrela shrugged. "If the inter-guild agreements fail, we will have something to worry about, but as it is, the Archive has proven itself utterly secure and discreet."

Tala did not understand, but she didn't have to. "Alright, then."

Atrela went through the process of adding Tala to the confidential rolls of the Order of the Harvest. Apparently, even the name of the Order was sealed from anyone who wasn't authorized within the Archive.

*I guess I'm glad that it's that secure.* She really should get an Archive slate for herself. *That should probably be my next big purchase, after expanding Kit, assuming that's reasonably priced.*

With no further business, Tala bid Atrela farewell and headed back down the tree, toward the work yard and the cargo-slot that she needed to empty.

\*   \*   \*

Within the cargo-slot room that she'd called her own for nearly two weeks, Tala didn't have much to consider. In the end, Tala took her bed, but that was about all she needed from the space.

Everything else of hers lived in Kit.

Blessedly, the bedframe folded to a size that would fit through Kit's opening, and the mattress, while incredibly firm, still flexed enough to be forced through.

After that addition, Kit was full. There was still enough room that Tala could pull out what she needed, but she didn't really have room to climb down in anymore, let alone room for a bath.

*Unacceptable.* Instead of going back to the training room, she returned to Jevin in the Constructionist Guild.

Mistress Odera was gone, as Tala had expected, and Jevin came from the back shortly after the pleasant ding announced Tala's arrival. It was still late afternoon, so it wasn't after business hours, thankfully.

"Mistress Tala? What are you doing back so soon?"

"I need to make my dimensional storage larger."

He nodded. "That makes sense. I assume you just need raw size, not any other feature?"

She frowned. "Yes? What do you mean?"

"Well, every additional feature or ability integrated with a dimensional storage is added complexity and expense. We do, however, have quite a few Mages and Archons who simply want to expand their storage devices, not to mention a host of mundanes who just want to store a lot of things."

"What are you getting at?"

"If you just need the extra space, we can expand it much more cheaply than the cost of a truly useful dimensional item containing the space we need."

She grimaced. "That's not what you conveyed before."

"I was conveying generalities and minimums. It's always better to set expectations of cost at a reasonable level."

"So…?"

He gave her a look. "I assume your new desire is partially inspired by your stipend from the Caravan Guild?"

"It is."

"Do you want to spend all of it?"

"No? I can probably spare…" She hesitated, taking a deep breath. "…thirty ounces gold?"

"We can triple your pouch's capacity with that."

"Is that the full cost? Or just for the construct that we need?"

"For item and combination."

"Great. Let's do that." She'd been hoping to at least double Kit for thirty gold; a tripling was almost enough to make her laugh in glee. "When can it be done?"

"We can do it now. It doesn't take that long." He motioned for her to follow him, and he led her into a backroom that she'd not seen before. That wasn't surprising as she'd not really explored this complex, despite her somewhat frequent visits.

She looked around, taking in the simple space. Most of the room was filled with a heavily inscribed construction of immense complexity. The clearly inscribed construct appeared to be made in sections, mostly of wood, cleverly latched together. As a part of the construct, there were two small platforms, each with an open, smooth circle of wood three feet across.

"Alright, what do I do?"

"Place your storage on the left side, and I will be right back."

She did as he asked, unclipping Kit and setting the pouch within the clear circle. After a moment's hesitation, Tala quickly topped off Kit's power reserves. *Better to be safe.*

Jevin returned carrying a simple wooden crate.

Physically, it was expertly crafted, the seams all but undetectable even with her enhanced vision. The dowels did stand out, pinning the sides together, but in a way that added to the beauty rather than taking from it. The leather hinges were obvious as well, woven through smooth holes in the lid and through the top of one side.

Dimensional magic was quite evident surrounding the box, and it was as simple as it was powerful. All that the magic ingrained into the artifact-like construct did was expand space within. There was no isolation, no organization, no protection. It was just a box that was bigger on the inside.

*I feel like it would look even prettier painted blue.* She shrugged at the odd notion. It was already a well-crafted container. There was no need to cover up the craftsman's work.

*It expands space like Kit does.* Tala paused at that. *Wait… if Kit just expands the space, the inside should always be leather, like the pouch.* She looked back toward Kit. Her magesight saw what she'd always seen, the magics ingrained in the pouch were directed at expanding the space within, defending the pouch, and axis, weight, and kinetic isolation for the expanded space. *And… there's more that I don't really understand. Something tying it all together.* Obviously, there were at least space manipulation aspects, otherwise Kit couldn't reorganize, or give her what she reached for. *Worth looking into further, but not now.*

She shrugged internally. Jevin had examined Kit's magic and hadn't seen anything of concern. So, it was fine.

"This, right now, has a bit more than double the capacity of your pouch. We expect a little bit of loss with most combinations." He set the crate down in the other circle of the larger construct. "This device," he patted the massive construction, "will hold the contents of your storage in suspension, combine the devices, and return your items to the newly created whole."

Tala nodded, feeling a bit nervous. "And that won't damage Kit?"

"No. We're very good at this, Mistress. No functionality will be lost." After a moment, when she was clearly still concerned, he continued. "We have a guarantee, but since it's been centuries since it was invoked, we rarely bother speaking of it."

That did make Tala feel better, at least a bit. She nodded. "So, what now?"

"Now? Since one of the storage items is magic-bound to you, you must power the merger." He pointed to a hand-shaped impression off to one side.

Tala walked up to it and placed her hand there. "Just… feed it power?"

"I would suggest creating a mental construct of your aim, but yes. I assume you understand dimensional expansion well enough for the mental model?"

She nodded. *So, the mental model that matters is the result, not the process.* That made sense. It wouldn't be very efficient, but it would work. "Let's do it."

Without further hesitation, she built a mental image of the end result she wanted: Kit, with greater spatial capacity.

She forged one large void-channel and connected it to the massive device through her mental construct. That wasn't giving enough power, so she made another, then another. Finally, she reached the needed flowrate.

Power ripped through her, moving in a thunderous tide.

Slowly, the copper lines on the great construct began to glow, her power suffusing the feat of magical engineering.

When the entire room was filled with coppery light, the air hummed with power. Kit and the crate slowly lifted up, floating on power and circled by activated inscriptions.

Both storage items seemed to become translucent, their magical matrixes fading into visibility even to Tala's mundane sight.

Just like she'd seen before, the crate was a simple, straightforward construct.

Kit's magics, on the other hand, were a mind-bending, interconnected masterpiece. If Tala hadn't known better, she would have said it looked like some sort of alien being, one that couldn't possibly exist in their world. That image wasn't helped when Kit's scripts shifted, unfurling like a great mouth opening wide.

It consumed the simple script as a cat consumes a tasty treat.

As Tala watched, the crate's spell-forms were pulled free of the physical object. As soon as the spell-lines separated, the wooden crate came back to easy visibility, settling back down within its circle.

The magics stolen from the crate were pulled into Kit, absorbed, digested, and integrated into the pouch. The result was a larger, slightly more complex, alien construct of interwoven spell-lines.

The empowered item that Tala was feeding with her void-channels slowly wound down. Kit and the crate floated down to rest where they had been, physically unchanged.

When the draw of power through her hand ceased, Tala broke down her void-channels, stepped forward, and examined the crate. *Nothing. Just a simple wooden box.*

Then she picked up Kit and looked inside.

There was so much room! Tala laughed. "That's amazing!" She turned to Jevin but hesitated when she saw the Paragon regarding her and Kit oddly. "Is everything alright?"

"That was... more animated than I usually see."

"The combining? That's exactly what I'd expected." She shrugged. "Well, I suppose I mean it seemed right to me, not that I really knew what to expect."

He visibly relaxed. "Ahh, that makes sense. This sort of combination often takes a form according to the caster's understanding." He smiled. "So, are you satisfied?"

"Well, I don't have a measuring tape on me, but it looks great."

He nodded. "You actually got just more than triple the capacity. You had a much better mental construct than I was expecting, and so the process was more capacity efficient than usual. That likely comes from your work as a Dimensional Mage. It took a bit more power, but you handled that with ease."

She shrugged and smiled. "Thank you."

"I am happy to assist. If you confirm the transaction, we'll be done. Though, of course, you are welcome back any time."

She smiled, examining the slate he held out to her. It allowed the Constructionist Guild to take thirty gold from her upcoming payment from the Caravan Guild. *Not ideal, adding to my debt even temporarily...* If she'd taken a moment to consider, she'd probably have waited until the stipend was given, but that option was past possible.

With a press of her thumb and power, she confirmed the new debt and forced a smile. "Thank you, again."

## Chapter: 24
## Reactions

The day after she'd gotten the dimensional tether, Tala was sitting cross-legged, deep in a meditative state, when the world trembled around her. Her magesight screamed a warning.

Her eyes snapped over, and with a thought, Flow was in her hand in the form of a sword. She was sweeping it outward before her mind processed what she was seeing.

First, her magesight registered the aura: Reforged. The being before her was filled with a perfectly controlled, deep blue aura, clearly a bit more purple than true blue. It didn't radiate out from him, but instead, was held precisely at the surface of his skin almost like a badge of authority or office.

Second, she recognized him: Xeel.

Third, he once again countered her. This time he simply hopped up, over her swing.

"Mistress. I apologize for the intrusion." His hands lanced forward, grabbing either side of her head. His power flooded through her mind, and she was utterly at his mercy.

The moment passed, and Xeel was gone. A second later, something slammed into the wall behind her.

She looked up and saw Force stopped in place where Xeel had been.

With a smooth motion, Tala stood twisting to face the other way.

Xeel was peeling himself off the far wall, which was miraculously intact. "I hate kinetic manipulators." He sighed, turning to face them. "Was that necessary, Master Rane?"

"Apologies, Master Xeel, but you were using magic against her. I struck before I fully recognized you." Rane had been meditating nearby and was now standing just behind and to her left.

*Fast reactions.*

"On her. I was using magic on her, not against." Xeel was brushing off his simple, dark Mage's robes.

Rane's tone was tinged with mild regret. "That's a hard distinction to make in a split second." He sheathed Force as he came to stand beside Tala. "What can we do for you, Master Xeel?"

"I needed a second point of comparison, to narrow in on her first encounter with the arcane."

Rane glanced to Tala, then back to Xeel. "Is it that important?"

Xeel nodded. "Mistress Tala, how sure are you that you've never left the city or academy until your first caravan trip?"

"I'm one hundred percent certain."

"Then we have a problem."

Rane was frowning. "What's going on?"

"We have two options. First, Mistress Tala did leave the city on her first day in Bandfast, but no longer remembers doing so, wanting to do so, or what she might have been intending to do while outside. I find this very difficult to believe. Such a thoroughly invasive erasure should be impossible to hide, even from casual inspection."

Tala swallowed, her mouth suddenly dry. "What's the second option?"

"The arcane encounter happened within the bounds of Bandfast."

Silence hung heavy in the air of the training arena.

"When?" Her voice was barely above a whisper.

"By your records, on your first day, after you exited the teleportation tower and before you went to the Caravan Guild."

"How can you possibly know that precisely?"

"Because Mistress Lyn has no evidence of mental tampering, and you were with her for the remainder of the day."

*Oh, that makes sense.* "Wait, you examined her mind?"

"I did. I must say, she was much less violent than the two of you."

"She leads a less violent life."

Xeel grunted. "True enough, I suppose."

"So what now?"

"Now? Nothing. You continue as you have, and I'll take this to the collective Archon Council."

"We're just supposed to continue, knowing that arcanes can get inside human cities?"

"What would you like to do?"

She opened her mouth to respond, but nothing came to mind. Rane placed a hand on her shoulder, and she glanced his way before closing her mouth.

"Master Xeel, I think what she means is: how can we be safe? What can we do to protect ourselves, and…?" He shrugged. "It's too big an issue to encapsulate all the implications."

Xeel's face softened, just a bit. "I understand this is… difficult. It definitely calls into question many things we thought certain. If such a manipulator has access to our cities, then many things become…" He shook his head. "It can't have been long standing, nor could too many of them have this capacity, or we would already have fallen."

"Are you sure? Couldn't they want us to exist for some reason?" Tala felt a building jittery energy. *What is true? Do I even have a family, or is that a fabrication? Is Xeel human, or do I just believe so?* Tala cut off both lines of thought. *No, that way lies madness.*

"As I said, I need to take this to the Councils."

Tala took a deep breath, but it was Rane who responded. "So what can we do?"

"Improve the strength of your will and your soul. Fuse, and be alone as little as possible."

She started scratching at her arms. It felt like something was crawling under her skin.

Xeel sighed. "Relax. Find some way to destress. When you get back to Bandfast, I'll meet with you and tell you what I've learned. I had a talk with Mistress Holly, and she gave me this." He held up an inscribed stone. "May I?"

Tala shifted uncomfortably. She recognized the stone, but Holly had never told her, precisely, what it did. "What will it do, exactly?"

"It will transfer the information directly to the Archive, locked to you and Mistress Holly." He hesitated. "Well, initially it will be locked to her, until she processes it. The encapsulated results will be available to you when they are compiled."

*Oh. I can get access to my own records?* That seemed a bit of a silly question. Of course she could. "Alright."

Xeel crossed the room with measured strides, and Tala bent her head forward to expose the scripts on the back of her neck. He placed the stone there, and she felt a strange tingle, like a dog was drooling on her then licking it clean.

"Gah!" She shivered, shirking away from the feeling, but the process was already complete. "I forgot how that feels." She shuddered again.

"The transfer is complete."

Tala had a thought. "You know, given the situation, it would be useful for me to have an Archive slate. Any chance you could get me one?"

Xeel gave her a long look. "You want me to give you an empowered item."

"If you wouldn't mind."

"No." He paused for a moment, as if he was going to go on, but then he shook his head without saying anything further.

Tala waited another moment, but when he didn't say anything else, she shrugged. "Worth asking."

Xeel snorted a suppressed laugh. "Take care of yourself, Mistress Tala."

He was gone.

Tala looked to the closed door. "How did he do that?"

Rane shrugged. "There are a lot of options, actually."

She turned a skeptical look his way. "Why would you know how it's done?"

He gave her a long-suffering look. "My master could do that, from the first day I trained with him, and he refused to tell me how. I've had a *long* time to try to figure out how."

"Oh, yeah. That makes sense." She shrugged. "Do tell."

He held up one finger after another as he went through a list. "One. Immense speed, while manipulating matter around himself to remove the sonic boom and prevent materials from breaking. Two. A soul-bound gate, with one fixed location and a second, untethered end. He could summon that end and move through to a fixed location."

## Millennial Mage, 4 - Bound

Tala's eyes widened at the idea. "Wait, gates? I thought those were only a theory."

He gave her an odd look. "They are, and we're theorizing."

She grimaced at him but didn't comment further as he wasn't done.

"Three. Untethered storage space with a tethered entrance to get out through." He shrugged. "That one *should* be possible, but like the gate, I've never heard of such a thing actually being done. Four. A partial transformation into, or merging with, light, which I believe is his element of choice. Five. A pulse of focused willpower to disrupt our perception for a moment to simply allow him to walk out. Six—"

"Okay, Okay. I get it. There are many, many ways someone could accomplish what he just did."

Rane smiled, letting both his hands drop.

Tala gave him a skeptical look. "You didn't have a sixth thing, did you?"

"Do you want me to go on?"

She scratched her lip, thinking. "No, that way lies madness. I don't want the full list. I want to work on my void-channels."

She returned to where she'd been sitting, two tungsten balls in front of her. In the past few days, she had expanded her abilities with her active gravity manipulation to let her target two items at once. She couldn't change their gravity as fast as when she focused on just one, nor could she affect them differently, but it was a start.

And it was exhausting.

It felt like trying to imagine someone juggling, actively tracking where every ball was, while noticing how every muscle moved and tracking the exact nutrient expenditure.

*No. It's not quite that hard...* She didn't sound convincing, even in her own head. *It's hard, just not that hard.*

She sighed, sitting down, locking onto the two targets, and closing her eyes. *Focus, Tala. One increases, the other reduces. It's not that hard. It doesn't violate reality.*

It was not destined to be a productive day.

\* \* \*

Two days later, Tala and Rane stood beside a simple, post-and-rail fence.

Rane wore a look of fascinated horror.

Tala just grinned.

They both ignored the almost overbearing power at ground level around Makinaven.

Before them, a large animal pen held a half-dozen pigs, frantically running around, and Terry. Tala had seen the pig-pen on her way into Makinaven, and she'd instantly wanted to do something like this for the terror bird.

Terry, just taller than Rane, went around from pig to pig, pinning one down then moving on, constantly drawn to the next.

Sometimes, he would crouch down and sprint after a fleeing porcine. Other times, he simply flickered from one to the next.

He crowed, trilled, and thrummed in abject joy.

The pigs squealed in terror.

The farmer had lent the field and sold Tala the pigs for a gold. Tala knew she'd overpaid, but Terry was living the dream.

She tried not to think about the pigs.

Rane's voice was hushed as he spoke. "He looks like a cat, toying with mice."

Tala glanced to the large man, then back toward her terror bird. "So he does."

The animals were churning up the large pen, but that was fine.

The enclosure was a hundred feet to a side, a perfect faux hunting ground… if the goal was purely entertainment.

After five minutes or so, Terry began to challenge himself. He ceased flickering around and attempted to catch more than one at a time without hurting them. That only lasted a minute or so before the pigs finally began to tire.

The animals, whether becoming tired, or realizing that Terry hadn't hurt any of them yet, began to slow their panicked racing.

Terry allowed them some rest.

Then he flickered to the largest, slowest pig, and ate it in one bite.

The newly refreshed pigs squealed in renewed terror, and the games began again.

Terry's jubilant, dominating trills drowned out the pigs' squeals whenever he lifted his head in a triumphant cry.

"This seems… cruel somehow…"

Tala regarded Rane skeptically. "How so?"

"He's terrorizing them. Why not just eat them?"

She turned to fully face Rane, one eyebrow cocked. "Terror. Bird."

"Well, yes, I understand that."

"Do you? I feel like he survives on terror more than meat… Actually, is that possible?"

"No?" Rane regarded Terry, continuing his one-bird, bloodless rampage. "I've no idea, and I don't know of any theory that would allow it." He shrugged.

They continued to watch as Terry gave the pigs another rest before eating a second and beginning again.

In less than an hour, Terry had a single pig left, and it lay shuddering on the ground, Terry curled around it, cooing contentedly.

"Okay, that's a bit… much." Tala swallowed. *That's how he sleeps next to me…* "Terry! Just put it out of its misery!"

Terry raised his head to regard her, then shook. He stood, used one taloned foot to pat the pig on the head, then flickered to Tala's shoulder, small once more.

"You're… not going to eat it?"

Terry regarded her for a moment, then let out a long sequence of trills.

Tala didn't understand at all.

Slowly, in the middle of the churned enclosure, the pig stood and hesitantly went over to the water-trough.

Tala turned to go, but Terry let out a short chirp, so she waited.

The pig slowly stopped shivering, drinking deeply. Then, seeming uncertain, it shuffled over to the only gate out of the enclosure, seemingly looking to be released.

Terry looked to Rane and squawked.

Rane, frowning, moved over to open the gate.

The pig perked up, patiently waiting to be released.

As Rane opened the gate, Terry flickered, appearing straddling the pig, his head now half again as high as Rane's.

Before anyone could react, Terry snapped up the pig, swallowing it whole. The avian then straightened and gave Rane a long stare.

Rane took a step back, hand unconsciously resting on Force's hilt.

Terry flickered back to Tala's shoulder, curling up to sleep.

## Millennial Mage, 4 - Bound

Tala swallowed dryly, regarding her avian companion. "Sometimes," she swallowed again, "you are rusting terrifying."

\*   \*   \*

The day after Terry's porcine adventure, Tala slammed her face into the wooden training floor, groaning despite the lack of lasting damage.

This was not the first time, and she knew it wouldn't be the last. What really grated was she couldn't blame anyone but herself.

She pushed herself up with her left hand, returning to her feet and readying for the next attempt.

Around her, filling about a third of the training room, Tala had built an obstacle course of a very strange variety.

There were the traditional obstacles: hurdles, climbing wall, balance beam, and such. In addition to those, there were a series of mundane tasks, some as simple as a cup of water to drink, some much more complicated, like lacing a shoe or writing a letter.

The mundane tasks were only worthy of the course for a single reason: she'd bound her right arm behind her back, simulating its absence.

That handicap made the entire process difficult beyond what she'd expected.

*Would have been easier with just my right arm, and my left bound.* But she hadn't lost her left arm, and she wanted to *feel* that loss, to come to grips with the cost that she'd almost paid. *Hah, come to* grips. *I'm hilarious.*

Puns aside, she was struggling, and her left hand was cramping… again.

She knew from experience that her scripts would sooth the muscle ache, and restore it to functionality shortly, but it was still deeply uncomfortable.

*I hate writing with my left hand...* It was especially difficult when she chose to do the writing challenge directly after one of the climbing obstacles.

Tala had come up with this idea while meditating on the loss of her arm... and after learning that the training complex had obstacles that could be added to a rented space at no charge. *Personal introspection, free of charge.*

Obviously, Tala had put together the more mundane tasks on her own, but none of those were overly complex.

Rane cracked an eye from the far side of the room. He was still covered in sweat and breathing heavily from his most recent series of forms. "I still don't get why you're doing that."

"I need to understand the injury I endured. If I don't, I'm going to become callous to damage I take on my body. I can't allow that. I need to feel both the loss and the relief that the loss was reversed."

Rane shrugged. "If you feel that you need to, but it seems like you already felt the loss, and you *are* relieved to have your arm back."

Tala thought about that for a long moment. Finally, she sighed and undid her belt, which she'd used to keep herself from cheating. "You're probably right." She took another deep breath and let it out slowly. Then, she glanced behind her and grinned. "Once more."

She whipped through the course, two good arms making each task trivial.

"That is so, so much easier." She remembered the guard whose arm she'd cut off to save him from the magical crystal contamination. She had a new appreciation for the time he'd spent without that arm, even if it had been his left. More than that, though, Tala felt a warm joy that she'd been able to help pay to restore the man's arm once they arrived in Makinaven. *Yeah, that was worth the coin.*

She'd have helped even if she hadn't been forced.
It would have just been the right thing to do.
No question at all.
None.

At Tala's request, the training complex's workers removed the obstacles shortly after her last run through, breaking them down with practiced speed, and departing with only a few words exchanged.

Rane stood from his meditation after the workers had left. "So, I only reserved this space through the end of today. We were supposed to depart today, but I figured I'd want the space the morning before we left." He shrugged. "The point is, do we want to try to renew, or should we look for another place to train?"

Tala thought about that for a long moment. *It would be nice to be higher up the tree.* But when their time here ended, she'd need to come to the bottom each morning for the last couple of days. *No reason to let that color the intervening weeks.* She nodded. "Let's find somewhere higher up. Maybe somewhere outside, or with a view outside?"

He smiled in return. "That sounds like an excellent idea."

## Chapter: 25
## Happy to Assist

Tala hesitated. She and Rane had each just finished up their weapon's form and were getting ready to depart, but something was eating at her. With a sigh, Tala turned to Rane. "I still need to thoroughly test these…" Tala lifted her arms, indicating the bracers that she'd dutifully put back on after every self-cleansing.

"Ready to tell me why you haven't practiced with the tether so far?"

"I only just finished reading the booklet on the items this morning."

He waited.

Tala looked down. "I don't know."

He didn't comment.

"It's silly."

Rane just gave a patient smile, lips sealed.

Tala grunted. "Fine…" She took a deep breath and let it out, slowly. "Most of the language in the booklet was lifted from that of the prison item's manual. I… I don't like thinking of myself as a prisoner, even a voluntary one."

He cocked his head but remained silent.

Her voice was small as she finally spoke, once again. "What if he made it wrong, and I'm trapped forever?"

Rane let out a long breath, then, clearly considering. "That sounds terrifying."

Tala gave him a skeptical look.

He smiled in return. "What? It does. That said, it comes down to one question: do you trust him enough to give it a try? If not, return it, and he might be willing to refund some of your funds. If so, why not give it a try?"

After a long moment, Tala nodded. *That makes sense...* She now felt a bit foolish for hesitating. Thankfully, she hadn't lost that much time. She really had just finished reading up sufficiently to empower the tether that morning. "Alright. I'll try it once we find a new training spot. Alright?"

"Sure." He glanced to the side. "You know, I'm happy to help, if I can."

Tala nodded. "I do know, yeah." She looked to Terry, seemingly asleep in the corner. "Terry?"

The bird opened one eye to regard her.

"Are you alright with relocating, higher into the tree?"

He lifted his head, then let out a soft, warbling note that conveyed indifference.

Tala grinned. "Fair enough; shall we go take a look, now?"

"Sure." Rane pushed himself up.

Terry flickered to her shoulder, and they departed together.

Once they'd exited the facility and were heading up the second tier's seventh spiral, they had a brief conversation about how they would approach finding a new spot to train. As part of that, they decided that they should walk through the third-tier marketplace, on the way up to a higher level.

The market looked much the same as the previous times Tala had walked through it, but this time she was firm in her resolve that she wouldn't buy anything else. So once they made it to that tier, she was focused more on the buildings and other, less sales-oriented, features.

"Caravan street?" Tala was looking at one of the street signs that she'd not really paid heed to before.

Rane looked at it as well. "Yeah. If I remember correctly, they had some fun with naming the streets, here: Caravan, Wagon, Courier, Fleet, Ship, and the like."

"Huh, I suppose it makes some sort of sense for a market area."

"Yeah. It doesn't fit quite as well with the services and restaurants here, but it lends a bit of amusement, I guess."

They continued walking down the road, seeing many of the roads that Rane referenced.

"Hey, there's a barber right there." She glanced to Rane. *Is his hair longer than usual?* Well, obviously it was, hair grew constantly. "Do you usually keep your hair short or was that just how you had it when we met?"

"Usually short."

"Do you want to get it cut?"

Rane reached up and checked his hair. "Maybe…" He glanced to the barbershop, frowning slightly.

"It looks like it's over a pie shop! I could get something to eat while you get your haircut."

Rane seemed to contemplate, but finally, he shook his head. "Not today. I'll probably get it cut short just before we leave again."

Tala shrugged. "Alright." She glanced back to the barbershop. "If you want to come back here, it looks like this one's on Fleet Street."

Rane shook his head. "I'm sure there will be barbers closer to where I'm staying. Thank you, though."

Tala shrugged, and they continued on, talking about the various establishments that they passed. Even as they climbed higher, seeking the upper tiers, they kept up the conversation, pointing out various oddities, or intriguing places as they went.

All in all, it was a fun way to pass the time.

## Millennial Mage, 4 - Bound

\* \* \*

Tala took deep breaths, striding purposely away from the anchor that she'd just empowered.

The wooden spring-clip rested on the floor in the center of their new training area.

Tala walked toward the outer wall, a large, transparent section of wood that showed a beautiful view to the east.

She wasn't getting closer to the window. She could easily see the dimensional power acting on the space in front of her, but that was the only evidence that she could see that anything was happening.

She looked down, and the wood beneath her seemed to stretch as she moved her foot forward, pulling back to normal as she continued with the other foot.

With a sudden motion, Tala dove forward, sensing the space around herself expand even as she rolled and returned to her feet.

She was no closer to the wall.

Tala pivoted, turning to face the simple item, laying on the floor.

"Hey! You're alive." Rane grinned from beside the anchor.

She glared back. "I wasn't afraid of dying." Her glare faltered, and her voice quieted. "I was afraid of being trapped."

Rane's smile softened. "You alright?"

She shrugged, then nodded. "I think so."

"Alright, how can I help?"

"Can you pick it up?"

Rane picked it up with ease. "Seems so."

"What happens if you move away from me?" She was currently ten feet away, at the edge of the range.

Rane took a step, and Tala felt the world warp.

It was a completely different feeling than when she tried to move away from the anchor but somehow exactly the same.

She was holding her breath as she looked down.

The grain of the wood in front of her feet was compressing between her and the anchor, keeping the distance she perceived between her and the anchor in Rane's hand the same. Her perception of the world to either side was warping, like she was looking through an increasingly compressed lens.

She pulled in a breath, and her expanding chest felt like it was grabbed and pulled along. It wasn't a painful feeling, but it wasn't exactly comfortable. She was looking down when it happened, and she watched the floor expand, sliding under her feet even though she didn't *feel* like she was moving.

*This is… incredibly odd.*

Rane was watching her, walking backwards.

"What does it look like from your perspective?"

He was thoughtful for a moment. "Like you're sliding along the ground after me."

"What if something is in the way?"

Rane thought for a moment, then walked over to her and pulled out a large rock. It was so heavy that he had to use two hands to get it out of his dimensional storage before setting it down in front of her.

"Why do you have that?"

"Thought it might be useful?"

She narrowed her eyes at him, then examined the rock. As she examined it, she noticed that it had interesting striations, and even what appeared to be a few fossils embedded within it. "You thought it looked pretty."

He shrugged. "I… suppose that's true too."

"You found a pretty rock and wanted to keep it."

## Millennial Mage, 4 - Bound

He scrunched his face. "Fine. What's wrong with that? It's not like other people don't pick up rocks they find interesting."

"Most don't choose boulders."

He grunted. "So, are you ready?"

Tala grinned but nodded. "Fine by me."

Rane walked backwards, watching her closely.

As he got far enough that dimensionality began to warp around Tala, she moved her eyes to the rock.

It seemed to flatten before her, becoming thinner and thinner, until… it was gone. She looked behind herself and saw it sitting there, whole and unaffected. "That's strange…"

"From my perspective, you compressed vertically, for a flickering instant, to move over and past the rock."

*Just like the booklet said. What would it do for a solid wall?* Did she really want to experiment when it could just splatter her against the surface? *No, the instructions said that it would either bypass any barrier or break the connection until the barrier was removed.*

Tala caught up to Rane and took the anchor from him. "Now, let's try something odd."

"If you're sure."

She went to the far side of the room, anchor in hand, turned, and faced him. "Ready to catch?"

Rane gave her a searching look before hesitantly nodding. "Alright."

She'd been working on her throwing accuracy under various levels of gravity for days, now. So, she felt reasonably confident when she pitched the anchor toward her companion.

The world warped around her, and she lost her sense of balance, stumbling forward slightly.

"Tala!" Rane caught the anchor, concern evident on his features.

Tala, herself, dropped to one knee, pressing her forehead to the other knee. "Oh… that was rusting terrible. I'd be painting the floor, if I could puke." Even so, she had enough presence of mind to realize that she was now, indeed, only ten feet from where Rane had been when she tossed the anchor. "Do you think I can acclimatize myself to that?"

Rane sat beside her. "Honestly? If it's possible, it will be *very* hard."

"What if my eyes were closed?"

"Do you feel like it was your vision that caused the nausea?"

"…no…"

"Then that probably won't help." He patted her shoulder. "Come on, let's get some fresh air."

There was a balcony for just that purpose off to the side of their large training room, and he led her out into the steady breeze. He clipped her anchor to her belt as they walked.

The moving, fresh air helped almost immediately. "Thank you."

"Happy to assist."

Tala looked over the railing, down at the couple hundred-foot drop. "What would happen if I dropped the anchor over the side?"

Rane gave her a long look. "You aren't recovered, are you."

She thought about it for a long moment. "That's fair. I still feel…" She rubbed her upper chest and made a face. She felt like she was about to puke, but once again Holly's inscriptions prevented that. *I wonder if I'm going to wear through those at a really inconvenient time…*

"How's Mistress Odera doing?" Rane was clearly trying to change the direction of her thinking.

Tala shrugged. She and Mistress Odera had gotten in the habit of grabbing breakfast together, but Mistress Odera deflected all questions about herself. Tala was left basically recounting what and how she was training if she spoke at all. "She's… distracted. I've gathered that she drops through the Constructionists' every few days." She snorted a half-laugh. "So, she's done that twice. But I guess she likes talking with Master Jevin."

"I don't blame her. He's brilliant. I just wish I knew what to ask him."

"Still nothing from the books?" She knew that he wanted to have a better understanding of things before pestering the Paragon with questions.

Rane growled in irritation. "I've got a countdown at least. Apparently, I have three days before my soul has finally settled…"

Tala sighed. "Mine just keep giving me snark."

He smiled back at her but wisely didn't comment.

"Let's go get something to eat, then we can come back and train some more. I'm going a bit crazy."

"No."

Tala had already half turned away. "What?"

"I said no." He was giving her a half smile. "You still haven't gotten a lock through the wire ball, have you?"

Tala growled this time. "No. It's ridiculous. It's a stupid training method." She knew she sounded petulant, but it was *irritating*.

"Tell you what; When you can do it, I'll buy you dinner and take you somewhere fun to celebrate. But you have to try again, now."

She cocked an eyebrow. She thought through the offer before shrugging. *Can't hurt to try.*

She walked back inside, pulling out the first ball in Jevin's training set.

Thin wire surrounded the wooden ball within the most permeable of the spheres. The wires were coated with something to prevent them from rusting or spreading iron around, and that added a slightly reflective sheen to the metal.

Tala sat down, cross-legged, placing the wire ball in front of her on the floor.

Her left middle-finger pressed into her thumb, and she focused on the wooden ball.

Her attempted lock broke on the iron cage as it tried to settle through it. *Just like every time before.*

Rane sat across from her. "I've watched you try this, off and on, for days now. I think the issue is that you aren't using one of your greatest assets."

Tala looked to the Archon, eyebrow cocked. "Do tell."

"What does your lock look like to your magesight?"

"It makes the target glow."

Rane shook his head. "You've described your abilities to me before, and that's not true. The lock highlights the target for you, that's not a function of your magesight."

She opened her mouth to object, then stopped. *Huh... He's... he's right.*

Tala frowned, refocusing on her spell-working. Almost absently, she pulled out a bit of jerky and flicked it to the side for Terry, then she drew out a simple notebook, setting it beside the wire ball.

Thumb and middle-finger still pressed together, she focused on the notebook. She pulled as much power from the working's visualization as she could, while adding power to her magesight, causing even the slight magic in the air to become almost painfully bright.

Among the normally faint, swirling lines of power, Tala saw her lock; the magic had the look of a hand, reaching out and grabbing the notebook. As the fist closed, the book began to glow, indicating a successful lock.

"It's a hand, grabbing onto my target." And Tala felt a smile tug at her lips. Of course, it was a hand. She grabbed onto her target with her power, then she had the power to manipulate it. What else would it be?

He nodded. "That's what I've seen while watching. So, why? Why is it a hand?"

"I'm taking the target in hand." She shrugged. It just made sense.

"Could you use a tether? Or something else?"

Tala glanced to her bracers. Their connection to the anchor, currently on her belt, simply looked like a faint line of power, even with her magesight enhanced.

"That seems to work well enough, right?"

Tala grimaced. "I suppose so…"

"Your spell-lines don't require the visualization of a hand. The use of such likely makes it less efficient, honestly. You just don't need such a complicated construct of will. All you are doing is marking a target."

She released her lock on the book and focused. *All I need to do is mark it.* That was true. *How would I mark something?* She could use a brush to paint a dot. *That would be a lot simpler.*

In her mind, she imagined stretching out and painting a dot on the book. It made sense. Then, her magic would know what to affect.

She felt herself grinning. Her eyes opened, and she magically reached out to lock onto her notebook once more. She felt a small bit of power leave her, and a small mark blossomed on the book to her magesight before the book blossomed with a secondary glow, indicating it as a designated target.

Tala jerked, her left eye twitching violently. "*Ow!*" It felt like someone was driving a spike into her temple. She curled in on herself, taking deep breaths as the agony passed.

When she finally lifted her head, Rane was still sitting across from her, contained concern evident on his face. "Are you alright?"

She knuckled her forehead furiously scratching at an internal itching sensation. "Yeah, that was a *deep* mental pathway that I just bypassed."

Rane gave her a sympathetic smile. "I actually had something similar that Master Grediv had to break me of."

"Oh?" She was somewhat interested, but more, she needed time to collect herself.

"Yeah, I was imagining my defensive scripts pushing me; I was picturing hands imparting the energy. It was slower, less efficient, less precise, and more jarring." He gave a self-deprecating smile. "It took me weeks of work to change my way of thinking, but mainly because I refused to have Master Grediv help. He'd pointed out a flaw, and I wanted to correct it myself." His smile faded as he shrugged.

Tala smiled at that, the pain mostly gone. "That sounds so unlike you."

He snorted. "It is exactly as I was, and unlike how I strive to be, now." He quirked a half-smile.

"Well, I'm glad I had help."

"It's painful, but so long as you don't fall back in your thinking, you should be fine. I'd recommend practicing your lock as much as possible over the next few days. If I may ask, what did you replace the hand with? I can see a small splash of power, but I don't know how you enacted it."

"I imagined marking it with a small paintbrush."

# Millennial Mage, 4 - Bound

"That's a good one. Yeah, I'd recommend focusing on *marking* your targets, instead of grabbing, or indicating, or… whatever you were conceiving, before."

"I think it was simpler than that. I used my hand to activate the target process. So…" She shrugged.

Rane grinned. "That would do it. So, don't do that."

She snorted another laugh. "Fine."

She released and retargeted the book a dozen times, and when she was satisfied, she turned her eyes back to the wire ball.

With the practice and the new mental image, it was trivially easy to reach out, her power lancing through one of the gaping holes to mark the wooden ball, within.

"*Ha!*" Tala held her arms up in triumph. "I did it!"

Rane's eyes snapped open from his meditation, and he gave a seated, smiling bow. "Congratulations, Mistress."

*How long was I working on that?* Probably close to twenty minutes. *It was kind of him to leave me to it.* Tala stood. "You're right. I want to celebrate, what do you have in mind?"

He stood. "Well, you mentioned missing plays, so I got us two tickets to a show tonight: Hypocratease, a comedy about… well," he gave a small laugh, "that's probably pretty obvious."

"That sounds great." She hesitated, frowning. "Wait, you said we'd go if I succeeded."

"I did."

"But you have tickets for tonight."

"I do."

She gave him a long look. After a lingering moment, a smile pulled at the side of her lips. "We have time to get cleaned up and changed?" She gestured his way. "I think the theater would object to your current outfit."

Rane looked down at his bare chest and mid-thigh shorts. He laughed. "True enough. It'd be like walking in with a bared sword. Meet back here in half an hour?"

"That sounds perfect."

# Chapter: 26
# A Mild Combat Application

Tala leaned on the balcony, beside their training room, the midnight-sky stunningly beautiful overhead.

Her stomach was pleasantly full after the feast she and Rane had shared.

Her cheeks had echoes of soreness, despite her scripts. She couldn't remember having ever laughed so much at anything. It had been a magnificent farce.

Rane had dropped her off at the training room and headed up to his rooms in the upper reaches of Makinaven, leaving her alone with her thoughts.

Terry hadn't paid much attention to the play except to give her odd looks whenever she laughed, though he'd remained on her shoulder throughout the entirety.

At the moment, he was curled up in the corner sleeping once again.

As Tala thought back, a contentment settled into her being. She'd only been in Makinaven for eight days, but she was already falling into a pattern. Even the change of training venue wouldn't disrupt that. *But staying up much later than usual will.* She almost laughed at that. She was up later than she liked, but that seemed to be happening almost as often as not, these days.

*If I'm going to be here for another three weeks or so, I should take a venture out of the city with Terry.* The more she considered that, the more she liked it. *Terry could get us out past the defenses quite quickly, it could be a great day-trip. I've been training in too sterile an environment, and some actual combat would help settle all that I'm working on.*

She grinned to herself. *Hunt some arcanous beasts, do some more active training.* It would be perfect. *Another week?* She nodded. *Another week of training.*

She yawned, stretching toward the stars. *But now, bed.*

\* \* \*

Three days of intense training interspersed with plays, meals, and walks through the upper reaches of Makinaven passed without great incident.

Tala was practicing her throwing when Rane let out a triumphant laugh. "It's open to me!"

She didn't complain about her spoiled shot. After all, she needed to practice while distracted. Even so, she shot Rane an irritated glance. Her irritation was spoiled when she saw him holding a book. "Wait… Is that…?"

"Yes! 'Soul Work' is finally open to me."

Tala frantically pulled Kit open and retrieved her own copy. Almost shaking, she opened it and placed her palm on the first page, giving the book a look at her magic.

To Tala's magesight, an almost invisible, interwoven network of spell-lines began to unravel, pulling back and leaving the book utterly exposed, at her mercy.

A manic grin split her face, and she immediately sat, reading ravenously, her throwing practice forgotten for the moment.

From the other side of the room Rane groaned. "Great… I need to make another star. It's time for me to bond with Force."

Tala shot him a self-satisfied smile. She'd been recommending he do that for days, but he'd wanted to wait. *He's right often enough that this won't hurt him too much.*

He groaned. "Most of this is work with a soul-bond."

Tala did *not* gloat. She was too busy reading. She had kept up her own soul exercises, pulling Flow to her from varying, decreasing distances, in regimented sets specifically designed to strengthen that aspect of herself.

The first chapter of 'Soul Work' was a detailed breakdown of doing just that, with a few additional, surrounding details.

*Huh, I've been pulling on the link between us, but Flow can pull, too.* Obviously, it wouldn't move her, but it would greatly extend her potential range, if the knife was adding to the pull. *Like a kite reeling itself in, while I'm winding the line.*

The question was how to do it.

*Start small.*

She set Flow as far as she could easily reach without getting up. She then focused on the bond, pushing her will through it

Once she had a good hold over the connection, she did *not* pull on it, to draw Flow to her. No, she tried to will the knife to pull itself to her hand on its own.

She focused as Rane put on more socially polite clothing and departed, presumably heading to the market for another sapphire for his new Archon Star.

She searched with her will; she dug deep with her consciousness; she probed the extent of her bond with her internally directed magesight; and she referenced the book more times than she could count, parsing through every sentence of the advice and descriptions associated with the modified technique.

Finally, an indeterminate time later, Flow *snicked* into her palm, the weapon having pulled itself to her hand, at her command.

## Millennial Mage, 4 - Bound

Tala jumped, spinning in a circle and laughing maniacally. When no one commented, she took in her surroundings for the first time in what had clearly been hours.

The transparent wall looked out on a nighttime forest; Terry was sleepily gnawing on a large, leather ball that Rane had picked up for the avian a couple of days earlier; and Rane was deep in meditation, a small sapphire held in his hand and power pouring from him into the gem.

*Oh… That took me quite a while.* She glanced down at Flow in her hand, and the open 'Soul Work' on the floor beside her. *Well, then, that's a good start.*

She sat back down to repeat the process and brainstorm on how to integrate it into her training.

\*     \*     \*

Tala looked nervously across the training hall at Rane.

He held Force in a ready position, awaiting her attack. He hadn't bonded the weapon, yet, though he had created the star the evening before. He said he wanted to have Jevin inspect the weapon and the star before he merged them, just in case. Tala hadn't fought him on it. It was his bond, his soul, after all.

Tala took a deep breath, steadying her nerves. She wasn't nervous to fight him; they'd been doing that, uncounted times each day.

No, what had her nervous was the anchor, sitting on the floor between them. She'd experimented with the paired devices. She'd even been using them to allow her to run in the mornings without having to find a route. Yet, she'd not fought with the anchor active, not yet.

Tala charged forward, past the anchor, and engaged Rane sword to sword.

She was getting better, both in her ability with Flow and in her understanding of her increased physical attributes. Rane still overshadowed her with talent, training, and experience, but she was narrowing the gap, if slowly.

Her minor errors finally built up to the point that Rane was able to hit her with a horizontal slash, her block *just* out of position.

She shot sideways, eyes locked on her opponent.

She stopped moving away from him, though the air still rushed by her for another instant. Dimensional energy warped around her, expanding the space before her and keeping her from getting farther from her anchor.

As she came to the ground, tumbling slightly before rolling to her feet, she found herself still close to Rane. Still within striking distance.

He didn't let that go to waste.

Force struck her again, throwing her backwards and up this time.

Rane took off after her in a dead sprint.

When she reached the back edge of her tether's range, it looked like she jerked to a stop midair, though she still felt air rushing past her, even as she began to drop.

Rane was there before her feet touched the ground, but Tala got Flow up to block this time.

The concussion of Force against Flow radiated out, even as her feet returned to the springy wood of their training room. Rane was grinning wildly. "Oh, this is going to be amazing."

A range of twenty feet was hardly an expansive battlefield, and Tala would need to figure out how to move her anchor tactically, but it had worked.

She grinned in return. *Not perfect, but it is a wonderful improvement.*

## Millennial Mage, 4 - Bound

Rane usually launched her into the walls, ceiling, or floor with ease, causing extra damage and often dazing her, even if just momentarily. Now, his only option was the floor, and she was becoming more proficient at blocking overhead strikes from his massive sword. After all, she deeply disliked being slammed against the ground.

They spent most of the remainder of the day, and the two following, sparring with her tether active, only taking breaks to recover their strength and mentally process the previous bouts.

\* \* \*

Dawn broke early, though marginally later than the day before, and Tala shot out of bed with special alacrity. *Today is Terry adventure day!*

Rane was going to go visit the Constructionists and finally bond Force, and Tala and Terry were going to take a daytrip into the surrounding forests to hunt and shake off the building feeling of claustrophobia.

"Good morning, Terry!"

Terry flickered to her side, even as she climbed out of Kit.

She tossed him a bit of jerky before picking up the pouch and hanging it on her belt. She gave him a bit more as she moved through her morning routine.

Terry was patient enough, snatching up the occasional bit of jerky she tossed out in a random direction.

Soon enough, she was done, and they headed out of the training facility.

She'd arranged with Mistress Odera to miss their breakfast that morning, so the Mage wouldn't have to wonder where Tala had gotten to.

"Let's go!"

They walked out to the city spiral, exiting the training complex, and Terry immediately grew to a rideable size.

Tala thought for a moment, then clipped her anchor to his collar. She then climbed up, holding the collar and tucking her feet under his wings. One of her hands on Terry's collar also held the anchor. *If he flickers away, he'll leave it behind, but this way, I'll keep a hold of it.*

As soon as she was situated, Terry took off down the inside of the tree.

They'd discussed it in the previous days and decided to leave through the southern gate.

Well, that wasn't quite accurate. Tala had proposed various things, and Terry had squawked and trilled until she'd said things that he was Okay with.

That was fine. A large part of this was to let the terror bird have some unrestrained time, so his input held a lot of weight.

They shot out of the tree's southern gate. Entering the power-heavy air there at ground-level felt like running into a wet blanket, at least to her spiritual self.

Something about beginning the fusing process seemed to have sharpened her magical senses, at least slightly, and she could now tell that all this power, this ocean of magical might, was already bound to and controlled by someone.

The sense of their influence felt… familiar, but she couldn't place it. *I'll figure it out eventually, or I won't.*

She grinned. Today wasn't for contemplation; it was for adventure. It was for battle.

Terry hadn't slowed, and they were out from under Makinaven's tree with surprising speed.

In less than an hour, they were past the reach of its magical drain, into the wild forest in truth.

Terry gave a soft trill of warning before flickering away.

Tala dropped to her feet, clipping her anchor to her belt as she dropped.

Terry regarded her from around ten yards away.

"Go, hunt, have fun. I'll call you by name if I need help."

He waited a moment longer, then trilled happily and vanished.

Tala pulled out one of the large jars of pig's blood that she'd purchased from a butcher. *One silver per gallon.* Not cheap, but effectively much less expensive than bleeding a gallon from herself.

She uncapped the jar and poured it out on various rocks around the center of the clearing in which she stood.

The clearing was just over a two hundred feet across, surrounded by trees in a rough ring.

She then let out a call of challenge, careful to keep any fear from the sound. She didn't want another human hearing it and coming to assist her.

Her powerful lungs, and reinforced vocal cords, allowed for a *very* loud challenge.

Wind moving through the forests rustled the canopy overhead, carrying the scent of blood through the woods.

Less than a minute later, she heard the first answering challenge.

The basso roar caused the ground to tremble and her bones to shake.

*It's Okay, Tala. You got this.*

A creature, twice her height, came into view. It looked quite a lot like Terry, but with armored plates instead of feathers, and teeth instead of a beak, and instead of vestigial wings, it had front arms, baring vicious looking claws. *So, not much like Terry at all.*

It let out the too-low roar once again, its throat vibrating visibly as it generated the challenge.

Tala pulled out one of the tungsten balls, which had its gravity already reduced to near nothing, and pitched it at the massive, bipedal lizard with all her strength.

A five-foot crater blossomed at the impact site. Shrapnel shot out in all directions from the tree just beside and behind her target.

The beast jumped to the side, letting out a sound that evoked irritation and startlement in equal measures.

Tala grimaced at the hole in the middle of the crater in the tree. *Well, rust. That's going to be a pain to dig out.*

She called Flow to her hand, pushing power to form it into a glaive, even as she moved through the motions to throw the weapon.

This attack flew true… at least mostly.

Flow ripped past her opponent, taking off one of its front arms and gouging a sizzling chunk from its side as it passed.

Tala called Flow back before it could go too far, and was about to charge in, when three smaller creatures leapt out onto her first opponent, tearing it apart and taking it to the ground in moments.

The fallen lizard let out a confused final cry before the three smaller attackers ended its struggles.

The scent of blood had only grown, and now the smell of cooked meat had been added.

Tala could hear sounds from various distances all around her as predators, large and small, moved to investigate.

*Huh… This might not have been the most well thought out plan.*

\*     \*     \*

## Millennial Mage, 4 - Bound

Tala rolled across blood-soaked carcasses, which coated the ground, striking out at any opponent that came close.

The little valley had devolved into a melee long ago, but the predators just kept coming.

At some point, Terry had returned, following the tide of incoming targets, and he was exuberantly flickering through the churning, primal gore-fest, trumpeting in glee.

To Tala's best guess, the sound of fighting, combined with the smell of blood, and the already powerful draw of a human presence was driving the creatures into mad battle-lust. Most still retained enough cognizance to not attack those of their own kind, but that was it.

On the negative side, Tala had suffered numerous injuries—all healed now, of course—but they had pulled from her reserves, and that would pull from her budget. She had void-channels to her elk leathers and Kit, along with those to Flow, keeping them in top form and preventing the mounting damage from being too much.

If she'd had a goal to reach, or anyone else to protect, she'd have failed utterly. The only reason that she was still living at all, aside from Terry's occasional intervention, was that her presence seemed only to increase the creatures' ferocity, not cause them to target her, specifically.

*Stars be praised.*

On the positive side, she was practicing every skill and ability she had which had even a mild combat application.

She was throwing with a fair degree of accuracy.

She'd been able to pull out gravity-enhanced balls and arches, dropping them at opportune moments. The first few had done little, but she was working out the kinks.

She'd used her gravity manipulation on a full four creatures at the same time, increasing two and reducing the other two. That had come after many failures, but even still, she felt like it was a tremendous accomplishment.

Her sword and glaive work had taken on new shape and meaning to her as she battled for her life. The sharp, crisp movements of the weapons' techniques had morphed into brutally efficient strikes, blocks, and deflections. Flow seemed to be thrumming with power alongside her, its shape shifting between the three forms as easily as water filled a cup.

And she felt *alive*.

Every movement was precise. Every mistake was punished, and every intuition tested.

It was glorious.

The ground couldn't absorb any more blood, though that quagmire was covered with no small number of bodies. The depression between trees was beginning to resemble little more than a shallow pool of dark red liquid filled with islands of the dead.

Still, arcanous beasts came.
Still, Tala, Flow, and Terry reaped a crimson harvest.
Still, the sun moved up the sky, ever closer to noon.

## Chapter: 27
## Murder Dell

Tala lay, sprawled out atop the heaving back of a massive bear as its breathing slowed and finally stopped.

*Last one.*

She jerked Flow out of the carcass, letting it shift from its glaive form back to that of a knife.

Tala tried to ignore the wet slurping sounds as Terry flickered around the clearing, devouring the mangled, blood-marinated bodies of the fallen.

She groaned and started stretching on the tangled hair of the great beast below her.

As the bodies disappeared one by one, the thrashed, soaking ground was revealed more and more.

The noon-time sun shone down on the canopy above, filling the space with clear green light, interspersed with shafts of untinted sunlight.

In the green light, the ground looked mostly black, and only the smell indicated what it really was. The interspersed patches of white light highlighted the crimson color of what lay below, making the terrain resemble blood-stars in a dark sky.

Some fur and detritus still smoldered, though Terry seemed to have prioritized those beasts. Apparently, he liked a smoky flavor. *That tracks with his love of jerky, I suppose.*

The smell of cooked meat was almost as strong as that of blood and gore. A surprising number of beasts had been able to augment themselves with, or breathe out, fire. *How a forest survives with so much fire magic within it, I've no idea.*

Additionally, her every cut with Flow had left cooked meat in its wake.

"You know, Terry, I was planning on harvesting some of those."

Terry looked her way, the tail of a massive lizard hanging from his mouth. He threw his head back and let the remainder of the creature slide down his gullet before returning his gaze to her. He trilled questioningly.

"I know you helped. I'm not asking you to starve. I just want to collect some things first." She looked around. "Well, at least from the few that are left."

Terry looked around at the few bodies remaining, then squawked and settled down to wait.

"Thank you."

Tala looked down on the carnivore below her. The bear had stood three times her height and breathed fire. *Probably called a Blaze Bear, or something silly like that.*

If she were being honest, this bear had killed the majority of opponents there at the end. The arrival of it, and one other like it, had heralded the final phase of the skirmish.

Tala had only slain this one by coming at it from behind as it roasted a wolf pack, which had tried to challenge it for some food.

"How am I going to move this?" She looked at her bracers and anchor. "You know, if I could get you registered as the target, then simply walk away with the anchor…" She bit her lip in thought. "What if I asked Master Jevin to make some target darts, or something. I could then use those to tie enemies to the same anchor I'm linked to. That would be useful in all sorts of ways…" She nodded. It was worth asking. "Include the inner defenses for those? Keep them from grabbing the anchor and running?" She clicked her tongue.

While promising, the *idea* wasn't particularly helpful to her current situation.

She gave the bear a weary sigh. "I don't really want to skin you in a blood-puddle." She glanced to Terry. "Are you willing to help me move these bodies?"

Terry let out a descending series of short trills, suddenly growing to twice the size of the bear.

With quick motions, he flickered to each body, picked it up in his beak and walked to a nearby rise before setting it down. Last of all, he came for the massive bear, and Tala had to hop off.

Her feet squelched in the thickening muck, the paste-like substance working its way between her toes. *What happens when blood dries and hardens when mixed with dirt?*

She scraped her tongue across her teeth, unconsciously trying to get an imagined taste off of it. "That's gross…"

She took high, long steps, trying to get out of the muck as quickly as possible. By the time she got to the rise, all the animals were laid out and ready for her ministrations.

*Now, Mistress Ingrit gave me a list of the best harvests in this area. Let's see how many I can find.* There were other things that would be of use to her, and even more that her magesight could guide her to. All told, there would be plenty for her to gather up.

She looked to Flow, in its knife form. *Shouldn't cook anything in this form.*

That decided, she went to work, directed by Mistress Ingrit's list and her own magesight and desires.

\*       \*       \*

# Millennial Mage, 4 - Bound

It was midafternoon by the time that Tala had finished harvesting, and Terry had eaten the last of the remains.

The bird didn't really seem to care what he ate, as he ate the gut piles as readily as the other organs and the meat.

Tala didn't really want to eat meat from carnivores, so she'd left that to Terry, but she had gotten two massive bear-hides. One from her final kill, and one that was barely smaller. The beast had been gutted, probably by Terry.

The hides were so heavy that she had a hard time moving them around, even with her enhanced strength. Not only did they have a heavy coat of thick fur that was far from clean, but the hide, itself, was nearly four inches thick.

They had been a *pain* to stuff into Kit. Though, she assumed that Kit would debride them for her, so that made it worth the effort.

*This might cost more than I'm willing to pay to tan...* She'd had that thought before, but she'd figured that she could probably pay a tanner one of the hides to tan the other for her.

In addition, she'd gotten a large number of bones and claws, which had drawn her attention due to the magic within them. She'd coated them in iron-salve and stored them within Kit. Some of those had been on Ingrit's lists, some hadn't.

Her list had contained other oddities, including the *left* eye of one of the creatures. Tala had looked closely and, indeed, the two eyes did have subtle differences to her magic sight. *The more you know.*

She'd collected everything she could and was quite satisfied with the haul. *It would have been better if Terry and I had talked first.* That was on her, though. She didn't feel any ill will toward Terry.

"Well, Terry?"

He flickered to her shoulder and head-butted her cheek.

"I'm glad you had fun." She almost turned to go, but her eyes passed over a tree with a large crater in it. "Oh… right." She wasn't used to having weaponry that needed to be retrieved after a battle. She'd not been one of those helping to get the guard's bolts back on the caravan trip, and so, she wasn't even used to retrieving *others'* weaponry.

Tala sighed. "Let's see how many we can find."

It took another two hours to gather up her tungsten balls and metal arches. Blessedly, she'd been able to find all of her weaponry. That was probably only because each had their gravity altered. Because of that alteration, they practically blazed to that portion of her sight. Thus, while it wasn't quick, nor easy, to scrape through the muck, as soon as the smallest portion was within her line of sight, she noticed the item instantly. She could even often catch a glimpse of the altered gravity through intervening barriers. *I should practice that portion of my sight as well.*

None of the gravity-altered items had been anywhere near clean, but Tala trusted Kit to deal with the filth, and just dropped the items in as she found them. Well, none had been clean except those from Terry.

Terry had helped by hacking up three of the balls that had apparently been embedded in parts of his feast. *Good to know that he can bring things back out…* She tried not to think about that.

Those three balls had come back to her practically scoured clean.

She didn't think she wanted to know what Terry had in his gut that worked so quickly. *No chance of getting harvest back, now…*

Tala turned her focus elsewhere, once again trudging free of the slowly hardening slurry.

She was *starving*.

While Tala hadn't taken any large hits, the cumulative damage that she'd had to heal had taken more from her reserves that morning than she'd used during the entire trip from Bandfast to Makinaven, even taking into account the regrowing of her arm.

*Yeah… this was not the wisest choice. I'll need to figure out a safer way of doing this for next time. Even if I get a lot of gold from this, it's going to take a lot of food to replenish, and I'll be vulnerable until then.*

One of her most obvious mistakes was that she'd only drunk a small amount of endingberry juice, thinking that she'd be doing small fights and could top off as needed in the lulls. There hadn't been any lulls, and the endingberry power she'd had was quickly spent.

"I need some food…" *And juice…* She drank a cup of the powerful juice to be safe. *My reserves are low. I do* not *want to get caught out without proper defenses.*

Terry cocked his head and trilled.

"Yeah, I do have some…" That was a good point. She should probably try some of her solo-venturing food. "Let's get away from that, though." She tilted her head to the pungent dell. "I'm sure something will come by, eventually, and I've had enough fighting for the day."

Terry squawked his agreement and flickered to stand beside her, sized for riding.

She mounted up, clipping her anchor to his collar again, and they were off in search of a more secluded spot, far from the murder dell they'd created.

*We could go back to the city, get this stuff sold, then eat?* No, she should eat sooner than that.

Less than ten minutes later, Terry trilled and flickered away, dropping her on the top of a hill with good sightlines. A splattering of dried blood and muck fell free as well. "Thank you, Terry."

She was about to start making her food when she caught a good look at her hands. *Oh, I'm the one who put all that on Terry...*

Her hands were quite literally blood-stained, caked with muck, and filthy beyond belief. "Bath first."

It took her over an hour to get truly clean. She really hadn't realized how pervasive the filth had been, as she'd had to scrub blood out of all sorts of places. She'd scrubbed, soaked, scraped, and scoured, and that was just for her skin. Her hair was a different story.

She had not been willing to risk her comb, as it was *not* designed to deal with such clinging filth.

In the end, all her efforts on that front were for naught, and she'd had to use Flow to shave her scalp, allowing her scripts to regrow her hair once more.

A quarter hour later, she was dressed and sitting on the little hill, feeling refreshed and untainted at last. She grimaced briefly at the memory of what she'd removed but didn't let it overshadow her much improved mood.

*Now, food.*

She pulled out the cauldron, setting it on a relatively flat patch of earth and wiggling it to settle the heavy cookpot into a stable position. She then took out her hot air incorporator and removed Flow from her belt. She set both into the cauldron, making sure they were in contact with each other, and used her bond to the knife to connect a large void-channel to the incorporator, causing fairly hot air to blast around the cookpot's interior.

*There, preheating the cauldron should help it cook the food faster and more efficiently.*

While she waited for the cauldron to heat, Tala looked through the little booklet that Atrela had given her to decide what she wanted to eat. Absently, she made herself some tea: mint this time. The process had become rote, almost meditative, for her over the past weeks. So, it didn't distract from her perusal of menu options.

She took her time, pulling out the dried or otherwise preserved ingredients and following the directions in the little book. *If you're going to do it, do it right.* She could modify the recipes later, once she knew how they would turn out when following the instructions.

In no time at all, she was ready to combine what she'd prepared.

She pulled Flow and the hot air incorporator from the cauldron, placing the latter into Kit.

The starter ingredients went into the now pleasantly warm pot, and she filled a good portion with near-boiling water from her hot-water incorporator.

She stirred those initial ingredients, realizing that she didn't really have a way to add more heat. *Oh… that's a bit foolish of me.* The hot air incorporator just wasn't hot enough, and she didn't want to constantly add water.

*Maybe if I had a larger pot, that this one fit inside? I could have more water around it…* No, that was just adding complication. *So, I need a hot air incorporator that's closer to a baking temperature. I seem to remember that people have tried baking with them before. So, there should be schemata for those higher temp ranges.*

She sighed. *Another expense.*

Still, the meal was coming along nicely.

It wasn't stew; stew would take hours to properly cook.

No, this was a thick, noodle soup with a selection of vegetables and a spice packet added.

The spice-pack was a simple, sealed waxed-paper envelope that Tala had torn open and dumped into the water.

Less than five minutes after adding the hot water, it was done, and she had nearly a gallon of tasty soup.

It wasn't as hot as she'd have liked, or as the ingredients really needed, so the noodles and veggies were a bit chewier than ideal, but it tasted *so good.*

Hunger really was an amazing spice, and Tala had that in gold.

There was some bread in her stores as well, and she used that to complement the soup, just as the little book had suggested.

In the end, she used the last of the bread to clean the final bits of soup from the cauldron.

A healthy application of incorporated hot water helped clean out the cookpot, and she placed everything back into Kit.

Her meal finally complete, she tossed another bit of jerky for Terry, and laid back, staring up at the canopy overhead.

"That was a good idea, Terry. Thank you."

The avian head-butted the top of her head.

"Yes, the battle was fun, too, but I think we might have jumped into the deep end with that one."

Terry trilled.

"Yes, you were amazing. You'd have been fine."

He let out a bit of a warbling note.

"Oh? That was more than you've tried before?"

He bobbed a nod.

"You know, I feel like I'm understanding you more and more."

He bobbed again.

"Good." She grinned. "You are a scary, terrifying creature, but you're *my* terrifying creature, my partner."

He trilled and head-butted her again before curling up beside her head and closing his eyes.

## Millennial Mage, 4 - Bound

Tala lay there for long minutes, on the edge of wakefulness.

*What should I focus on when I get back to Makinaven?* She needed to sell her harvests, get the hides to a tanner, and meet back up with Rane. *And eat more. So much more.*

That reminded her that she needed to get an oven-hot air incorporator.

She thought back on the melee. Her excellent memory let her move through the battle again, in slow motion, and she critiqued herself, giving silent praise for wise or skillful maneuvers and sighing at points where she'd made mistakes.

Whenever she came to one of the mistakes, she would pause her recollection, analyzing what had led to the action or choice. Usually, the correct choice presented itself, and she was able to work through her thinking and reactions that could lead to a better choice in the future, adding that to her mental training regimen.

In some cases, she was forced to admit that, mistake though it was, it had been the best she could have done in the moment. That led her to go back through the moments leading up to the incidents, searching for where she'd gone wrong among her good choices.

*Turns out you can back yourself into a corner with purely good reactions.* She'd known that, obviously, but it had never been as apparent as it was now, looking at the ordered chaos of brutal conflict.

She passed an unknown amount of time in that meditative state of purposeful recollection and critique.

A screech resonated through the woods, coming from the direction of their murder dell.

Tala's eyes snapped open, and she was on her feet before she registered moving.

A second screech resounded between the trees, and Tala was sure she knew what made the sound.

She'd been sure with the first, but she'd hoped she was wrong.

Leshkin had found the murder dell.

# Chapter: 28
# Choose Wisdom

Tala quickly swept her rest spot, tucking the couple of odds and ends that she'd left out into Kit.

"Terry."

Terry was already beside her, sized for riding.

Tala wanted to go, investigate the Leshkin, and slay what she found. *But that's not the wise course. I have no one out here to protect, no goal other than survival. I should go the other way.*

In her mind, the juggernauts loomed large, exuding terror.

That fear made her want to charge toward the unknown Leshkin, to prove that she wasn't afraid with each slain member of their cursed race.

*No, Tala. That is not courage. That is just letting your fear rule you in a different way.*

Tala growled, clipping her anchor to Terry's collar and swinging up onto his back.

The terror bird looked back to her, a clear question in his eyes. *Which way should we go?*

She'd watched the Leshkin harm so many, even killing some of those under her protection. She wanted revenge.

But that was foolish. Even if the exact Leshkin who had caused those deaths were, indeed, near the murder dell, destroying their bodies wouldn't do anything permanent to them.

She could go, hunt down their hatchery, or nursery, or wherever their heartseeds were stored.

*And that is even more foolish, Tala. You could do that once you've elevated yourself another few steps and you've equipped yourself properly, but even then, it would still probably be foolish.*

She thought of Jevin, then. A powerhouse, equipped with the best the Constructionists could put together, and a truly god-like being, at least within a certain radius.

*If he hasn't wiped them out, there must be a reason. It must be harder than I'm imagining.*

She thought about that for a long moment. What was she imagining?

In her mind's eye, she pictured herself and Terry breaking through and around juggernaut guards and into a long building, full of pulsing, fleshy seeds.

She would run down the aisles, Flow outstretched, wreaking havoc and a harvest of death upon the enemy of humanity.

She snorted a laugh. *Yeah… I'm definitely oversimplifying the task.*

She sighed. The wise course was obvious. It was also obviously not what she wanted to do.

*Wisdom. I have to choose wisdom to grow in wisdom… even when I don't want to.*

"Makinaven, Terry. Let's go."

Terry bobbed a nod even as he turned, crouched low, and took off at a sprint, heading north, back toward the city-in-a-tree.

\* \* \*

They passed the draw-down line without incident, but Tala stayed vigilant, keeping a wary eye on the surrounding trees.

Terry continued to sprint through the woods without slowing.

It was only then that Tala remembered that Terry didn't really have any recourse against the Leshkin. He must have wanted to leave from the moment they heard the first cry.

She leaned a bit farther forward and patted the avian's neck. "Thank you, Terry."

He turned his head slightly to the side to glance back at her momentarily.

"Thank you for staying with me and being willing to let me come to the wise choice."

He trilled in happy acknowledgement.

Soon after, they came into the clearing around the great tree, and Tala took a steadying breath. *I know running from your fears makes them worse, but it was still the right call.*

It was mid-afternoon, and mundane citizens were working all throughout the vast open expanse.

The strong scent of mint was carried on the breeze, and Tala found herself grinning. *Right, wasn't the tea-brick seller connected with a large farm to the south? Lots of mint, indeed.*

She didn't stop or seek out the source of the scent. There would be no real point.

The power in the air was, again, almost smothering. *I swear the signature feels familiar.*

It was hardly the time to investigate that, so she pushed it to the back of her mind.

Tala asked Terry to slow as they approached the southern gate, and she called out to a guard. "Hello there!"

"Greetings, Mistress. How can we assist you, today?"

"I'm looking for a skilled tanner for beast hides."

The man looked up, clearly considering. "I'm sorry, Mistress, but I don't know of one. If you can wait, I can go ask our Master Sergeant. She should know."

Tala nodded. "Thank you; I don't mind waiting. Are you sure it's alright? I don't want to get you in trouble."

He smiled and gave a half-bow. "It would be my pleasure, and duty, to serve." He turned and went through a well-hidden door, just inside the gate's arch.

Tala had only waited for about five minutes before the guard returned with a scrap of paper.

"Here you are, Mistress. Just east of us, here." He gave her further directions, then handed her the paper with another description of how to find her destination.

"Thank you, guardsman. Take care."

He waved goodbye as Terry turned and took off toward the tanner. *A business fully outside the city proper.* She shook her head. The forest cities had many, many oddities it seemed, and Tala was starting to enjoy most of them quite a bit.

\* \* \*

Tala found the tanner to be quite reasonable, and they did settle on a payment of one hide to tan the other. When she returned, she would get to select between the two hides and take the one she preferred, so Tala didn't really see any way she could lose out.

That accomplished, she and Terry returned to Makinaven, thanked the guard, and entered through the southern gate.

It was still late afternoon, so she wasn't sure where Rane would be.

*He'll probably be either with Master Jevin or back in the training hall we're using.*

She decided to drop through the Constructionist Guild. If nothing else, she needed an oven-air incorporator. Thankfully, the stipend had come in, and her debt with the Constructionists had been cleared.

In no time at all, Terry had flickered to her shoulder, and Tala was pushing open the door into the Constructionists' third tier compound.

"Mistress Tala?" The greeting mostly overrode the standard chime sounding in the back rooms.

"Master Grent?"

"Hello! Welcome." He gestured expansively. "Good to see you back here." He said a few quiet words to the assistant he'd been dialoguing with upon Tala's entrance. As the assistant departed, Grent turned back to Tala, a genuine smile across his face. "How can I assist you today?"

"Well…" She thought for a moment, then shrugged. "I have some harvests to sell, an incorporator to buy, I'm interested in what watches you have on hand, and…" She contemplated for a moment. "I think that's it."

He nodded to her. "Certainly. Right this way. I'll take you to an acquisitions room. You can lay out your harvests there, and we can go over what they're worth."

Ten minutes later, Tala, Terry, and Grent regarded two large tables covered in a single layer of harvests.

"What did you do, Mistress?"

She frowned his way. "What do you mean?"

"There are harvests here from a half-dozen species, all predators. Did you go hunting or something?" After a moment, he shook his head. "No, that's silly. Why would you track down all of these individually…? They don't seem to have any magic about them any longer, so are you selling them just as materials? Did you find them in some uber-predator's den?"

Tala picked up one of the claws and scraped off the layer of iron-salve.

Grent took it from her and sighed. "Why the rust would you coat these in iron?"

"To preserve their power?"

"Why not get an iron box?"

"This is more efficient?"

"Power-wise, yes, but you can't reuse this…" He ran his thumb over it. "Salve? A box is a one-and-done purchase." He looked around. "I suppose you'd need a lot of boxes…" He frowned. "So, have you been hoarding these? Bringing them all at once to… what? Get a higher rate for the lot? That's not usually how it works."

"No, I killed these today."

He stopped, set down the claw, and turned to face her. "Mistress Tala."

"Yes?"

"I think you have a story to tell."

She hesitated, then grinned. "For the right price, as an addition to the sale? I can work with that."

Grent laughed. "Sure." He went through every item, only scraping holes in a few random layers of salve to verify they all had the same level of power held within. He then carefully smoothed over the breach to keep the power well contained. "Well, these are all of the highest quality, but I would expect that even from unsealed harvests the day of their acquisition."

"So? How are we looking?"

"I don't know what sort of behavior I'll be encouraging if I buy these…" He gave her a searching look.

"I'm not telling you the story before I sell."

His mask broke, and he grinned. "Twenty gold for the harvests, and ten for the story."

She narrowed her eyes at him. "These are worth at least thirty gold, without the story."

He nodded, waggling his head noncommittally as he scratched his chin. "So then, thirty gold for the harvests, and I'll buy you coffee? You tell me the story while we drink."

She huffed a laugh, shaking her head. "You said, yourself, that these are from a wide variety of creatures. These have to be worth more than thirty."

"Oh, of course they are, and if you'd like to hunt down individual buyers, you could easily get forty, maybe even fifty, but we can't pay you that."

Tala tsked. "The seal on them is near perfect. They won't degrade, so you won't take a loss, even if it takes you a long time to find a use or a buyer."

"True enough."

"Forty."

"Thirty-five, and the story."

Tala groused for a moment. "Wait! We still need to look into the incorporator, and the watch."

Grent paused. "Ah, right." He picked up the slate he'd been working on and searched through. "What temperature do you want?"

"I don't have a specific temperature that I want. The most efficient?"

He hesitated. "What do you want it for?"

Tala explained what she wanted it for.

After a moment's contemplation, he nodded. "Well, if you don't want to go the most efficient route, we have a masterwork schema that might interest you."

"A masterwork?"

"Something a master Constructionist devoted their career to perfecting."

"Like the failed coffee incorporator."

He quirked a smile at that. "I suppose you could consider that in the same vein, but for it to be truly considered a masterwork, they would have needed to keep going, perfecting it, and making numerous versions until it worked the way they wanted."

Tala nodded. "Ahh, I see. So, what's this schema?"

"If you've got an output that can handle fifty mana per second, then—"

Tala held up her hand, stopping him, and sighed. "At my *best*, I can manage just more than that, but not for long."

He quirked an eyebrow at her. "Ahh, right. Not Fused yet."

"What's that supposed to mean?"

He grinned. "It's not a secret, not really. Once you're fully Fused, you're better able to pull power into this world; your gate is more 'physical,' and your body more 'spiritual,' and all that. Your throughput will at least double. It usually does great things for capacity, too."

*And I've another motivation to finish crocheting myself together.* "Good to know."

"Well, when you're Fused, we've a masterwork schema that we can make for a gold."

"That's a bit expensive."

"It's a variable temperature, breathable air incorporator. It can generate consistent temperature air, anywhere in the baking range."

"I thought changing temperatures caused the entire schema to have to be reworked."

He grinned. "That's why this is a masterwork. It has many interlocking and interlinking layers that connect and lose contact as you rotate one of the outer rings, forming the desired incorporator for the various temperatures."

Tala found herself nodding. "But it's not very good at any of them. Hence the efficiency issues."

"Precisely."

"Well, I'll keep that in mind. Maybe I'll upgrade later."

"Sure. Then with only one temperature, I'd recommend the hottest possible. You can then treat it like a fire and just feather the throughput to manage cooking temperatures. It's not precise, but you probably don't need it to be."

"Sounds good to me."

"Great, I've got one on hand. We made it a couple of days ago for a potter who wanted to do low-temperature glazing, but it turns out that his Mage son wanted to go into a different line of work. I won't bore you with the details, but suffice it to say I've got one that should work for you. A hot bit of slag, honestly." He clicked his tongue. "I'll throw in a set of tongs; I don't want you burning yourself on our products. This is *broiling* temperatures, you understand."

"That sounds great. Is it a standard incorporator?"

"Yup, standard rate."

Tala nodded. "And for a watch?"

"Well… what do you want it for? Do you need to know what time it is, all the time?"

"No, I just want to be able to tell, when it's important."

"Then, why not get an Archive tablet? It can do that, too. Plus, they're dead useful."

Tala considered for a long moment, then sighed and shook her head. "I need to talk with… a friend before I buy an Archive tablet. Something tells me she'll have a *lot* to say on the subject." *Mistress Holly has a set of inscriptions, which I think allow her to act as an Archive-connected tablet without the device. It's about time I got the story behind that, and maybe the same functionality.*

"As you say." He shrugged. "Do you want to see what else we have available?"

"No, but thank you. I think your idea's a good one; I just need to wait." *I wonder what all I'll be able to do with it, and what exactly it will require.*

He nodded. "Alright, then. These harvests and your story to me; thirty-four gold, seventy silver, a broiler-incorporator, and tongs to you."

"Thirty-*five* gold, incorporator, tongs, coffee, and pastries, then you get the story."

He scratched the side of his chin, then gave a half-smile. "Done!"

"A sufficient quantity of coffee and pastries for me."

He hesitated. "Why do I get a feel that that means something more than I realize?"

"Are you a gambling man?"

He gave her a long look. "No. Maximum four cups of coffee and half a dozen pastries."

Tala sighed. "Fine…"

His eyes widened. "How many would you have needed?"

"You'd have had to buy out a bakery." She gave him a wink. "Do we have a deal?"

He held out his hand. "Deal."

\* \* \*

Tala leaned back, washing down her sixth pastry with the last of her final cup of coffee. "So, I decided I didn't want to risk a fight with Leshkin and returned home."

Grent was staring at her with obvious incredulity.

"Any questions?"

"How… How are you alive?"

"Was I not clear in the story?"

"Oh, I understand how you survived today, but how does someone who'd do *that* survive long term?"

Tala grimaced at that. "I don't do things like that often. I was trying to give Terry, here, a nice day out."

Terry trilled happily, without moving.

Grent gave the terror bird a sidelong look. "And he's not your familiar, yet?"

"Nope."

He grunted. "Okay." After a moment, he asked, somewhat hesitantly, "You know, from your story, you should have had a *lot* more harvests than you brought in."

Tala hadn't wanted to divulge that Terry could eat as much as he had, or much else about the terror bird that wasn't required for the story. "Well, the Leshkin did arrive before I could harvest from more than I brought to you." Technically true.

He gave her a long look. "So it seems." He seemed to consider for a long moment. "You know, not many people can engage that number of opponents and leave harvestable materials."

"Oh?"

Grent nodded. "There are tons who could eviscerate, immolate, disintegrate, or otherwise obliterate so many enemies. Most much faster, actually, but none would leave a harvest to be reaped."

"What's your point?"

"You could make a killing as a harvester." He grinned. "Pun very much intended."

She huffed a laugh. "I've thought about it, but I don't know that I want that much danger, constantly."

"Well, think it over. Harvesters don't get any base pay, but they still can make a lot of coin…"

Tala cocked her head. "What's the rest?"

He sighed. "The saying is that harvesters are like gilt paper, they are inundated in gold, for as long as they last."

"Low survival rate?"

## Millennial Mage, 4 - Bound

"Very. That is actually one of the chief reasons harvests still command such a sum. There are usually only a couple of harvesters per city, and that's a maximum. Here? We've one, that I know of, though a few wanderers come through now and again."

"So, why form a guild? Why should I even consider joining such a guild?"

"Ready market for the harvest?" He shrugged. "You seem to have good info, but some of the most expensive harvests are hard to find buyers for, and many of the most common ones aren't always in demand."

Tala scratched her cheek. "I'll consider it, but I think I'm happy as I am, for now." *Might be worth doing some harvesting day-trips, though, between caravan runs.* "Well, thank you for the coffee and pastries."

They stood, and Grent offered her his hand. "Mistress Tala, it's been a pleasure."

"Likewise, Master Grent. I hope we see each other again, sometime."

He paused before asking in a rush, "What about tomorrow?"

Tala hesitated. "Oh?"

"We could grab coffee again, maybe in the morning. I'd love to hear about your other ventures."

Tala shrugged. "I'm sure you've done more exciting things than I have."

"Well, we can swap stories then?"

She paused, considering. *It's just coffee, Tala.* "Sure. Meet at the Constructionists' compound?"

"That sounds like a plan. Nine?"

"I have a breakfast appointment. Could we do ten?"

"Sure. See you then."

They walked to the door, side by side, both feeling a bit awkward at having finished their conversation then heading in the same direction.

Blessedly, once they were outside, Grent headed down and Tala headed up.

"Take care!"

Tala waved over her shoulder, Terry already standing beside her, ready to ride. "See you tomorrow."

## Chapter: 29
## Together

Tala stood up as Rane entered their training room. Rane pulled to a stop, seemingly not having expected to find her here.

She grinned. "So…? Can I see Force? Were there any changes?"

After another moment's hesitation, Rane grinned. "You spoiled the big reveal I was planning."

She shrugged. "Sorry, but I want to see it."

He snorted a laugh and pulled out his sword. There were, indeed, changes.

If someone had taken the large weapon, shattered it, and rebuilt it with liquid sapphire to hold the pieces together, Tala would expect a similar result.

The wood of the weapon seemed to have been refined, somehow, and there was a blue tint to that part of the sword as well. The entire weapon *almost* seemed to glow.

Tala nodded appreciatively. "That is beautiful."

"Care to test? Force against Flow?" Rane was smiling quite happily.

Tala drew Flow, immediately forming it into a sword.

Rane lifted his hands in mild panic. "Wait! Training scabbard."

Tala glanced at her weapon and sighed. She'd still had it freed from the fight, earlier. "Right…" Flow returned to the shape of a knife, and she bound the sheath around it. Again, the weapon grew. "Shall we?"

## Millennial Mage, 4 - Bound

Rane responded by throwing his sword. Tala easily side-stepped the attack, giving Rane a quizzical look.

Realization struck, then, and she spun to deflect Force coming at her from behind... only to see it laying in the corner, having slid across the floor.

Frowning, she turned back just in time for Rane's fist to land, high up on her cheek.

She was momentarily dazed as she took a single, staggering step backwards. Rane, for his part, shook out his hand even as he tripped her.

Tala had recovered enough to execute a controlled fall, rolling back to a standing position a few feet away.

Rane was cursing under his breath before giving her a mild glare. "Ow! What are you made of these days?"

Tala grimaced rubbing her cheek. "Same as before." She shook her head. "I can't believe I fell for that. Can you even call your bound weapon to you?"

Rane grinned, holding out his hand.

"I'm not falling for that—"

Force slammed into her back, throwing her forward and back to the ground.

Rane laughed as he caught his weapon. "I can't do it more than a couple times, but Force's magics make it a pretty useful attack."

Tala groaned in agreement, pushing herself back to her feet once again. Flow could cut on a return path, maybe burn a little, when not sheathed, but that was pretty much it. The way Force was designed, it would be almost as effective in flight as when wielded by Rane, himself.

She narrowed her eyes. "Force was designed for use as a soul-bound weapon, wasn't it." It really wasn't a question.

"I told you so, didn't I?"

She tsked. "Yeah, I suppose you did. Any new functionality?"

"Aside from the bond, I can alter the edge and shape of the… force." He quirked a half-grin. "I have it blunted, now, but I seem to be able to refine it into a true cutting attack."

Tala nodded. "Impressive."

"Thank you."

"Again?"

"Again."

They sparred uncounted bouts as the afternoon faded toward evening.

Tala picked herself up off the floor, vaulting back to her feet one final time. "I thought I had you there."

Rane wiped sweat from his forehead, even as he sheathed Force. "You are getting much better. I want to meditate on our matches, then I'll head to bed."

Tala glanced to the darkening sky, just visible between the edge of the canopy overhead and the trees surrounding Makinaven. "That's fair, I suppose." She replaced Flow onto her belt.

Rane took a deep breath and smiled. "So, what are your plans for tomorrow?"

\* \* \*

Tala rolled her eyes as Rane paced back and forth.

"You have a date, with a Refined?!"

"You can say that as many times as you want, it doesn't make it any more true."

"Coffee," he ticked items off on his fingers, "pastries, talking. That's a date."

"It's two people learning from each other."

He turned toward her, meeting her gaze. "Is that how he sees it?"

"How should I know? Why should I care?" Her eyes narrowed. "Why do you care?"

Rane growled. He opened his mouth, then closed it several times, before he turned and he continued to pace. Finally, he groaned. "It's taking time from our training…?"

*That sounds inaccurate. He doesn't even believe that himself.* "You don't have to tell me why it bothers you, Rane, but I don't need your permission. Now, aside from that, and my breakfast with Mistress Odera, I've got nothing planned. That *is* what you asked, right?"

Rane had stopped his pacing and turned toward her once more. After a moment, he grimaced, then took a deep breath and let it out slowly. "That is what I asked… yes."

"Well, alright, then. Why do you ask?" She tried to steer the conversation from the oddly touchy subject.

He seemed to war within himself, before sighing. "It might be a bit silly, but I've bound Force, and I wanted to celebrate tomorrow. There's a series of plays in the tier four park. Tons of food and people. It should be a lot of fun."

*Food and plays sound good. People are inevitable, I suppose…* She shrugged. "Sure. When does it start tomorrow?"

"It starts just after lunch."

She smiled. "Then no conflict."

Rane hesitated, then sighed. "Fine." He looked around. "I still need to meditate."

*You are the only reason you haven't.* "Be my guest."

Tala, for her part, immediately dropped into a cross-legged, seated position and took out two tungsten balls. Both had altered gravity, one with it raised, one lowered.

This one particular variant of her ability's use was giving her trouble.

She could grab onto two targets, if they had the same starting gravity, and alter them together.

She could now grab onto any two targets and manipulate their gravity independently.

But she couldn't grab two differently gravitized items and alter them at the same time, in exactly the same way.

Oh, she could fake it, by altering them separately in the same way, but it didn't *feel* the same, and it took more power.

While she struggled with that, she also reviewed her fights with Rane. Every so often, her full attention would come back to the balls before her.

Finally, she thought she had it. *Increase.*

Their gravity increased… separately.

*Why won't you move together, rust you!*

Something clicked into place in her mind, resonating with her power, and something entirely different began coming together.

*Together. I should be able to move them together.*

Gravity was the interaction of all mass with all other mass, not just mass with the planet below.

*They are two points. I've been increasing their gravity, as connected to the planet. What if I increase it relative to each other?*

Excited beyond belief, she *dumped* power into that mental construct. *Collide.*

She wasn't altering the balls' gravity with the planet. She wasn't making them pull inward on themselves, though that thought was tucked away for later study.

No, she was only increasing their attraction to each other.

After just more than two minutes, the spheres began to wobble. In less than three, they suddenly rolled together, hitting with a satisfying *click*.

Rane's eyes snapped open. "Mistress Tala?"

## Millennial Mage, 4 - Bound

Tala was staring at the balls, wide-eyed and her mouth open in an ear-to-ear grin. "I did it, Master Rane. I discovered a new use for my ability, all on my own."

Rane tilted his head. "Oh? Do you want to share?"

Tala narrowed her eyes, pulling out one of the balls that she'd reduced to have near zero gravity. *As regards the planet,* she amended. She could almost feel her mind radiating through all her preconceptions and mulling over what this could mean.

While she did that, she locked onto Rane and the ball in her hand. *Collide.*

Rane... shrugged off her lock, likely without him even noticing her attempt. *Opposing will?* She could probably force it, but she might not need to. The ball didn't reject her manipulation, and *something* was growing.

"Mistress Tala?"

"One moment. I suggest you get ready." There was already a slight pressure, as the ball tried to pull from her hand, toward Rane. It was minute, but it was growing rapidly, now. *With the mass so low, I'm having to massively ramp up the effects.*

Rane slowly stood, drawing Force. "Alright..." He seemed, understandably, hesitant.

Tala just smiled. She had utter confidence in his abilities. *His defenses will keep him safe, if it gets past his sword.*

After four minutes, Tala was starting to have trouble holding onto the ball. "Head's up." And she released the ball.

It zipped across the room, heading straight for the area between Rane's navel and sternum, his center of mass.

Rane's eyes widened, and he struck at the ball on reflex. The ball flew away, but rapidly slowed, arching around to come back toward him. It acted similar to a ball in a funnel, where Rane was the spout. Any movement was quickly redirected into an unstable orbit.

*An orbit, eh? I wonder if I could actually use that, somehow… Could I place balls or armored plates in stable orbit around myself? Would that even be useful?*

Tala found herself laughing, continuing to increase the 'Collide' of the ball toward Rane.

Rane, for his part, was battering the ball around with increasing ferocity, but it kept coming back, faster and faster.

"Mistress Tala." His breath was coming more rapidly, now. "I actually can't do this forever."

*Oh… Oh! Rust!* "Ah, right! Sorry." She immediately went to decrease the pull but found that her mental image of that was… lacking. "Oh… rust. Rust!"

"Tala!"

She thought furiously. Finally, an odd image came to mind and clicked. It just felt right.

*Diminish.* She poured power through her void-channels into the mental construct, and through that into her spell-forms, but she'd been upping the ball's draw toward Rane for close to five minutes by that point. "It's reducing, but it'll take almost as long to come down as it took to ramp up!"

Rane made a small grunt of beleaguered irritation, but nodded, focusing fully on the ball and his repulsion of such.

With a moment of inspiration, she also dumped power into a Collide for the ball to one of the walls. The 'Diminish' was already taking all the power it could handle, so it didn't slow that part. Thus, the ball started moving more toward that wall with each deflection, until, finally, it was drifting as slowly as a leaf across the ground before a slight breeze.

Rane was panting by that point. "That… was… insane."

Tala grinned, now Diminishing the ball's link to both Rane and the wall, allowing the tungsten to drift lazily toward the floor.

"What was that?"

"I increased its gravity toward you."

He gave her a confused look. "What? How does that apply?"

"Gravity is every mass pulling all other mass." That was an oversimplification, but she felt that it was accurate enough for a short-hand explanation.

Rane cocked an eyebrow, then jumped, returning the floor. "I came down, I didn't go to the ceiling."

Tala smiled, instantly understanding what he meant. "Ahh, but you came down *slightly* slower than you would have if you had been outside, without the roof over your head. Gravitational accelerations are really a combination of accelerations toward every mass around you."

He was clearly still skeptical but seemed to have decided not to argue. "Well, you are the gravity Mage, I suppose…" After a moment, he grinned. "I actually think that was pretty good training for me, but I don't want to repeat it… Not exactly. We can work something out, though, right?"

"Sure." She glanced to her ball, now sitting on the ground, its gravity returned to normal, except as relating to the planet. That gravitational relationship was still reduced to near non-existence. The ball, itself, was cracked and warped. "Wow, you did a real number on this."

"Well, I asked politely, but it wouldn't leave me alone."

Tala glanced his way and saw him grinning with an obviously self-satisfied smile. "Yeah, yeah." She couldn't keep a smile from her face, or a chuckle from her tone.

Rane's breathing had returned to a more normal pace, and he scratched the side of his head a bit awkwardly. "So… mind if I finish meditating? It's fully night, and I need to get some sleep soon."

Tala waved assent and focused back on the tungsten balls before her. She'd remained sitting throughout the test against Rane. *This would be a great distraction for any one-on-one fight.* Assuming it didn't just slam into the enemy, killing them.

She reassured herself. *Rane's defensive inscriptions would have kept him safe.* Even so, she'd been a bit hasty on the test.

*What else should I test?* She thought through the ideas that Jevin had given her.

*I can do groups; I can increase one target while decreasing another.* She grinned. She could even increase one aspect of an item's gravity while decreasing another for the same target.

*I know that the change is compounding.* She hesitated at that, cursing silently. She'd unintentionally latched onto a ten percent increase, compounding each second, as how she envisioned it.

*Now, I need to break my mental construct of a fixed number.* She growled.

Rane shifted but didn't open his eyes.

*I can't change the direction of the resulting acceleration, but I can change what it is accelerating toward.* That said, she was at a massive disadvantage when dealing with gravity not relating to the planet.

*All that mass really is useful to me.* She grinned at that.

# Millennial Mage, 4 - Bound

*I still need to test if I can target just a part of something, but I should be able to.* What else did she need to test?

*Affecting an area… I don't think I can target an area. I just don't believe that gravity works that way.* She had to smile at that. She had *seen* other gravity Mages at the Academy doing area of effect gravity manipulations, but it had always struck her as wrong somehow. *What else?*

*Something held by an opponent, and opposed enactment.* Rane had shrugged off her lock, just by his nature as a Bound. She hadn't tried to force the connection, but it was one of the first times she'd ever had an issue locking onto someone.

*He must have been working on his power-density.* As she thought about it, she realized there was a second, more likely explanation. *His fusing is giving him greater magical weight.*

Her own fusing immediately took a massive leap up in priority for her.

Finally, the last thing she wanted to test, eventually, was what would happen if she increased an item's gravitation toward itself. She couldn't think of a use for it, as it wouldn't change the mass, nor affect anything else, but it would be interesting to see if she could.

*Well, that's quite the list. What first?* There was no question in her mind at all.

She began to crochet.

Rane finished up and bade her goodnight, but she only gave him a cursory good-bye, her focus directed almost entirely inward.

\* \* \*

It was after midnight when Tala flopped backwards with a groan.

"There! Are you happy? I tried."

Terry gave a sleepy, grumpy squawk from her folded bedroll in the corner of the training room.

"I can't do areas. It just makes no sense to me." She groaned again. "I bet all area gravity Mages are Creators, and they just create gravity fields in defiance of *all logic*!" She almost yelled the last two words.

Terry groused some more but didn't otherwise participate in the conversation.

"Fine. I'm done."

She'd worked on fusing for a few hours then decided that she should at least *try* to affect an area, instead of a specific target.

"On the plus side, I know I can affect just one part of something…" She'd been raising and lowering the effective gravity of a section of floor for the last hour. Nothing she could think to try had any effect on the items atop that floor, however.

From her prone position, she kicked up to land on her feet. "I want a bath."

She topped off Kit with power even as she took it from her belt.

Once she'd drawn the near-scalding bath, Tala let herself soak but didn't indulge for too long.

Much more relaxed, and fully exhausted, she crashed into her bed, set up in one corner of Kit's expanded interior. She increased her gravity almost absently, until the bed had a comfortable give for her current position.

She was asleep before another thought could flicker through her mind.

Tala woke some time later, sitting bolt upright and looking around.

*Was that just a dream?*

She'd felt like something was about to eat her.

She shivered, reflexively refilling Kit's reserves.

*Well, I'm awake...* She climbed up the short ladder and looked out into the training room.

The bit of sky she could see was gray but lightening toward dawn.

Tala growled. "Not enough."

She dropped back down, flopping back onto her mattress and curling up, asleep again near instantly.

"Mistress Tala?" Mistress Odera's voice floated down from above. "Mistress Tala!?"

Tala groaned, not fully awake, rolling out of bed and slapping into the ground. "What."

"Are you down there?"

"Yes." Tala spoke a bit louder this time.

"I'm not going to even try entering that... item. Please come up. I'd rather get breakfast *before* lunch time."

Tala jerked upright. "Oh! What time is it?"

"Half past seven, dear."

Tala growled. "Too early."

"Well, I can always eat by myself. I just thought you'd prefer to join me."

Tala's stomach let out a gurgling roar that Tala would have sworn echoed throughout Kit's interior.

After the sound settled down, Tala cleared her throat. "I'll be right up."

## Chapter: 30
## Great...

Tala's head was thrown back as she downed her fifth cup of coffee.

"That really isn't healthy for you."

Tala set down her mug, giving Mistress Odera a long look. "I was up 'til after midnight."

"Would you be drinking less, if you'd gone to bed earlier?"

Tala didn't respond, instead simply refilling her mug as she munched on a few pieces of bacon. Out of the corner of her eye, Tala saw Terry flicker briefly, and the pile of sausages was a few links shorter. She grinned but didn't address the mild thievery.

"I thought not." Mistress Odera pushed her plate back, having just finished her own, small meal. "Now, how is your training progressing?"

Tala shook her head. "Nope."

"No?"

"Nope. We talk about me every morning. It's time you answer some questions about you."

Mistress Odera cocked an eyebrow but didn't comment.

"So, why don't you go teach for the academy? That's where some Mages retire, right?"

She took a long breath, shaking her head. "Aside from the rudeness of the base assumptions in your question, the academy is for those who fear death more than they love magic."

"Care to explain?" Tala was using the opportunity to continue her breakfast.

"The island is a natural fountain of eternal youth." Mistress Odera smiled. "Well, in a sense."

Tala leaned forward, eating more bacon. "Wait, is the fountain of youth a fount?"

"Hmm? No, no. It's just often referred to as a fountain of water in the tales."

"Ah, Okay."

"Now, the legends are actually due to that place. It prevents the degradation of living creatures. You can grow up, but nothing will move past maturity, not while there. It won't reverse aging, however. That's just a myth."

"That sounds useful."

"It is, it is."

"So, what's the catch?"

Mistress Odera nodded appreciatively. "It suffuses you. Eventually, if you stay long enough, you don't even have to stay on the island to keep the stasis."

Tala found herself nodding. "It imprints upon your magic."

"Precisely, and conflicts with any inscriptions, slowly rendering them worthless."

She frowned. "Then why put so many Mage initiates there? Wouldn't that cripple their foundation?"

"No, it doesn't act upon those who have not reached maturity. Your magic cannot resonate with what does not act upon you."

Tala grunted. "The teachers refused to explain, and even led me to believe they didn't know what was going on."

"It is a shameful thing," Mistress Odera shook her head, "to fear death so completely that you would cripple yourself."

"Aren't they doing a noble thing? Giving up magic to teach?"

Mistress Odera snorted derisively. "Hardly. The academy is just a convenient use of the fearful old codgers."

Tala tilted her head in thought. "So why not offer it to mundanes?"

"The magic draws on your gate, and it takes more power than a mundane has available."

"So, it only works for Mages?"

"Worse."

"How could it be worse?"

"What happens if you use more power than your gate can draw?"

"It pulls from my reserves."

Mistress Odera nodded. "And when your reserves are emptied?"

"The spell-working ends?" Tala frowned. *Right?*

"Yes and no. What would happen if the spell-working was an inscription?"

"It would burn through the metal, exhausting it to give the working a few more moments of activity, leaving the Mage uninscribed," Tala answered instantly and easily.

"Yes, so, what is the equivalent of the inscription in this case?"

"The island?"

Mistress Odera huffed a laugh. "Then would it need a person's power to function?"

"No…" Tala frowned, once again. "It's enacted on their flesh… is that the answer?"

"In this case, yes." She smiled. "The history behind the island is thus: humanity negotiated for a source of eternal life. We are one of the shortest-lived races, after all, but we were deceived. The trade was magically locked, and our 'partner' was held to the letter of the trade, but that's all. We were given a poison pill, useless to the point of detriment to mundanes and Mages alike, while still, technically, doing as promised."

"What did we give up in trade?"

"That is lost to history, as far as I am aware."

"Seems like this is something that should be taught."

"Oh, you've heard of it."

"I have?"

"Who is the primary antagonist in all tales of the fountain of youth, among others?"

Tala's eyes widened. "The Arcane King."

"Precisely."

Tala sat back, thoughtfully eating a hash-brown patty. "Wow... Rust that guy."

Mistress Odera laughed loudly before covering her own mouth, drawing the eyes of some customers at the other end of the restaurant.

Tala smiled as she continued to eat.

"Truer words, Mistress." Mistress Odera shrugged. "He did follow through on the entirety of the request; humanity is safe there, from all outside threats. The gods and hostile arcanes are utterly incapable of setting foot on the island or affecting it in any way." She smiled. "The protections are really quite ingenious, actually. From what I've been told, they extend to maintaining the surrounding environment, so that even when the sun goes nova in a few billion years, that island will remain perfectly habitable. Assuming that humans still live there, I suppose."

"That's... quite something, actually."

"There's a reason people still seek the Arcane King, despite his known duplicity."

Tala frowned. "Arcane King…" She scratched her chin, remembering what Xeel had told her of arcane power rankings. "He's a Sovereign."

"Yes? Kings are a type of sovereign."

"No, I mean the arcane equivalent of a Transcendent."

"Ahh. I suppose? I've not really given him too much thought." She gave a sad smile. "Well, not since my grandchildren outgrew fairytales."

Tala was frowning, considering. "Are there any human Transcendents?"

"That is a question that I honestly thought you'd ask weeks ago. Though it is a bit of a tangent, now."

Tala grimaced. "Other things have been on my mind."

"That's fine, Mistress. I'll ask a question in return."

Tala sighed. "I should have expected."

Mistress Odera grinned. "Are there any adult babies?"

"What? No? But there are babies who become adults."

"Precisely. Those who transcend have transcended. They are *more*. They are not what they were."

Tala rolled her eyes. "You know what I'm asking, Mistress. Are there any Transcendent who *were* human, then?"

"No."

"No?"

"No."

"I find that very hard to believe."

Mistress Odera shrugged. "You don't have to believe me."

Tala sighed. "How can you be sure? Our society isn't exactly big on sharing such secrets."

"Because we are still at war."

She frowned, leaning back. "Explain, please."

"If a human transcended, they could either take us all away, making a new world and moving us there to ensure our safety, or they would try, and their equals would stop them. That would be… less than ideal for life on this planet."

"Couldn't you make the same argument that, since we are still at war, we have to have at least one Transcendent keeping the others from obliterating us?"

Mistress Odera snorted. "If one of them wanted us dead, they'd kill us all."

"The Arcane King?" Tala tried to think about all the stories she'd heard involving the creature.

"He enjoys messing with humans but doesn't actively hate us."

She considered. "The Hollow Queen?"

"She cares only for her own physicality. Isn't she usually a part of stories against harmful self-love and narcissism?"

"Mansa the Gold?"

"Only wishes for greater treasury. His tales usually end with him digging toward the core of Zeme, seeking ever more wealth from the earth."

"Krol the Conqueror."

"Dead? Isn't that what the stories say?"

Tala considered. *Yeah, there was a uniting of ancient heroes that died to stop the Conqueror.* "Reine of the Deep? Dauphin the Enduring? Mirza Far Sight?" Tala frowned, trying to remember all the most powerful, nonhuman figures in the ancient tales. "Padishah of the Plains? Basileus the Betrayer?"

Mistress Odera shrugged. "I cannot tell you the dispositions of the powers in the world at large, Mistress. I know the same stories as you, though I imagine you know them better." She gave a small smile. "For all I know, most, if not all, of these are purely fictional."

"What of the gods?"

She let out a long sigh. "Mistress Tala. In my life, I have only ever seen one creature classified as a god. The Leviathan."

"When did you see the Leviathan?" Tala's voice was just above a whisper.

"When I was at the academy." Mistress Odera quirked a smile. "It is one reason I sought answers about the origin of the place. I was on the library's tower-top, just after a storm. A ship, not of human make, had been driven into the waters around the island, and the magics were forcing it away."

Tala had paused her eating to listen.

"As the magics finally compelled the vessel out past the area of safety, a hole opened in the ocean, and the ship dropped from sight, like a stone from the tower-top." She shook her head. "Moments later, after the hole had closed and all traces of the ship were gone, an eye rose up to regard the island. The eye was larger than a wagon, and the power of the being was so great that I could see the magic even without my magesight active. A single tentacle reached out toward me—well, probably toward the academy—but slid off of an invisible boundary."

Tala swallowed and shivered. She'd never really been interested in sea travel. Now, she was sure she'd avoid it at all costs. "So, that's a god."

Mistress Odera laughed. "No, no." She shook her head. "As the tentacle slid off the boundary, I saw sudden fear enter the great eye. A bellow of terror shook the academy and turned the sea into a froth. In an instant, that ship destroyer vanished inside a great maw. Teeth larger than the library tower I stood upon tore through cleanly and dragged the creature under. The ocean was red and thick with blood for a month after that."

Tala took a deep drink of her coffee. "Yeah… no sea travel for me."

# Millennial Mage, 4 - Bound

"Wise choice. Most gods on the land are easier to ignore, assuming you don't violate their sense of what is right." Mistress Odera nodded sagely. "The Forest Spirit walks these very woods. He only interacts with mortals if they attempt to harm the forest at large, or wipe out one of its species."

"The Leshkin."

"Yes. They put themselves under his protection by becoming creatures of the forest."

Tala frowned. "That seems like cheating."

Mistress Odera laughed. "He doesn't care if you kill the creatures, only if you threaten the species as a whole. The Leshkin cannot be killed outright, so he only cares if their heartseeds are threatened."

*Well, that explains why no one has wiped them out yet.*

"He isn't vengeful, though. He simply stops the attempts. Very few have actually ever seen him, but those who recorded the experience recall feeling overwhelming shame, like disappointing a cherished mentor. It is theorized that, at his core, the Forest Spirit is a Conceptual Creator, but that is obviously speculation."

Tala grunted. "I don't really understand the conceptual side of magic."

"Most humans can't, really. That's one of the reasons we can't use it."

Tala laughed. "That makes sense. I don't even know the divisions of that side, though."

"What do you mean?"

"Well, humans use physical magic:; Material and Immaterial."

"That's right."

"So, what are the divisions of conceptual magic?"

"Ah, Abstract and Concrete."

"I don't know what that means."

"Well, I can't explain it to you."

"How can a concept be concrete? Aren't they all abstract?" Tala was mainly talking to herself.

Mistress Odera didn't answer, instead sipping her tea.

After a moment, Tala cocked her head. "Wait a second."

"Hmmm?"

"I was trying to ask questions about you."

"Were you now?" Mistress Odera managed to hide most of her smile behind another sip of tea.

Tala narrowed her eyes at the woman. "Yes."

"Well, I'm sorry to say that our time is all but done."

"Oh?"

"You said you were meeting someone else at ten, right?"

"Yes."

"It's half past nine."

Tala grimaced. "That's not fair."

"What isn't fair?"

"You know how to play my curiosity, deflecting me from what I intend."

"That's called being a good conversationalist, dear." She then muttered into her tea, too quietly for her to have expected Tala to be able to hear. "You should try it some time."

Tala glared but didn't comment.

"So? Get going, Mistress. I've got the bill covered."

Tala sighed but stood. "Thank you for breakfast, Mistress Odera."

"It was a pleasure."

Tala grabbed a double handful of bacon and sausage, wrapped it in a napkin and headed for the door.

Terry flickered to her shoulder, and she gave him a sausage as they left the restaurant.

\*　　\*　　\*

Tala finished up her load of meat just as she got to the Constructionist Guild office.

The standard scan and *ding* heralded her arrival.

"Tala!" Grent walked out of the back hall, arms wide.

*Well, rust...* Tala folded her hands in front of herself and gave a half-bow. "Master Grent."

He seemed to almost miss a step, but his smile never wavered. "How are you, Mistress?" He stopped just out of arm's reach and gave a half-bow in return.

"I am well, thank you. And you?"

"I am very well, thank you."

"Shall we?"

It was an awkward second breakfast.

\* \* \*

Tala grimaced as she entered the training room, only to find Rane already there. Terry flickered to his corner, seemingly not wanting to get involved.

"So? How did your... not-date go?"

Tala grimaced. "I have nothing to say to you."

Rane quirked a smile but nodded. "As you say."

She sighed, stretching in a back-and-forth twist. "I need to hit something. Spar?"

"I thought you said you need to hit something." He had a mischievous twinkle in his eyes.

She glared. "You are testing me, sir."

"Not yet, I'm not." He drew Force.

Tala drew out two gravity-reduced balls, tossing them to either side and immediately beginning to increase their effective gravity toward Rane.

"Mistress Tala?" His eyes flicked between her and each of the balls, the previous night's events clearly still on his mind.

Tala growled, drawing Flow in its training sheath. She lunged for him, transforming Flow into a glaive even as she charged.

Rane barely brought Force across in time to deflect the strike, but Tala switched paths at the last moment.

Flow shifted into the form of a sword, causing Force to sweep through empty air.

Rane was too skilled to be thrown off balance by a missed block, but he was definitely caught off guard.

Tala capitalized by immediately returning Flow to the form of a glaive and driving it toward the left side of his chest.

His defense activated, spinning him out of the way, and Force whipped around in a tight circle toward her head.

Flow's long shaft came up to parry Force, and a concussion of power radiated out.

Tala held the glaive angled down, so the blade was nearly between Rane's legs. With savage power, she ripped the blade upward.

Had he been without his defensive inscriptions, and if Flow had been unsheathed, she'd have split him groin to crown.

As it was, he flipped over her, lancing out with strike after strike as he passed overhead, skimming the ceiling a bare thirteen feet up.

She expertly parried each thrust with the staff of her polearm, causing consecutive concussions of power.

As his feet touched down, Tala flicked her anchor past him, transforming Flow into a sword even as she was forcefully pulled forward by the dimensional compression.

She gritted her teeth against the incoming nausea, set on her goal. *I will beat him, today.*

## Millennial Mage, 4 - Bound

The anchor would have caused *her* to bypass Rane, but Flow was out before her, Tala holding it perfectly still.

Rane's defenses acted by matching his velocity to any incoming attack. Tala and her gear had no velocity of their own. Dimensionality was warping around her, causing her movement.

Flow struck his chest with a meaty *thunk*, throwing him backward.

His eyes widened in shock, even as the wind was driven out of him.

Rane stumbled backwards, up against the wall. Tala's dimensional travel ended less than ten feet from him, and she was already sprinting for him.

As he lifted his off-hand to his obviously bruised chest, Rane looked down and saw her anchor. He thrust Force into the circle of the spring clip and flicked it away.

Tala's eyes widened, but she reacted on instinct, throwing Flow.

As the weapon flew, it transformed back into a knife, threaded the anchor, and pinned it in place, barely five feet to Rane's right.

Before he could react further, Tala closed, attacking him from the left to drive him toward her anchor.

She ducked and wove around his strikes with precision, speed, and skill that she'd never been able to combine before. That, and he was moving slower than he was usually capable of, sucking in each breath.

As his next slash came in at shoulder height, Tala ducked and struck at the inside of his knee.

As he flipped out of the way, she stood, jumping with all her strength toward his center of rotation.

Rane's inscriptions moved him away from her, slamming him into the ceiling. He groaned, his hand spasming and allowing Force to fall toward the floor.

Tala's anchor dimensionally expanded the space above her, preventing her own impact with the ceiling.

She slowed and lightly dropped to the floor just before Rane fell.

She called Flow to her, ripping it from the floor and transforming it into a glaive for a sideways sweep, again at Rane's center.

His inscriptions moved him out ahead of Flow's strike, slamming him into the wall this time.

Tala stepped forward, feinting with thrusts threatening enough to cause his defenses to activate, jerking him against the wall and up just enough to keep him from returning to the floor.

His eyes opened, and something changed within them.

Force whipped up from the floor, clipping her leg on the way to Rane's hand.

A spray of blood splattered the wall, and she momentarily lost that support. She had no time to fully register the injury.

Without a moment's hesitation, Rane's blade licked out.

One.

Two.

Three.

Four.

Five strikes in less than a second, and Tala only blocked two of them.

The other three drove spears of force through her, painting the training floor behind her with her blood and bile.

Her leg returned to functionality just as Rane hit the floor, his eyes a hard, solid blue.

He lunged for her; a rictus of concentration locked on his face.

## Millennial Mage, 4 - Bound

Tala stumbled backwards, shifting her weapon fluidly between its forms to block every strike.

She wasn't able to regain her footing, even as she hit the edge of her anchor's radius.

Sensing the dimensional energy, she dropped backward into what was effectively an in-place-roll, deflecting a downward strike from Force in the middle of the maneuver with Flow's glaive staff.

The next exchange was too fast for thought.

Tala couldn't have said if they battered back and forth ten times or a hundred, but she managed to hold her own.

Rane was fighting with a ferocity she'd never witnessed. That gave him speed and reactions near what she, herself, had, but his skill was proportionally lessened, making it much closer of a fight than it had ever been.

She tried to press toward her anchor, so she could get it and retreat, but she had no luck.

Finally, she growled out, "Terry, I need the anchor."

The terror bird flickered into being beside the device. He picked it up in his beak and tossed it, then vanished back to his corner.

As the anchor sailed through the air, Rane saw it. Lancing out with Force, he struck the device, sending it streaking across the room and toward the door out onto the balcony.

Tala's eyes widened, even as motion sickness overcame her, and she likewise shot across the area.

Terry flickered into being for just an instant, catching the anchor, and dropping it so it would land within the room.

*Bless you, Terry.*

Tala stumbled to a knee as the dimensional energy dispersed.

She kept her head up just enough to keep an eye on Rane.

He stood with perfect form in a middle, hanging guard. His eyes blank and fixed on her.

"Master Rane?"

He took one careful step toward her.

*What happened to him?* "Master Rane. Enough."

One step became two, then three, then he was rushing her.

"Rane, stop!"

His foot hesitated for an instant, but his momentum continued, causing him to stumble and dropping him into a roll. He smoothly came up to a knee, just more than a dozen feet from her.

"Master Rane?"

His calm, even breathing broke, and he was suddenly panting, shivering, and heaving. Sweat broke out across his entire body, and a shudder went through him before he collapsed to the floor, seemingly unconscious.

"Great…"

# Chapter: 31
# What Is Happening to You?

Tala watched Rane slowly stir.

She sat in a meditative position, having just finished looking through herself with her magesight. Thankfully, her scripts had cleaned up all the damage and contamination within her body. Tala really needed to thank Holly, once again, for the beautifully designed scripts.

Rane groaned and pushed himself up. "Water." His voice came out in a harsh croak.

Tala slid a waterskin to him.

"Thanks." He guzzled down the whole thing before wiping his mouth with the back of his hand. As he set the empty skin to one side, he wrinkled his nose. "What is that smell?"

"Oh, that? That's my bile and blood."

"What?" He blinked at her owlishly, clearly not fully mentally present yet.

"You put three clean thrusts into my abdomen, through my digestive system, and out my back. Anyone else would be dying of peritonitis and sepsis, if they didn't just bleed out."

He paled. "Wha— How?"

"I was finally, *finally* getting the upper hand, and something about you changed."

He groaned, putting his head in his hands. "I remember you hitting me." He looked up. "How *did* you manage that, by the way?"

She grinned. "I figured that your defense somehow read the velocity of the incoming attack, in order to mirror it. So, I didn't move Flow. I kept it perfectly still while my anchor dimensionally pulled me past you."

"Ahh… yeah, that's a hole in my defense." He frowned. "Not that there are many who could exploit it…" He sighed. "I'll have to take time to consider that."

"So… do you want to tell me what happened?"

"I… have a temper."

She gave him a flat look. "No, I'm not chalking that up to temper. You seem to have some memory loss surrounding it, and that was more than just an emotional reaction."

He groaned again. "Many of my family have a blessing, or a curse depending on who you ask. When we are truly threatened, a more primal portion of our mind takes over. I wasn't lying; it is very tied to my anger, to my temper, even if it is triggered by damage."

"Well, I don't like you when you're angry." She rubbed one hand on her abdomen, remembering the pain. It had felt like… There was no good comparison, but it had felt *wrong*.

"I am sorry about that." His face showed genuine remorse.

"It was pretty rusting terrible, honestly."

Rane sat up straight, then executed a seated bow. "My deepest apologies, Mistress Tala, both for my provocation before our bout, and for losing my temper and attacking you so lethally."

Tala gave a half-bow in return. "Apology accepted, but you really should have told me about the danger."

"I planned on it, but, with all due respect, last time we fought you were *far* from being able to hurt me enough for the danger to be present."

She quirked an eyebrow.

"Clearly something's changed." He frowned, looking around as if searching for something. "Wait, you started the bout by tossing those balls out to the sides. They never actually attacked me."

She grinned. "Best case? The fight would have lasted long enough that they could come into play. As it was, they were a great distraction."

Rane laughed, then. "Too true." He groaned, rubbing his chest. "You hit *hard*."

"You better believe I do."

"No, I mean, you might have left a lasting mark." He looked down. There was, indeed, a light purpling of his flesh across his upper chest. "That's going to be rusting awful for days." He cocked an eyebrow at her.

"You throw me into walls all the time."

"You heal." He shifted and winced. "Plus, I'm pretty sure I have worse than this on my back."

Tala nodded, having seen his shirtless back. "Yeah, you'll be sleeping on your side for a while."

He sighed. "I'll just go to a healer." He glanced toward her stomach. "We can get you looked at, too. I know you've good healing scripts, but I don't want something to be amiss, and we don't realize it."

Tala hesitated. "What would that cost to take care of?"

"My injuries? I think the standard for a simple heal is ten silver, and this should qualify. For you? I don't know what a diagnosis will cost, and any healing that might be needed would probably be more than simple."

She grimaced, again, at the remembered pain. "Yeah… having myself looked at might be wise." She bit the side of her lip, considering.

He stared, giving her time to think.

After a moment, a sly grin spread across her face. "Want to gamble?"

Rane tilted his head in interest. "What do you have in mind?"

"I pay for your healing, and you pay for mine."

"That hardly seems fair."

"You said I might not need it."

"Oh, I know. That is exactly the problem. I mean that it is not fair to you. You'll be paying for my wounds, and I probably won't have to pay anything."

She almost laughed, then. "Alright. Then, what if you clean the training hall?" She gestured to the blood-splatter and streaks of stinking bile.

He scratched the back of his head, considering and grimacing at his injuries. "Deal, but I would have done that regardless."

Tala just shrugged. She honestly felt a bit bad about hurting him and wanted to pay for the healing. She knew that she shouldn't. He hurt her in sparring far more than that all the time, but she had designed herself to recover from such things. She'd purposely bypassed his protections.

*Which I'm supposed to do in sparring.* Even so, she felt it was right to pay.

She smiled, bringing her thoughts back to the present. "So, your defensive, temper thing: Magical?"

Rane grunted. "Yeah. Some ancestor earned a boon from Basileus and asked for his descendants to be protected against death."

"Wait… Basileus the Betrayer?"

"That's the one. Apparently, he hadn't earned the moniker yet."

"That's… rough."

"A bit, yeah. He kept his bargain, though. For mundanes, the berserk rage is actually really useful, and unlike psychedelic-induced rages, we can always distinguish friend from foe."

"Assuming your friend isn't attacking you."

Rane scratched the side of his head. "That's not usually an issue?"

Tala snorted. "I suppose."

\*   \*   \*

Rane took nearly half an hour to clean the mess. He even had to request a batch of pretty strong cleaning chemicals from the facility staff.

While he did that, Tala bathed. She used the privacy to focus on her abdomen and cement in her own mind that she was whole, once more. *Getting hurt and healed so rapidly is doing a number on me... Do I want to get used to it?*

She further centered herself by crocheting another stitch within her innermost self. *Progress. Always progress.*

When she came out, Rane was in his normal clothes, rather than his training gear, and stretching. "Ah! You're done." He smiled. "I just finished getting cleaned up, myself. Ready to go?"

"Yeah. Terry?"

Terry joined them, and the three headed toward a healer recommended by the training center's staff. Apparently, training accidents weren't uncommon, so a healer had set up shop just down the spiral.

Tala opened the door to the healer's shop and a little bell *dinged* over the door. She held the door for Rane. *He's the patient, after all.*

Rane hesitated for the briefest of instants, then shrugged and walked in ahead of her. A kindly man greeted them from a comfortably looking chair in the back corner. "Master, Mistress, how can I serve today?" He set down a book as he stood, after placing a bookmark in it.

Tala immediately picked up on his magic, the inscriptions were entirely oriented toward Material Guide spell-forms. Holly's inset assistance helped Tala understand them as focused on flesh, bone, blood, organs, and other internals. *Makes sense.*

He was clearly unbound.

Rane bowed to the older Mage. "Master. I am Rane, and this is Mistress Tala. I took some injury while sparring, and I would appreciate healing." Rane grinned. "She's paying."

The Mage laughed. "Well, Master Rane, Mistress Tala, I am Cris." His eyes flicked to Terry, on Tala's shoulder. "Who is your small friend, there?" He gave a professional smile as he waited the answer.

Tala reached up to scratch Terry's head. "This is Terry. He's my partner."

Terry trilled happily but didn't otherwise react.

Cris bowed toward Tala and Terry, then faced Rane. "Now, Master Rane," he regarded the much bigger man, "it is common practice to ask others to wait outside, or in here, while we go into a back room."

Rane shook his head. "That's not necessary."

"If you're sure?"

"I'm sure."

"Very well." He held out his hand. "May I?"

"Certainly."

He touched Rane's head and a pulse of magic swept through the Archon. "Oh, yes. That looks painful." Cris winced in sympathy. "Nothing's broken, thankfully, but both your flesh and bones are bruised. My standard fee is ten silver, and this isn't complicated enough to require more."

They both looked to Tala.

She shrugged. "I'll trust your expertise, Master Cris."

Cris smiled, giving a nod of thanks. "That is kind of you." He tapped Rane's head once more and a different, more extensive set of inscriptions activated.

Healing energy moved through Rane like a cool breeze.

Cris leaned in close to Rane's ear, speaking low enough that a normal person couldn't have heard him in Tala's place. Of course, she heard him anyway. "Your urine will be brown and foamy for a couple of days. That is normal for instant healing of such injuries. If you have any concerns, you can come back whenever you like. If you want a second opinion, you may go to any other healer, and if they find issue with my healing, I will pay for their work on you."

Rane nodded in thanks, then his eyes flicked to Tala, and he reddened, slightly.

Cris didn't comment. "Now, Mistress, would you like a diagnosis? It's free of charge. I am happy to take a look at your companion there, too, though I don't know avian biology as well as human."

Tala was about to protest, but then she shrugged. *Might as well verify Holly's work.* "Sure, I suppose." *Might be good to check on Terry, make sure nothing's off.* "You can check Terry first, if he's interested."

Terry lifted his head, trilling questioningly.

Tala smiled at her friend. "Yes, if it's Okay with you."

Terry regarded Cris for a long moment before bobbing his head. He extended his neck so that Cris could reach him more easily.

After a soft tap, power rippled through the avian, and Cris frowned. "Did someone shrink you, my friend? Are you… under a curse or something?"

Terry squawked, then looked to Tala.

Tala quirked a smile. "He shrunk himself."

"Ahh… Okay, then." Cris seemed to be looking at something they couldn't see. "Well, he seems in good health, though much of his biology seems to be sequestered in a dimensionally expanded, inertially isolated space?"

Tala regarded Terry. "Is that how you get smaller and get lighter? I was curious."

Terry shuffled happily, curling back up.

"Well, I can't say I've ever seen anything like it, but you seem healthy enough." Cris seemed a bit uncertain, but finally just shook his head. "I can say with certainty that you have no living parasites within you, nor any infections or unaddressed injuries."

Tala smiled. "Thank you, Master Cris."

He gave a nod. "Certainly." He took a deep breath, seeming to recenter himself. "Alright then. Mistress Tala?"

"Sure, I'm ready."

He looked to her and gave a bow. "I'd normally have Master Rane depart."

She waved him off. "He's fine."

"It's up to you." Cris tapped her on the forehead, and she felt power ripple through her. As she felt the power move through her, she thought she detected a pattern. *It's following my circulatory system. Using the iron in my blood to reflect the investigative spell more efficiently through my body?* That seemed reasonable.

The healer's eyes widened in a mix of shock and horror. "Mistress Tala… what… what have you done to yourself?"

"What do you mean?" She frowned, coming back from her contemplations.

"Do you have active inscriptions on all your internal organs?"

Tala shrugged. "Yeah, most of those are regenerative, but every system has scripts working alongside it to improve its function."

"Well, yes. With this, you'd only need to defecate… monthly? Maybe less than that, if I'm understanding correctly, which is doubtful, because you seem to be almost as much inscription as biology."

Rane was giving Tala a questioning look, but she was focused on the Mage. "I know that my digestive system is more efficient, and my cleansing organs recycle more than they expel."

"Yes, there is that, and that work is quite ingenious. Honestly, I look forward to the designers of those inscriptions publishing a paper with their findings."

Tala frowned, but he continued before she could comment.

"But that really doesn't explain what's happening to your liver and kidneys."

"What do you mean?"

Cris was clearly a bit off his usual routine, but he leaned forwards, concern obvious across his kindly face. "Are you… an alcoholic?"

"What? No!" Tala straightened, stepping back and raising her hands in negation.

He shook his head. "Then, I can't easily think of what could be causing such a strain on those organs."

Rane spoke up, then, interjecting into the brief silence. "Coffee."

They both turned to him, and he shrugged.

"What? She drinks an *insane* amount of coffee."

Cris turned to regard Tala. "How much coffee have you had, today?"

Tala considered for a moment. "Ten… no, fifteen cups." She glowered. "Second breakfast wasn't ideal…"

Rane suppressed a grin, but Tala decided to be the bigger person and ignore him.

Cris held up a hand, making a small circle with his index finger and thumb. "Like… small cups?"

Tala shook her head. "No, I'd bet we're talking… sixteen-ounce mugs?" She nodded. "Yeah, I think the first five were from twenty-ounce tankards. That place was amazing." She scratched her temple, considering. "I should really go back there. They have great portions."

Cris gaped at her.

"What?"

"Mistress Tala." He swallowed. "That is more than two gallons of coffee."

She thought for a moment, then nodded. "Yeah, that sounds about right."

"How are you breathing? Your liver is obviously breaking down the caffeine, but it's not like you can pee out the metabolites… where do they go? What is happening to you?" He leaned forward. "Two of those byproducts are stimulants in their own right. How are you not overstimulated, all the time?"

Tala frowned. "Well, my neurology is also reinforced and regulated with scripts. Would that explain it?"

Cris just stared at her for a long time. "You let someone… inscribe your brain with magics that can alter function?"

She opened her mouth to say, 'No.' but stopped herself. "Yes? Well, yeah. I had to alter brain function, or I couldn't support my increased senses and reactions."

He just stared back at her, a look of genuine horror dawning across his features.

Rane cleared his throat. "I think we are getting off topic, just a bit."

"Right, right. You're right." The Mage gave Rane a searching look, seeming to be pulling himself back together. "Is that much coffee… standard for her?"

Rane snorted. "From the sound of it, today's a slow day."

Cris pulled up a chair and sat down. "I'm going to be sick."

Tala was feeling a bit uncertain. "What's the problem? I have inscriptions that keep my organs functioning properly."

He lowered his head into his hands after he waved a hand dismissively. "Yeah, sure; it looks like they even enhance functionality. Good for you."

Tala cocked an eyebrow. "That's a bit snippy."

He locked gazes with her again. "Do you use inscriptions to boil water immediately before you drink it, just because your throat can take it?"

"No?" *Might help warm me up, if I'm ever somewhere really cold, though…*

"No! Of course not! Why waste the inscriptions? Why put that stress on your system? Why are you doing this to yourself?!"

Tala took another half-step back, glancing toward Rane.

Rane, for his part, seemed to be uncertain how to handle the situation.

"Please, for the love of… every human. Drink. Less. Coffee."

Tala swallowed. "I'll… consider it?"

Cris narrowed his eyes at her.

Rane stepped forward, clearing his throat. "That's actually quite a concession from her, Master Cris, and if she says she'll consider it, she genuinely will."

Cris sighed, slumping back. "I suppose I'll take what I can get."

Tala shifted. "So… other than that?"

The healer waved. "Oh, you're in perfect health, from my perspective. You *should* be two hundred pounds, by what my detection spells are saying, but you clearly aren't."

"Well, I am."

He gave her a look. "Ahh, apologies. My… professionalism seems to have left me utterly. Please forgive my imprecise language. You should be very overweight, but clearly, your fat stores are well proportioned to your body, however they function now. Your bones are denser than I would expect, but they haven't calcified through the marrow, so there is no loss of function there. Your blood pressure should kill you, but there you stand. Your blood volume shouldn't fit inside your vascular system, but I suppose that explains at least part of the pressure, which I've already addressed. Do you wish for me to go on?"

Tala cleared her throat. "That… that won't be necessary. Is there anything you'd recommend I get healed?"

He sighed. "You are healthier than I could make you, and anything I did would risk interfering with the unstable equilibrium you seem to have achieved."

"Alright then. Thank you, Master Cris. I think we should pay you for your time and be on our way."

They departed a couple minutes later, leaving the healer in a mild daze.

Rane was smiling widely, clearly containing laughter while Tala really didn't know what to feel.

Terry was content to remain on Tala's shoulder.

Rane cleared his throat, "So… still up for seeing the plays? It's barely lunch time, so we should be able to make it easily enough."

"That would probably be a nice distraction. Sure."

It had been a *strange* morning.

## Chapter: 32
## Foundational Understandings

Tala and Rane walked down the spiral side by side, weaving their way through slower foot-traffic or those traveling the other way.

They could have asked Terry for a ride, but they weren't really in a hurry. This was meant to be a mental break, and a celebration of Rane's soul-bond to Force.

As they walked down the spiral, they talked about small things, only occasionally falling back on talking about magic and combat, and Tala occasionally flicked out bits of jerky. *I'll need to get more of this, sometime soon.*

After nearly a full circuit of the city, they passed one of the large shafts that Tala had occasionally seen. This time, a woman was standing next to it, and the entire shaft glowed incredibly oddly to Tala's vision.

*Gravity. I'm seeing the manipulation of gravity, there!*
"Excuse me, Mistress?"

The woman tsked. "I've no time for tourists. Please move along." She didn't turn, dismissing them out of hand.

Tala cleared her throat.

The woman turned, rolling her eyes, but stopped when she saw them. "Ahh, Mistress, Master, feathery… creature. I apologize, I have my work interrupted all too often by the… curious. What can I do for you?"

## Millennial Mage, 4 - Bound

Tala grinned at her. "I'm Tala. I'm curious what you're doing." She winked, then continued, "I dabble in gravity magic a bit, myself."

At first, the woman looked a bit irritated, but she brightened when Tala explained further. "Ahh, Mistress Tala, good to meet you. It is always fascinating to discuss magics with a fellow practitioner. I'm Haiba."

"Good to meet you, Mistress Haiba. So, I'm an Immaterial Guide."

"Immaterial Creator."

"I see." Tala actually did. "So, what is your foundational understanding?"

Haiba snorted a laugh. "Ahh, I haven't heard that question since the academy." Her voice got much deeper, in an obvious imitation of someone she'd known. "Rock is hard and heavy." Her voice went higher. "Wind moves around and within us all." Her tone became flippant. "I don't know… light is bright, I guess?" She giggled, her voice returning to normal. "Gravity accelerates all, equally."

*Solid for area of effects.*

"You?"

"All mass attracts all mass."

Haiba frowned. "Huh… I don't mean to… question your foundation, but no? It takes stellar-scale mass to create gravity fields."

Tala grinned. "It takes that much mass to create *noticeable* gravity fields. Magic aside."

Haiba waved her hand. "Magic aside, of course." After a moment's thought, she shrugged. "Is this some Guide-nonsense, like 'the air always has dust, which is just very small rocks?' No offense intended."

Tala sighed. *Typical Creator thinking, if it's too small for me to notice, it doesn't matter.* "Sure, something like that."

"Ahh, Okay. Neat." She turned back to the shaft. "One moment." A large cylinder shot up through the altered gravity, and Haiba watched it closely as it passed, muttering to herself. "Good stability and acceleration."

Rane was gaping. "Wait. You can make gravity go up?"

Haiba gave him an odd look. "Of course."

Rane turned to Tala. "You can make gravity go up?"

"Of course not, gravity isn't a repulsive force." After a moment's consideration, Tala shrugged. "I could increase gravity of the object toward the top of the shaft. That would do effectively the same thing."

"That's ridiculous. Gravity is an area of effect, it affects all things equally."

"We'll have to agree to disagree on that one. Though, your own actions prove that wrong. Gravity is affecting that shaft differently."

Haiba shook her head. "Magic excepted."

"Well then obviously gravity affects all things equally, but we were discussing the application of magic."

She opened her mouth then closed it, considering After a moment, she shook her head again. "True enough, but even so."

Rane was looking back and forth, a question clear in his mind. Finally, he addressed Haiba. "So, you must be an incredibly effective warrior. Simply reverse gravity and throw your opponents into space."

Haiba laughed far more than the comment deserved and patted Rane on the shoulder. "Oh, no. I can't make an altered gravity field that reaches space. Rust, I doubt anyone could. I can reverse gravity in a ten-foot by thirty-foot column, though." She said the last with obvious pride. "That's why I'm head of gravitational transport…" She hesitated. "Well, one of the divisions."

Rane frowned. "So, you could throw an enemy sixty feet up?"

"If I had to, yeah. It's pretty power intensive, though. I can only do it a few times a day, and the inscriptions are *expensive*. More so if I use more than the standard force of gravity to do so, but that would get a higher throw."

Tala was trying to hide her smile. *Exactly why I didn't pursue that sort of foolishness.*

"Wait…" Haiba turned to regard Tala with a quizzical look. "When did you graduate?"

"Not too long ago."

A light of understanding entered the woman's eyes, and she gasped. "I remember you!"

Tala frowned. *I don't know who this is.*

"I graduated," she glanced toward Rane, then back to Tala, "more than five years ago. There was a new student, making all sorts of fuss about gravity and how the teachers were silly for how they were teaching it. They asked me to talk to her, to you!"

Tala slowly shook her head. "I'm sorry, but I don't remember that at all."

Haiba laughed. "Of course you don't! You refused to meet with me." She grinned. "As soon as you were told that I was a Creator, you said I had nothing to teach you."

*Oh… That's probably right…* "Oh, sorry about that."

She waved Tala off. "It's fine. We clearly have utterly different foundational understandings. How'd yours work out?"

Tala shrugged. "Pretty well."

Rane grinned. "She can crush one massive enemy in the middle of a horde of allies."

"Crush?"

"Oh, yeah, I've seen massive opponents just go *splat*." He clapped his hands together.

"There's no way. To ramp up the gravitational field that much would take a ridiculous amount of power. What, do you increase gravity…" she seemed to be grasping at what she wanted to say, "six times?" She said it like a joke, even chuckling a bit.

Rane was giving Tala an odd look.

Tala gave a small smile. "Something like that."

"Incredible. You must have an incredibly high magical density to do that even a couple times a day."

Rane opened his mouth, but Tala gave him a quick look, which Haiba didn't seem to notice.

"Well, I need to watch for the next shipments, and keep them from wobbling. We do our best to balance the loads, but center-mass is never *exactly* in the same place." She gave a half bow to each of them. "Thank you for stopping, and for the chat. It's been interesting."

Tala returned the half-bow. "Good to meet you. Take care."

As they walked away, Rane leaned close. "Why didn't you correct her?"

"It's the same argument I've had a thousand times. Most gravity mages stop at 'gravity accelerates things equally, regardless of mass.' Or some derivation of that."

"That's true."

"It is, but it's also a bit simplistic." Tala laughed. "Though, I'm sure my understanding is far from perfect. It works for me, though."

"Seems like their understanding has its uses."

"You'd be surprised how few creatures will die from a sixty-foot fall. Gravity, as they use it, isn't combat capable, except as support magic."

"Why?"

"Power consumption. Even in the best case, they have to undo their working after they're done, else they'd throw off the planet, or slowly fill up the world with wonky gravity fields."

"Ahh, yeah, that would be bad."

"Just a bit."

"And you don't do that?"

"Nope. I attach my alteration to the identity of the target. I'm basically writing an exception to the universal laws, pointed at that one thing. Doesn't change anything else, and once that thing is gone, the exception has nothing to point to, so it ceases to exist. Nothing left to clean up."

"That's clean." He gave her a small smile.

"Exactly."

"So… how did you come to your understanding?"

"What do you mean?"

"Well… your teachers disagreed with you."

"In a sense, but not really?"

"Alright, you have to explain that."

"Well,"—she wrinkled her nose, thinking for a moment—"let me give an example. What's the most important part of a sword?"

Rane frowned. "Well, it's the blade that makes it a sword. Replace that with something else, and it's a knife, or mace, or hammer."

"That is a good point. I think it's the handle, because without the handle, it's just a blade, and you can't use it at all. At least with the other options you mentioned, there is still utility."

He opened his mouth to argue, then stopped. "I see. The argument isn't between two *wrong* points of view. It's between incomplete points of view."

"Precisely."

"So, why not complete your perspective?"

"Two reasons. First, incomplete perspectives allow things that better understanding would not. Power fills in the gaps."

"Example?"

"Mistress Haiba, if she added my understanding to hers, she wouldn't be able to reverse gravity."

"Alright, so what about yours?"

Tala gave him a slightly embarrassed look. "I just don't understand gravity as a field. It makes no sense to me."

"What do you mean?"

She nodded. "If I told you that two feet in front of me there was a three-foot sphere of increased gravity, what would that mean?"

"That if I put something into it, it would fall faster?"

"Precisely, but that's gravity *acting* on a mass, not the field itself."

Rane frowned, then slowly nodded. "Like some kinetic Mages can 'throw force.'"

"Throw… force? How would that even…? What?"

He laughed. "I know, right? Force is a force! It's not a thing that can be made into a wall, or thrown at something…" He scratched above his ear, frowning. "It's frustrating, because I would *love* to be able to do that, and in a sense, it is correct, but it just makes no sense to me."

"Yeah, I think that's a good comparison." She smiled at him. "Different interpretations are better for different styles and use cases. And we are each hampered by what we are capable of understanding."

"That makes sense." He smiled in return, and they fell back into a companionable silence.

As they walked, Tala was thinking through the conversations, checking what she'd said and heard, to see if she'd said anything that she didn't agree with, or missed something important. As she did so, one of the things that Rane had said in their conversation with Haiba was tickling the back of her mind. *I can crush my enemies. I even have an amazing mental construct for it.* "I'm an idiot."

"What now?" Rane frowned her way as they continued walking down the spiral.

"I already have a perfectly serviceable mental construct for nearly instantly quadrupling an object's effective gravity." She pulled out a copper coin.

She put her left middle finger to her thumb, locked onto the coin, and invoked her gravity manipulation. *Increase.*

This time, however, she used her mental construct for Crush.

She felt the need for power and connected a few large void-channels to the working.

The coin instantly quadrupled in gravity, then again.

Again.

Again.

Again.

She released the working, then, holding a copper ounce that weighed more than five and half pounds. It had taken less than five seconds.

She laughed. "It worked!"

"What worked? You pulled out a copper coin, then started laughing…"

"I made it heavier much, much more quickly."

Rane was frowning. "Isn't it illegal to increase the weight of currency?"

*Oh… he's right.* "Fine, I'll put it back, but this is *huge* Rane. I can use my Crush almost at will, now." She looked internally at her inscriptions and almost stumbled. *Well, rust.* She'd used up a good chunk of her remaining spell-lines' material in that invocation.

*Right… fast takes more power and material.*

Tala groaned. "Well, at least I know it works."

"What?" He had a concerned tilt to his head.

She sighed. "That took much more of my inscriptions than I realized it would." She was already reducing the coin's weight once again, the slow way this time. It took just more than thirty seconds to return effective gravity to normal on the coin.

"How much faster was it?"

Tala thought, doing calculations on how her normal method of increase would have worked. "Five seconds versus almost forty."

Rane grunted. "That's a big difference."

"Yeah, but still not something I want to use casually." Some of her joy came back. "But it does do exactly what my Crush did."

"Hey! That's great. You had a non-destructive alternative too, right?"

"Yeah, Restrain."

"Does it replace that?"

"No, it won't directly, but that's Okay."

Rane glanced her way, cocking an eyebrow.

She smiled back and shrugged. "Restrain stole my opponent's momentum, and then calculated exactly what level of gravity was required to put them in a stable orbit, just above the ground."

"Ah, yeah, that's quite a bit more complicated."

"Just a bit, yeah." She shrugged again. "But I haven't used it in a good long time, and these days I feel like anything I need to use less than lethal force on, quickly, isn't really an immediate threat."

Rane grunted. "That's true enough." He quirked a smile. "You can still just reduce their gravity, right?"

"I can, yeah. I can probably even use a portion of the mental construct from Reduce to do it quickly, if necessary, but it will be a slagging inefficient thing as it is."

"Worth meditating on?"

Tala snorted a chuckle. "I'll add it to the list."

Rane nodded in understanding. "You're spread pretty thin, right now."

She sighed, her shoulders dropping just a bit. "Yeah. I feel like I'm scrambling from one important thing to another."

He seemed to contemplate for a long moment as they continued their leisurely stroll downward. Finally, he nodded. "Something Master Grediv would say seems to apply here."

Tala straightened, speaking in a faux serious tone. "Please, Master Rane, share with me the wisdom of Archons."

Rane grinned back at her. "If you insist, Mistress Tala." He gave a slight bow of his head. "Things can be urgent, important, both, or neither. Does that make sense?"

"I think I understand the difference. Urgent needs to be handled right away. Important just needs to be handled." She frowned. "So… how could something be urgent, but not important?"

He nodded. "Good question. If you ordered food, and it is ready to be picked up, that is urgent, but not important."

"Speak for yourself."

He laughed. "No, really. If you don't pick it up, you might have to buy other food, but it isn't the same as breathing, and no one will die."

She bit the side of her lip in thought, then nodded. "Okay, I can understand that. So what are you driving at?"

"That which is urgent and important, do first. If it is important, but not urgent, plan for. If it is neither, don't do it. If it is urgent but not important, find someone else to do it."

"Wouldn't finding someone else take more time?"

Rane shrugged. "Many Archons, as well as many older Mages, hire at least one assistant, and that is who they have do the urgent, but not important, things." He waved a hand, dismissively though. "But that isn't the point. You have a massive spread of things that you are working on. Which are both urgent and important? What should you be focusing on, *right now*?"

Tala had an instant response. "Fusing."

"Perfect. Can you fuse constantly?"

"No."

"So, what do you need to do when not fusing?"

"I... don't know... Improve my abilities in martial fighting? Expand my spell-form utility and efficiency? Grow Kit's capacity? Figure out what else I want to do to Kit? I think it's time for me to bind my elk leathers, but I just haven't had time. And—"

Rane placed a hand on her shoulder, halting her.

She stopped speaking immediately, taking a deep breath. Thankfully, they were off to one side of the walking path, so they wouldn't really be an obstacle to traffic.

Tala hadn't realized that the speed of her speaking had been increasing as she continued listing out what she had to do. She let out her breath in a long, slow exhale.

"Are you alright?"

She looked toward her feet, nodding and breathing deeply. Eventually, she looked up and smiled. "I think I'm avoiding thinking about all I have to do."

Rane nodded, giving her an encouraging smile. "So, you can't fuse all the time."

"That's right." She tilted her head slightly, wondering where he was going with a return to the topic.

"Why?"

She blinked at him a few times. "It's mentally exhausting. It strains my magical control and takes a lot out of me." She knew her tone was defensive.

He was nodding. "Alright. So, since fusing is your highest priority, when you aren't fusing, what can we do to recharge your mind and let your magical control rest?"

Tala turned and started walking again without comment. *Why didn't I think of that?*

That was hardly relevant. *What can I do?*

Exactly what Rane had been encouraging: plays, walks, eating outside the training room. She gave Rane a searching look, but he continued to walk beside her quietly, giving her time to process.

Terry was utterly unaffected by their conversation.

"Relaxing." She went with the short answer.

"Alright. How can we help you relax?"

She gestured vaguely in front of them. "Food, plays." She swept a hand through her hair. "Sparring? Is that odd?"

"Not at all. Physical exertion can help with mental strain, and food is needed for anything and everything, more so for you, and stories about others help us to disconnect from our own lives, our own problems, and return to them with fresh eyes and the energy required to do what's needed." He quirked a smile.

"So, keep doing what I've been doing?"

"Maybe, but if you do, do so because you know it is the best course you can take, not just because it's the only thing you can think to do."

She thought about that as they continued walking, and Rane gave her the space to process in silence.

She had been hurt, but she had seized her own path.

Tala nodded to herself. *I can't just be wounded and ignore it.*

She had people who cared about and depended on her, and she wouldn't let them down.

*Not again.*

Tala would keep improving, now matter what it took, and the next real step required an alignment of body, mind, and soul.

Internal turmoil had to make that harder.

*I can't run from my issues forever.*

She needed to face the things that were bothering her and deal with them.

Whatever it took, it was time that she truly started Fusing.

## Author's Note

Thank you for taking your time to read my quirky magical tale.

If you have the time, a review of the book can help share this world with others, and I would greatly appreciate it.

To listen to this or other books in this series, please find them on mountaindalepress.store or Audible. Release dates vary.

To continue reading for yourself, check out Kindle Unlimited for additional titles. If this is the last one released for the moment, you can find the story available on RoyalRoad.com for free. Simply search for Millennial Mage. You can also find a direct link from my Author's page on Amazon.
There are quite a few other fantastic works by great authors available on RoyalRoad, so take a look around while you're there!

Thank you, again, for sharing in this strange and beautiful magical world with Tala. I sincerely hope that you enjoyed it.

Regards,
J.L. Mullins

Printed in Great Britain
by Amazon